D0638258

A FEAST OF CRIME

JEANNE M. DAMS
DENISE DIETZ
CYNTHIA P. LAWRENCE
VALERIE S. MALMONT

WORLDWIDE.

TORONTO • NEW YORK • LONDON
AMSTERDAM • PARIS • SYDNEY • HAMBURG
STOCKHOLM • ATHENS • TOKYO • MILAN
MADRID • WARSAW • BUDAPEST • AUCKLAND

A FEAST OF CRIME

A Worldwide Mystery/May 2005

ISBN 0-373-26527-1

DARK FÊTE Copyright © 2005 by Jeanne M. Dams.

EVERYBODY DIDN'T LIKE SARA LEE Copyright © 2005 by Denise Dietz.

DEATH TO DONUTS! Copyright © 2005 by Cynthia P. Lawrence.

TORI MIRACLE AND THE TURKEY OF DOOM Copyright © 2005 by Valerie S. Malmont.

Printed in U.S.A.

CONTENTS

DARK FÊTE

Jeanne M. Dams

ONE

"ONE DAY that woman is going to get what she deserves!" said Jane, setting down her cup with a thump that rattled the other dishes on the tea tray.

Both cats woke from their naps and decided to go elsewhere, and Margaret and I looked at each other, eyebrows raised. Jane Langland not only showing temper but expressing it in a complete sentence? Something was badly wrong.

Margaret Allenby, wife of the dean of the Cathedral, had joined me and Jane, my best friend and next-door neighbor, to talk over the church fête held the day before. We had barely recovered from the experience, but after a hectic month of preparations and an exhausting day, I thought we deserved a congratulatory tea and a relaxing postmortem. My husband, retired Chief Constable Alan Nesbitt, had retreated to his den and left the parlor to us women and our tea and talk.

As far as I knew, the fête had gone splendidly. The weather, for a nice change, had been perfect. The quality of goods donated for the jumble sale had been unusually high and sales had been brisk. That stall had been set up near the tea tent, so I'd had a ringside seat. Fortunately, I'd restrained myself. I didn't really need somebody's old whatchamacallit, no matter how charming.

I had, during a brief period when it seemed no one wanted tea, taken a turn around the Cathedral Close to look at the other delights the fête had to offer. There were the usual games for both children—a sack race was going on when I wandered past—and adults—"Test Your Strength, Ring the Bell!" The range of things for sale was amazing: bottled fruit, knitwear, baked goods—involving a competition—home-made candy, pickles and chutneys, and a great deal more. It was hardly to be wondered at that several children looked quite green by the end of the afternoon. Then there were the fortune-telling tent and the bingo tent—I didn't bite—and the handicrafts stall—I did: the loveliest tea cozy I'd ever seen. I'd listened to the Cathedral Choir at one end of the Close and the Salvation Army Band at the other. They didn't clash too badly, but then the Close is big and the air was still. I'd had a good time and gone back to my duties a few minutes late.

I related it all to the others and they told me their stories—the dog that made off with all the pork pies from the baked-goods stall, the nonagenarian who got into what very nearly became a fistfight with another old lady over a knitted shawl both wanted.

We'd been enjoying it until Jane's explosion.

"Jane, have another scone. Your strawberry preserves are to die for, and we really must eat up the clotted cream. If Alan sees it in the fridge, he'll want some, and it's so bad for his arteries. What has Rachel done to get your dander up this time?" I pushed the tray of goodies closer to Jane, refilled my own cup and sat back.

The tale of Rachel Spry's iniquities was apt to be long and entertaining. Rachel, a woman in her forties with a highly shellacked hairdo and a personality to match, had lately moved to Sherebury. With, apparently, time on her hands, or else ravenous social ambitious, she had quickly established a presence in most of the town's women's endeavors.

"Humph!" said Jane. "Set the whole fête by the ears, didn't she?"

"Well, I knew she wanted to run it," I said mildly. "I thought that had been smoothed over."

Margaret smiled ruefully. "We all thought it had, Dorothy, after we managed to avoid putting her in charge. That wouldn't have answered, of course."

Jane snorted. "Bossy, opinionated…" She took a bite of her scone and subsided into mutters.

"For someone new to Cathedral circles, she's made a good many waves, hasn't she?" I commented, neatly mixing metaphors.

"The bookshop," Margaret said, ticking Rachel's sins off on her fingers. "I did think Willie was going to resign as manager when Rachel tried to reorganize the shop, stock, volunteers *and* schedule. It took all Kenneth's tact to settle that one."

"Poor man. Enough to do, without that," Jane growled. "Fearful job, dean of a Cathedral."

"How did he solve the problem?" I asked. I was really curious. Squabbling women have been known to defeat even the wisest of men.

"Actually, it was rather clever," said Margaret with a grin. "It just worked out that, on the Sunday when things were at their worst, the Gospel was the bit about Mary and Martha. You know, the two sisters? And Martha did all the toiling and moiling around the house while Mary just sat and listened to Jesus, and Martha resented it?"

"I've always thought Martha had a point," I said. "Nothing would ever get done if everyone were a Mary."

"Ah, but Jesus praised Mary, you remember. And so did Kenneth. He went up to Rachel after the service and told her how much he admired her work with the bookshop, but he thought really she was better suited to more spiritual pursuits, that God meant her for a Mary."

Even Jane laughed at the idea of worldly, officious Rachel sitting piously at Jesus' feet, but we could easily imagine that she would lap up the dean's flattery.

"It backfired, though," Margaret went on, "when Rachel

elected herself to the Flower Guild. Apparently she thought flowers more 'spiritual' than books and souvenirs, but…" She spread her hands and rolled her eyes.

"Yes, well, we could all see the results of *that*," I said, sighing. "Those awful 'modern' arrangements, all spiky twigs and exotic flowers in containers that looked like pieces of old drainpipe. And just after Easter, too."

"Grateful it wasn't *for* Easter," said Jane. "Wanted to be reimbursed for the flowers, as well."

"Good grief, I didn't know that! But haven't the flowers always come out of people's gardens?" I asked.

"Nearly always," said Margaret, "except when the weather turned cold and killed everything, or when it was frightfully hot like that dreadful summer when all the gardens dried up. Then we've had to buy a few. And of course for Christmas and Easter, when so many flowers are needed. But for the most part we've muddled on in the good old-fashioned way, with good old English flowers, as the parish churches do."

"That's one thing I love about the Cathedral," I said. "It *is* old-fashioned and it *is* like a parish church. I mean, take the fête. Cathedrals don't usually have them, do they?"

"Great pity, too," said Jane. "Raise lots of money. Bring people together." She had finished her scone and returned to her usual telegraphic style. Her mood appeared to have mellowed. I didn't pursue the subject of the infuriating Rachel.

"Well, at least we did raise a good deal of money this time. We don't have a firm total yet, but Kenneth says it's well up in the thousands. Jeremy *will* be pleased. Added to the money from the appeal, it should be enough to put us over the top for the organ restoration."

"Jeremy Sayers is the best organist-choirmaster I've ever known, and he deserves a proper instrument," I said. "I'm glad we made lots of money, though it nearly cost the two of you your sanity. Me, I just helped in the tea tent, but you two both ran your feet off, organizing everything and then actually running things yesterday. Jane, how did your stall do? I don't suppose you had anything left over, did you?"

Jane had worked tirelessly organizing the food stalls, the one with baked goods, the one with snacks, and her own specialty, the one with jams and jellies. She had put up I don't know how many jars of lemon curd and current jelly and apricot jam, as well as quantities of the strawberry preserves we had scarfed down with our tea. She had dunned all her friends for their most delectable concoctions and had manned the busy stall all day.

"One pot of lemon curd—a mistake. Set it under the counter. Woman never came back. Forgot about it."

"I'll buy it," Margaret and I said simultaneously.

"Bought it myself. Want to make some tarts for Walter. Growing boy."

Walter Tubbs had been a waif of a boy when Jane took him in some months before. Or a young man, really, in his early twenties, but a waif, all the same. Thin and forlorn, a university student with very little family, he had appealed to Jane's love of the young and her passion for the underdog, and she had bustled him from his comfortless boarding house and established him as her pet. She had also discovered that he was her grandson, the child of her long-dead illegitimate son. I was one of the few people alive who knew that.

Walter had thrived on Jane's love as much as her good food and seemed to have shot up a good six inches as well as filling out. Not surprisingly, he adored her.

"He'll know where to put them," I said, smiling. "And how did he do yesterday? I saw a lot of teenagers at his stall."

Jane didn't smile back. She scowled, in fact, and when she spoke, her voice was jerky.

"Did all right. Nearly sold out. No thanks to *that woman*."

Uh-oh. Were we back to Rachel? I looked a question at Margaret, who shook her head.

Jane's frown deepened. "No right to make accusations like that! Walter's a fine boy. So're his friends."

"What sorts of accusations?" I asked.

"Not true, any of them."

"I'm sure not, but what? Surely, Rachel didn't think Walter was taking any of the money for himself, did she?"

"Worse. Piracy."

I was lost, but Margaret was quicker on the uptake. "Rachel accused him of stealing the music?"

Jane nodded and I shook my head to clear it. "Wait a minute. Let me get this straight. Walter was selling used CDs, right?"

"Right. His own idea. Said young people wouldn't come for the sort of thing one usually finds at a fête, but they'd come for cheap music. Collected all sorts from his friends. Sold well, until she put her oar in."

"She thought he was selling stolen goods? Pirated disks? What, off the Internet?" Margaret asked.

Jane shrugged. "Don't think she knew herself what she meant. Ranting and raving. Drove the customers away. Sheer nonsense. Disks had proper labels. Plainly legitimate. I weighed in and made it worse. Created a scene. Only jealous because his stall was doing business and hers wasn't."

Margaret lifted her hands in a despairing gesture. "Well, what did she expect? We gave her the bookstall, thinking she couldn't do much damage there, but she offended everyone who tried to contribute. Told them their books were rubbish and they'd do better to throw them in the fire. I heard her myself. I believe she stocked the stall with her own discards, and my dear! They were treatises on avant-garde decorating and cooking and politics—anything stark and tasteless and unpleasant. Of course they didn't sell!"

I shook my head again. "Is there anyone in this town that she hasn't infuriated?"

"Quite honestly I can't think of anyone. Did you hear about the fracas at the Women's Institute?" Margaret replied.

"Not there, too!"

"Indeed. She went in as a newcomer and proceeded to tell them their ideas were antiquated, their programs pathetic, their procedures inefficient. Oh, dear, I do hate to gossip about the woman, and Kenneth would scold me if he were here. It can be trying to be the wife of the dean. One has to try, all the time, to exercise Christian charity. Which is all very well, but how *are* we to cope with her? I admit I do wish she'd go back where she came from."

"And where was that, do you know? And why in the name of common sense did she come to Sherebury? A sleepy cathedral town isn't at all her sort of place. She seems the London type, all brisk efficiency and executive attitudes," I said.

"One would think so. Unless she liked the idea of being a big, important frog in a small pond. Even then, a new city would be more her style, all cement and angles and edges and people with no sense of tradition—"

"—who'd do as she told them," Jane finished. "Like to send her there myself. Or send her someplace. Anywhere but here."

"I agree, but where *did* she come from? Does anyone know?" I asked again.

Jane shook her head. "Can't talk to the woman without wanting to strangle her."

Margaret didn't know, either. "I did try to draw her out a bit when she first came. Most people like to talk about themselves, but she only wanted to talk about how badly we did everything. Since then it's taken all my time to try to soothe the feelings she's wounded. I've never met anyone with so little tact. And she blows hot and cold, one moment sweet to the point of smarmy, the next blowing a fuse over nothing at all. Truthfully, I've wondered sometimes if she were quite... well—"

"Sane?" asked Jane bluntly. "Shouldn't think so, myself."

"I wonder," I said thoughtfully. "Are all nasty people a little insane? Or are they just nasty? If sanity means knowing what one is doing, then I'd say she's perfectly sane. I've not seen her in action very often, but I watched one confrontation with poor Willie in the bookshop. It seemed to me that Rachel knew exactly how much she was upsetting Willie and she was enjoying it. It wasn't pleasant."

"Well, I suppose Kenneth would say we mustn't judge. Dorothy, are there any more preserves?" Margaret asked.

"I'm afraid we've eaten them all. I'd hoped Jane might have some left from the fête, but I should have known better."

"Rachel was sane enough to buy two pots," Margaret commented. "I saw her, Jane, when you were taking a break. So perhaps she has some sense."

Jane snorted and poured herself another cup of tea.

TWO

THE NEXT WEEK was one of those supremely lovely stretches of weather that made you forget England is noted for its rainfall. June came into its own after a wet, cold spring, and everything bloomed at once, even flowers that weren't supposed to be out together at all. The lilies of the valley were just going, red berries appearing where the tiny bells of flowers had been, but in shady patches the flowers still flourished, their scent competing with the lilacs. The rhododendrons seemed to explode like fireworks in every shade of red and pink and white, with an orange hybrid now and then to set an exotic note. And the roses! One thing nobody has ever criticized about England is its roses. If transplanted Americans like me long, now and then, for some really good plumbing, we forget it when the roses are in their full glory.

The strawberries thrived, too. Jane had made her preserves out of last year's frozen berries—and I don't know how she kept them from getting watery; I never can—but I was trying to make some from this year's crop when Jane tapped on my back door and walked into the kitchen.

"Smells good," she commented.

"They *smell* all right," I said darkly. "The question is how they'll turn out. My results with jam and fudge have a certain family resemblance. I always seem to end up with either soup or concrete. How do you get your preserves to come out so perfectly every time?"

"Seventy years practice. And throwing out the failures. Any coffee going?"

"I'd be glad to make some. Actually I was just about to have some lemonade. It's hot for coffee, or I'm hot, anyway. Been standing over that kettle for ages."

"Don't leave it now. It'll gel and you'll never forgive me. Your sort of lemonade?"

"Heavens, yes. Homemade. I can't stand the fizzy kind you Brits drink."

"Not this Brit." She found the glasses and poured us each a glass, adding ice to mine as a concession to my peculiar American habits. Of course the jam was ready before we'd taken more than a sip and she helped me pour it into the sterile jars and seal it with wax.

"Looks all right," she said when we'd finished, holding a jar to the light. "Right color, not too thin."

"It's only because you're here. It knows who's boss."

She made a face and drank her lemonade in silence.

"How's Walter been?" Usually, when Jane found it hard to begin a conversation, there was something worrying her. As the joy of her heart, Walter was a likely subject for anxiety.

"All right." More silence.

Well, I was happy enough to sit and relax and wait for her to tell me why she came over.

When she did speak, she surprised me. "Seen Rachel Spry about lately?"

I blinked. "No. I haven't exactly sought her out, though."

"Don't suppose so." She paused and cleared her throat. "I have. Tried to phone her. Just went to visit. Not home. Don't know where she's got to."

I opened my mouth a couple of times, but nothing I could think to say seemed very sensible. I didn't like to ask Jane straight out why she was going looking for her worst enemy.

"Expect you want to know why I want to see her."

"Well…I did wonder, yes."

"Want to apologize."

"You? Apologize to her? What on earth for?"

"Lost my temper, at the fête. Said things I shouldn't. Wanted to make amends."

"Good grief, Jane! Didn't she give you cause?"

Jane studied her lemonade glass. "Got to thinking. If she's not quite—whatever—then not entirely her fault. No harm in an apology. Hate to hold a grudge."

I grinned. "Jane Langland, you are a saint. No matter what anybody says."

She looked at me and shook her head. "Crabby old woman. Hate crabby old women. Scourge of the earth."

"Oh, right. I'm sure Walter thinks you're a real pain. And the kids you used to teach. I notice they only visit three or four times a week these days. And the W.I. ladies. Obviously they just put up with you. It must be all of a month since they asked you to take on a new project. Then there's the RSPCA, the old folks' home, the church youth groups—"

She held up a hand. "Point made." Her face had reddened. "Finger in lots of pies. Still crabby."

"Okay, have it your way. And if I see Rachel, I'll let you know. Just don't ask me to talk to her. I can't get beyond 'good morning' with that woman without it turning into an argument. More lemonade, or would you rather have some toast and jam to sweeten you up?"

"No, thanks. Have to get home. Haven't made lunch yet."

"Why not have it here? It's just a salad, but you'd be welcome."

"There's Walter. Working today. Needs a good meal."

I knew better than to press her. Cooking for Walter, tending to Walter, spoiling Walter was the greatest joy of her life. And Walter, bless him, was made of the stuff that laps up love and returns it in full measure, without turning greedy and demanding. He had accepted Jane as an honorary aunt and was beginning to forget the "honorary" part. It was a great day for both of them when those two found each other. She would probably never tell him their true relationship, but he understood that he was cherished.

It was Walter, two days later, who brought the news. I was pulling a few weeds out of the flower bed at the front of my house—my gardener being on one of his periodic benders— when Walter came out of Jane's house on his way to his job at the town museum and paused to chat.

"Have you heard about Mrs. Spry?"

"Oh, no! Don't tell me she's gotten on the wrong side of somebody else!"

"Well, not exactly. She's dead."

I straightened, with a sharp crack of both knees and a groan. "You're serious? Good grief, you are! An automobile accident?"

"Drug overdose. Legal drugs, I mean. They found a bottle of some kind of capsules, tranquilizers or something, and they think she just took too many. They found her yesterday, but she'd been gone quite a while. She lived alone, so nobody knew she was dead. They don't know if it was an accidental overdose or suicide."

"Oh, poor woman!"

"She was a b—a real witch! I can't work up much sympathy. I'll bet there isn't a human being on the face of the earth who'll be sorry she's gone."

"That's why she deserves sympathy. If I thought nobody'd miss me when I died, I'd be tempted to suicide, too."

Walter looked shamefaced. "I never thought of it that way. But she really upset Aunt Jane. It's hard to forgive her for that."

"And what about you? If Jane was upset, it was because Mrs. Spry insulted you."

He waved that off. "I knew I was right and she was wrong.

She made a fool of herself. I was angry at the time, but it wasn't important."

"Well, Jane has forgiven her, as well, so try to let go. It's a great mistake to cling to bitterness toward the dead. Believe me, I've done it often enough to know."

He gave that sententious speech exactly as much attention as the young usually do, waved and went on his way.

That was in the morning. I weeded for another half an hour, pondering how terrible it would be to die unloved. We grieve over the deaths of those we love, but when we cannot grieve, and feel we ought to, it's almost worse. I decided I had no right to be sanctimonious with Walter. I'd disliked Rachel Spry as much as anyone and hadn't been any nicer to her than I could help. Did it matter that it was her own fault people couldn't stand her?

A sudden rain storm put an end to both gardening and unprofitable contemplation. I gathered up my tools and repaired to the kitchen with a cup of tea, and stopped thinking about death and remorse.

The day passed, slowly, as it does when one is idle. It was early afternoon and Alan and I were just finishing our leisurely lunch in the kitchen when someone pounded on our back door. Pounded and kept on pounding. The cats looked up from our plates, which we had set on the floor for them, and Alan threw down his napkin with a frown of annoyance.

"All *right!* Stop that row, I'm coming!"

He flung the door open, letting in a gust of wind and rain and Walter.

"You have to do something," the young man said without preamble. "They've arrested Aunt Jane!"

Alan is good in a crisis. He made Walter sit at the kitchen table. He poured out a small tot of brandy. Then he sat himself, deliberately crossed his legs in a casual attitude, and said, "Now. When you've got that inside you, tell us what's happened."

The boy swallowed the brandy in a gulp, made a face and told his story. "They came just now. I'd come home for lunch and I was just ready to go back to work when they arrived."

"'They' being the police, I assume." Alan's voice and attitude were formal and business-like, the policeman in him all on top.

"Yes. And they said there were some questions about Mrs. Spry and they took her away!" Walter was trying very hard not to cry.

Alan was all business. "Did they caution her?"

"What d'you mean?"

"The standard caution. 'Anything you say may be taken down as evidence,' et cetera."

"Oh. No. At least not while I was there. They took her fingerprints, though. And mine, as well! But I didn't hear them say anything like—what you said."

"Then she isn't under arrest. They've taken her in as a material witness. That's not good, but it's not as bad as it might be. Go on. Did they ask her anything?"

"I don't know! I was—oh, wait. They asked if she had any more strawberry preserves."

Alan frowned. "And does she?"

"No. She sold them all at the fête. She's going to make some more…" His voice faded out and he looked again as if tears weren't far away.

"Alan?"

That was all I said, but my husband knew exactly what I was asking. He nodded.

"I'll find out everything I can. Walter, you'd best get back to your job. Try not to worry too much. I'll keep an eye on the situation."

"They can't think Aunt Jane had anything to do with that bitch's death!"

That was strong language for Walter. Well, he had a right to be upset.

Alan remained calm. "We don't know enough yet to jump to any conclusions. Off you go. I'll talk to you later this afternoon."

"But isn't there something you can do?"

"I'm retired, Walter. I have no authority to do anything. I can only ask questions, and they will be answered only if the investigating officers choose to do so."

"But they will," I broke in. "They always do."

Alan gave me a look. "Even if they do, there may be some information I will have no right to share. But rest assured, Walter, that I will do all I can. As for you, you can best help Jane by staying calm and doing what you're paid to do. You know how she'd react if you lost your job."

"But—oh, all right. But no one will show up at the museum today, anyway. They never do when it rains."

"You can study, then," said Alan with a trace of exasperation. "Now off with you!"

I waited until Walter had gone—with an eloquent bang of the door—before I said, "You might have told him everything would be all right. He needed some comfort, poor child."

"How could I say that, Dorothy? I have no idea whether things will be all right. If they've asked Jane about her preserves, it must mean they've found something suspicious in some preserves, somewhere. What I didn't tell Walter is that they wouldn't have taken Jane to the station for questioning unless something very serious had come up. I hate to say it, Dorothy, but it's looking as though they suspect something other than accident or suicide in Rachel Spry's death. And Jane hated the woman and was publicly heard to threaten her."

THREE

"Alan Nesbitt! You don't mean to tell me—you can't *possibly* mean that you think Jane killed Rachel Spry!"

Alan smiled. A bit tepidly, it seemed to me. "Simmer down, darling. I don't mean any such thing. I don't think Jane could be a murderess any more than you do. I do think, and I say, that Jane could be in trouble. The police don't haul people in for questioning for frivolous reasons, you know. There must be something, some evidence, that makes Derek and co. suspicious."

"Oh," I said, somewhat mollified. "Well, just as long as you don't plan to join the prosecution team. You think Derek is in charge, then?" Derek Morrison is the detective chief inspector who usually directs homicide investigations in our neck of the woods. He's also a good friend.

"Probably, if it's turned into a murder investigation."

"Well, that's good. He's a careful man."

"Careful enough not to tell me too much, considering I'm Jane's next-door neighbor. However." He pushed himself back from the table. "I told Walter I'd find out all I could, so I'd best be off to do just that. I think this is a case when I'd fare better in person."

Alan, in person, can be rather formidable. He's a big man, tall and substantial without being fat. His calm exterior hides a keen intellect and a powerful will. "Yes, dear, I agree," I said with a grin. "Phoning wouldn't be a bit the same. If Jane's still there, maybe you could talk to her. I know it would make her feel better."

"Certainly, I will, if I'm allowed. I'm neither a member of her family, her solicitor, nor her clergyman, you know. Just remember I'm limited, now, in what I can do and how much weight I can throw about."

"I know what you told Walter. I also know you still have a fair number of markers to call in from those people."

Alan rolled his eyes. "You Americans and your language! 'Markers to call in,' indeed. Seriously, love, I'll do all I can, but you know there are lines I cannot cross. It might behoove you to do a little nosing around yourself. You have no official status, of course, but that means there are also no legal strictures about the people you may approach and the kinds of questions you may ask."

"There's also no reason why anyone should answer any of those questions."

"No. But for some reason they often do, don't they? I'm off. Home for tea, I hope."

He shrugged into his raincoat and departed, leaving me to stare out the window into the rainy garden and wonder what to do next.

Why had they taken Jane in? That was at the heart of the matter, and until Alan found that out, I was speculating, with no data to work from. And when, I asked myself, had that ever stopped me?

Strawberry preserves. It had something to do with the strawberry preserves. Therefore the police were thinking about a poisoning. At least, that was the only reasonable conclusion. You could, in theory, choke somebody with jam, but then the maker of the jam wouldn't be suspect. You could hit them over the head with a large jarful. You could break the jar and stab them with the shards.

You could, Dorothy Martin, pull yourself together and start thinking sensibly.

Very well. Suppose I wanted to poison some strawberry

preserves. How would I go about it? Surely I could dredge up enough snippets, from the ragbag I call my memory, of mystery plots I had read in a long lifetime. Agatha Christie was good with poisons, Dorothy L. Sayers used them occasionally, Ngaio Marsh—all the classics. I racked my brain.

Well, if I were an efficient murderess, I decided, I'd use one of the chemical poisons. Arsenic is nice. Readily available in the form of rat poison, tasteless, odorless, fast.

The trouble was, arsenic produced pretty distressing symptoms. If Rachel Spry had died from the ingestion of arsenic, she would have been sick as a dog first and there would be plenty of evidence in her house.

Unless her murderer cleaned it all up.

Well, keep arsenic in my back pocket, so to speak. What else?

Cyanide, naturally. Quick, nasty. Used in photography; my first husband had been a very fine amateur photographer and had had about a pound of potassium cyanide in his darkroom. He used it, infrequently, as a bleach, when retouching. Nowadays, with digital photography taking over and retouching done on the computer, I wondered if anybody still used the stuff.

I also wondered if any of Rachel's many enemies was a photographer.

Strychnine. Now there was a truly unpleasant poison. Causes dire convulsions, extremely painful, and the victim doesn't die for a while. Off hand, I couldn't think of quick, easy ways to obtain strychnine, but doubtless there were sources.

Wait, though. There was a problem with any of those poisons. The police had first thought that Rachel had died of a drug overdose. "Tranquilizers or something," Walter had said. Now that would surely imply that she was found in her bed. Again, a murderer might try to hide the evidence of his—or her—activities, but would anyone stick around long enough to clean up vomit, or throw away the broken china that might well result from violent convulsions? Would a murderer then tidy up the victim and put her neatly into bed?

No. I was looking at this from a skewed angle. The murderer wouldn't even have been there. The whole point of poison is that it is planted long before the victim takes it. Then the murderer is long gone. If he's made sure he's left no evidence of his presence behind, he's home free.

Or she. I thought for an unpleasant moment of Jane and jam, and decided to take another tack. There was really no point in speculating about the symptoms of various poisons. If Alan could find out what poison was used, then I'd have a better idea where we were. And anyway, that kind of forensic speculation was what the police did best. No, what I needed to do was to go and talk to some people. But what people?

I could start with the ones who had disliked Rachel. That seemed to include everyone who had ever met her, but I might narrow it down a bit to the people I knew well enough to approach.

First of those was certainly Willie, formally Ariadne Williamson, manager of the Cathedral Bookshop. I had done volunteer work there for a few months before my marriage to Alan, and Willie had become a fast friend.

The rain was coming down harder than ever, so I put on my Wellies, along with my raincoat and yellow plastic hat, told the cats to behave themselves, and let myself out.

It wasn't a long walk, or wouldn't have been in good weather. The Cathedral is almost literally in my backyard. I live at the end—the bottom, the English would say—of one of the streets that lead to the Close. There is no access for vehicles, but a gate opens to admit pedestrians and then a path across the grass leads to the south choir transept door of the Cathedral. Not many people use that door, but it's very convenient for those of us who live in Monkswell Street.

I went in, shook the water off my garments and walked

through the transept to the south aisle. I should have turned left and walked toward the back of the church to the bookshop, but I couldn't resist going on into the nave for a moment.

I live next door to this church. I go to service there every Sunday morning, and to a fair number of weekday evensongs, too. I participate in some of the women's activities, and Alan and I attend concerts here quite regularly. But familiarity, in this case, never breeds anything except increasing love. Sherebury Cathedral or the Cathedral Church of St. Peter and St. Paul at Sherebury—to give it its proper name—is, I think, the most beautiful church in the world and it would take quite a lot of argument to convince me otherwise.

When I had gazed my fill, for the moment, of the vaulted roof, the columns, the glass that, even on a rainy day, seemed to radiate the very light of heaven, I deliberately turned my back on all the glory and walked to the small, stuffy little corner near the south porch where space had been set aside for the bookshop.

There were actually quite a few books among the souvenirs and what a priest friend of mine used to call "holy junk" on the crowded shelves. The tourists didn't often buy any of the books except the lavishly illustrated color booklets about the Cathedral, but Willie didn't care. Every now and then a scholar would find something to delight his heart and Sherebury residents knew that when they wanted to find their pet poet or essayist, Willie would likely have the work. In her own way, Willie is a purist.

And where, in fact, was Willie? The shop was small enough that I could see at a glance she wasn't around. I approached the volunteer at the cash register, a woman I knew only slightly.

"Hi, Dorothy. Looking for a book?"

"Looking for Willie, as a matter of fact. Is she not here today?"

"Taking a tea break. Go on back."

A flimsy partition has created a tiny staff room at the back of the shop. Somehow Willie had, a few years ago, bullied the authorities into putting in plumbing for a sink—no small job when one is dealing with fifteenth-century walls a couple of feet thick—so she could make tea. As bidden, I went to the room and poked my head through the curtain that did duty for a door.

"Willie, it's me—Dorothy. Can I come in?"

"Do, but I've just finished the tea. Shall I make you some?"

She was sitting on the room's lone chair, which had grown several degrees more dilapidated since I'd seen it last. It seemed to be even harder to get out of than it used to be. Probably several more springs had gone. I extended an arm to Willie, who seized it and at last struggled out of the chair's clutches.

"Whew! One day it's simply going to eat me alive."

"The original Venus chair-trap," I agreed. "No, don't bother with the kettle. I don't want any tea. Alan and I finished lunch just a little while ago, isn't it disgraceful?"

"You'd be here to ask me about Rachel, I expect."

I've lived in Sherebury for a number of years. I've grown used to the fact that news spreads by some sort of bush telegraph, especially when the Cathedral is in any way involved. I nodded. "And you've heard about Jane?"

It was a pro forma question. She raised her eyebrows. "And in an attempt to prove that Jane is innocent, which she surely is, you've hit upon me as the next most likely suspect."

I've also grown used to the fact that Willie can be very direct. "Not exactly. If disliking Rachel made one a suspect, the police would have to rent a football stadium to hold everyone. No, I just wanted to talk to you about her. I barely knew her, myself."

"You can count yourself lucky. Look, it's time for Bar-

bara's tea break. Let's go into the shop. There won't be any customers on a day like this, so I can be as indiscreet as I like."

She established herself on the stool behind the cash register. I leaned against a case displaying various wares with the Sherebury crest on them, and began to ask questions.

"Willie, nobody seems to know where she came from, or anything about her. She's only been here since...when? Sometime after Christmas, wasn't it?"

"Just after. I don't know when she moved to town, but she showed up here, wanting to volunteer, on Epiphany. I knew she was trouble the minute I saw her."

I said nothing, but raised an interrogative eyebrow.

"I can't explain. It was the look of her. Intelligence and temper and a short fuse, and...something else. Oh, she was very smooth. Explained that she had some experience in retail work, and I looked as though I could use some help, and she had time on her hands. We still had tourist traffic left over from Christmas, and I did, in fact, need volunteers. She could see that for herself so plainly that I couldn't very well turn her down. I wish I'd forgotten about tact and just said I couldn't use her."

"I'll want to hear all about that in a minute, but...she said she had experience in retail. Where?"

"She didn't say. In fact, I doubt that she had. She was an experienced businesswoman, there was no question about that, but not, I think, in retail. She knew nothing about display, for one thing, nothing about customer service. I could imagine her as a particularly unpopular manager in an office in some big company. She loved to give orders and hated to explain why."

"Hmm. Maybe she'd been in the army."

Willie laughed. "That's one explanation that never occurred to me. But I can tell you that I think she came from London. She knew London well, anyway. She used to talk about restaurants she liked, shops, that sort of thing."

"I thought she was closemouthed about her background. That was the impression I got, anyway."

"She was. But when she got off on her favorite subject, which was how wonderful she was, she couldn't help saying things about 'the best restaurant in London, of course very few people know about it' or 'charming little shop in Soho, chic and extremely exclusive.'"

"A place-dropper."

"Of the worst kind. Nothing anyone else mentioned was any good at all. I tried her out on tea at the Ritz once. You should have heard her! Several steps down from Disneyland, according to her."

"I love tea at the Ritz," I said.

"So does everyone else. Except dear Rachel. It was almost as if she set out to get everyone's wool up."

"It's been suggested that she might have had mental or emotional problems."

"Now that's interesting. That's very interesting. Because she certainly took a lot of pills. She dropped her handbag one day—she claimed someone had knocked her elbow—and my dear, the number of little bottles that rolled out! I wouldn't have believed it. She didn't like it that I saw them, either. I offered to help her pick them up and she was downright rude, literally pushed me away." Willie shook her head.

"I don't suppose you noticed any of the labels."

"No. They were all prescriptions, though, nothing over-the-counter. I do remember that particularly, because I thought at the time that so many different drugs could be dangerous together."

"Did you say anything?"

"You're joking. Actually I might have done, if she hadn't been so snippy. As it was, I rather felt that the more pills she took, the better. Oh, dear!" Willie heard what she had just said and looked conscience-stricken.

"Don't feel guilty. We all think things like that from time to time, and Rachel certainly invited the reaction. Anyway, the police apparently think, now, that it wasn't the pills at all," I told her.

"Do they know—no, I mustn't ask you that sort of question, must I?"

I grinned. "I couldn't tell you even if I knew, but in fact I don't. I'm hoping Alan will have something for me when he gets home, but there's no guarantee now that he's more or less out of the loop. Meanwhile, I'm going around in circles. I have no idea if I'll turn up anything useful, but I did want to talk to some of the women in the Flower Guild."

"More of your suspects," said Willie.

I nodded. "Under just as much suspicion as you." We both smiled, but with the underlying knowledge that it wasn't funny, really.

FOUR

SINCE IT WAS LATE on a Saturday afternoon, I expected to find a few of the Flower Guild women about, doing the flowers for Sunday. I had reckoned without the rain. When I could find no one working, I went to the small room at the bottom of the tower where the vases and so on were kept. The head of the guild, a Mrs. Little whom I knew only slightly, was busy polishing brass and seemed shocked when I asked where everyone was.

"Oh, but one can't pick flowers in the rain, Mrs. Martin! Or at least, one can, but they'll never be at their best. If they're cut wet, they get spots and sometimes actually mold. If it's still raining this evening, we'll have to wait until sunup tomorrow." She smiled condescendingly. I had just betrayed my ignorance of the finer points of gardening and confirmed her decision not to invite me to join the guild. There were other reasons, of course. The biggest one was that, although I had lived in Sherebury for some years now, I was American, and therefore more of an outlander even than Rachel Spry.

How was I to raise the topic of Rachel? Perhaps if I could get a conversation going… "Oh, goodness, I didn't know. Though I should have, I suppose. I used to cut wet flowers back in Indiana and they never did very well. I thought it was just because the flowers themselves weren't exactly spectacular. Gardening has never been one of my strengths, I'm afraid."

Mrs. Little unbent a trifle. "Well, we can't all be good at

everything, can we? Although there are some who think they
are," she added darkly, picking up an oddly shaped vase and
putting it down again.

That looked like my cue. "Mrs. Spry certainly seemed to
be competent in a good many areas. Isn't that one of the vases
she donated to the Cathedral?"

"Donated, ha! She picked them out and had the face to
charge me for them! Charge the guild account, I mean. We'll
never use them again."

"Poor woman," I said deliberately. "I do really feel rather
sorry for her. She didn't have much of a gift for making
friends, did she?"

Mrs. Little pursed up her mouth. "I wouldn't waste my
sympathy on her, if I were you. One ought not speak ill of the
dead, but the plain fact is, that woman was a troublemaker.
And I'd say more if we weren't on consecrated ground."

Blast consecrated ground! I needed some good old-fashioned gossip and Mrs. Little looked ill-natured enough to
provide it to me. I had a sudden inspiration. I looked at my
watch. "Goodness, it's much later than I thought. No wonder
I'm perishing for a cup of tea! I don't suppose—that is, Alderney's isn't far away, so we wouldn't get very wet, and I'd
love some company. I know you're terribly busy, but have you
time to join me? My treat."

Mrs. Little was three inches shorter than I and weighed at
least twenty pounds more—and I'm no fashion model. I was
gambling that she couldn't resist tea at Alderney's, where
they have a special butter-and-cinnamon-drenched tea cake
that would tempt the most rigorous dieter.

"We-ell," said Mrs. Little, and I knew I'd won.

Twenty minutes later, seated in a cozy booth with steaming
teacups in front of us, she and I were rapidly getting chummy.

"It's my belief, Mrs. Martin," she began, and then paused
to apply a napkin to the butter on her chin.

"Dorothy, please," I said with my best smile.

"Oh, good. I do hate formality, don't you? I'm Isobel."

"And you were saying, Isobel?" I took a bite of my own tea cake. And I'd meant to diet! Oh, well, it was in a good cause.

"Well, I suppose I shouldn't say it, but it's my belief that woman had a Past."

The capital letter sounded clearly. Isobel wasn't a woman I'd want to get on the wrong side of, and she'd never be a bosom friend. But I had to deal with her on her own terms if I was to learn anything. "Really!" I said. "How exciting! You don't mean..." Since I had no idea what she meant, I let the sentence dangle and she picked it up on cue.

"What I mean is that anyone that closemouthed has something to be closemouthed about, if you take my meaning."

I suppressed a sigh. This was getting me nowhere. "Well, I suppose there's a skeleton or two in everybody's closet."

Isobel looked at me sharply. "I hope you don't think that of everyone, Mrs. Martin."

Oops. I hastened to make amends. "Oh, of course I don't mean people like you and me. But when a woman comes to town, and no one knows who she is or where she's come from..."

"Yes, that's just it! Where did she come from? I hinted and hinted, and finally asked her straight-out, and do you know what she said?"

I raised my eyebrows.

"She said she couldn't imagine why that was any of my business. Now, I ask you!"

"Hmm. That's interesting." It was, too. Anyone might refuse to respond to hints from an Isobel Little. I might, myself. The woman rubbed me the wrong way. But a direct question about something as harmless as one's previous place of residence—most people would answer that, if only to get the questioner out of their hair. "That's really very interesting. So you were no more successful than anyone else in finding out anything about her background."

"I didn't say that," Isobel said coyly.

I had picked up my teacup. I set it down and looked across the table. If a cat had been sitting across the table from me, a cat that had just polished off the last of the clotted cream, it couldn't have looked more smug and satisfied than Isobel. Her eyes glittered, her face shone with malice.

I looked inquiring and waited.

"It was pure accident, really," she said in a self-excusing tone of voice. " I needed to go up to London that day anyway, and by coincidence I took the same train as Mrs. Spry."

Noticed her at the station and followed her, I thought. "Really," I said, a little too dryly. I sipped some tea and coughed. "Sorry. Frog in my throat. Well, that was a lucky chance. At least if you happened to see where she went. London's a big place."

"And I did," she announced triumphantly. "I had a doctor's appointment, and there was such a long queue for taxis that I decided to take the Underground. The Regent's Park station is quite near Harley Street, you know."

"I do, as it happens."

She hadn't expected that, and looked somewhat taken aback.

"When I broke my leg," I went on remorselessly, "I had it seen to by a doctor in Harley Street. Naturally, I never took the Underground, not with a broken leg, but the taxis passed by the station on the way. I seem to recall that it's really rather a walk from Harley Street. And the street itself is quite long, isn't it?" I was about to point out that the far end of the street was at least half a mile from the Regent's Park tube station when I caught myself. I might not believe a word of her "coincidences," but it was definitely not smart to tell her so. "So fortunate that your doctor's office is at the top of the street, isn't it?" I beamed at her.

"What is more to the point," she said, ignoring my digression, "is that Mrs. Spry was also going to Harley Street, and her doctor's office was on the very corner, just as one turns from Marylebone Road into Harley Street itself. And what sort of doctor do you think he was?"

I shook my head.

"A psychiatrist, that's what! I consider that proves it."

"Proves what?" I was completely at sea now.

"That she was off her chump, of course."

"But…" Once more I restrained myself. Going to a psychiatrist may mean a great many things, but this was not the time to lecture Isobel on the subject. "But you said you found out where she lived. Had lived, I mean. And just because she was seeing a doctor in London—I mean, you go to a London doctor, yourself."

"A specialist," she said. "He understands my Condition."

She was dying for me to ask about it. I didn't. "How nice for you. But how did you find out—oh, more tea?"

She had finished her bun and drained the teapot. I ordered more, along with a plate of jam tarts.

"Oh, dear, I shouldn't, but if you really think…"

"The jam tarts here are some of my very favorite things," I said firmly. "You were telling me how you discovered where Mrs. Spry had lived."

She fiddled with her napkin. "Well, you see, I—I realized that I was wrong about my doctor's appointment. I just happened to look at a newspaper, and it said it was Thursday, and I'd been thinking all day it was Friday, which was when my appointment was." She trilled an artificial laugh. "Silly of me, wasn't it?"

"Understandable," I said. I had my attitude under control by now. "I've done it myself. So you followed Mrs. Spry?"

"Not to say *followed*. I have always enjoyed that part of London, Wimpole Street, you know—dear Elizabeth Barrett, so romantic—"

"Yes, and I believe Dr. Watson had a surgery there at one time," I put in.

Isobel looked blank.

"When he wasn't living at 221B Baker Street with Sherlock Holmes."

"Oh. Yes. Well, so I walked about a bit—it was a lovely day and I had time to spare, because I'd set aside the whole afternoon for my appointment—but I grew tired, and I had just decided to go and get some tea when Mrs. Spry came out and started walking up the street. And—well, yes, I suppose I followed her. I was curious, you see, because she wasn't going back to the Tube. And you can imagine my surprise when she went into *another* doctor's office."

"Another? Surely not another psychiatrist?" But suppose she was abusing some kind of drugs. If she went to several doctors and none of them knew about the others—

"No. At least the brass plate didn't say anything about psychiatric practice. Well, I was trying to decide whether to wait or not, when what do you think I heard?"

"I can't imagine."

"I heard Rachel Spry screaming!"

"Screaming! You mean, someone was attacking her?"

"No, no, not that kind of screaming. If anything, it was she who was doing the attacking. Such carryings-on as you never heard, and a man's voice trying now and then to get a word in edgewise."

"Good heavens! What on earth? Why would she have a fight with her doctor?"

"Aha! I asked myself that same question. And do you know what the answer is?"

Numbly I shook my head. I was tired of the guessing game and wondering if Isobel would ever tell me anything that was worth the cost, in money and health, of the tarts and tea cakes.

"She was screaming at him because he was her husband!"

"Her husband! I didn't know she had a husband!"

Doling out her information as if each item were worth five pounds, Isobel told the rest of the story. The man in question, it turned out, was not Mrs. Spry's husband anymore, but a former husband. Isobel had overheard the word "divorce" and a loud dispute about money. Then the man had apparently succeeded in quieting Mrs. Spry, because after that only bits and pieces were audible. Isobel had heard agitated talk about "the house in Belgrave Square," from which she had concluded that Mrs. Spry had lived in London, and had been well off, to put it mildly. Finally, as Mrs. Spry left the offices—and Isobel, I gathered, had hastily retreated from her listening post— a last remark was flung.

"'So do what you want with that little tart!' Her very words, and I don't think," Isobel concluded, "that she was talking about this sort." She scooped up the last jam tart, which I had been eyeing, and stuffed it into her mouth.

It turned out that Isobel was the sort of person who enjoys telling stories over and over. She rehashed the whole thing several times, over more tea and a piece of rich fruitcake for her. I passed on that one. When I finally managed to escape and waddle home, it was nearly six. The first thing I did was beat it upstairs to the bathroom.

Alan, seated in the parlor, gave me a quizzical look when I returned. "Feeling poorly?"

"Fine, now. I had at least six cups of tea at Alderney's. And I'm sorry, but I haven't the slightest interest in dinner. Ever."

"Ah. That'll lighten the household bills a bit."

I stuck my tongue out at him and plopped down on the couch.

"You were sleuthing, I take it?"

"I was. And I learned some things, too, if the source is to be relied upon. But you first. Did you get anything out of Derek?"

He studied my face, his head to one side, and then got up

and went to the kitchen. When he came back he carried a tray with two glasses and a bottle.

"Uh-oh. If you think I need some Jack Daniel's, the news must be really bad."

He poured the amber liquid into both glasses, handed me one and raised his own in a toast. "Here's to you, love. And the news isn't quite disastrous, but you won't like it. They found Prozac in the strawberry jam at Rachel's house, and it's unquestionably Jane's jam."

FIVE

ALAN WAS RIGHT. I didn't like it. I took a sip of my drink, which burned with a gentle warmth all the way down. "I suppose we knew that, really. But it's absurd to think Jane put it there. I doubt she even knows what Prozac is. I'd bet money she's never taken any, so where is she supposed to have gotten it?"

Alan sighed. I took another sip and waited.

"Rachel was taking the drug," he went on. "There was a vial of it on the table next to her bed. The prescription had been filled just last week. The vial ought to have been nearly full. It was nearly empty."

"She could have taken the overdose herself."

"Except why would she go to the trouble of mixing it up in jam?"

I clutched my head with both hands. "Alan, that's crazy! Nobody with any sense would have chosen that way to kill someone! Now look here. Prozac isn't poisonous, right?"

"Not in normal doses, no."

"All right. What happens if someone takes a mild overdose, say twice as many as prescribed?"

"Dorothy, *I* don't know! I'm not a doctor, nor a pharmacist, nor yet a forensics expert."

"Well, I do happen to know. I read about it once in some mystery. Any of those tranquilizers, antidepressants, any of that kind of thing, they have to be taken as directed, because a small overdose will have just the opposite effect. The patient goes bonkers."

"That, I take it, being a medical term."

I made a face. "I don't remember the details. Excitement, agitation—bonkers, as I said. It's been a while since I read the book, but I think the victim in that case threw things and in general caused a big scene. The point is that a moderate overdose wouldn't kill anybody. I don't think even a hefty one would, unless they were taking something else and the two drugs didn't mix. And, Alan, how much Prozac could anyone get from a tablespoonful or so of doctored strawberry preserves?"

I was waving my hands and almost shouting by the time I ended my little tirade. "Sorry," I murmured, and picked up my glass.

Alan took a healthy swig of his own drink. "That's one of the reasons they're not charging her. For now."

"Oh! You mean, she's home? I want to talk to her, right now!"

I started to rise from the couch, a feat that takes more and more effort as the years go by. Alan shook his head. "I wouldn't, not just now. She's very tired and out of sorts, and Walter is looking after her. Wait a bit."

I got up anyway. I needed to pace. "Alan, none of this makes any sense," I said, waving my arms in frustration. "Think about it. Suppose Jane did want to kill Rachel. I don't suppose any such thing, but for the sake of the argument. Now, Jane is an intelligent and methodical woman. If she did plan a murder, she'd do it efficiently. There are any number of nasty little poisons she could have put in that jam if she'd wanted to. Why would she go to the trouble of doing something so risky?"

Alan didn't attempt an answer.

"And another thing. What do the police propose as a scenario for this murder? Jane goes over there, taking a jar of carefully altered strawberry preserves, when Rachel has already bought two at the fête? Or she goes over hoping she'll find something at hand that she can stir into the jam while Rachel's not looking? Or does she fix up a jar of very special jam and take it to the fête on the off chance that Rachel may happen to buy it?"

"Two jars," said Alan.

"What do you mean, two jars?"

"Didn't I tell you? Derek and co. found the other jar in the kitchen. It was still sealed, but it had Prozac in it, too."

"Still sealed? What do you mean, still sealed?"

"Well, with the bit of cloth tied on top and the wax beneath, actually sealing the jar."

"But, Alan, it would be child's play to take off the cloth, pry out the paraffin, put in whatever one wanted to, and then just put everything back. It's not like a Mason jar of home-canned beans or tomatoes or whatever. Those really are sealed, and when you open them the middle of the lid pops up and it's easy to tell they've been opened. But preserves aren't put up like that. Do you suppose they looked really carefully at that extra jar? There would be signs, if it had been tampered with."

"I expect they did, you know, Dorothy. The forensics people aren't amateurs."

"And I am, but I'll bet I was learning to preserve food before any of them were born or thought of. And now there's no point in looking. They've opened the jar and ruined any evidence that might have been there."

Alan didn't argue, just nodded toward my glass, which was empty. "Another?"

"No, thanks. Alcohol is a depressant and I don't need to get any more depressed. From all you've told me, I think it's a wonder they didn't charge her. There's so much suspicious stuff. Even though it's all nonsense."

"Lots of suspicions, no proof. Derek needs to make a case, and Jane's not going anywhere."

"I see," I said a little bitterly. "Give her enough rope...is that it?"

"Be fair, Dorothy. And let's drop that end of the case for a while, and you can tell me about what you learned in your trial by tea."

I made a face. "Ugh. I'll go up shortly and take a bath. I hate gossips, Alan, and I had to pretend to be one."

Probably wisely, Alan said nothing. I responded to his silence.

"Well, I'm not one, really, and you know it! I do enjoy talking about my friends, but not…not maliciously. I'd *never* go out and try to dig up dirt—"

Alan grinned and held up a hand. "Peace, woman. I haven't accused you of anything. Go on. You had to pretend to gossip."

"Well…to encourage it, anyway. I decided to follow your advice and nose around, and my nose led me to the Cathedral. I talked first to Willie, but she didn't have much to offer, except that Rachel took a lot of pills. They spilled out of her purse one day. I suppose Derek will assume Jane knew about that."

Alan looked patient, and I let it go.

"So after I struck out there, I went to find someone in the Flower Guild."

"Ah. And I suspect, from your reaction, that you unearthed Isobel Little."

"You know her?"

"There is not," said Alan dryly, "a policeman within twenty miles who does not know her. She's a complainer. You know, the sort who watches her neighbors every minute and calls in the law when darkly suspicious things begin to happen."

I nodded. "A light goes on at the wrong time."

"Or off. Or a strange car shows up."

"Or goes away. Or the cat yowls, or doesn't, or the dog barks in the nighttime."

"Or the parsley sinks into the butter. Dorothy, what are we talking about?" Alan asked.

"Aside from proving we know a little Sherlockiana, we're

talking about Isobel Little, and a less attractive subject I can't imagine. And now I *am* being malicious."

"In her case, entirely justified, I'd say. Did your tea and conversation result in anything positive?"

"Something for you to follow up, maybe. Or Derek, I mean. Isobel thinks she found out that Rachel used to live in London, that she was rich, and that she was married to a doctor."

"Married? She didn't wear a ring and her will—yes, Derek looked into that, of course—her will left everything to the Cathedral."

"Good heavens! Maybe the woman had some redeeming qualities after all. Anyway, she wasn't married when she died." I relayed Isobel's story.

When I had finished, and had excused myself again, I came back downstairs to find Alan tenting his fingers and frowning.

"I see the great brain is at work. Okay, what startling conclusions has it drawn?" I asked.

"No conclusions, just questions," he said. "The first is to wonder just how much of what Isobel told you is fact and how much the product of what is, I promise you, an extremely active imagination."

"Derek will have to find out."

"He *will* be pleased," said Alan dryly. "And my second question is something else for Derek, probably, though we might be able to help him a trifle. Dorothy, since when do doctors list their specialities on their brass plates?"

"Well, I don't know! I've only ever been to one doctor in London, and you took me there, the first few times, anyway. I never paid attention to whatever was on his front door."

"I can tell you. It has nothing but his name. Nor does any other doctor's plate I've ever seen. They don't expect people to be roaming about Harley Street shopping for an orthopedist or a pediatrician or whatever."

"Then how," I demanded, "did Isobel know that the first doctor Rachel went to was a psychiatrist?"

"Precisely."

I caught up with him a second or two later. "Because Isobel had been to the same man, or someone else in the same practice."

"I'd think so, wouldn't you?"

We mulled that over for a little while. I finally said, "Well, she's certainly odd enough to need a psychiatrist, I'd say. And she hated Rachel Spry. Maybe Derek should look into her movements just a little."

Alan sighed. "Motive, as you very well know, is the least important factor in making a case. Besides, name me someone who didn't hate Rachel Spry."

"Jane Langland," I said firmly. "And I've changed my mind about another drink, please."

I did eventually get hungry, but I didn't feel like cooking, so we decided to go to the Rose and Crown, which is nearby in the Cathedral Close and is one of our favorite hostelries. At my insistence we knocked on Jane's door to see if she and Walter wanted to come with us.

Jane answered the door, looking very much like herself. Hers is not the sort of face that goes haggard in hours. She did look tired. I would have loved to give her a hug, but she's not a huggy sort of person, so I restrained myself to a discreet murmur about how sorry I was.

She shrugged. "Natural enough, I suppose. Police got the wrong end of the stick. Hope they realize it in time. Come in out of the wet."

"Yes, well, we're doing our best to get the police to see sense, Jane," I said. We shook out our wet things and sat in her front room. I detailed my afternoon.

Jane snorted. "Isobel Little. Wrong name for her, eh? Of course…" She looked disparagingly at her own contours.

"You're not fat, Jane. Just—solid."

Jane is not the sort of person to take offense at remarks like that. She nodded matter-of-factly. "Eat too much, for a fact."

"Which reminds me. What we really came for was to invite you both to dinner at the Rose and Crown."

"Good of you, but having supper at home. Walter's cooking."

I raised my eyebrows.

"Has to learn sometime, doesn't he? Make someone a good husband one day."

A smell of burning came from the kitchen, followed by a muffled expletive. "It's all right," came the shout. "Only the toast."

"You're sure you won't join us?" I asked.

Jane shook her head. "Take more than burned toast to kill me."

She showed us to the door. The rain had stopped while we were inside, or rather, had paused. It was certainly going to rain some more, but for now there was only mist in the air. Jane stepped outside with us and inhaled deeply.

"Air smells good. Lilies of the valley, roses, violets."

That was all she said, but I pictured her behind bars, far from fresh air and the garden she loves. A lump formed in my throat and I couldn't reply.

The rain began again. Jane stumped back inside while we put up our brollies and sploshed through the Close to the pub.

I didn't have enough appetite for the exquisite and expensive food in their dining room, but we happily ordered cottage pie in the bar and chatted with the Endicotts, owners of the establishment and long-time friends.

Peter was a little cool with Alan. "I hear Jane Langland's been arrested," he said as he set our beer down on the oak table. "You'd think the police would have more sense."

Alan sighed. "I'm not 'the police' anymore, as you know perfectly well, Peter. And your information is inaccurate. They did not arrest her. They asked her to come to the station for a few questions."

"Right, a technical difference," he said with something very much like a snort.

"But an important one," I pointed out. "They've let her come back home, you know. We invited her to supper with us, but she was tired. Walter is coping. Goodness knows what she'll get to eat."

"Doesn't matter much, does it? What she needs is cosseting, and she'll get it. A good lad, that Walter."

"He's a nice boy," I agreed, and sipped my beer.

"So what are the police doing to track down the real killer?" asked Peter, a trace of belligerence still in his tone. Custom was slow that rainy night and he seemed prepared to stay and talk to us.

"Oh, sit down, Peter, and climb off your high horse," I said, pulling out a chair for him. "They're doing all they can, and Alan's put me to work, besides. That should make you happy."

He grinned, a little ruefully. "Sorry. Didn't mean to be rude, but Jane's rather a special person. If she—and you, Dorothy—hadn't believed in Nigel, I might never have had the most wonderful grandchild in the world."

Well, that led to baby pictures. "Pulling himself up in his cot, and not even eight months old yet," said Peter proudly. Alan and I had to counter with stories and pictures of his first great-grandchild, a little girl who was unquestionably the most beautiful child on the planet.

Peter's wife Inga brought us our meals, and then the pub got busy, and we had finished our totally wicked but lovely portions of summer pudding before Peter had another chance to talk.

"You asked what's happening about the murder, Peter. I found out some interesting things today." I queried Alan with my eyes; he shrugged. It was all gossip, the shrug seemed to say. No reason not to pass it along.

"So did you know Rachel had been married?" I asked when I'd finished my recitation. "You did know her, didn't you?"

"To my sorrow," said Peter. "She was a regular. Our beer was no good, mind you, our food was barely edible and our service was nonexistent."

"Then why did she keep on offering her patronage to your humble establishment?" asked Alan with heavy irony.

"Finally asked her that, in so many words. 'If you don't like it here, why don't you find another pub?' I said, and I meant it. Hoped she'd stomp out and never darken our door again."

"What did she do?"

"Tore me off a strip, said I didn't know the meaning of hospitality, left without paying her bill, and was back again in two days. I left her alone after that." Peter jerked his head in the direction of the bar, where a chipper little man was serving. "Bill's got a hide like a rhinoceros. I let him wait on her. It all rolled off his back."

"But did she ever talk about a husband? Or an ex-husband?"

"She was almost always alone. Once or twice she came with another woman. Never with a man, that I recall. I didn't notice what they talked about. Too busy trying not to catch her eye or get too close."

"No wonder she found the service terrible."

"Right. Another round?"

"Please," said Alan as I said, "No, thank you. Just coffee." Peter went off to fetch them and when he came back I was ready with another question.

"Peter, did you know any of the women she dined with?"

"Sure. Cathedral types. Willie Williamson, one time, and some of the Flower Guild."

"Mrs. Little?"

"Not that I ever saw."

"Did you ever see her acting erratic? As if she might have been under the influence of drugs?"

"She did drugs?" Peter was clearly astonished.

"Only legal ones, so far as we know."

"Well, that's a relief. I don't like drugs in my pub. Oh, I know a lot of people do them, but they cause trouble. You get users, sooner or later you get drug deals going down, and I won't have that on my premises. I could lose my license, and besides, I hate rows."

"Very wise of you," I said soothingly. "But you never saw Rachel Spry acting oddly?"

Peter raised an eyebrow. "Given the sort of personality she had, how would you expect me to have known?"

We went home, full of food but just as empty of information as when we'd left.

SIX

THE NEXT DAY, Sunday, we went as usual to church in the morning and then spent most of the day with Alan's oldest granddaughter, Cynthia, her husband, and her adorable new baby. One of the many things I love about being married to Alan is that I get to revel in the joys of grand- and great-grand-motherhood, a neat trick for a childless woman. Little Caroline and I had a wonderful time smiling and cooing at each other, and I completely forgot about murder and suspicion and all the dark things of life.

My mind apparently profited from its respite, because Monday morning an idea popped into my head before my eyes were open. I turned over and tried to go back to sleep, but it's almost impossible to sleep on a fine June morning. The early sunrise wakes the birds, which make a racket like fifty orchestras tuning up. They, in turn, wake the cats, who then decide they're hungry and hammer on the bedroom door in search of their slothful human servants.

As the noise continued, accompanied by assorted yowls, Alan yawned, sighed and opened his eyes.

I patted his shoulder. "Never mind, love. I'm awake anyway."

He grunted and turned over, and I got up to begin the day.

Once they had my attention, the cats were willing to wait until I made coffee before they renewed their demands. By the time I'd fed them and drunk the coffee and nibbled some toast, it was nearly six and I was wide awake. It was a really gorgeous day. The cats had long since slipped out the cat door to chase those tantalizing birds, so until Alan appeared I was free to sit and think.

Ideas that come when one is half asleep often don't seem as good when looked at in the cold light of day. But this one still seemed to have possibilities and I intended to run it by Alan the moment he'd ingested enough caffeine.

He got up a little later and he wasn't even into his second cup of coffee when I asked, "Alan, was the stuff cooked?"

He'd been looking over the *Times*. He put the paper down with that wary expression a man gets when he fears he's missed part of a wifely dissertation.

"Sorry. You're coming in in the middle. I've been thinking. The Prozac, in the jam. Could the police tell if it was cooked in?"

Alan thought about that for a moment and then gave me an entirely different look. "I have no idea, but it's an interesting question."

"You see the point, then. If it was cooked in with the preserves, then it puts Jane in a worse jam than ever. Oh," I said as Alan groaned, "no, it wasn't intentional, I didn't even see it coming. But if it *was* cooked, or heated, anyway, who but she could have added it? And then she could have deliberately sold Rachel the poisonous preserves. Not that she would, but I mean that's what the police would think. And it would be much easier to stir something into hot jam, before it sets. But if it was added when the jam was cold, how did it get in there?"

"It's not a definitive argument, you know," said Alan, moving the newspaper aside and devoting his whole attention to the matter. "For all we know, heating might alter the effect of the drug."

"But do you know that's true with Prozac? More to the point, would Jane know?"

Alan made no reply. He refilled his coffee cup. Apparently he wasn't minded to argue, at least not without more stimulant.

"Anyway," I said as I got up to make breakfast, "I absolutely refuse to believe in Jane going to all that elaborate and unnecessary trouble just on the off chance that Rachel Spry would come by her stall and buy two jars of jam. For heaven's sake, she hadn't even quarreled with Rachel, or not seriously, until that day!"

"There's that," Alan agreed, and went back to the *Times* while I whipped up some French toast.

"What are you going to do today, love?" he asked when we were washing the dishes later.

"I thought I might learn something useful from Rachel's neighbors. Oh, I know," I said as he opened his mouth. "The police will have asked them all the usual questions, but if I know any of them, I might be able to get more information than someone official could. Where did she live?"

"Now, where would you think, given her taste?"

"Oh. The awful new housing estate, of course. Up by the university."

"Of course. I can give you the address. It's rather a rabbit warren up there. Would you like me to drive you?"

My uncanny ability to get lost in England, even in my own town, is legendary. I fight it constantly. "Certainly not. I will find my own way."

He grinned. "I have every confidence in you, my dear. But make sure you have the mobile, just in case."

I stuck my tongue out at him.

As I got ready to go, putting on one of my most flowery hats for confidence, I had an idea. I could shorten the odds considerably with one side trip. "I'm running over to see Margaret for a minute," I called to Alan, and left the house.

The dean of the Cathedral and his wife life in a very beautiful fifteenth-century house within the Cathedral Close. When I admired it once, Margaret closed her eyes briefly and said, "Yes, it is rather nice, but you can't think what a trial it is entertaining guests. There's only one bathroom, you see, and positively no way to add another one." Americans, with our reverence for the antiquity of English houses, don't always consider these things.

I found Margaret in her garden, tending her roses. "Busy?" I said.

"Not really. Mostly just reveling in June. It's so short, and often so rainy and cold. This is a perfect day, isn't it? I only hope it doesn't turn into another summer like that frightful one in 2003."

"Mmm. My American friends could hardly believe me when I wrote to them complaining of a heat wave in England."

"At any rate, it's lovely now. Did you come by to admire my roses, or is there something I can do for you?"

"I do need something. Who do I know who lives up in the modern horrors near the university?"

"Let's see. Priscilla and—no, they moved to Birmingham a year or two ago. Then there are the Ridgeways, but I don't believe you know them." She cocked her head interrogatively; I shook mine.

"There aren't a lot of Cathedral parishioners up that way. Oh! I know! Jeremy Sayers has moved there."

"Jeremy! But he has a house in the Close." The Cathedral organist/choirmaster was the very last person I'd have suspected of modern tastes.

"Yes, I know, but it developed dry rot. Hadn't you heard? It's having to be completely redone, and meanwhile Jeremy's fallen in love again, someone named Alistair, I believe. And since the man had a perfectly good house on the hill, it made sense for Jeremy to move in with him while the repairs were being done."

I nodded. "I see. It won't do me a lot of good, though. I was hoping to find someone who lived close to Rachel and would have been home most of the time. A witness, in fact."

Margaret beamed. "So you're digging again. Well done! And in fact you're in luck, because although Jeremy isn't home a great deal during the day, his partner is. The man is writing a book," she added as if that explained everything.

"Oh well, then, he might be just the person I want. I've only ever known one writer, but from what I could gather, she spent every possible moment trying to figure out things she could do that would keep her from having to sit down and actually write. Does this Alistair live near Rachel?"

"I don't know, but Jeremy would. Why don't you pop in and ask him? It's officially his day off, but he's looking over the organ one last time before the restorers come in."

I found Jeremy laying out music in the choir stalls. He was very helpful. "Oh, yes, cheek-by-jowl with the late unlamented. It's a perfectly horrid house, and I've told Allie so, but he's absolutely barmy about minimalist architecture. Myself, I prefer beauty and comfort. But Allie's a dear boy, and quite, quite dishy, so I put up with black glass and white leather."

"Does he keep track of his neighbors?"

"The original Paul Pry, I assure you."

"Wonderful. What's his full name?"

"Alistair Carmichael III."

"Heavens. I hope I'm aristocratic enough to talk to him. Now, Jeremy, can you tell me *exactly* how to get there? Because you know me. I can get turned around in the High Street."

So Jeremy drew me a very accurate little map, and I actually managed to find the place without one false move, a new record. It was on a cul-de-sac that had only three houses, one at the end and one on either side. I parked in front of the one on the left and rang the bell.

Alistair Carmichael III turned out to be a very nonintimidating man of about forty, somewhat older than Jeremy. He answered the door in black jeans, a clean but somewhat tattered T-shirt and bare feet. His hair was standing straight up in front, a look I found reminiscent of my writer friend.

"Yes?" he said, looking at my hat with an expression of mild shock.

"I'm awfully sorry if I'm interrupting, but I'm a friend of Jeremy's and he thought—"

Alistair ran his hands through his hair. "You have been sent from heaven, dear lady. Any friend of Jer's—and in any case the book is going badly, *very* badly, and I was pining to stop work. Would you like a cup of tea? We could take it out in the garden. *Such* a heavenly day—and your hat would fit right in."

I accepted with gratitude, and when we were settled on a couple of oddly angular lawn chairs, in a garden that consisted of raked gravel, I looked across to the next house. "Jeremy tells me you live near the house where Rachel Spry died. Is that it over there?" I pointed to the house at the end.

"It is. You can't imagine the number of policemen who have been haunting the neighborhood. I finally had to take my laptop and go away and hide, or I would have got no work done at all, and as it happens they came when I was in particularly good form. It doesn't happen that often," he added gloomily.

"Ah. Well, I'm on the same sort of errand, I'm afraid. I don't believe I've introduced myself properly. My name's Dorothy Martin and—"

Alistair raised a dramatic hand. "No! Not Sherebury's very own Miss Marple, right here in my garden! I ought to have known the moment I saw that magnificent chapeau. I am honored, dear lady. What, pray, can I do for you?"

I laughed. "Well, you can come off it, for one thing. I'm sure you're not always quite so—"

"Mannered? Wildean? No, not really." He slumped back into his chair. "Only when I am absolutely at my wit's end.

Which I was until you came. But now that I have a perfectly good excuse to take a break, I can relax. It's hell to try to write when there's nothing in one's head."

"I've never tried to write, but I can vouch for trying to teach thirty or forty squirming nine-year-olds when one has no ideas. Hell is the word." We raised our cups of tea in a toast to mutual misery and sat for a moment or two in companionable silence.

"I suppose," Alistair said eventually, "that you want to know what I know about the dear departed."

"I did think your views might be useful," I admitted.

"You will find them somewhat prejudiced, I'm afraid, and based on very little information. We didn't know her, really. She scarcely showed her face. Of course she lived here only about six months. She arrived a bit before Christmas. I remember, because the house had sat empty for months and I'd hoped someone would move in who would add a bit of Christmas cheer to the place. Nothing too twee, but a holly wreath, perhaps, and a lovely little tree in the window?" He sketched a lovely little tree in the air.

"And did she?"

He made a face. "Not so much as a candle in a window. Well, one tried to be charitable. Perhaps she was Jewish, or Muslim, or whatever. But then she turned up at the Cathedral, so that idea was no good. Jeremy thought she might not have had time to do any decorating, so he made some mince pies—he's the cook in the family, you know—and took them over, just as a neighborly gesture. We thought it might put her in a holiday mood."

"And how was that received?"

"Well, she took them—greedy cow—but she didn't ask us in, much less offer something in return. Not that we wanted a quid pro quo, mind you, but a cup of tea would have been a civilized way to greet her new neighbors. But not a bit of it.

She very nearly slammed the door in our faces. And that was the only conversation we ever had. If you can call it a conversation, when we nattered on and she said yes and no and thank you."

"You know, that's really very interesting, Mr. Carmichael."

"Alistair. Or Allie."

I nodded. "And I'm Dorothy. Anyway, it's very interesting indeed, what you said. Because Mrs. Spry made all sorts of efforts to get 'in' in Sherebury. The bookshop, the Flower Guild, the Women's Institute, the Fête. One would have assumed that she was lonely, trying to meet people, make friends. And yet she was rude to you when you attempted to be friendly."

Alistair looked at me pityingly. "My dear lady. Your surprise shows your heart in a far better light than your head."

I looked at him, completely lost.

"Are you really not aware that there are vast number of people to whom a gay couple is anathema? Actually, I'm surprised she took the tarts. Some of the bigots think we're catching."

"Oh. Oh, dear. Well, no, I didn't think of that. I mean, I'm so used to Jeremy, and he's such a good friend, and such a fine musician, and there were lots of students back home..." I ran down and started again. "I'm in danger of saying something like 'some of my best friends are gay,' aren't I?"

"Close," said Alistair, but he didn't sound offended.

"Well, in any case, I wonder if you're right. She spent a lot of time at the Cathedral. Did Jeremy ever mention any rudeness to him?"

"No. But then he never mentioned any encounters with her at all. Thank the Lord for small favors."

"Well, I suppose your explanation may be the true one, but I'd like further evidence. She offended nearly everyone, you know, male or female, gay or straight. An equal opportunity offender."

Alistair chuckled.

"Anyway, what I really wanted to know about was comings and goings at her house. You can see her front door, I notice. Did she have many visitors?"

"None, really, up until the last week or so. Although there were times when I was working and might not have seen."

I waved away those times. "What can you tell me about what you did see?"

"It was just after the fête. Not the next day—that was a Sunday. No, it was the Monday. I remember, because that's Jer's day off—usually—until Evensong. A man and a woman came to visit in the afternoon. Jer was still home and we were having our tea out here, early because he had to leave soon and chivvy the little monsters into shape for the service."

The little monsters, I assumed, being the angelic-looking choir boys. Once I would have quarreled with the description. That was before I met any of them. I grinned. "He seems to have them well in hand, at least when they're actually singing. So tell me about the couple who visited."

"Well, we didn't see much, because they were evidently expected. At least the door opened almost the moment they rang the bell. So we only saw them getting out of the car and again when they left."

"What kind of car?"

"Oh, my dear!" His tone became reverent. "The loveliest Jaguar, a silver XJ. A beautiful, beautiful car."

"But good grief, Alistair! Those things cost a fortune, don't they?"

"They start at forty thousand quid, or did the last time I priced them."

I raised my eyebrows at him. "Writers must make a lot more than I thought."

Alistair grinned. "I am, dear lady, what is vulgarly known as independently wealthy. I didn't make enough on my last book to keep Jeremy in shirts, but my papa made a great deal in his line of business, and was considerate enough to leave it all to me, even though I was a great disappointment to him. He wanted me to go into partnership with him. Off-the-peg men's clothing. I ask you!"

"Okay, so you could afford a fancy Jag if you wanted one. But the point is, so can these people who called on Mrs. Spry. What did they look like?"

"Like people you'd expect to see driving that sort of car. I would imagine the combined bill for their clothing would hit four figures, easily. And she was glossy. You know, that sort of sheen you see on the ladies who lunch?"

I nodded and he went on.

"The funny thing—the thing Jer and I noticed most of all—was that they both seemed nervous. Or maybe that's not the word. Hesitant, perhaps? They didn't want to be there. At least that's the impression we got. A sort of 'once more into the breach' kind of thing."

His body language was eloquent. Shoulders back, head up, eyes front, the hint of a sigh.

I considered that. "How old were they?"

"He was about Rachel's age, late forties, maybe early fifties. She was much younger. Not much over thirty, I'd say. And quite, quite lovely. Slim, carried herself well, knew how to dress."

"Blonde? Brunette?"

"Oh, didn't I say? Redhead. A true strawberry-blond, and her own, if I'm any judge. She had the clear skin to go with it."

"You saw a lot in a few seconds."

He shrugged. "One observes beauty."

"I don't suppose you happened to notice the license plate."

Alistair dismissed license plates with an airy wave of his hand. "Of no interest, my dear."

"Well. And you said you also saw them leave."

"I did. Jer was gone by that time, slaving over a hot organ console."

"Did they stay long?"

"Not so very. I didn't keep a stopwatch running, but let's see. We were just finishing our tea when they arrived. Then Jer showered and changed and left. I suppose that took about fifteen minutes. I mooched about clearing up the tea things and tidying the bathroom. You can't *imagine* the mess that man can make! So that was about another half hour, I'd think. And then I took a glass of sherry out to the garden again, with a book, and I'd just got myself settled when the beautiful people left."

"What did they say to Rachel?"

"They weren't the linger-at-the-door sort. The door opened, they came out, they went to their car and drove off."

"Did they come back?"

"Not that I saw. They were the only visitors I'd ever seen next door, and there was only one other—before the police came swarming over the place, that is."

I glanced again at the house next door. "Good grief, Alistair, a police car pulled up just now!"

Alistair took that in stride. "Yes, they come and go. One doesn't know why. I wonder if they know what they're about, or simply present themselves from time to time to make an impression."

I wondered, too, but I let it go. "I see. Alistair, tell me about the other caller."

Alistair shifted in his chair and pressed his lips together. He sighed. "The other caller was Jane Langland."

SEVEN

I SWALLOWED. My mouth was suddenly dry.

Alistair got out of the awkward chair in one graceful, fluid motion. "You'd like more tea. I'll make a fresh pot."

I rose with more difficulty and followed him inside. "Do you mind if we sit in here? It seems kind of hot outside."

"Come through to the kitchen. It's frightful. I haven't re-done it yet. But it's reasonably comfortable."

The kitchen was much more my kind of place and it had a perfectly normal kitchen chair that fit my contours a good deal better than the modern ones Alistair preferred.

"Alistair, tell me about Jane's visit."

He filled the electric kettle and pressed the switch. "There isn't a lot to tell. It was about a week after the fête."

I nodded. "I remember the day. She told me she'd been to see Rachel. Or, to be accurate, she said she'd tried to visit, but found no one home."

"Well, as to that, I can't say. I didn't actually see her arrive. I was working. I do sometimes work, you know."

"I'm sure you do."

"It's going to be a great book when it's done," he said serenely. "On the days I can write, I write very well indeed. That day everything was coming together, so well that I forgot to eat lunch. It was a Thursday, Jer's busiest day, so I hadn't seen him since the morning. And in the middle of a paragraph I suddenly felt ill. Then I realized it was only hunger, so I came downstairs—my office is upstairs, at the back of the house. I came down to find something to eat. It was a lovely day, so I took my sandwich and a bottle of Bass outside, and I saw the car parked in front of Rachel's door. Not much of a car, is it?"

Jane drives a venerable old Ford. I smiled. "It gets her where she needs to go."

"Yes, well…at any rate I wasn't interested in the car. But then I saw Jane come around the corner of the house and get in it. I know Jane, of course. Anyone who's spent any time about the Cathedral knows her."

"Nearly everyone in Sherebury knows her, I should think. You say she came around the house? Not down the front walk?"

"I thought she'd been to the back door. If I thought about it at all. My mind was still on that scene I'd abandoned. That's why I didn't speak to Jane. I could easily have invited her over for tea, or beer, but I wanted to get back to work."

"What time was this?"

"My dear Dorothy, I haven't the slightest idea. I was engrossed in my book, and time had ceased to exist. I went straight back and worked the rest of the day. I vaguely remember Jer coming home and thrusting a plate of something before me, and I suppose I ate it. I was afraid that if I stopped writing it would all go out of my head. And how right I was. The next day there was nothing there, nothing at all. I think I'm going mad." He thrust his hands through his hair, making it stick straight up again.

"How much of this have you told the police?"

He shrugged. "I answered their questions. I was rather brief. As I said, they intruded on a day when the book was going well again, at last. I suspect I was rather rude to them."

"Well, you've been very helpful to me. I don't know exactly how we'll go about looking for a silver Jaguar—what did you say the rest of it was?"

"Jaguar XJ. Dull silver, with cream leather upholstery. I'd know it if I saw it again."

"You may have to swear to it. Because they might have valuable information about Rachel's mental state, whether suicide seemed a possibility, that sort of thing. Apparently they were the last people to see her alive, and the police are going to want to talk to them. I'll bet you a Jag on that."

But Alistair had suddenly stopped paying attention to me. "Yes!" he murmured to himself. "A bet! That would be why she made such a nit of herself that evening. And then when she tells him, he'll want..." His eyes focused on me for a moment. "Sorry. I can't—I have to—"

"You have to go write. Scoot."

I turned off the kettle before I let myself out.

Alan, when I got home and told him what I'd learned, was all for calling Derek and suggesting he send someone out to interview Alistair. He was rather hot on the subject. "Dorothy, he had no business withholding this information. Does the man have no sense of responsibility?"

"Very little," I said, "when he's trying to write. My friend in Indiana used to say the rest of the world just didn't exist when she was deep in her stories. She had real problems with writer's block, I gather, but when the ideas were coming, woe betide anyone who interrupted her. That's why there's absolutely no point in anyone trying to talk to him now. He's got the bit between his teeth and he intends to ride those ideas as far as they'll take him. He won't let anyone in. He might even go somewhere else to work. He's already done that once to elude the distraction of the police."

Alan rolled his eyes. "Artistic temperament! And what do you suggest doing until the young pup climbs out of his literary trance?"

"He's probably forty," I pointed out. "But anyway, he's told me enough to be going on with. Why don't you just report to Derek? He can ask me whatever he wants to, and he can get a start tracing that car. There can't be that many silver Jaguar X-whatevers in a town the size of Sherebury."

"If in fact its owners live in Sherebury," Alan said, still annoyed.

"And there's the description of the people," I added. "They'd stick out a bit, as well. It's a pity no one else saw them. You'd think, on a lovely afternoon, that people would have been out and about."

"There's only one other house on the cul-de-sac, you'll remember, and the people who live there have been away every time the police have called. They're probably on holiday. It's June, after all."

"Well, then, it does look as if Alistair's our only hope. And I promise you, the police will get nothing out of him if they pester him now."

Alan sighed and ran a hand down the back of his neck. "I suppose you're right. Derek won't be happy."

"I *did* get some information that might be useful," I said with some asperity. "And it occurs to me—has Derek checked out those London doctors?"

"He's undoubtedly working on it. I'm not entitled to a daily report, you know."

"Because a Harley Street doctor might very well drive a Jag," I continued, ignoring his comment. "And from the description of the female visitor, someone like Rachel might very well describe her as—what was it?—a 'little tart.'"

Alan unbent. "You're right. It's worth following up. I'll call Derek."

He went into his den and I shook my head at his back. It was taking Alan a long time to adjust to his amateur status in criminal investigations.

I was preparing a salad lunch in the kitchen when he finished talking to Derek. "Well?" I said, putting plates on the table.

"Well. Not the happiest conversation I've ever had. If I

were under Derek's authority, he'd have torn a strip off. As it was, he controlled himself rigidly, but he came very close to telling me to butt out."

"He's got a nerve! When you've given him the best lead he's had in the whole case."

"I'm afraid he doesn't see it quite that way. He still thinks Jane is the likeliest suspect, and I'm sorry, love, but I think he's about to make an arrest."

"Why?" I demanded. "What new evidence can he possibly have?"

"He didn't say. In fact, he said as little as he could and remain deferential. I feel a bit sorry for him, actually. It's a difficult position he's in."

"He's put himself in it, being so stubborn. I'm not going to waste my sympathy on him. Things would be much easier if he'd help us out, but if he won't, we'll just have to do it ourselves."

Alan sighed and got out the bread and butter. "Do what?"

"Track down that car, of course."

"Darling, do be reasonable." He sat and looked at his salad. "Is that all you're putting on it?"

"No dressing except a little oil and lemon juice. We've both gained far too much weight."

He grinned. Alan knows me very well. My diet kicks usually last about three days, or until I can't resist something delectable. He picked up his fork. "As I said, how are we to trace a car with no license number, no address and no help from the police?"

"You've forgotten the excellent resource we possess right in the family."

"And what might that be?"

"Two teen-age grandsons. More lemon juice?"

Alan's grandsons—mine, too, now—attend an excellent boarding school just outside Sherebury. They wouldn't be home right then, I knew. English schools don't break for the summer until the end of June, as a rule. But the boys are day students, so they'd be home for dinner. I was counting heavily on their ability to recognize, and remember, a spectacular car. And since they've lived in Sherebury all their lives, it was a good bet they'd know who owned the Jag and where it lived. I planned to call on them the minute they got out of school.

After I'd tidied the kitchen and done one or two household chores, I baked a quick batch of brownies as a bribe for information. My special brownies, made with chocolate ice-cream syrup, are rich and moist to begin with, and by the time I add chocolate chips and walnuts to them, they're a chocolate-lover's dream, if a cardiologist's nightmare. I almost never make them for us anymore, but teenage boys have a long time before they have to worry about their arteries. I added some marshmallows to the batch, in consideration of adolescent taste, or lack of it. Once the pan was out of the oven and cooling, I sat to consider how I should spend the rest of the time until I could reasonably go see the boys. I hadn't yet talked to any of the Women's Institute ladies. I've never been involved in the W.I., so I don't know many of the members. Jane, of course, and Margaret. I didn't really want to bother Jane, so the best thing was to call Margaret and ask who would tell me all about Rachel's run-ins with the good ladies.

I had my hand on the phone when it rang. I jumped and picked it up.

"Hello, Dorothy?"

"Yes." I said it tentatively. The voice, tense and male, was a strange one.

"This is Walter."

"Good heavens, I didn't recognize you!"

"Dorothy, we're at the police station. We're allowed one phone call, and we don't have a solicitor, not that sort, anyway, so I thought it had better be you."

"Solicitor! Allowed one call! Walter, what *are* you talking about?"

"They've arrested both of us." His voice was thick now with tears he couldn't suppress. "Aunt Jane and me, they've taken both of us in. Dorothy, you've got to help us!"

I stood there for a moment with the phone in my hand before assorted noises reminded me to press the off button. I very carefully put the instrument back on its charger.

I don't know how long I might have stood there paralyzed if Alan hadn't come into the room.

"Who was on the—Dorothy, what is it?" He crossed the room and took my arms in his strong hands. "What's happened? Is it one of the kids?"

"No," I said, trying to clear my head. "No, nothing's happened in the family. It's—oh, Alan, they've arrested Jane! *And* Walter!"

"Arrested? You're sure?"

"Walter just called. He was making his one permitted call from the police station."

Alan doesn't waste time on emotion when action is required. "Why didn't he phone their lawyer?"

"He says they don't have one—or at least, not a criminal lawyer. I don't know what you call them over here."

"I suppose you mean a barrister, but they're briefed by solicitors. We'd better ring up Carstairs. Walter was probably too rattled to think of him. He's Jane's lawyer, too, I believe, and no, he doesn't handle criminal work, but he'll know who can deal with it."

Mr. Carstairs is our solicitor. He deals with wills and other legal documents, not criminal cases, but he has a sense of adventure. He'd find someone to aid Jane and Walter. Gratefully, I sat and listened while Alan called him and explained the situation. I wasn't up to much of anything.

"Well, that's done." He came and sat beside me on the

couch. "Buck up, old dear. Help is on the way. Carstairs is sending a man from his firm to the police station to find out what's prompted this and petition for their release. Until he finds out what's going on, there isn't much we can do."

"Can't we go see them?"

"Probably not, if they've been charged. We'll know soon enough, love. Try to be patient."

"But they didn't do anything! How can two perfectly innocent people—"

"The police make mistakes, Dorothy. We try not to make them very often, but we're all human. We very, very seldom bring an innocent man to trial. Rather the reverse, if anything. I wish I had a pound for every wide boy I had to let go in my time because we didn't have enough evidence to make a case."

"Will they be allowed to come home?"

"Probably, though it may not be until tomorrow. These things take time."

"Tomorrow!" I wailed.

"Or even the next day. My dear, I know you're upset. So am I. But there has to have been some reason for this action. New evidence of some kind. Now we both believe Jane and Walter to be innocent. I don't think, in fact, that Derek is very happy about the idea of Jane as a murderer. But until we know the reasons for the arrest, there's very little we can do."

"And I don't suppose Derek will be following up any of the leads I've uncovered."

Alan just shook his head.

"Then I'm going to do what I can." My initial numbness had been replaced by nervous energy. "I can't just sit here and do nothing. I'm going to go over and talk to Mike and Dennis and see if they can't identify that Jaguar."

"I'll drive."

I opened my mouth to protest, but thought better of it.

Mike and Dennis might be more forthcoming with me than their grandfather. They are, after all, teenagers, whose family is often viewed as a necessary evil. And I am not quite family, therefore more acceptable. But I was in no mental state to drive, and getting lost or having an accident wouldn't help Jane and Walter.

I went to the kitchen for the brownies.

EIGHT

OUR TIMING was good. The boys had just come home and were about to begin their homework, the household rule being "homework first." Alan went to have a word with their mother about why the rule needed to be broken this time while I went to the boys' bedroom and handed the brownies to Mike.

"Gosh! Thanks, Gran. Wow, your special ones, right?"

"With marshmallows as an extra treat."

"Brilliant!" Mike shot a conspiratorial glance at his brother. I intercepted it.

"Is this forbidden fruit?" I asked.

"Well—it's only that Mum is on a health binge just now," said Dennis, at fourteen the younger boy. "She's trying to get us to eat tofu and nuts and that sort, you know? She'd go spare if we brought home something like this, but as it's a gift, she'll only sniff a bit. I think."

"I won't tell her if you don't, and what she doesn't know—"

"—won't hurt us," finished Mike. "Want one?"

"I don't mind if I do," I said, and sat to eat it while Mike and Dennis each took two and then stashed the tin in a back-pack. I was corrupting the young and would have to apologize to Elizabeth, their mother—but later.

"Now, kids," I said when their mouths were no longer full, "I've come on a mission, and it's serious. You know our neighbor, your grandfather's and mine, Jane Langland?"

"Everybody knows Miss Langland," said Mike.

"Well, she's been arrested in connection with the death of Rachel Spry, and so has Walter, the boy who lives with her."

"Gosh! When?"

"Just this afternoon. We know almost nothing about it, Alan and I, but our solicitor is trying to find out what's happened. The thing is, I think you can help."

They nodded earnestly, their eyes big.

"Mrs. Spry had a visitor, or rather visitors, two days after the fête. That was not long before she died. A man and a woman. I don't know anything about them except that they look well-to-do, and she's a very attractive redhead, and he drives a Jaguar."

"A Jag!" said Mike, sounding even more impressed than Alistair.

"A silver XJ. I don't know the license number, or even if it's from around here. I was hoping you might have noticed it."

Mike's face fell. "Jag's are pretty thin on the ground in Sherebury, and I've never seen a silver one," he said with absolute assurance, and Dennis nodded in agreement. "We're at school all day and haven't a lot of time to go about town."

I sagged back in my chair. I'd been counting heavily on one of them identifying the car.

"The police can find it, Gran," Dennis said consolingly.

"They're not looking. They think they have their criminals." My tone was somewhat bitter and the boys picked up on it.

"So it's up to us?" Dennis sounded excited, and too late I realized my mistake.

"You're not to get involved," I said hastily. "I asked you a question, and you didn't have an answer for me. I'm disappointed, but that's the end of it. Alan would have my head if anything were to happen to you, and it's apt to if you go poking about into murder."

"You poke about in murder all the time," said Mike with devastating logic. "Nothing's happened to you yet."

"I've had my leg broken and your grandfather was nearly killed once, not to mention all the other near-misses. I flatly forbid you to take one single step in the direction of looking into this! And if you go ahead and do it anyway, I'll tell your mother you bought the brownies yourself."

"Now, Gran," said Mike soothingly, "we're not stupid enough to get into trouble. All Dennis meant was that we know lots of people. We're not the only day students at St. Barnabas, you know. And one or two of them know about cars. We can track down your car for you, don't worry. And we won't let any cats out of any bags. *Will* we, Den?"

Dennis sighed. "I suppose not. I mean, no, of course not," he said hastily as Mike glared. "We'll get on it straightaway, and we'll ring you up as soon as we know. And, um, we won't tell Granddad, right?"

"I'll tell him you're trying to identify the car," I said. "I do appreciate it. You have a network of informants I can't access. But do any other snooping, or tell anyone why you're interested, and I'll see you grounded until you're twenty-one. I mean it."

"Right!" They smiled beatifically and took a few more brownies out of the backpack. "But we'd best get to our homework. The sooner we're finished, the sooner we can go talk to people."

With profound misgivings I went to report to Alan and Elizabeth and admit my sins in the culinary department. Elizabeth chided me, but gently, and offered us tea. It was accompanied by some strange-looking biscuits that she assured us were excruciatingly good for us. I claimed to be full—which was in fact true—but Alan manfully took one.

"Cardboard, flavored slightly with a substance I was unable to identify," Alan said when we were back in the car. "Elizabeth was always prone to strange enthusiams. She could be rather trying at times. Did you have any luck?"

"Not yet." I reported the conversation. "I hope they find out something soon. I got the idea they were going out to ask questions the moment their homework was done."

"Going out to play cricket, most likely. But that means a large collection of young males. There's a chance they may learn something."

"You don't think they'll think they're the Hardy Boys and start sleuthing, do you? I warned them in the strongest terms I could."

"I don't know the Hardy Boys."

"The male version of Nancy Drew. You *have* heard of her?"

Alan smiled. "Barely. No, they're sensible kids. I think they'll do exactly as you asked them, but it may be a day or two before they turn up trumps. Dorothy, why don't we stop at Carstairs's office on the way home? He may know something new and he'll feel more free to talk in person than on the phone."

Alan is a calm, deliberate person who likes to let matters take their course. I knew then that he was every bit as worried as I was.

Mr. Carstairs—the man must have a first name, but I've never known it—was in his office and did, in fact, have news for us.

"It isn't good, I'm afraid," he said when he had settled us and offered us sherry, which we both declined. "It seems that young Walter has been up to some mischief."

"Walter?" I said in disbelief. "He's not the mischief sort. A very serious young man."

"This was serious mischief. He broke into Rachel Spry's house."

"What?" Alan and I cried in unison. "When?" I added.

"Last night, apparently. The police went 'round to the house this morning on a routine check—"

"Good grief!" I said, interrupting. "I actually saw them arrive."

Mr. Carstairs nodded and continued, "—and found the seal on the back door broken. So they went inside and found things out of order. Not trashed, but obviously searched since they'd sealed the house. They also found an empty prescription bottle with most of the label torn off. However, the word Prozac was still visible. The police are prepared to swear it wasn't there when they searched the house before."

He paused to let that sink into our shocked minds and then continued. "They took fingerprints, and when they were matched to both Miss Langland and Walter—well." The lawyer spread his hands in a gesture that renounced responsibility.

"But—" I stopped and shook my head. This was too much.

"What does Walter say?" asked Alan.

"He admits going to the house and leaving the pill bottle. He could hardly deny it, could he, with his prints all over the shop. Really, if he was going to do such a thing, one would have thought he'd at least have the sense to wear gloves."

"But why?" I found my tongue. "Why would he do a criminally stupid thing like that?"

"He says he found it in his dustbin. He knew Miss Langland never took any such thing and was convinced someone must have planted the bottle. He knows, he says, that she could not have murdered Mrs. Spry, so he was simply putting the bottle back where it must have come from."

I groaned. "And all he did was get them both into a lot more trouble."

"What are they charged with?" asked my husband, the practical policeman.

"Walter with breaking and entering and criminal trespass and tampering with evidence, for now. Miss Langland with aiding and abetting—again, for now."

"Did your man have any luck about getting them released?" Alan was still docketing procedure in his logical mind.

"Not yet. I gather the police are going over the house again, very thoroughly, to make sure Walter didn't leave any other little surprises behind."

"I still can't believe he would do such a thing." I shook my head and sighed heavily.

"My dear Mrs. Martin, when human passions become involved, one can never predict what a person will do. Walter is very much attached to Miss Langland."

He looked at me blandly and I thought, *He knows.* Jane had probably changed her will in favor of Walter and she would have had to explain their true relationship then. She must have told him that I knew about it, but that Alan did not.

I returned the look, saying simply, "Yes. They are very fond of each other. He must have thought he was doing the right thing."

"Nevertheless, the young man did commit a criminal act. He admits as much. And in view of the circumstances, it will take us a little time to persuade the police that neither of them represents a danger to the public, and that this firm will be responsible for seeing that they appear for trial. When we have made that case, they will be released under bond—and not before."

"May we visit?"

Alan shook his head as Mr. Carstairs said, "I'm afraid not at this point."

After that there seemed nothing for us to do but go home and wait for word from the boys. I did think about going to see one or two of the W.I. ladies, but I couldn't seem to work up the energy.

So we sat, trying to read, or pretending to, and watching the clock, and waiting for the phone to ring. I even picked it up once to make sure it wasn't out of order. Alan began on the *Times*'s crossword puzzle, but threw it aside after ten minutes with not a single word filled in.

I gave up after a while and went to the kitchen. Neither of us was hungry, but it was well past dinnertime, and one has to eat. I scrambled some eggs and threw together a salad, and we sat and picked at the food. We weren't even interested in strawberries and cream for dessert. They reminded us too much of Jane and her preserves.

Nine o'clock came and nine-thirty. The cats sat on the windowsills, lazily watching the birds circling and settling for the night. It was still quite light outside. We were only a few days from the longest day of the year, and it wouldn't get dark until ten, at the earliest.

"Surely they must have stopped their game by now," I said when I could bear the silence no longer. "Don't they have bedtimes?"

"Elizabeth's pretty much given up on a bedtime for Mike. He's nearly seventeen, after all. As long as his schoolwork doesn't suffer, she lets him set his own schedule, within reason. Dennis is supposed to be in by nine, but on a beautiful summer evening the rules are stretched. Don't forget they may have nothing to report. They'll keep on asking at school tomorrow."

The phone rang. We both jumped for it, but I got there first.

"Hi, Gran." It was Mike's voice. "We've got it for you. A lad we know knows a chap whose dad runs a garage. He specializes in posh cars. So, anyway, we tracked it down. It belongs to a woman, not a man. Her name is Annabel Barrington, and she lives at—half a mo'—at The Larches, Crescent Hill."

"The Larches, Crescent Hill," I repeated, looking at Alan and raising my eyebrows. He nodded. "Good, your grandfather knows where that is. That's fast work, Mike. Consider yourself commended."

"Well, it isn't much, just a name and address. We thought we'd try tomorrow to find out something about her and who else lives there and—"

"Whoa! You promised, remember? No more sleuthing!

You've done splendidly, but any more and you could get into trouble. In fact you *will* get into trouble—with me and your grandfather. Right?"

"Right," said Mike, entirely too cheerfully.

"Yes. Well then, what would you like as a reward, more brownies?"

"Afraid not. Mum's nixed any more of those. Would it run to some cricket gear? Ours is pretty antique, and the mice got into the pads and that over the winter."

"It would. You'll have to come with me to pick it out, though. I haven't a clue."

"Brilliant! Saturday?"

"Saturday it is."

"Um, Gran, is Miss Langland all right? I mean, is she…are they going to—"

"She and Walter will be coming home soon." I didn't add *I hope* except mentally. "Alan and I have talked to her solicitor. Things are a bit sticky, but we think they'll come right. You've helped a lot, you know."

"I hope so. I have to go. Mum's making dire signals. 'Bye."

"Too late to go and see tonight, I suppose," I said to Alan as I hung up the phone.

"Definitely too late, but first thing tomorrow."

"Alan, do you really think Mike will take me seriously? About not getting any further involved in this thing, I mean? I'm beginning to feel awfully guilty for getting him into it at all."

"Elizabeth has always said he was an unusually obedient child, never disobeyed a direct order."

"Well…but he's nearly seventeen. I don't know a lot about boys that age, but wouldn't he be feeling his oats a bit?"

"My love, I'm less worried about him than about you. I'm sticking to you like glue for the next few days."

NINE

I HAD TROUBLE getting to sleep, and I suspected Alan did, too. I was restless, while he lay perfectly still—usually a sign he was awake. We woke early and didn't say much as we crumbled our toast.

"It's too early to go, isn't it," I said when the kitchen was clean. It still wasn't even seven.

"It depends," Alan replied. "If they're working people, they're up and maybe even off to the train by now, if they work in London."

"I think he might be a Harley Street doctor," I reminded him.

"Yes, but we don't know that. With an address like Crescent Hill, it's fairly likely that they don't have to work at all."

"I don't think I know where Crescent Hill is."

"South of the river. It's actually outside Sherebury proper, but it's a Sherebury address, and a posh one indeed. There are only two or three houses in the area, all of the manor-house type. Not quite Lynley Hall, but a close cousin."

"Mmm. Not far from the railway station, then."

"No." He looked at me and grinned. "You want to try the station?"

"Well, if he's a doctor, he'd be leaving soon, wouldn't he? And somebody'd have to drive him to the station."

"And they might use the Jag. All right, my dear. Off we go."

Sherebury is a very small town, but it is designated a city by virtue of the Cathedral. Also by virtue of the Cathedral, and the tourist traffic it generates, railway authorities have

kept our station open through the devastating mess of priva-
tization. The station is located, for reasons best known to
long-dead Victorians, some distance outside of town. It was
a pretty drive on a perfect June morning. At least, I suppose
it was. I was too keyed up to notice very much.

We got to the station just as the 7:32 to London pulled in.
The car park was a snarl of traffic; we avoided it, parked up
the hill in a good spot for observation, and waited.

There was not one Jaguar to be seen, silver or any other
color. We watched and waited until the train had left and the
car park had cleared. We waited a few minutes more in case
the Jag owner, running late, came anyway in the vain hope of
catching the train.

"It was a good idea, Dorothy," said Alan. "It just didn't
work out."

"Yeah, right," I muttered.

"Next stop, The Larches," Alan went on with forced cheer.
"But I think we'd best stop somewhere for coffee first. The
idle rich don't rise at this hour, as a rule."

I sighed. "But not here. I am absolutely not up to railway-
station coffee."

"Certainly not!" Alan sounded shocked. "The King's Head
isn't far, and they have excellent coffee. They also do breakfast for nonresidents. We didn't actually eat anything this
morning."

The inn was crowded, but we found a small table and ordered coffee and, seduced by the aroma of bacon and sausages, a substantial breakfast, as well. There was too much
noise to talk quietly, and we didn't want to discuss murderers and silver Jaguars in raised voices. So we ate and waited
until we got back to the car to discuss our next move.

"I've had an idea," I said, belting myself in. "What if we
go see if Alistair Carmichael is willing to come with us? He
could identify the car for certain."

"If you think he can leave his precious book for so long," Alan replied in a grumpy tone. He had taken a dislike to Alistair, sight unseen.

"Oh. There's that. And he might not be up yet."

"If we can't verify the driver of that car within a few hours, I'm going to Derek to throw my weight about." Alan sounded downright testy. "I still have a *little* influence, if only because of the people I know, and the only *sensible* approach to your temperamental author is a proper police interview."

I held my peace. Alan's rare bouts of temper almost always have to do with police work, when he feels out of things. He hasn't adjusted easily to retirement. It's a problem he has to work out himself; I can't help. But I do know enough not to argue with him when he's in one of those moods. We crossed the river and drove in silence through narrow, winding lanes.

"There's the drive," said Alan in a few minutes, slowing the car to a crawl and finally stopping on the wide, grassy verge of the road.

A steep gravel drive on our left wound up out of sight into a grove of oak trees. To either side a dense hedge defeated prying eyes and barred any intruder larger than a rabbit. A wrought-iron gate sported a neat white-on-black metal sign: The Larches. The gate was firmly closed.

"Oh," I said blankly. "Now what?"

"There's probably either an electric eye arrangement or a bell one can push. They have to have some accommodation for tradesmen, unless there's a back way."

"'Servants and tradesmen use the back entrance,' you mean? In this day and age?"

Alan shrugged. "Some people like to keep up appearances, even if they have to answer the back door themselves."

"The more fools they. Anyway, I don't think I'm up to a hunt for a back entrance, not in this terrain. Shall we try for a bell push here somewhere?"

Alan didn't move an inch. "And what did you propose to say to anyone who answers the bell?"

"Oh." Yes, he was right, I hadn't thought about that. "How about the truth? Say we're friends of Jane Langland and would like to talk to them for a moment."

"And if they do know something about Rachel's death? What then?"

"If they're honest, they'll invite us in and talk to us."

"Dorothy, if they were honest, they'd have come forward before now to say they'd seen Rachel shortly before her death. There's some reason why they didn't speak up."

He let that sink in. I said slowly, "And you think the reason is that they are the ones responsible. That they are murderers."

"Not necessarily. They may simply have had some past contact with her that would put them under suspicion. If your theory is right and he's Rachel's ex-husband, that fact alone would make Derek want to talk to him."

"So if we try to go barging in there and ask questions, we might start alarm bells ringing," I concluded glumly. "Why didn't you tell me this sooner?"

"I didn't remember the layout here. This house is quite new, built since I retired, and I suppose I've driven past, but I never noticed it particularly. I had envisioned arriving, spotting the car, noting the plate number, and going away again. The security precautions they've taken make that approach unworkable. Besides—" he grinned and took my hand "—I didn't think about how to approach them, any more than you did."

"That makes me feel better." It did, too. Alan was over his snit. "But it doesn't solve our problem. So to repeat myself, now what?"

"I think I'd be inclined to search for that back entrance. It's likely we're dealing here with a wish for privacy, coupled with a strong desire to show off, rather than a true need for strict security. It'd be my bet that the back way is unguarded and we might at least be able to look over the house—and the car, if it's there."

"Lay on, MacDuff." I didn't complete the quotation. Alan had inspired me with uncharacteristic caution and I had the uneasy feeling I might well be the first to cry "Hold, enough."

I could never have found the track—scarcely a drive—that led off from the road at an impossible angle. The hedge was so close on both sides that our car scraped leaves and small twigs off the bushes as Alan made the sharp turn. What the hedge did to the car's paintwork was something I preferred not to consider. Our vehicle was a far cry from a Jag, but Alan liked to keep it pristine.

The path was deeply rutted. I wasn't at all sure Alan knew what he was doing, but I didn't dare open my mouth to find out. I was keeping my teeth tightly clenched so as not to bite my tongue off when we hit particularly bad bumps.

Eventually the wood thinned and opened into a clearing. I suppose it would be called a stable yard. Certainly there was a horse. It poked its curious head out the open top half of the stable door, decided we weren't worth bothering about and disappeared again. That building was on our right. Straight ahead was a building I could identify as a three-car garage, the more easily since one of the overhead doors was open.

The sun was high now, but still far enough to the east to shine into the garage and reveal the silvery surface of a Jaguar XJ. Its license plate was clearly visible.

Alan let out an almost soundless "Ah," and reached for the notepad he keeps in the car.

I glanced around nervously. No one was in sight, and the house was some distance away, but anyone might have been watching us. "What are we doing here, Alan? In case anyone asks?"

"I doubt anyone will, but just in case—let's see. Ah, it must be those confusing directions your friend gave you. This is plainly not the cattery where we hoped to find a nice Silver Tabby. We did think it odd that there was no sign at the turning."

He backed and turned the car smoothly and we drove down the hill undisturbed.

We were halfway home before I broke the silence. "Alan, what are we going to do? We have to find out what those people were doing at Rachel's house. Or rather, Derek has to find out, but I don't think he's going to try."

"I've been thinking about that, too. Derek isn't merely being stubborn, you know, although I've been somewhat annoyed with him in the past few days, as I know you have."

"Humph," was my only comment.

"Yes, but you remember the perpetual problem—shortage of both staff and money. With a great many other matters to deal with, he can't afford to ignore a pair of suspects who are handed to him on a plate, no matter what his personal feelings may be."

"So he's going to pretend he believes Jane and/or Walter guilty, no matter what other evidence turns up?"

"No, Dorothy, he won't disregard new *evidence*. So far there has been none against anyone except Jane and Walter, only supposition. Yes, he'd like eventually to talk to the people in the silver Jag, but for now he's concentrating on the certainty that Walter committed one crime and the probability that he—and/or Jane, as you put it—committed others."

"Then somehow he has to be presented with new evidence."

"Preferably something that will stand up in court." Alan sighed. I wasn't sure if it was a comment on Jane's and Walter's disastrous situation, or my probable course of action. Because I intended to take action. I just wasn't sure what, not yet.

I pondered it all the way home and for the rest of the morning. Alan got on the phone to one of his friends and tracked down the license number. The boys had been quite right. Annabel Barrington.

We waited for a phone call from Mr. Carstairs saying Jane and Walter had been released. It didn't come.

We'd had a large breakfast and weren't hungry again until midafternoon, so I decided to combine lunch and tea. I got some scones out of the freezer and toasted them while I made a few fairly substantial sandwiches and retrieved a pot of my strawberry jam from the pantry.

"It isn't as good as Jane's," I commented after I'd taken a bite of a scone. "Hers always has more flavor, for some reason—oh!"

Alan waited.

"I've just had a thought. You said their house was new."

We've been married long enough to read each other's thoughts. He didn't have to ask whose house. "Only a few months old, I think," he replied.

"Then they haven't lived there long."

"No."

"Then—the Women's Institute!"

Alan blinked.

"She needs to be invited to join the W.I.," I said patiently.

"Are you sure they actually invite people? I thought women simply joined up."

"I don't have a clue, but the point is, if she's from London, she won't know, either. I'll have to ask someone."

"My dear woman, I don't pretend to know what you're talking about, but if it involves a way to get into the Barrington house, I'm coming with you. Not negotiable."

"Well…but you'll have to stay in the car. She may be urban and gullible about country ways, but I can't see her swallowing you as a representative of the W.I."

He grinned at that. "Very well."

"And we take my car. Just in case someone saw us this morning."

Alan groaned. He hates driving my ancient VW Beetle,

which I love because its left-hand drive makes me feel secure. "Suppose you drive. I'll navigate," he said.

"Um, are there any roundabouts? You know how I feel—"

"We can avoid them. When do you want to go?"

"As soon as I call Margaret and find out how I can pass myself off as a W.I. type."

Alan shook his head, but made no protest. He wanted to find out about the Jag couple, as I was calling them in my head, as much as I did.

Margaret, a stalwart of the W.I., revealed so far as she knew there was no Annabel Barrington among the membership, and that they didn't usually call on women to invite them to join, but she didn't see why I couldn't. Beyond the fact, of course, that I wasn't a member myself. I ignored that small detail. After I'd taken a fresh jar of strawberry jam from the pantry and added a pretty ribbon and so on, I set off, a nice summer hat on my head and an apprehensive husband by my side.

It took a little longer to get there than it had in the morning, partly because the traffic was heavier, partly because we took a circuitous route to avoid a roundabout I hate. As we approached the impressive gate, I took a deep breath. Alan patted my hand. It was reassuring to have him along.

The gate opened as I turned off from the road. Alan was right; the gate was for show, not security. I drove up the steep, well-maintained drive slowly, trying to note any significant details. "Not a larch tree in sight," I commented. "Just oaks."

"'The Oaks' must not sound impressive enough," said Alan with a grin.

However, when we made the last turn and came in view of the house, he pointed. There were two small evergreen trees in pots on either side of the front door.

"Oh, really, now! That's too much!" I giggled at the display and discovered that I had regained my nerve. I could deal with any woman who would consider a couple of four-foot trees in pots a reasonable excuse for naming a house.

"Now you stay put," I said. "I may be a while. I want to find out as much as I can about this woman. I already know she's silly and affected."

"Don't underestimate her on that account," cautioned Alan, reasonably.

"Don't worry." I straightened my hat and stepped out of the car, carrying my oversize handbag with the jar of jam in it.

There was a speaker arrangement at the front door. More ostentation. "Yes?" said a female voice in response to my ring.

"My name's Mrs. Nesbitt." I'd thought it wise to use Alan's name, though I don't usually. Not exactly a lie, but not a name she would ever have heard before. "I'm calling on behalf of the Women's Institute. We thought you might be interested in joining."

"Oh!" She sounded pleased. "Oh, yes, just a moment."

She was every bit as lovely as I'd been told, even dressed casually in slacks and a shirt I imagined belonged to her husband. "I'm sorry about the way I look," she said, eyeing my hat as she let me in. "I wasn't expecting anyone."

"I ought to have phoned, but I was a little later getting started than I'd planned, so I just took the chance you might be at home. What a lovely room!" She had showed me into the living room—lounge, parlor, whatever—and it was indeed lovely if a trifle sterile for my taste. "You haven't been here long, have you? The house looks brand-new."

"It is. It was only finished in January. We—it was my wedding present."

"Oh, then you're a bride. How lovely! And what a generous husband."

"Actually…well, I meant it was my gift to him." She looked self-conscious.

"Oh, how silly of me. Is your husband at home? I'd love to meet him. But no, I suppose he's at work."

"No, actually he came home a bit early. He's a doctor, you know, in London."

Aha.

"Today's his half day, so he was here a bit earlier, but he…he had to go out. Would you like some tea?"

She was nervous, but I couldn't tell what about. More probing was in order. "Thank you, my dear, it's very nice of you, but I took my tea early today. So your husband is a doctor. He must have qualified very young." I smiled broadly at her, hoping she would catch my implication that she was very young herself.

She returned the smile, but mechanically. "Oh, I'm older than I look. And James is older than I. It's a second marriage for him, you see."

As soon as she said it, she looked horrified. *She didn't mean to tell me that,* I thought.

She rushed back into speech. "It's so very kind of you to invite me to join the Women's Institute. I haven't met many people in town yet. We're a bit isolated out here, and we've been busy getting settled and…are you quite sure you won't have some tea?"

I'd learned enough to confirm most of my ideas. I'd also learned enough to make me feel very sorry for this lonely, wealthy young trophy wife. It was time to spring my surprise, but I felt bad about what I had to do.

"Well, if you insist, I wouldn't mind a cuppa. In fact, I brought a little gift, just as a welcome to Sherebury. It might go nicely with tea."

I brought out my jar of jam and held it up in the ray of afternoon sunshine that streamed through an open window. The light clearly showed the streaks of a white powder mixed in with the strawberries.

Mrs. Barrington stood and gasped, her hand to her mouth. "How…how did you know?"

"I don't know what you mean," I began when the cell phone in my purse started to warble. The timing could not have been worse. "I'm sorry. I won't be a moment."

Pale and terrified, she began to edge away from me as I spoke into the phone. "Yes?" I said in an irritated voice, turning away from Mrs. Barrington.

It was Alan. "Love, you'd better come. I've had a call from Mike, and we need to leave right now."

"But I'm just—"

"Now, Dorothy."

"But—oh, very well." I turned back to explain to excuse myself to my hostess.

There was no one in the room.

I wondered mightily where Mrs. Barrington was and what she was doing, but I couldn't traipse all over the house trying to find her. "I'm sorry, I've had a call and I have to go," I called. There was no answer.

Thoroughly put out, I stalked back to the car. Alan was sitting in the driver's seat. "What—"

"Get in, darling, and we'll talk on the way."

I did as I was told, slamming the car door with unnecessary force. "I hope you realize I ought to stay here. Things were going beautifully. Another minute and I would have had her admitting—well, I don't know what, exactly, but something incriminating, I'm sure. So what *is* all this urgency about?"

"Mike called on the mobile. He's tracked down the Jag."

"What do you mean, tracked it down? It's here."

"Apparently not. Was Mr. Barrington at home?"

"Dr. Barrington. And no, he wasn't. His wife said he had been, but had had to go out. Oh! And took the Jag, I suppose. But what do you mean, Mike tracked him down? He promised—"

"He says he was out biking and happened to see it. And as it happened to be going the direction he was, he couldn't be said to be following, could he?" There was the hint of a smile in Alan's voice.

"He can't keep up with a Jaguar on a bike."

"Not on the open road, no. But in winding streets, in late-afternoon traffic, a bike has the advantage. And Mike's done some racing."

"Well, we have to catch up with him before he gets into trouble."

"My thought exactly. He told me where he was heading and promised to keep in touch. That's why I was so peremptory back there. Now tell me what you were able to learn."

"He's a London doctor and she's his second wife. And she didn't like mentioning his earlier marriage. It scared her. But what really scared her was when I produced my jar of strawberry jam."

"Why?"

"Because I added some crushed-up aspirin to it, just before I wrapped it up."

"But why—oh."

"Exactly. Alan, I haven't told anybody about the drug in the jam at Rachel's house. And I can't imagine that you have, or Derek. And it's ridiculous to assume that either Jane or Walter has talked about something that makes them look so suspicious. So why would Annabel Barrington be frightened out of her wits at the sight of white powder in strawberry jam?"

"Because she's seen it before. Or at least, that's your theory."

"It is. And if Mike hadn't interfered, I'd know a lot more by now."

Alan's cell phone rang. It was tucked down between the seats. I picked it up.

"Oh! Gran, is that you?"

"It is," I said ominously. "And where are you, young man?"

"I know you're mad, but listen. I haven't done anything stupid, really. And I can't follow the Jag any farther, because it just turned into a cul-de-sac and I'd look pretty silly riding in circles. But Gran, it's the one Rachel Spry lived on!"

"Got it. Hole up somewhere nearby and we'll be there as soon as we can."

I punched the phone off. "Alan, you'd better stop the car so we can change drivers and you can make a call. I think you're going to want to phone Derek."

The Jag was parked in front of Rachel's house when we pulled up a few minutes later. I parked awkwardly, virtually blocking the entrance to the cul-de-sac, and Mike pedaled up almost as soon as we stopped.

"I was in the drive next door," he said in an excited whisper. "What do we do now?"

"Nothing," said Alan crisply. "We wait."

We didn't have to wait long. Two police cars, blue lights flashing, pulled to a stop behind my VW, and a minute or two later, a man walked out of Rachel's front door, his perfectly tailored shoulders slumped. He didn't even attempt to get into his Jag, but went straight to one of the police cars and got in.

TEN

"IT WAS ALL an accident." Alan and I, Jane, Walter, Mike and Dennis sat around our kitchen table, a few pieces of pizza left in assorted boxes. It was nearly midnight and, on a school night, but we and the boys' parents had agreed unanimously that they deserved be in on the session. Alan had spent the evening at the police station and was now giving us his full report.

"John Barrington was, indeed, married for a time to Rachel Spry. When he began to recognize the signs of growing mental instability, he sent her to a psychiatrist, but she refused to admit there was anything wrong. The rages got worse and finally John divorced her.

"He told Derek a long, rambling story, but the gist of it was that he met and married the beautiful Annabel, who just happened also to have pots of money. They moved to Sherebury, partly to get away from Rachel. She found out about it, though, and followed them. Barrington assumed she wanted revenge of some sort. At any rate, she couldn't find out where they lived—they're ex-directory and have kept a pretty low profile—so she joined every women's group in town hoping to come across Annabel. They'd never met; Barrington had been able to keep them apart.

"Finally, Rachel succeeded, at the fête. She invited her to tea, giving a false name, and Annabel, desperate for company, accepted. When she told Barrington, however, he recognized Rachel from the description. Annabel couldn't be dissuaded from accepting the invitation, saying that Rachel had been very sweet and perhaps she'd changed."

"You'd think a doctor's wife would know that psychotics have changeable moods," I put in.

"Hasn't been a doctor's wife very long," said Jane.

"At any rate, Annabel was determined to go, but Barrington insisted on going along."

"I can relate to that." I grinned at Alan. "So what happened?"

"One will never know what Rachel intended. Probably she meant to make Annabel's life a misery for her, that afternoon and for a long time after. But when she—Rachel—saw her ex-husband walk in the door, she lost it completely, began shouting and throwing the china about. Barrington says she'd probably been taking far too many Prozac. He found, later, a prescription bottle that should have been nearly full, according to the date, and was half empty."

"I thought Prozac was an antidepressant," said Walter.

"It can, I understand, be used to treat a number of emotional disorders. But in large doses, as my wife reminded me a short time ago, it has just the opposite effect, creates wild agitation, excitement—all sorts." Alan paused, but nobody else had a question.

"Well, you must remember that Barrington is a doctor and that he knew Rachel very well. He had suspected that she might get out of control, and he'd had the forethought to bring some medication with him. So when she started ranting and throwing the tea things, he caught hold of her arm and kept her still long enough to give the standard treatment for psychotic rage, an injection of Haldol."

"What's that?" asked Mike.

"A powerful psychotropic drug. It's used in emergency rooms quite often when a raving patient comes in. However, it's dangerous because—"

"Drug interaction!" said Mike and Walter together. They grinned at each other.

"Got it in one. You have to remember that Barrington didn't know, at that point, about the Prozac. He had expected the Haldol to take effect fast, so he wasn't surprised when Rachel calmed down and became sleepy. He led her to her bedroom, helped her undress, and put her to bed. Then he and Annabel tidied up a bit; they didn't want Rachel stepping on broken china when she woke up. Before they left the house, he went in to check on her and found her in a profound coma. That was when he spotted the half-empty bottle of Prozac and realized what he'd done."

There was silence in the room. Alan went on. "There was nothing he could do for her. She stopped breathing while he watched, and there they were with a big problem on their hands."

"Why?" asked Mike. "He didn't mean to kill her."

"I think I can answer that one," I said. "He's a doctor, Mike, but not her doctor. He had no business giving her that injection in the first place, let alone giving it without knowing what she'd already taken. Besides, they were not on good terms and had just, in fact, had a plate-throwing fight. Would anyone believe his story? At the very least he stood to lose his license and his reputation. At worst…" I shrugged.

"That's more or less what Barrington said," Alan continued. "He had to keep out of it. At first he thought he'd just pour the remainder of the Prozac down the toilet and hope the death would be put down to an overdose. But, as is the way with guilty consciences, his began to work on him and he thought of a better idea. Jane Langland had been heard to threaten Rachel, and there was a dish of strawberry preserves on Rachel's tea table. Mrs. Barrington went into the kitchen, found the jar, and recognized the preserves as Jane's. There was also a plate with toast crumbs and a smear of jam on it.

Rachel had evidently eaten some for lunch or had a snack before the Barringtons arrived. So why not empty the remaining Prozac capsules into the jam?"

"But…wait a minute." I shook my head to clear it. "The police found that bottle, on her bedside table or wherever, and there was still quite a lot of the drug in it. So—I guess I don't quite follow."

"Well, this is where the plot gets rather nasty. Dr. Barrington still had in his head that Jane must be blamed, and he wasn't sure the doctored jam was enough, even though he very carefully opened the sealed jar and stirred some of the drug in that, too, and then made it look as though it had never been opened. He was afraid the police would wonder just what you did, Dorothy—how would Jane get hold of Prozac?

"So he wrote a prescription for Prozac for Jane Langland and went to a pharmacy later that afternoon and filled it. Then he artistically tore the label at the top, where the date was, emptied the contents of the bottle down a drain somewhere, and slipped the empty bottle through Jane's mail slot late that night."

"Found it in the morning," said Jane. "Had rolled into a dark corner. Didn't really look at it. Thought one of the dogs had picked it up somewhere. Threw it out."

"And I found it in the dustbin," Walter took up the tale. "Yesterday, when I emptied the wastepaper baskets. I knew someone else had put it there. Well, I mean, I know now that Aunt Jane *did* put it there—but I knew it couldn't mean she did anything wrong. Because she wouldn't. So I made an utter fool of myself, picked the thing up, tore off the bit of the label with her name on it and then went and broke into that house…"

He slumped down in his seat. Jane, sitting next to him, put her arm around his shoulder. I saw the young head and the old one, side by side, so unlike and yet stamped at that moment with a strong resemblance. I saw Mike look at them, too, and saw an idea dawn in his mind.

"Well," I said hastily, "I hope Dr. Barrington gets what's coming to him, if only for that attempt to incriminate Jane."

"He probably will," said Alan with a yawn. "It was going back today that put the final nail in his coffin. Thanks to the alertness of young Mike here."

"Who must never, ever, do such a thing again," I said severely.

Mike just grinned. "Why did he go back, anyway? It was a stupid thing to do."

"Making doubly sure. Just checking to make certain he hadn't overlooked anything. You know, the old 'murderer returning to the scene of the crime' cliché. But it does happen. It turns out his wife saw us this morning, when we explored the back of the house. She panicked and called him in London and he thought he'd best just take another look at the house." Alan yawned again.

I followed suit and our guests took the hint and left, Jane and Walter with expressions of profound thanks.

"What's going to happen to Walter?" I asked as Alan and I were putting away the remains of the pizza. "He did commit a crime."

"The charges will probably be dropped, after Derek tears him off a strip. He doesn't want to make a habit of that sort of thing."

As we were about to climb into bed, I said, "I hope Mike doesn't make a habit of playing detective, either. He's an observant youngster, and it was all right this time, but he could get hurt."

Alan chuckled. "Oh, he had a word with me before he left."

"And?"

"He asked me how one goes about getting into the police force. I think you've permanently influenced a young mind, my dear."

I groaned and Alan turned out the light.

RECICPES

DOROTHY MARTIN'S SUPER-DUPER BROWNIES

½ cup butter, softened
1 cup sugar
2 eggs, at room temperature
1 cup flour
¼ teaspoon baking soda
¾ cup chocolate ice cream syrup
(Dorothy uses Hershey's, when she can get it.)
1 teaspoon vanilla
¾ cup chopped walnuts
¾ cup semi-sweet chocolate chips

Preheat oven to 350°. Spray 8- or 9-inch square baking pan with nonstick cooking spray and dust with flour.

Cream butter, add sugar and cream together. Beat in eggs. Combine flour with baking soda and add to batter mixture alternately with chocolate syrup. Stir in vanilla, nuts and chocolate chips. (When she's making these for the young, she sometimes adds a ½ cup of cut-up marshmallows.) Pour carefully into prepared pan.

Bake at 350° for 45 minutes, or until brownies pull away from sides of pan and a toothpick inserted in the center comes out clean.

These would probably stay moist for several days, but they seldom last that long. They are cakey rather than chewy brownies. Dorothy almost always makes a double recipe, which can be baked in two square pans or a 13-by-9-inch cake pan.

They're sinfully rich, but everyone needs a forbidden treat now and then!

EVERYBODY DIDN'T LIKE SARA LEE
LIKE SARA LEE

Denise Dietz

ONE

ELLIE BERNSTEIN like to clip coupons. Not that she ever used them. Every three or four months she'd clean out her purse and trash the outdated vouchers. And yet, clipping coupons gave her a weird sense of purpose.

On the Classified Ads page she struck gold. A fifty-cents-off coupon for a giant bottle of diet mayonnaise. Near the coupon was a chimney sweep ad, a "free puppies to good home" ad, and a personal ad that hyped "candlelight dinners and long walks on the beach."

Beaches in Colorado Springs were a tad hard to find, Ellie thought with a grin.

Above the Chimneys R Us ad was an open-auditions announcement for the John Denver Community Theater's production of *Hello Dolly*.

Ellie thought about trying out—briefly.

Only one thing would impede her audition.

Actually, two things.

She couldn't sing and she couldn't dance.

SARA LEE—nee Sarah Leibowitz—liked to tell everyone that she was a cold-blooded killer. "I killed the 'h' in my name when I was thirteen," she liked to say. Then she'd laugh. She had a unique laugh, a cross between a puppy's playful growl and wind chimes. Her laughter was contagious. Nobody ignored it and most people joined in—laughing with her, not at her.

Her smile was contagious, too.

A month or so ago she'd bumped into one of her regulars at the supermarket. He said, "You're not smiling, Sara Lee," and she said, "I'm off the clock."

Although she hadn't clocked out yet, Sara Lee scowled. Damn Tim and his phone calls! If he called again during a busy shift, she'd be off the clock for good.

Her hand shook as she fished her compact from her apron pocket. Ignoring the compressed powder, she stared into the little round mirror and saw Barbra Streisand. Oh, she didn't have Streisand's magnificent nose. But the rest of her face was comparable, especially her mouth. Lips that looked vulnerable and kissable. Lips that opened up to pour forth Broadway show tunes, R&B, country-western, punk rock, acid rock, you name it. Everything but rap. Sara couldn't get a handle on rap. "Obscene poetry," she told her husband Tim, who couldn't get a handle on anything except Elvis.

Last week Tim had seen The King at a truck stop outside Denver. The week before, at a carwash in Colorado Springs. Elvis had been stolen by aliens then brainwashed, Tim told Sara. Uh-huh, she said. Sure. Whatever.

Twenty-three years ago she'd been adopted; there was no doubt in her mind. Sandwiched between kid number three and kid number five, total seven, she was the only Leibowitz who could sing. The others were tone deaf, excruciatingly so.

Mom said no, Sara hadn't been adopted. Mom said, "Are you out of your freaking mind? Why would Daddy and me adopt when we breed like rabbits?" Mom wanted "her Sarah" to become a word-famous singing star and support her family, like Shania Twain. Instead, Sara had cashed in Uncle Ira's high school graduation gift, a U.S. Savings Bond, flown to Vegas and married Timothy Zachariah—a big mistake.

Tim had a temper. Tim had a jealous streak a mile long. Tim didn't believe her when she said she had to work double shifts at Uncle Vinnie's Gourmet Italian Restaurant. Tim liked to use her body as a punching bag.

If everything went according to plan, Tim would soon be roadkill.

Returning the compact to her apron pocket, Sara retrieved a mangled pack of cigarettes. She was on a smoke break. Vincent, the chef who owned Uncle Vinnie's Gourmet Restaurant with his brother Al, didn't allow his waitresses to smoke inside the building. So she stood outside, in an alley behind the kitchen, sharing her small space with two puke-green Dumpsters. She smelled rotting lettuce. And tomato sauce. She hated the smell of tomato sauce, almost cheered out loud when one of her customers ordered shrimp scampi or fettuccine Alfredo. One of her *guests,* that is. Vincent insisted his wait staff call customers "guests."

The cheap guests ordered spaghetti and meatballs. With a side salad and garlic-buttered Italian bread, it was the lowest-priced entrée on Uncle Vinnie's overpriced menu. Sara had nothing against spaghetti, although the price of one spaghetti-and-meatballs dinner could feed a family for a week, assuming they ate spaghetti and meatballs. But the cheapies drank water with lemon, rather than wine or beer or soda, keeping the tab—and tip—to a minimum.

She desperately needed every cent she could scrounge; money for clothes and cigarettes; money for her secret singing lessons—if Tim knew about the lessons he'd slice her throat; money for a hush-hush plan she called "America the Beautiful." *Let freedom ring!* As "Sara Lee," she'd take Broadway or Nashville or Hollywood by storm. But she needed a grubstake first; the bigger, the better.

One of her fellow servers always earned big bucks. She had asked him how and, for weeks, he'd refused to tell her. When she'd finally wheedled it out of him, his fail-safe scam wasn't exactly legal. It wasn't fail-safe, either, even though he said restaurants never prosecuted because of the bad publicity.

If things didn't pick up, she'd try his scam. Except, with her luck, she'd probably get caught. And prosecuted.

Sara heaved a deep sigh. She climbed on top of the sturdy wooden crate that short waitresses used when they tossed bloated trash bags into the Dumpster. As she tap-danced in place, her cigarette punctuated the sky with exclamation points. She mentally shed the black slacks that didn't show stains and the starched white shirt that did. In her mind's eye, she unknotted the skinny strings that kept her cranberry-colored apron moored to her waist. Then the tie that strangled her throat like a noose. Vincent left the choice of necktie motifs up to his waitresses—waiters wore black bow ties—and Sara had opted for whimsy. Today: Daffy Duck.

Still pensive, still fully clothed in her waitress uniform, she imagined her supple body sheathed by a long, glittery gown. She added a tight corset so that her ample breasts threatened the gown's low-cut bodice. She hid her blond-streaked ponytail underneath an elaborate wig. What else? Jewels. At her ears and throat. How about a diamond choker? She'd seen one in Wardrobe. The fake diamonds would shimmer and call attention to her bosom, assuming the person who worked the spotlights knew the difference between up and down, left and right.

Ray Morass had volunteered to do the lighting for the John Denver Community Theater's production of *Hello Dolly*. But, as a member of the theater committee, Sara had nixed his request. Ray was a klutz.

During the J.D.C.T.'s production of *The Pajama Game*, Sara had soloed with "Steam Heat." Clothed in black tights and leotard, she had thought herself sexy, seductive, cute. Unfortunately, Ray's focus—and spotlight—had still been on "Hernando's Hideaway," an earlier production number. What a bonehead!

She had altered her choreography, scrambling to stay in the light's beam, and one nasty newspaper critic had called her performance "awkward."

Tomorrow night she'd audition for the starring role of

Dolly. She had every song down pat, sounded more like Streisand than Streisand. She'd get the part, and while she was strutting on stage—the perfect alibi—somebody would ambush Tim and—

Come to think of it, she could have planned the hit for tomorrow night. Her audition would make a good alibi, too. She shook her head. She didn't want to know when it happened. She'd take her curtain call and sing an encore and the cops would be waiting in the wings, looking sorry-ma'am-solemn, and she'd play the grieving widow with nary a pause. After all, Dolly was a widow and Sara, who believed in omens, took that as a good o—

Lord have mercy, her tie was *killing* her! Her friend Nico had perfected a Windsor knot that suddenly pressed against her throat. And her shirt collar felt way too tight. She'd have to buy more shirts at the Salvation Army's thrift shop.

Maybe, on her way home, she'd stop at the supermarket. She didn't have to work tonight, thank goodness, so she'd cook up some pork chops. Tim liked pork chops, the swine. She had tried to leave him once, but he said he'd kill her if she tried again. He'd get away with it, too. Tim was a good ol' boy, an ex-football player, the quintessential personification of an adorable redneck. He coached a kid's football team and made sure every kid played—as long as his team was ahead by fifty points. He hawked used cars at one of the dealerships owned by a retired Denver Broncos quarterback. Everybody loved Tim.

Turning her face away from the Dumpsters, Sara tried to do a Baryshnikov. She had watched *White Nights* a bazillion times, watched Mikhail—in sneakers!—dance on his toes. However, her sneakers gave way at the last minute and she landed, flat-footed, on top of the crate. She glanced around, hoping no one had caught her "awkward" performance.

Uncle Vinnie's Gourmet Italian Restaurant anchored a pet supply store, a beauty salon, a video rental shop and a real-estate office. The restaurant was easily visible from Interstate 25, and easily accessible if one exited the interstate and/or drove east along Austin Bluffs Highway. Across the highway, golden arches pierced the vista, and Sara, who swore she'd never eat pasta again as long as she lived, was addicted to Ronald McDonald's fries. A temptation-laden breeze carried the succulent scent of seasoned grease. Maybe tonight she'd—no!

Tim would skin her alive if she served him fast food.

Instead she'd cook up some Rocky Mountain Chili, her own, original recipe. It was easy to prepare and she could rest her tired feet while it simmered. All she had to do was to brown a pound of ground beef in a large pot, add onion, garlic and pepper when the meat was half done. Then, later, after a soak in the tub, she'd add a cup of stale Coors, two bouillon cubes, a chopped green pepper, a minced banana pepper, kidney beans, canned tomatoes, basil, oregano, thyme and a cup of ripe, chopped olives. What made her chili special— and moist—was the beer. And, God knows, there was plenty of warm, stale Coors around her house.

Yes, chili made more sense than pork chops. Her chili tasted even better the second day, and Tim could scarf it down while she attended the *Hello Dolly* auditions. Too bad she couldn't add rat poison.

As Sara's mind wandered, she loosened the Windsor knot at her throat, wriggled the necktie free from her collar and flung the end over her shoulder. She lit a second cigarette, then shoved the pack and lighter inside her apron pocket, where it joined car keys, loose change, pens, her compact and a corkscrew. *And a partridge in a pear tree,* she thought, her Streisand lips morphing into an Elvis sneer. She unbuttoned her shirt collar and—with profound relief—inhaled. She sucked in the smell of pungent tomato sauce, gagged and felt the osso buco tidbits she had snitched during her lunch shift tickle her throat.

She coughed, swallowed and glanced toward the restaurant's back door. She really should go inside before Micki, the tattletale hostess, ratted on her.

First, she'd finish her cigarette and practice one song.

Nico—fellow waiter, friend, lover—was keeping an eye on her last two tables. After her guests paid their tabs, she could clock out.

"I'm the greatest star," she sang.

She felt arms encircle her waist. Leaning back against a body that smelled of hairspray and sweat, she said, "Darling, we don't have time."

One arm draped her chest like a beauty contestant's banner.

"Darling, you're baaaaad," she said.

She felt something press against her throat.

Not diamonds...

Not even a fake diamond choker...

The necktie she'd flung over her shoulder!

Dropping her cigarette butt, Sara clutched at her throat. She clawed at the tie but couldn't get a fingerhold. She waved her hands, as if she were a mime pressing against an imaginary piece of glass.

Her motion slowed, grew sluggish, as if she waved from a parade float.

Sara Lee—nee Sarah Leibowitz—did not see her life pass before her eyes. All she could see, in her mind's eye, was Daffy Duck's loony smirk.

TWO

ELLIE BERNSTEIN thought she'd die laughing.

On the other end of the phone, in his office, in his precinct, Lieutenant Peter Miller said, "What's so funny?"

"Sssssscout," Ellie managed to hiss the word out between giggles.

"Gesundheit."

"No, no, honey…Scout…dog. I told you about her last night."

"Right. You're dog-sitting for one of your diet club members. And she just did something funny." Peter's last six words sounded triumphant, as if he'd solved a *Murder She Wrote* rerun before the third commercial. "The dog did something funny, not your Weight Winners member."

"I picked up Scout an hour ago. She was fine in the car, very attentive, as if I were a kidnapper and she wanted to map the route in her brain. She peed in the front yard, then sped into the house…" Ellie paused to glance at an old patchwork quilt, scrunched near the fireplace. "Rachel gave me a quilt. And dog toys. Scout curled up on the quilt and—"

"Jackie Robinson," Peter guessed.

Ellie nodded, then realized Peter couldn't see her. "Before I could close the door to the kitchen," she said, "Jackie Robinson pranced into the family room, king of the manor. Have you ever seen a black Persian cat do a double take?"

"I don't think I've ever seen any cat do a double take. Is it different from a human double take?"

"No. Exactly the same."

"So…Jackie Robinson hissed. Clawed. What?"

"At first he looked as if I'd plugged his tail into a light socket. Then he looked like Elsa Lancaster as Frankenstein's bride. Then he just stared. Scout stared back. They've been like that for fifteen or twenty minutes. Staring at each other. Both waiting for the other to make the first move. It's really funny, Peter, but I guess you'd have to be here."

"Why don't *you* make the first move, sweetheart? Let Scout out into the backyard."

"Scout's a guest."

"Scout's a dog!" He groaned. "Please don't tell me you think dogs are furry little people."

"No. Of course I don't. They're furry little animals." Even to her own ears, her voice lacked conviction. "I've never owned a dog, Peter. My mother…well, she said she was allergic. My son wanted a dog—"

"But your ex said no."

"Tony liked the image, man, dog, very macho. But he said a dog would be too much of a responsibility, would restrict our freedom, meaning his freedom." She sighed. "You've owned dogs."

"Dozens. I grew up on a ranch."

"I'll need your help."

"Okay."

"Let's start with this stupid staring contest."

"Carry Jackie Robinson into the kitchen. Shut the door between the kitchen and the family room. Are you writing this down? There'll be a test later," Peter said, teasing.

"Very funny. I'm having a major crisis here and—"

"Hold it, sweetheart. My other line's buzzing."

Ellie cradled the receiver between her ear and shoulder. Afraid to move and disturb the peaceful standoff between her black Persian and Rachel Lester's black sheltie–Border collie, she tapped her fingernails against the polished wood of the telephone table. At the sound, both animals focused on her hand. Then they went back to staring at each other.

"Gotta go," said Peter. "See you tonight. Love you."

Ellie shook the receiver as if, by that action, she could re-connect the fragile lifeline to her significant other. At the same time, a proverbial goose walked across her grave and the hairs at the nape of her neck prickled. She shivered. She wasn't the least bit chilled, but Peter's abrupt hang-up could only mean one thing.

A mystery to solve.

DENVER'S DOCUMENTED felonies fattened the national stats, but Colorado Springs had been on cruise control. No one had robbed any banks or convenience stores. Gangs had apparently signed, initialed or spray-painted a truce. It was as if September, rather than January, had ushered in a new year. Topical, ripped-from-the-headlines TV shows and a slew of hot-off-the-press whodunits by her favorite authors were the only mysteries Ellie had solved lately, if one didn't count a three-point Denver Broncos loss to the Chicago Bears.

"It's not that I want to see anyone hurt or, God forbid, murdered," Ellie told Jackie Robinson, uncontested winner of the staring competition. "But if someone has been hurt or murdered, it's only fair that Peter should consult me. Two heads are better than one, especially if one of the heads has been solving fictitious mysteries her whole life. And the reason the Broncos lost to the Bears is because the coach called a quarterback sneak on fourth down when the obvious call was a slant pass over the middle, then a quick spike."

Ellie's NFL-sanctioned Denver Broncos T-shirt, tie-dyed orange and blue, was neatly tucked into a pair of faded-from-washing designer jeans. Her waist pressed against the kitchen counter as she attacked a chopping block. Her knife's honed blade left scars in the wood, but somehow her carrots and celery ended up diced, her fingers intact.

She had always been a good if lazy cook, forsaking health for convenience and, admittedly, caloric gratification. Her ex-husband Tony and son Mick never minded her excess sugars and carbs, especially when she served potato pancakes and homemade peanut brittle. But Tony, more often than not, ate out with his playmate of the month and Mick metabolized by running up and down a basketball court, or by hula-hooping his hips while he strummed a guitar, shedding sweat and pounds until he was as thin and wiry as his idol, Mick Jagger.

Ellie—also known as "Big Mama" and "the little woman"—didn't believe in waste. Most of the time she couldn't remember swallowing, much less tasting, leftovers. Despite several quick-fix diets, her weight ballooned until she looked like the turkey that flew above the Macy's Thanksgiving Day Parade, assuming the turkey was stuffed with something other than helium.

Last she'd heard, Tony had turned vegetarian, more into tofu than toffee. Married to an ex-Dallas Cowboys cheerleader who subsisted on low-fat cottage cheese—when she wasn't binging and purging—Tony had packed up his Armani suits and his young wife's pom-poms and moved to L.A.

Following her divorce, Ellie had joined Weight Winners and lost fifty-five pounds. Hired as a group leader, her leftovers now went from table to garbage disposal. Or, when waste-management kicked in, the freezer.

Her cooking skills had improved, as well. It was more difficult to cook healthy meals, but much more gratifying, and her favorite accolade had come from Mick. "Hey, Mom," he had said, gobbling down her Weight-Winners-sanctioned Short Ribs Borscht and Judeo-Christian Coffee Ring. "You should open a franchise."

Ellie slanted a glance at the kitchen clock. As she added the carrots and celery to the transparent onions that sautéed on top of her stove, she said, "Of course, the Broncos wouldn't have been behind three points if their lame-brained coach hadn't called for a prevent defense. Which, by the way, never, ever works."

Creasing the cushion of a kitchen chair, looking like a black wreath, Jackie Robinson lifted his furry head and yawned. He wasn't into football. He wasn't into baseball, either, even though he had been named for one of the greatest baseball players of all time.

Tempted to hum Simon and Garfunkle's "Mrs. Robinson"—her cat's favorite song—Ellie hummed "Homeward Bound" instead. Soon a minced garlic clove, oregano, celery seed, thyme, rosemary, basil and one teaspoon of chili powder joined her onions, celery and carrots. Then she scrubbed the preparation dishes while the hands on her clock inched, second by second, toward the five-minute mark.

"Homeward bound...I wish Peter were...homeward bound," she sang off-key, her hips swaying like Elvis at a county fair.

Yummy aromas filled the kitchen as she added canned tomato sauce, mushrooms and two tablespoons of honey to the pot. She stirred vigorously, then turned the stove to simmer. Later, she'd cook six lasagna noodles and spread a thin layer of her seasoned, simmered sauce over the bottom of an oiled pan. She'd add layers of noodles, cottage cheese, cheddar cheese and more sauce, ending with mozzarella and a little sauce on top. Her directions said to bake for fifty minutes and cool for ten—more than enough time to interrogate her lieutenant.

Peter would also play guinea pig since this was a brand-new recipe, donated by Charlene Johnson, one of Ellie's diet club members. If it tasted as good as it smelled, Ellie would type up the recipe and thumbtack it to the "inspirational" bulletin board at the Good Shepherd Church, her Weight Winners meeting site. Charlene, who had lost forty pounds and was halfway to her goal weight, called the dish "Veggie Lasagna." Ellie had renamed it "Honey Lasagna." Peter wouldn't touch anything that included the word veggie, not even vegetable oil. However, in all likelihood her carnivorous detective would detect a lack of meat. If he did, she had microwavable pork sausages on hand.

She heard Peter before she saw him. He had been trained by his nana to take off his shoes before entering a home. He didn't remove his shoes inside a crime-scene house, of course, but at the start of his career he'd automatically bend to one knee and reach for his laces. Some of his colleagues still called him Shoeless Pete. *Lieutenant* Shoeless Pete. Lieutenant Shoeless Pete, *sir.*

Strolling into the kitchen, he straddled a chair catty-corner to Jackie Robinson and said, "Something smells good."

"Sauce. Dinner. *Honey* Lasagna." Ellie stared at his gray sweatshirt and white socks. "You changed your clothes."

He pressed the heels of his hands against his faded blue denim thighs, as if he planned to do push-ups. He was trying to appear relaxed, Ellie thought, but his hands betrayed him. So did his tense shoulders.

"These are locker clothes," he said. "I decided to leave the precinct early for a change. I was about to tell you that when a call came in…" He clamped his mouth shut. His gaze touched upon Jackie Robinson, the stove, the sink, the refrigerator and the refrigerator magnet that stated, People Who Are Forced To Eat Their Own Words Will Reduce Their Big Mouths. Opening his mouth again, he said, "Where's the dog?"

"Outside. In the backyard. Staring at a squirrel." Ellie strolled over to the stove and stirred her sauce with a wooden spoon. "Tell me," she said, making an about-face.

"Your spoon's dripping," Peter observed.

"Jackie Robinson will clean it up. He loves tomato sauce. Tell me."

"I should introduce myself to what's-her-face. The dog."

"Scout. She was named for the little girl in *To Kill a Mockingbird*. Played in the movie by…Mary Badham."

"How do you remember things like that?"

"Trivial Pursuit should have been called 'Eleanor Bernstein.'" Ellie placed the wooden spoon on top of the chopping block, then splayed her hands across her hips. "Tell me."

"Tell you what?"

"Don't play innocent, Lieutenant. You were talking to me on the phone when you got another call and…?"

He ran his hands through his thick, dark hair, a stall tactic.

"Don't you know," she said, "that running your hands through your hair like that will make you bald?"

"Says who?"

"Says my mother. She also says overweight people should starve themselves to death so they can live a little longer."

Rising from his chair, Peter strode across the kitchen. Squeezing his eyes shut, he lightly scuttled his fingertips over her breasts. "And, according to your mother, messing around in the bathroom will make you blind."

"My brother Tab has twenty-twenty vision," she said as liquid fire slid through her belly.

Peter's silver-streaked mustache grazed her forehead. His blue-gray eyes, when open, usually sparkled with tender mischief. His nose, once broken then reset incorrectly, angled toward the left of a mouth that enjoyed kissing. Those same lips that could caress her into a kaleidoscope of oblivion could assume a frowning line of professionalism while announcing, "You have the right to remain silent." A detective with the homicide division of the Colorado Springs Police Department, Peter helped—or hindered—when she played part-time sleuth.

"My brother doesn't even need reading glasses," Ellie continued, "which proves my mother doesn't know everything, even if she thinks she does."

"Forget Tab, forget your mother." Peter opened his eyes and grinned. "*Jeopardy* is about to commence."

Peter liked to neck in front of *Jeopardy*. For some dumb reason, the sound of Alex Trebek's voice turned him on. The fact that Ellie knew ninety percent of the questions to the answers stoked his flames. She had tried to explain that she'd always been a walking, talking trivia machine and that she was a complete dud when it came to geography, but it didn't matter. Shortly after their first encounter, during the diet club murders, they'd made love in front of *Jeopardy*. Now it was a ritual.

"Tell me about the phone call first," she said. "If you don't," she threatened, "I'll turn the channel to a local news station."

He started to run his fingers through his hair again. Then he stopped and said, "A waitress was murdered."

"Holy cow! I had hoped for something less…irreversible. Where?"

"In an alley, behind the restaurant where she worked."

"And that restaurant is?"

"Why do you want to know the name of the restaurant?" he asked, his voice filled with suspicion.

"The local news will tell me if you don't," she said, her voice smug.

"Uncle Vinnie's."

"Uncle Vinnie's Gourmet Italian Restaurant? I've been there. Time of death?"

"Sometime between two-thirty and three-fifteen."

"Two-thirty and three-fifteen? No one noticed she was missing?"

"The deceased had finished her cleanup, they call it sidework, and during her absence a waiter collected her tips and stuck the money in an envelope. The owner, Vincent, said the deceased often left spur-of-the-moment."

"Was he terribly upset?"

"Who? Vincent? Yes. But he seemed more upset over the loss of two waitresses than he was over the death—"

"*Two* waitresses?"

"Could I taste your sauce, Norrie?"

That brought a grin to her face. Peter had nicknamed her Norrie, short for Eleanor. Because, he said, she ig*nored* his advice. "The sauce isn't done yet, honey. Why two waitresses?"

"One's dead. It's a bit difficult to wait tables when you're dead, Norrie, unless you're Tom Hanks."

"Tom Cruise, if you mean *Interview With a Vampire*. What happened to the second waitress?"

"She found the body and lost it."

"She lost the body?"

"No. Her marbles. Vincent said the customers at the McDonald's across the highway could hear her screams."

"Where was the body found?"

"I told you. In an alley behind the rest—"

"On the ground? Hidden behind trash cans?"

"Nope, but good guess. The deceased's body was found inside a Dumpster. The waitress who lost her marbles was standing on top of a wooden crate. She wanted to trash some trash. Her eyes were half shut and she held her breath, hoping to expunge, or at least dissipate, the smell of the garbage. She opened her eyes, glanced into the Dumpster, screamed bloody murder, fell off the crate and suffered a concussion. She'll be out of commission for a couple of days, but Vincent doesn't think she'll come back. He says waiting tables is a killer job to begin with and murder puts a strain on…employee relationships."

"He suspects another employee?"

"I didn't say that."

"You didn't have to."

"Vincent thinks the deceased was messing around with a waiter named Nicholas. Nicholas vehemently denies it."

"Of course he does. What's her name? The second waitress? The one who found the body?"

"Theodora something...Mallard. Why?"

"No reason. Curious."

I know her, thought Ellie. *She was a cheerleader in high school and she briefly dated my brother, Tab, when they were in junior high.*

Peter said, "Stay away from this case, Norrie. Leave it to the C.S.P.D. We're dealing with a cold-blooded killer and—"

"What was the murder weapon?"

"Daffy Duck."

"Excuse me?"

"The deceased was wearing a Daffy Duck necktie."

"Stop calling her 'the deceased'!" Ellie glanced at the kitchen clock. "You've got less than five minutes, if you want to watch Alex Trebek."

"I don't want to *watch* Alex Trebek," Peter said with a Groucho leer and the flick of an imaginary cigar. "Okay, here it is in a nutshell. Sara Zachariah, also known as Sara Lee, was taking a smoke break. The restaurant owner doesn't allow his waitresses to smoke inside the building. Someone crept up behind the poor kid and strangled her with her Daffy Duck necktie. We figure she was standing on top of the wooden crate."

"How do you know that?"

"She lost control of her sphincter muscles and, er..."

"I get the picture."

"So unless the murderer was standing on a second crate, he was fairly tall. And before you say 'or she,' that's the empirical he."

"*Was* there a second crate?"

Peter shook his head. "There's a stepladder—"

"In the alley?"

"No. The kitchen."

"Could two people fit on top of the crate?"

"Yes, but it would be a tight squeeze. And if the deceased—if Sara struggled, they'd fall off."

"When the wind blows," Ellie murmured, "the cradle will rock."

"What?"

"Nothing." She glanced toward her window. Outside, the wind had begun to blow and her café curtains were dancing a Judy Garland-Mickey Rooney jitterbug.

"We don't know yet if Sara was sexually abused, but there were no obvious signs of that. And that's all I'm going to tell you."

"Fair enough, Peter. Was the motive robbery?"

"Nope. She had sixty-some-odd dollars in her pants' pocket."

"Her tips," Ellie said, "and her bank."

"Bank?"

"My brother Tab waited tables one summer. He was forgetful and clumsy. He was also cute and charming, so he did okay, money-wise. People always asked if Tab was his real name. He'd say yes, he was named for Tab Hunter, which is true. Then he'd schmooze his tables by quoting from Tab Hunter movies, especially *Battle Cry* and *Operation Bikini*. A bank is the money you start out with—short for bankroll. At the end of the shift you turn in everything except your bank and tips. Do you have a suspect, other than Nicholas?"

"Nope. Everybody liked Sara Lee. And that's all I'm going to tell you."

"*Everybody* didn't like Sara Lee. Is—was she married?"

"Yes."

"Zachariah. *Tim* Zachariah?"

"Yes. How'd you know that?"

"He used to play for the Minnesota Vikings. He was traded to the Broncos, lasted one season and was dropped from the team. No other team would touch him with a ten-foot pole.

He wasn't a bad player, but he kept piling up penalties for personal fouls. Late hits, unnecessary roughness. He could have carried that attitude off the field, roughed up his wife."

"We're checking that out, sweetheart. There were no emergency calls to 9-1-1, but we'll talk to the deceased—to Sara's family. And the neighbors. And that's all I'm going to tell you."

Ellie opened her mouth to ask another question, but Peter scooped her up into his arms and gave her a kiss that left her gasping for breath. His motion was aggressively tender rather than rough, and had she been an NFL referee she wouldn't have thrown a flag. Not that she possessed the strength to throw a flag. Peter's second kiss had jellyfished her whole body. She could almost smell her desire, musky and warm.

Peter took the stairs two at a time, entered the bedroom and transferred her from his arms to the water bed. His face was tense with arousal. As he turned on the portable TV, she heard the familiar music, heard the announcer say, "This...is *Jeopardy.*"

THREE

RACHEL LESTER STARED at the mountains through the cabin's plate-glass window. Like millions of other children, she had been taught that George Washington could not tell a lie. Neither could Rachel. If she tried, her lips would quiver, her pinch-me-please cheeks would flush, her cornflower-blue eyes would tear up and her voice would stumble over the simplest syllable. Even the forehead beneath her bangs and the scalp beneath her perky pageboy would sweat.

"I cannot tell a lie," Washington had supposedly said when confronted with his hatchet job. And, as a kid, Rachel had wondered if "cherry tree" was a sexual innuendo. She made the mistake of asking one of her teachers at Sacred Heart and the nun had rapped Rachel's knuckles so hard, three fingers broke. Rachel's parents didn't have the money for physical therapy, so over the years her right hand had curled into a claw. During moments of stress she could actually *feel* it stiffen and coil. Although the sadistic nun was long dead, Rachel's husband had adamantly insisted she call Jonah Feldman, the famous—some said infamous—attorney. Jonah had filed a class-action lawsuit. Apparently, Rachel wasn't the only student crippled by sharp rules and razor-sharp rulers.

Comfortable with the knowledge that she was in the right, that the broken fingers hadn't been *her* fault, Rachel had finally fabricated a falsehood and gotten away with it—"gotten away" being the operative words. At age thirty-seven, she had, at long last, lied. She had cooked up a teensy distortion, a little white lie that couldn't possibly hurt anyone, and, miracle of miracles, everybody believed her.

So why did she feel so guilty, so conscience-stricken, as if she'd been caught with her hand in the cookie jar?

Because Ellie Bernstein had been so trustful, that's why. When Ellie liked someone, she tended to ignore a fib, even if it bit her on the butt. How many times had Rachel heard Ellie tell a Weight Winners member that he or she had hit a "plateau" when Rachel—and everybody else—knew darn well that the member had spent the week cheating like crazy?

Charlene Johnson was a prime example, always sucking up to Ellie by donating recipes, always cheating and bragging about it. "I lost three pounds and I cheated like crazy," she'd whisper after she stepped off the scale. Charlene cheated on her husband, too.

There was a lot of that going around. Probably because of the Internet. It was so easy to arrange an assignation on the Internet. Not that Matthew used the Internet. He liked to use the phone, and he liked to cheat close to home. Maybe the danger of getting caught spiced his two-timing stew.

She had ignored Matthew's "little indiscretions" for years. But this time he'd gone too far. This time three so-called friends had cornered Rachel. Chittering like Woodstock, Snoopy's bird-pal in *Peanuts,* they'd given Rachel lurid details she preferred not to hear. Last week her three so-called friends had been lunching at Uncle Vinnie's Gourmet Italian Restaurant and they'd seen, with their own six eyes, the way a waitress named Sara Lee flaunted her "assets." Matthew had left his business associates and wandered toward the back of the restaurant. One of Rachel's so-called friends had had to "go potty." The bathrooms were located at the back of the restaurant and the so-called friend just *happened* to accidentally catch a glimpse of Matthew and the waitress in the alley behind the kitchen. The so-called friend didn't want to tell tales after school, but if Rachel really wanted to know what Matthew and Sara Lee were doing, think Monica Lewinski.

Her husband had been caught with his pants down once too often, Rachel now mused with a grimace. And just like her favorite country-western singers, she couldn't forgive, nor forget, Matthew's cheating heart.

Not anymore. Never again.

And yet, before she accused him face-to-face, she needed to consider her options.

Which was why she had lied.

She had told Matthew that her sister Margee, who lived in Houston, was very sick, practically at death's door, and she needed Rachel to baby-sit her three kids.

To tell the God's honest truth, Margee's illness wasn't a little white lie. It was a whopper. Margee, who worked part-time at a bookstore called Murder By The Book, was alive and kicking and healthy as a horse.

And she didn't have three kids.

During the ten years they'd been married, Matthew had never asked Rachel one question about her family. It was as if she were a puppy he'd adopted from the pound. On the day she and Matthew eloped, she became his property, duly licensed with a marriage certificate rather than dog tags.

So when she told him she had to nurse her sister and baby-sit the kids, he simply gestured toward Scout and said, "You'd better take that damn mutt with you. I'm not going to walk and feed him."

"Her," Rachel had said. "Not him, her. And I've made arrangements to leave Scout with a friend."

"I didn't know you had any friends," Matthew had said with a nasty laugh.

Well, she did. The three so-called friends from her book club, the ones who had told her about Matthew's waitress. And Ellie, her friend as well as her diet club leader. And Cee-Cee Sinclair. Three years ago Cee-Cee had discovered Scout, all skin and bones, abandoned at a roadside souvenir stand. Cee-Cee had become a friend. A good friend. Such a good friend that she'd loaned her Pikes Peak mountain cabin to Rachel, even though—due to a *real* family emergency—Cee-Cee couldn't dog-sit Scout. So Rachel had asked Ellie. Which, in retrospect, had been silly. She could have put Scout in her car and driven off to Zanzibar, for all Matthew knew or cared.

Scout would love it here, she thought with a sigh. Although she felt totally isolated, as if she'd landed on Mars or the moon, she was less than two hours from downtown Colorado Springs. Her nearest neighbors were a rinky-dink gas station and a small grocery store. Both charged like wounded bulls.

Surrounded by acres of foliage and trees that touched the clouds, the snug cabin was a port in a storm, a haven in every sense of the word. In Cee-Cee's words, "an accommodation that offered the most favorable opportunities."

Rachel desperately needed an opportunity to think.

Cee-Cee called her cabin "nouveau rustic." Clean as the proverbial whistle, its kitchen and bathroom were up-to-the-minute, brand-spanking new. The living room and bedroom, however, were straight out of a historical romance novel. A fireplace. Wood-hewn furniture. A double bed with a fairly decent mattress. A sofa that looked and felt like a church pew.

The cabin had no TV or computer, but it did have a phone, and Rachel had brought her cell phone, so she wasn't totally disconnected from the outside world.

She really should call and check up on Scout.

Whoa! Was she losing what little remained of her mind? She'd only been gone a few short hours and she was supposed to be winging her way to Texas.

Inside the cozy kitchen, inside a copper-bottomed Revere saucepan, a couple of all-beef kosher hot dogs boiled merrily. Rachel knew it was silly, but when she cooked franks she always pictured them as cartoon hot dogs, the kind that drive-in movies would put up on the screen during intermissions. Magnified, the hot dogs would be smiling as they merrily leaped from grill to bun.

But then, they never got burned.

Sauerkraut simmered inside a second saucepan. Rachel loved sauerkraut, despite her tendency to retain water.

She felt so virtuous. Everything on top of the gleaming-white stove was "legal" Weight Winners fare, even though, technically, she could cheat. Didn't people cheat when they were on vacation? Wasn't she on vacation?

Well…no.

She was on a mission. She needed to write a Mission Statement. She needed to get her priorities straight. She needed to get her head on straight. As soon as her broken-fingers-lawsuit was settled, she'd have money. Granted, the lawyer would keep a goodly portion, but there'd be lots left over. *And guess what, ladies and gentlemen of the jury? For reasons I'm sure you can understand, I didn't want Matthew Lester Scrooge to get his dirty, cheating hands on one red cent of my payoff.*

The sauerkraut smelled delicious. The sauerkraut smelled burned!

Rachel raced to the stove and turned it off. Oh, well, she wasn't really all that hungry. Of course, she could always eat the hot dogs without sauerkraut, but why bother? Her hot dogs didn't look happy. They looked old and shriveled and dead.

Returning to the family room, she sat on the floor. Her knees supported her chin as her spinal column pressed against the pew/couch. For the umpteenth time she wondered how a girl who had been voted "most likely to succeed" had ended up in a time warp. Of course, no one had ever told her what she was supposed to succeed *at*. And while infidelity was practically Noachian, she felt like such a cliché. Maybe she'd cut her hair, get rid of the Prince Valiant pageboy she'd worn since nursery school.

Next to the wooden sofa were neatly stacked books: romance paperbacks and hardcover mysteries. Her sister had boxed up and mailed some new mysteries, but Rachel preferred romance novels, especially historical romance. She liked to lose herself in the eighteenth and nineteenth centuries, where women were beautiful and gutsy and *slender.* Where men were, for the most part, faithful to their wives.

Matthew didn't know he'd been caught with his pants down.

Rachel was a good Catholic, so divorce was out of the question.

Rachel was a good Catholic, so she couldn't kill Matthew. *Thou shalt not kill.*

But the Bible—and, as far as she knew, the Pope—had never said anything about waiting until one's two-timing husband was asleep, then cutting off his...

What did Marty Blue, her favorite romance author call it? Oh, yeah. His "turgid organ."

FOUR

WHEN ELLIE AWOKE from her post-*Jeopardy* catnap, a local TV reporter was asking tall, burly, thick-necked Tim Zachariah how he *felt* when he'd heard his wife had been strangled to death.

And Peter was nowhere in sight.

As the stoical Tim said he felt "bad," Ellie fumbled for the remote and pressed Mute. Then, cocking her head, she listened carefully but didn't hear any bathroom sounds. No running water. No singing. Unless she and Peter shared the bathtub, he'd sing. Nonstop. He sang in the shower. Heck, he sang while he brushed his teeth. Privately, Peter imagined himself Mario Lanza. Too bad he sounded more like Mario Langur. Although he didn't have the chin tufts of a langur monkey, Peter possessed the bushy eyebrows. And the voice.

His jeans and sweatshirt had disappeared, too.

There'd be a note downstairs.

And a missing pair of entrance-hallway shoes.

She heard branches whap-whap against the half-open bedroom window, stirred *and* shaken by a gusty breeze. The earlier, cradle-rocking kite wind had apparently swallowed a growth-hormone capsule.

Daylight was rapidly diminishing and she could smell September. There was no other smell like it. She loved September, when the iridescent aspens shimmered like gold aluminum foil and the air smelled of burning leaves, even though, nowadays, sated leaf-blowers blasted one's eardrums with boisterous belches. Best of all, September ushered in a new football season. True, the Broncos had won one game and lost one game, but they had fourteen more to go and they'd clinch the AFC championship.

Outside, it sounded like Tin Pan Alley. City workers had begun tarring the main boulevard's potholes and her usually traffic-free street served as a detour route. Car horns honked like bronchial geese. Competing with the horny geese, piano music wafted from a neighbor's open window; Gershwin's "Rhapsody in Blue." Another neighbor was listening to Bette Midler belt out "Boogie Woogie Bugle Boy." Despite the miscellaneous overtures, Ellie heard the fluty whistle of the wind as Aeolus somersaulted over her roof and around her eaves. Crisp, cool draughts blew away any leftover dregs of torridity, abolishing, until next year, the lazy, hazy dog days of sum—

Dog! Scout!

She hoped Peter had let the dog inside. She hoped Peter had fed the dog. She checked the bedside clock. Five forty-five. Holy cow! She was supposed to feed Scout at five o'clock.

As she clicked the remote, negating Mute, she saw that the reporter was now interviewing two men. Both wore black-and-white-teensy-checkered pants, white chef jackets, and stiff, white, shirred-paper chef hats. One man looked droopy and mournful, the other bright-eyed and bushy-tailed, as if he planned to make the most of his fame-filled fifteen minutes.

Ellie clicked the volume louder.

"Tell us, Vincent," the reporter said to the mournful man. "How did you *feel* when you heard that one of your waitresses had been strangled to death?"

Vincent and his companion stood under an awning. Both were practically plastered against the double doors of Uncle Vinnie's Gourmet Italian Restaurant. When Vincent tried to step backward, away from the microphone, he had no place to go. The reporter waved her mike in his face until it was parallel with his upper lip. Shaded by his beaky nose, it looked like a metallic mustache.

The other man snatched the mike away from the reporter. "I'm Al," he said, "and I own Uncle Vinnie's Gourmet Italian Restaurant with my brother Vincent. My brother, the 'Vinnie' in Uncle Vinnie's Gourmet Italian Restaurant, is our certified gourmet chef and tonight's special is osso buco…braised veal shanks. Sara Lee, whom we all loved dearly, tasted a sample this afternoon, the last food she ever ate. She said it was 'heavenly,' and it makes all of us here at Uncle Vinnie's Gourmet Italian Restaurant feel really good to know that Sara Lee's tummy was full of yummy, gourmet food when she joined God's angelic choir."

Al raised his eyes heavenward. Apparently, Ellie mused, he could see God's angelic choir through the green-and-white-striped entrance awning.

"If you mention you caught my brother and me on the news," Al continued with a wink, "we'll take twenty percent off your dinner tab, liquor not included. We're located on Austin Bluffs at the corner of—"

Furious, face contorted, the reporter grabbed the mike back before Al could finish his spiel. Almost spitting, she said, "And how did *you* feel when you heard…" She paused, shifting gears. "I assume you and your brother were questioned by the police?"

"Of course. We told them the truth, that everybody liked Sara Lee, that she was one of our finest waitresses and that she treated our customers—"

"Guests," Vincent muttered.

"—like royalty."

"And yet you plan to open tonight?" the reporter asked, raising her eyebrows as high as they could go, which wasn't very high, considering that they had been plucked and penciled in. Her wrinkled forehead looked like a monkey's.

"We *are* open," Al said, ignoring the sarcasm. "We open for lunch at eleven and shut down at three. But we unlock our doors again at five sharp, six days a week. We're closed on Sunday. Sara Lee would want us to stay open tonight, to go on with the show. She was an actress, you know. Why, only this afternoon she was rehearsing for the John Denver Community Theater's *Hello Dolly* tryouts, and she sounded more like Streisand than Streisand. The auditions are tomorrow night—there's a detailed flyer at our hostess stand. Uncle Vinnie's Gourmet Italian Restaurant supports the Arts. If you buy tickets to a show and want to eat out first, we'll give you half off your second meal, liquor not inclu—"

"Tell me, Al," the reporter interrupted, her voice even more derisive. "Will you shut down for Sara's funeral?"

"Absolutely. If the funeral's on a Sunday."

Invading the space beneath the awning, a colossal gust of wind seized the two chef hats. Vincent and Al, in unison, grabbed at their heads, then chased their paper hats down the path, away from the restaurant. The reporter giggled as her cameraman followed the Buster-Keatonish-pursuit with his camera. Ellie turned off the TV.

She had noted that Vincent was tall, well over six feet, and that his hands were huge, oversize, almost clown hands—totally out of proportion to the rest of his skinny, small-boned body.

FIVE

ALTHOUGH THE MISCHIEVOUS wind mussed his mousse-drenched hair, Nicholas Vladimir Nureyev waited until the TV reporter and cameraman moved away from the restaurant's front doors.

Ordinarily he'd enter through the kitchen. The Rules said to enter through the kitchen. But tonight the alley that led to the kitchen was blocked by yellow police tape.

He didn't want to be on TV. That was for suckers and Nico Nureyev wasn't born yesterday. He knew his tall, muscular body, his dimpled chin and his smoldering black eyes were identifiable, especially to women, but the last thing he needed was for some jerk to look at the TV and say, "Hey, Mabel, I've seen that guy somewhere before!"

As Nico strolled toward the restaurant's entrance, he imagined a red carpet unfolding and trumpets heralding his approach. If you acted like royalty, people treated you like royalty, his mother had always said. He couldn't swear those were her last words because sometimes he forgot things, but he thought maybe they were.

Upon entering, he immediately walked up to the hostess and planted a kiss on her pale, chapped lips. "Hi, Shelley," he said. "You look beautiful tonight."

She flushed beneath her acne. "I'm not Shelley," she said. "I'm Micki...M-i-c-k-i."

M-o-u-s-e, he sang silently.

Damn, it was hard keeping the hostesses straight, especially since they all seemed to be named Michelle. This one was young, scrawny, flat as an ironing board beneath a blue sweater that revealed sweaty half-moons at her armpits.

Hadn't she worked the lunch shift? Yes. He gave her his best smile and said, "I'm terrible with names."

"Michelle Lopez," she said, pointing at herself like Tarzan. "They call me Micki. You know, for short?"

"Any relation to Jennifer Lopez?"

She giggled. "I hardly think so."

"The reason I asked was because you look like her. I swear, you could be her twin sister."

"Aw, Nico, you're lyin'. My hair's different."

True, he thought. Micki Mouse's dark brown hair was long, like J-Lo's, but coarse and dull rather than sleek and shiny.

"That's because Jennifer Lopez can afford to hire professionals," he said. "If you don't mind, I'm gonna call you M-Lo."

"I don't mind." She blushed again. "You'd better get on the floor, Nico. We're really busy tonight."

He nodded. "Ordinarily, I don't work doubles."

"Ordinarily, you don't work *lunch*," she said, batting eyelashes that looked like the wispy hairs on a caterpillar.

He shrugged. "I covered Jon's shift. Tonight was supposed to be my night off. But we're so short-staffed, Al asked me to come in."

"It's like that restaurant in California," she said. "The one O.J.'s ex wife ate at before she got herself killed? They were busy, too. People are weird."

Surprising him, she palmed his face, French-kissed him, released his face, took a couple of steps backward, and blushed for the third time.

The mouse has a tongue, he thought, *and she knows what to do with it. Interesting...*

He flashed his pearly whites at her, then wended his way toward the kitchen. He adjusted his smile to friendly, rather than personal, as he snaked around tables garnished with red-and-white-checkered tablecloths, glassed-in candles and small vases filled with artificial flowers. The salt and pepper shakers had once been wine bottles; Sterling Chardonnay for salt, Monterey Peninsula Black Burgundy for pepper.

Straightening to his full height of six-feet-two-inches, Nico walked through waist-high, swinging doors. He entered the kitchen, where he greeted Vincent and Al, both cooking up a storm. Prep cooks were making salads and stuffing dessert plates into a stainless-steel refrigerator. The dishwasher, who couldn't tell the difference between cannoli and cannelloni, was busy stirring tomato sauce.

Vincent and Al barely acknowledged Nico's presence, but later Al would give him a free meal, a reward for coming in at such short notice. Nico, who had worked at more restaurants than he could count, actually *liked* the food at Uncle Vinnie's. Licking his lips, he remembered Micki's tongue. He might forget other things, but not tongues.

He grabbed a freshly laundered apron, tied it around his waist, then stuffed its pockets with two sets of car keys, loose coins, pens, an order pad and a corkscrew.

"I am invincible," he sang under his breath, before he remembered that it was a woman's song, sung by Helen somebody. He prodded his memory, a trick he'd learned from one of his high school teachers, just before he quit school.

Ready, set, go…Helen Ready?

His father said he was dumb as a stick, but a person didn't have to be a genius if that person knew smart people. Nico would soon be able to invest in some kind of computer gizmo invented by a friend. All he needed was twenty-five thousand dollars. His grandfather had once been offered stock in a new company, but he had to buy a minimum of ten thousand shares at a dollar a share. Gramps had barely weathered the Depression and he didn't have ten grand, so he'd said no, sorry, can't scrape up the money, maybe next time. The company came out with a camera that developed its own pictures and Gramps never stopped talking about his "wasted opportunity." On his deathbed, his last toothless hiss had been, "Ten thousand shares of Polaroid at a dollar a share."

Slithering sideways into the narrow waiters' station, Nico clocked in on the computer and patted Kelly's butt.

Kelly liked to have her butt patted. An older waitress, forty-something, she had cornered him one night in dry storage, after their shift, and he had almost killed her by pressing his hand against her face. He was afraid someone would hear her happy moans, but she couldn't breathe and she fainted and he had never been so scared in his life.

She hadn't said anything, probably afraid she'd get fired, too. One of Vincent's strictest Rules was, Don't mess around with the staff.

Which, to Nico, meant, Don't get caught.

The only other Rule he broke was a stupid one. The menu said there'd be a twenty percent gratuity added to tables of eight or more. Vincent insisted servers tell the person paying the bill that the tip had been added. Nico never did that and, more often than not, he'd get double-tipped. Which, in his opinion, was the fault of the guests. Most never looked at their bills. The majority flipped him a credit card. At the end of his shift, he'd pay out the total amount of food and beverages ordered, tip out the bartender and busboy, then pocket the rest. So Nico would add his gratuity to the top line on the credit card slip, leaving the tip space open. Sometimes people said, "Has the tip already been added?" A square shooter, he'd say, "Yes, sir—ma'am—but you can add more if you like." Frequently, they liked.

Damn, he'd better get his butt on the floor. His station was filling up fast. Wait a sec! Micki Mouse had seated rugrats at one of his tables. He'd have to suck up to her again, teach her *Nico's* Rules.

No small children.

No old people.

No prom kids—unless, of course, they numbered eight or more.

Strolling over to the hostess's stand, he draped his arm around Micki's shoulders and said, "What are you doing after work, pretty M-Lo?"

"Nothing," she said, her irregular teeth pulverizing a wad of green chewing gum. "Why?"

"Why do you think, silly girl? I'd like to take you out. For a drink."

"Me?"

Now she looked like a cow chewing its cud. "No," he said. "Jennifer Lopez. Of course, you."

"I'm not a very good drinker, Nico. I drank champagne once…at my cousin's wedding. But I got sick as a dog and threw up all over the bride and groom and—"

"You threw up on the bride and groom?"

"Yes. No. Yes. The bride and groom on top of the wedding cake. My cousin was so mad, she swore she'd never speak to me again."

"We'll go to my place. No champagne. No wedding cake. Just vodka. You can't get sick on vodka."

"You can't?" Her tongue darted out to lick the spittle at the corner of her lips and he thought he'd burst. "But you can get drunk, Nico. Yes?"

She was practically melting at his feet. If she had any breasts, they'd be straining against her sweater. She wanted to get drunk. She wanted him. He had never seen any woman want him as much as this mouse, not even Sara Lee.

Micki Mouse was tall for a girl, maybe three inches shorter than Nico, and yet she couldn't weigh more than a hundred-ten pounds, dripping wet. Three double shots of vodka and she'd pass out cold.

Should she need more, he had more.

"If you get drunk," he promised, "I'll take care of you."

SIX

ELLIE DONNED panties and a white terry-cloth robe. Belting the robe, she raced down the staircase and entered the family room.

Scout slept on her scrunched-up quilt and…

Jackie Robinson slept in his usual wreath position, curled up against Scout's tummy!

Grinning from ear to ear, Ellie tiptoed into the kitchen. Almost immediately she saw signs of Peter's recent occupancy. Unless, of course, a hungry, benevolent burglar had turned off the stove, left an open loaf of bread and a wooden spoon on the counter, freckled the stovetop with lasagna sauce, then burgled…what?

Aside from her TV and computer and first-edition mystery novels, the only items of value she owned were paintings by Wiley Jamestone and Garrett Halliday.

She gazed longingly at the coffeepot. It was too late in the evening for caffeine. With a sigh, Ellie filled the teakettle and set it atop the stove.

Peter's note rested against a mug that read, Diets Are For Those Who Are Thick And Tired Of It. Inside the mug was an herbal teabag—peppermint. Her handsome lieutenant's thoughtfulness far outweighed his messiness. Ellie read the note:

My darling dog-napper,
I was going to feed your "guest" but your friend Rachel forgot to include dog food. Dog toys, yes. Dog food,

no. Answer: A supermarket. Question: where does one buy kibble? I don't know when I'll be back. Please don't wait up. I might pay my apartment a visit and catch a few Zs. Love you.

Translation: you will NOT *get involved in this waitress murder.*

And I love you, too, Ellie thought with a sigh.

A tad chauvinistic, and more than a tad anachronistic, Peter insisted on maintaining his own apartment until she agreed to marry him. But she liked things just the way they were, thank you very much. On her own for the first time in her life, she valued her independence...what her generation had called "more space." Peter's latest marriage bribe had been free health insurance. "If you keep sticking your lovely nose in my cases," he had said, sounding like the narrator of a Nostradamus documentary, "you'll need all the health insurance you can get."

Right now, she had to stick her nose in her purse and find Rachel Lester's neatly printed instructions list. She didn't bother checking the box Rachel had filled with toys, food and water bowls, a leash and Scout's patchwork quilt. If there had been any food, Peter would have found it. After all, he was almost as good a sleuth as Eleanor Bernstein, mature girl detective.

Rachel's list wasn't long or complicated. It included feeding instructions, her cell phone number and her vet's phone number. She used Dr. Ben Cassidy, Jackie Robinson's vet, so Ellie knew that number by heart. However, one of Rachel's directives stood out like a sore thumb.

"There should be more than enough dog food," she had written. "But if you run out, Reigning Cats & Dogs has Scout's special formula on file. The pet shop is on..."

Austin Bluffs. Right next door to Uncle Vinnie's Gourmet Italian Restaurant!

With that thought, Ellie slid the list underneath a fridge magnet that stated: The Perils Of Eating Duck Are Great, Especially For The Duck. As she began shoveling her lasagna sauce into a couple of Mason jars, she mapped her agenda for tomorrow. Among other things, she wanted to talk to Theodora Mallard, the waitress who had found Sara Lee. Then Ellie planned to follow Sara Lee's up-to-the-minute agenda—the agenda that had led to her death. But right now, this very minute, Ellie's main concern was Scout.

The dog had trailed Jackie Robinson into the kitchen, and Ellie could almost swear Scout looked up at the clock. Could dogs read clocks? Or did they have an internal clock? *Hey, lady…tick…it's way past…tick…my feeding time…tick.*

With a lithe leap, Jackie Robinson claimed his usual chair. Scout sat, her rump inches away from the legs of the chair, her tail sweeping the floor. Mouth open, panting, she seemed to say, *Cat would make a great dinner, especially skinned and deep-fried. If you're squeamish about cooking Cat, a pesky rodent inhabits your backyard. I believe you humans call it Squirrel.*

Ellie looked out the window. Obese raindrops had joined the swirling wind. Her windshield wipers were on their last legs and she didn't relish a drive to the supermarket. If Peter had been here, he would have copped a "me man, me battle storm and club fierce kibble" attitude. But she had a feeling Peter planned to avoid her like the plague…until he caught Sara Lee's killer.

Ellie debated calling Rachel in Houston. But what could Rachel tell her?

Where the damn dog food is, that's what!

"Holy cow, Jackie Robinson, can you say overreacting? A simple phone call to Rachel's husband will solve this particular mystery."

Her most recent Weight Winners roster, situated next to her kitchen phone, included fax and phone numbers.

Pressing the receiver against her ear, Ellie listened to an answering machine. "If you want Matthew Lester, Rachel Lester, or Scout Finch Lester," Rachel's electronic voice sang out, "please leave a message at the sound of the beep."

Trying to keep her frustration at bay, Ellie left her name, number and a brief message. Then she tried Rachel's cell phone number. No answer.

"We'll have to improvise," she told Scout, whose expression more than hinted that Ellie's tibia might make a tasty bone.

Cat and Squirrel were out of the question, but unless Scout had been brought up kosher, Pig wasn't.

Retrieving Peter's sausages from the fridge, Ellie headed for the microwave.

SEVEN

RACHEL LESTER couldn't believe it. Her cell phone was utterly, thoroughly, categorically *dead!*

God's will? The nearness of the mountain range? Karma?

I shouldn't have lied. I figured I'd go to hell for my Margee whopper, but I didn't figure my cell phone would croak.

The cabin's phone didn't work, either. She had automatically picked up the receiver upon her arrival and there'd been a dial tone, but that was before the windstorm, and now it was raining, and she felt miserable.

And, darn it, hungry!

A little voice inside her head whispered, *Dammit, hungry,* but she couldn't say the word "dammit" out loud. The nuns had done their jobs well, reinforced by Rachel's mom. To tell the God's honest truth, Rachel had pictured her mom as Carrie's mom when she'd read Stephen King's *Carrie.* Thanks to the nuns and her mom, Rachel didn't swear. Instead, when she wanted to cuss, she substituted the names of the seven dwarfs.

"Sleepy, Sneezy, Grumpy," she muttered, marching around the living room. "I should have stayed home. What made me think an isolated mountain cabin would clear my mind? That's like saying you can win the national spelling bee if you watch *Wheel of Fortune* every day."

Tripping over a piece of braided rug, Rachel looked down and saw that a folded piece of lined notebook paper had fallen from her purse. Or her pocket.

A shopping list?

Yes, ma'am, yes, sir, yes, we have no bananas. That's what it was all right.

Directly under bananas, topping the list, two words seemed to leap off the paper and hit Rachel square in the eyeballs.

Scout's food.

"Doc, Dopey, Bashful and...oh, darn, I can never remember the seventh dwarf. Sleepy, Sneezy, Grumpy, Doc, Dopey, Bashful and Vanna White!"

Tears stung Rachel's eyes. She had never used Vanna White, her personal role model, in a litany of cusses before. It just showed how upset she was, and for no good reason. Logic said that Ellie, planning to feed Scout at five, would see that the food was missing and drive to Reigning Cats & Dogs, which closed at six. No big deal.

Except, it *was* a big deal.

Rachel had always prided herself on her organizational skills. She might not have much else going for her, but she was undeniably methodical. How could she have forgotten to buy Scout's food?

She hadn't bought the bananas that topped her list, either.

As a matter of fact, she hadn't bought anything on a grocery list that was as long as the Gettysburg Address. Milk. Eggs. Dog biscuits. Cereal—

"Dopey, Sleepy, Grumpy," Rachel swore. Matthew would be livid.

Well, that settled it! She'd leave the cabin tonight. No. First thing tomorrow morning. She'd say her sister was much, much better and—*oh, gosh, how lucky can you get?*—she'd been able to book a red-eye flight.

Tonight she'd pack the suitcase she had unpacked, dump the burned sauerkraut, heat up the shriveled hot dogs, wash the pots, try to sleep and—

Was that the *wind* making such a commotion outside the cabin?

Or was it…oh, dear God…could it possibly be…a bear?

No way! A bear's paw couldn't grasp the doorknob and turn it slowly—

I didn't lock the door!

First the neglected grocery list, now the unlatched door. Ms. Methodical was definitely losing what little remained of her mind.

Mesmerized, her heart pounding in her ears, Rachel watched the door open.

A man walked inside. Spying Rachel, he raised his shotgun and said, "Who the hell are you?"

As she burst into tears, she remembered the name of the seventh dwarf: Happy.

EIGHT

ELLIE AWOKE exhausted. Her restless slumber had been infested with dreams—images that, this morning, were as substantial as cotton candy.

She had envisioned Sara Lee and Louis Armstrong singing "Hello Dolly"—that much was clear in her mind. Sara had been welcomed in heaven by Armstrong's angelic choir of musicians and waiters... *It's so nice to have you back where you belong.*

Catching last night's late edition of the local news had, in all probability, contributed to Ellie's twitchy sleep/dreams. The reporter had edited the effusive Al's promotional pitch and substituted a photo of Sara Lee, contributed by her inconsolable mother.

"Yes, but how did you *feel*, Mrs. Leibowitz, when you heard your daughter had been strangled to death?" the reporter kept asking the distraught woman, and Ellie had wanted to strangle the monkey-faced newscaster.

The family photo had depicted a teenage Sara. She wore a T-shirt, grungy jeans and a pair of unlaced combat boots. She looked tough, but in a good way, as if she faced the world with invisible boxing gloves. Her eyes and mouth seemed familiar.

Barbra Streisand, Ellie had thought. A young Barbra Streisand, although, to be perfectly honest, Streisand had never looked old. Still didn't.

Speaking of the news...

First, a quick shower.

Her wet auburn hair lashed her shoulders as Ellie toweled herself off. No time for a blow-dryer.

Craving caffeine, she donned a pair of black slacks and one of her son's touring T-shirts. Since all tees nowadays seemed to advertise something, she'd rather promote Mick's new rock group, Jade, than Old Navy or The Gap. Jade had scored a modest hit with a song called "Walk On Water." But their second release, "Jade and Jasmine," was rapidly climbing the charts.

With an apology to Scout—and the promise of a long pre-dinner walk—Ellie let the dog out into the backyard. Jackie Robinson followed. Maybe, together, they could trap Squirrel.

The aroma of fresh-brewed coffee tantalized Ellie's taste buds as, mug in hand, she turned on the kitchen TV and surfed until she found a local newscast.

A more recent Sara Lee photograph filled the screen—a *The Pajama Game* cast photo, Sara's face circled by a white grease pencil. Once again, Ellie noted the resemblance to Streisand.

Holy cow! Before he lost his chef's hat, hadn't Al said something about Sara sounding more like Streisand than Streisand? And that she'd be auditioning for *Hello Dolly,* the John Denver Community Theater's next musical production?

Ellie snapped her fingers. *The Louis Armstrong dream! That's where it came from!*

But why had her subconscious focused on that particular piece of Al information? A portent? An ethereal "handwriting on the wall"?

Should she call Peter? And tell him what? "Yesterday I saw an announcement for *Hello Dolly* auditions. Last night I dreamed about Louis Armstrong and this morning I remembered that Sara Lee was planning to audition. Maybe she was killed by an insecure Dolly hopeful."

And maybe Eleanor Bernstein, mature girl detective,

should add more clues to her arsenal before shooting off her mouth to Lieutenant Peter Miller.

Retrieving Rachel's instruction list from underneath the fridge magnet, Ellie dialed Rachel's cell phone number. No answer. She tried Rachel's home number and got the answering machine. Okay. First stop, Rachel's house.

If I can't get in, or can't find the food, I'll drive to Reigning Cats & Dogs. And maybe, if the timing's right, I'll eat lunch at Uncle Vinnie's.

She wanted to talk to Nicholas. And Vincent.

And Theodora Mallard, the waitress who had found Sara Lee's body.

There was no listing for Theodora Mallard in the telephone directory, not even initials, but surely Vincent and Al kept an up-to-date list of phone numbers so that, when the schedule came out, waiters could call each other and trade shifts. Where would they keep it? In an office, if they had an office. Or…

She had been inside Uncle Vinnie's kitchen…once. She and Al's wife had organized a fund-raiser for Canine Companions. Wasn't there an employee bulletin board near an employee bathroom? Yes. Ellie pictured a hand-printed warning, tacked to the cork: Giveing Out Enployee Phone Numbers Is A Fireing Offence. She remembered the sign so well because of the typos. So all she had to do was find an excuse to visit the kitchen, glance at the bulletin board, memorize Theodora Mallard's phone number, then call and arrange an interview.

Easy as pie, right?

Assuming Theodora's head injury hadn't blighted her memory.

If memory served, Tab's junior high school girlfriend had always been a tad wonky—even without a killer concussion.

NINE

MATTHEW AND RACHEL LESTER lived on the west side, not far from Manitou Springs, where the homes were old, well-land-scaped and well-tended—at least from the outside.

Yesterday, Rachel and Scout had met Ellie at the curb, so she'd never been inside the Lester's two-story brick home. Which, today, looked deserted.

Of course it did. Rachel was in Houston and her husband probably worked a nine-to-five job.

Because a house looks *deserted, that doesn't mean it* is *deserted.*

And...there's a car in the carport.

Ellie knocked, waited, rang the bell, waited, rang again. About to turn away and return to her Honda, her gaze touched upon the upstairs windows.

Open!

Ordinarily, that wouldn't have bothered her. Last night's wind and rain had given way to a crisp, autumn, sunshiny day. But even from a distance she could see that the curtains were soaking wet. A person might forget to close one window during a windy rainstorm, but not three. Maybe Matthew hadn't come home last night and Rachel, in a hurry to catch her plane, had left the windows o—

No! Not a chance! Rachel was too grounded, too orga-nized. At diet club meetings she took copious notes and she read every single word on a food label.

And yet she *had* seemed a tad edgy yesterday afternoon,

which Ellie had attributed to preflight jitters and sister Margee's sudden illness.

Rachel had also mentioned calling a cab, which, in all probability, meant her husband hadn't been home, and when Ellie had offered to drive her to the airport, she'd said no thanks, if the cab didn't show she'd leave her car in short-term parking.

Had the cab arrived on time? Was the car in the carport Rachel's car?

Matthew could have come home and opened the windows, then left again before the storm, but something didn't feel right.

Woman's intuition? Or too many cop shows?

A gate led to a fenced backyard. As Ellie stepped into the yard, she felt as if she'd landed in Oz; gone from black and white to Technicolor. A pinwheel of color assaulted her senses: verdant grass, uncut; red and orange leaves, unraked. A shrine to Scout, the tiny yard boasted an Emerald-City-green dog house, doggie toys and chew bones, an ultramarine water bowl, a green garden hose, its nozzle resting inside the water bowl, and a flower-decaled kiddy wading pool, drained, a relic from the summer's heat wave.

As Ellie walked toward the back door, she saw that it was ajar. In this neighborhood, one might leave a door unlocked but not ajar. Unless one slammed it shut then didn't wait around to see if the bolt caught.

Weak bolt notwithstanding, a concerned citizen should investigate.

Entering into a kitchen, the first thing Ellie smelled was dog. That explained the open windows. Rachel, who spent most of her time at home, probably didn't notice the odor, but her husband might have used her absence to air out the house. And he hadn't shut the windows when the storm hit because…?

Because he left suddenly.

Or been compelled to leave suddenly.

Ellie spotted a carton of 2% milk, an empty Denver Broncos Superbowl XXXIII coffee mug, and a clean spoon on the kitchen counter. There was also an open box of take-out chicken, untouched, a spilled can of coffee and a broken sugar bowl, knocked to the floor by...whom? Matthew or his assailant?

Although she couldn't swear there'd been a scuffle, and she didn't see any sign of blood, the open back door and upstairs windows told her that Rachel's husband had been caught by surprise.

Conjecture, a little voice inside her head whispered.

"Right," she said. "Not even enough proof for a search warrant. Of course, one doesn't need a search warrant if one wants to search for dog food. Does one?"

There was no dog food in the laundry room, the half bath or the family room. No sign of a scuffle, either. Ellie entered a study, neat as the proverbial pin.

Correction: neat as the proverbial pin except for a messy stack of papers spread out across the surface of an open rolltop desk. Unpaid bills? Yes. Next to the scattered invoices were envelopes and stamps. Peter had taught Ellie how to bank online, but it was in character for Rachel to pay her monthly bills the old-fashioned way. Unless her husband paid the bills.

No. This was definitely Rachel's room. The French Provincial writing desk with its decorative sliding cover wouldn't be a "real man's" option, and Rachel had described her husband as "someone who would rather starve to death than eat quiche." One full wall of bookshelves held hundreds of romance paperbacks, alphabetized by author. A Fran Baker romance, bookmarked, sat on a small, round, doily-infested table. Nudging the Baker book was the latest Marty Blue romantic suspense, also bookmarked.

Ellie felt her lips crease in a smile. Rachel, the most focused person she knew, read more than one book at a time. A chink in her systematic armor?

Under an ornately framed van Gogh reproduction was a hinged wooden shelf. Ellie imagined she heard Don McLean's "Vincent" as she scrutinized two silver-framed photographs. The first showed Scout, wearing a Santa hat, standing in front of a beautifully decorated Christmas tree. The second depicted Rachel and a man standing in front of the same tree. Rachel looked as if she'd pasted a smile on her face—*with eyes that know the darkness of my soul.* The man, doubtless Matthew, was attractive, assuming one lusted after Richard Gere. Matthew was shorter and thinner than his wife, so a hefty assailant—or Rachel, for that matter—could easily overpower him.

Ellie half expected to find a dead body upstairs, but the rooms appeared vacant. No Scout food materialized inside the master bedroom, full bath, second bedroom, or a storage room filled with unopened cartons and what could only be described as "garage sale schlock." Nor was there doggy food inside the closets, which she first scanned with trepidation, then searched thoroughly. Matthew's clothes, rather than Rachel's, smelled of perfume.

Was that another clue? Did Matthew sleep around? Had he been assailed by a jealous husband/lover?

As she approached a fifth room, at the end of the hallway, Ellie thought she heard the low hum of conversation behind a tightly closed door. Was Matthew talking on the phone?

"Matthew?" She cleared her throat. "Matthew," she said, upping the volume of her voice a couple of notches, "it's Ellie Bernstein...Rachel's friend."

No response.

"Your back door was wide open," she continued, practically shouting.

"Ajar," she amended, grasping the doorknob.

"Ordinarily, I wouldn't walk upstairs, uninvited, but Scout's out of dog food," she said and immediately realized how pathetic she sounded.

The room, an exercise/sewing room, smelled of sour sweat. If Rachel sewed in here, she'd have to stop breathing. Or breathe through her mouth.

A tabletop TV faced a treadmill. A sports channel televised an interview with the Broncos coach, his face both tanned and ruddy as he spouted cliché after cliché. The host of the show wore a tie and a smirk. Ellie often watched the same show while she dusted and vacuumed. Soon the host would interview the smiley Chicago Bears coach, then all the other NFL coaches, and the interviews would replay ad nauseam until next week.

Tempted to turn off the TV, Ellie decided she'd better not touch anything. Except the doorknob. She had already touched the doorknob. And the closet doorknobs. Damn!

Returning to the kitchen, she spied a portable phone. On the counter, next to the phone, were what looked like a thousand business cards, most still shrink-wrapped. Attached to one stack of cards was a yellow copy shop receipt.

Matthew Lester worked for a real-estate firm.

Ellie picked up the receiver with her thumb and third finger. She stared at the number pad. If the Lester house evolved into a crime scene and the cops couldn't get fingerprints off the receiver, there'd be no prints on the numbers. Right? Of course, right.

The receptionist's voice was colder than a frozen pizza as she stated that Mr. Lester wasn't at his desk, sorry. He had left yesterday, just before lunch, and never returned. He hadn't even called in for his messages, so it wouldn't do any good to leave a… No, she couldn't check his appointment book. Not without a subpoena.

Another *Law & Order* addict, Ellie thought with a grimace. She identified herself and was in the middle of explaining her Scout dilemma when the receptionist said, "Ellie Bernstein? Weight Winners?"

"Yes."

"Ohmigosh! My name's Andi—" the voice thawed "—and I've been planning to join your diet club since January. It was my New Year's resolution."

"Tell you what," Ellie said. "If you come to Friday night's meeting, I'll waive the registration fee."

After a thoughtful silence, Andi said, "What, exactly, do you need to know?"

"You said Mr. Lester left the office around lunchtime. Was he meeting anyone?"

"Wait a sec." Long pause. "Here's his appointment book. Yes. An associate."

"And that associate is…?"

"It doesn't really say who it is, just the initials C.J."

Ellie tried to stifle her impatience. "Do you happen to know an associate with the initials C.J.?"

"I suppose he could have meant Charlene Johnson. She's another Realtor, and she's the one who suggested I join Weight Win—"

"Does it say where they planned to meet?"

"Sort of."

Ellie swallowed a frustrated sigh. "Define 'sort of.'"

"The appointment book says 'UVIR.'" Silence. Then, "I'll bet that stands for the University of Virginia."

No, you ninny, thought Ellie. *It stands for Uncle Vinnie's Italian Restaurant.*

"Maybe that's why he's not here today," Andi continued. "Mr. Lester goes out of town for seminars and quite a few are held on college campuses."

"Are there any appointments for today?"

"Today? How could…yes! S.L. at 8:00 a.m., a multiple listing inspection at 10:00 a.m., and J.D.C.T. at 7:00 p.m. I guess he didn't fly to Virginia, after all. I wish Matt…" She paused and Ellie could practically hear her blush. "I wish Mr. Lester wouldn't use initials. It makes it hard to track him down. I have his private cell phone number, but—"

"Would you give it to me, please?"

"Oh, I couldn't. That number's for emergencies only."

"If you sign up Friday night, I'll give you a Weight Winners food scale. And a package of diet club breakfast bars."

Still holding the receiver between her thumb and third finger, Ellie tapped out Matthew's private, emergency-only cell phone number. A voice-mail voice told her to leave a message.

The voice inside Ellie's head said, *He was supposed to meet S.L. at 8:00 a.m. Sara Lee? The initials J.D.C.T. sound familiar. Jewish something-or-other? J.D.C.T.…J.D.C.T.… oh, well, if I don't obsess, it'll come to me.*

Wasn't there an apropos line in Don McLean's "Vincent"—the song her son Mick called "Starry, Starry Night"? She hummed her way through the chorus until she remembered the words.

"'Perhaps they'll listen now,'" she murmured, phoning Peter. Then she amended the line to, "Perhaps they'll listen."

Peter picked up on the first ring, as if he'd already fished his cell phone from the depths of his pocket.

"Honey," she said, "I really hate to bother you but—"

"Where the hell have you been?"

She blinked. "I've been scouting for dog food. I drove to Rachel's house and—"

"Where's your cell phone?"

"I didn't take it with me."

"The phone's in your purse. Don't women take their purses everywhere they go?"

Ignoring his chauvinistic remark—for now—she said, "Didn't your nana ever tell you that women change their purses to match their shoes?"

"What shoes? You wear sneakers."

"Not to Weight Winners meetings." She looked down at her sneakers. "Group leaders have a dress code."

"I've been trying to call you for hours."

"Blatantly untrue. I haven't been gone for 'hours.' Maybe you called when I was in the shower. Then you waited and called again after I left."

"Where are you now?"

"I told you. Rachel Lester's house."

"You're *inside* the house?"

"No, Peter, I'm standing inside a phone booth. With Superman. It's a tight fit, but it would have been much tighter if I hadn't joined Weight Winners."

"This is no time for sarcasm."

"Really! What's a good time? And before you respond, Lieutenant, chill out!"

"You're right. I'm sorry. I haven't had more than three hours' sleep."

"Why were you trying to call me?" Ellie asked.

"I need your friend Rachel's contact number."

"Why?" Ellie could practically hear him running his hands through his hair. "What happened to Matthew Lester?"

"How do you know something happened?"

She told him about the wet curtains, repetitive TV broadcast and messy kitchen. "I wasn't breaking and entering, honey. The door was open. Not just unlocked. Ajar." She chewed her bottom lip. "It's a homicide, right?"

"Yes. We found Lester's body in the trunk of a car. But we're not releasing any information, Norrie, not until we notify his next of kin."

She gave him Rachel's cell phone number. "I've called it so many times, I've got the damn thing memorized. But there's no answer, Peter, and no voice mail. I have a feeling her phone's not working."

"Do you know where she's staying?"

"With her sister, Margee, but that doesn't help. I don't have a last name and I'm fairly certain Margee's a nickname for Margaret."

"Aw, Norrie, don't cry."

"I'm not crying. I'm just…frustrated. Poor Rachel. Does Matthew's murder have anything to do with Sara Lee's murder?"

"We don't know."

"C'mon, Lieutenant, what aren't you telling me?"

"I'm telling you we don't know. Lester was last seen at Uncle Vinnie's. He ran up a sizable tab, mostly drinks, and he left a huge tip on his credit card. But Sara Lee didn't serve him, Nicholas did, so her 'service' didn't generate the big tip. Lester ate lunch with an unknown woman and—"

"I'll save you some steps, Peter. The woman is a real-estate agent named Charlene Johnson. And while Matthew might have last been seen at Uncle Vinnie's, he came home." Her gaze touched upon the open box of fried chicken and the broken sugar bowl. "So if he was killed because he witnessed the murder, he had more than enough time to call the cops. If he was the murderer, his death could have been a form of retribution. Where was Sara Lee's husband during the murders?"

"He has an ironclad alibi. Two ironclad alibis. During Sara Lee's murder he was with a potential customer. A dozen salespeople and mechanics can vouch for him. He took the client for a test drive, but that was *after* the murder occurred. Last night Zachariah locked up his house and mourned at a local sports bar. He got rip-roaring drunk and stripped down to his underpants. He solicited the cocktail waitress, who thought he was disgusting. A pal took him home and swears Zachariah spent the rest of the night on his knees."

"Praying?" Ellie asked dryly.

"No. 'Barfing into the crapper.' Quote, unquote. I have to go, sweetheart. I'll check in with you later. Love you."

As Ellie hung up the phone, she thought, *Peter confided in me. He gave me crumbs, rather than the whole loaf, but that's an improvement over his usual "don't get involved, Norrie."*

She was grateful for crumbs, even though crumbs weren't allowed on her diet. Once upon a time she had believed that cake crumbs didn't have calories.

More recently, at a Weight Winners meeting, shy Rachel had risen from her chair. "If you stand in a dark kitchen," she had said, "and eat ice cream straight from the container by the light of the refrigerator, it shouldn't count as a cheat."

Then she had laughed and everyone joined in the laughter and she'd looked so happy.

Ellie felt tears sting her eyes. *Poor, poor Rachel.*

TEN

RACHEL LESTER felt happy. Happy, happy, happy. Nude as an artist's model, seated atop the kitchen counter, she watched a naked Kurt Gordon prepare Hollandaise sauce for a breakfast dish he called "Eggs Gordon."

Kurt was very attractive—Grizzly Adams with a well-trimmed beard and the most incredible ice-green eyes. Despite his age, late fifties, he could have played the hero in one of Rachel's romance novels.

Instead he sequestered himself inside a mountain cabin and wrote romance novels. For Harlequin. Under the pseudonym Victoria Gordon. When he'd told Rachel that, she thought she'd died and gone to heaven. Except for Marty Blue, Victoria Gordon was her favorite author.

Kurt also played unofficial cabin caretaker, the reason why he had grabbed his shotgun and investigated the light in Cee-Cee's cabin.

Rachel had always believed stories of love at first sight were pure fiction, engineered by book publishers, sappy musicians, movie moguls and cosmetics manufacturers.

Not anymore.

Kurt owned—or as he said, *was owned by*—a Springer spaniel named Lady and two cats, Little Missy and Miss Kitty.

Last night he had dumped Rachel's burned sauerkraut and shriveled hot dogs, then whipped up something he called Quiche Gordon. As she'd watched, he preheated the oven to 425° and fried some bacon. He'd crumbled the bacon into a prepared pie crust. With a wire whisk he beat four eggs, two cups of heavy cream, a teaspoon of salt and a pinch of nutmeg. Then he stirred in a quarter pound of shredded Swiss cheese. He poured that mixture into the crust, baked it for fifteen minutes, then turned the oven to 325°. While the quiche baked for another thirty-five minutes and cooled for ten, Rachel told Kurt her life story. When she had finished, he'd stuck a knife in the middle of the quiche, held the knife up for her inspection, and said, "Clean."

"Are you saying," she'd asked, "that tonight is a clean start? A clean slate?"

"Yup."

"Then I shouldn't eat heavy cream," she'd quipped. "I'm on a strict diet."

He'd put down the knife and said, "I like women with meat on their bones."

"But you write romances, Kurt, where the women are always slender."

"Underfed," he'd amended. "Rachel, in the real world very few women look like the women I write about, nor should they. It's like saying Barbie and Ken are anatomically correct."

"Holy sh—sneezy! Are you for real?"

He'd laughed. "If I'm not, you'd better adopt Lady, Little Missy and Miss Kitty."

"I'll bet your heroines don't have *this*," she'd said, her voice bitter.

He'd gently grasped her proffered claw-hand and kissed her palm.

By the time she'd eaten the Quiche Gordon, it was cold rather than cooled and Margee's recovery had been put off for a few days.

Now, gazing at her romance author/hero, she slid from the counter and stretched like a cat. "I prefer my eggs cold, Kurt," she said, pressing her body against his.

"Yes," he said, "I've noticed that."

"And for the record, Hollandaise sauce doesn't have any calories when you eat it cold."

ELEVEN

Uncle Vinnie's Gourmet Italian Restaurant served home-made, seasoned croutons on their salads and, just like cake crumbs, croutons were a no-no.

With that thought, Ellie turned right, exiting the highway. Then she drove a few feet, made a sharp left turn and parked in the strip center's lot.

Her gaze touched upon the restaurant's green-and-white-striped awning.

First, Scout's food.

Reigning Cats & Dogs's window display included a chess set with dogs as queens, kings, rooks, knights, bishops—thirty-two pieces in an assortment of the most popular breeds. To Ellie, the exhibit conjured up an Ogden Nash proverb: "Happiness is having a scratch for every itch."

Inside, the shop was more a boutique than a pet supply out-let. A human boutique, to be exact. A boutique for *wealthy* humans.

Glancing at two clothing racks, she wanted one of every-thing, especially an appliquéd and embroidered blazer. The appliquéd cats were so cute, so colorful. She could wear the blazer, over skirt or slacks, to Weight Winners meetings.

And it only cost…$99.95!

Why had she come here? Oh, yes, Scout.

In the corner of the shop, almost as an afterthought, were small decorative barrels filled with doggie biscuits. Shaped like hearts, diamonds, clubs and spades, their labels boasted ingredients such as "wheat flour" and "cultured whey."

Ellie's gaze touched upon a large, gingerbread-flavored, all-natural biscuit that actually looked like a dog biscuit. Manufactured by Old Mother Hubbard, the sticky tag read Peace. *Oh, heck,* Ellie thought. *Why not? It costs a lot less than the blazer.* Just to be fair, she snatched up a rubber mouse flavored with nothing.

The saleslady was more than happy to pull "Scout Finch Lester's" index card. She disappeared into a back room and soon returned with a kibble-filled brown paper bag, as if Ellie had purchased a contraband copy of Playdog. The plain brown paper bag was, in fact, the boutique's only basic, unadorned item.

Ellie paid, exited the shop, placed the food-biscuit-mouse sack in the back of her Honda, and checked her watch—10:40 a.m.

Uncle Vinnie's opened for lunch at eleven.

She entered a video store. In the children's section she found *Lassie* and *The Incredible Journey.* She had a feeling dogs and cats didn't give a rat's spit which movies their humans deigned to show, but she paid the rental charge.

At 11:05 she pulled open the door to Uncle Vinnie's, then stood behind a Please Wait To Be Seated sign.

The hostess was tall, very thin, very pale. From the expression on her face she suffered from a migraine, or a hangover, and she kept patting her head.

"My friend told me about a waiter, Nicholas," Ellie said. "I'd like his section, please."

"I'm sorry, ma'am. Nico doesn't work the lunch shift."

"That's funny. I'm sure my friend said Nicholas—Nico worked yesterday. At lunchtime, I mean."

"Yes, but he cov...covered for...for another waiter."

"Are you all right?" Ellie asked.

"Yes. No. Sorry..."

The hostess pressed her hands against her mouth and ran toward the back of the restaurant. Ellie followed, opened the ladies' room door, guided the girl inside a stall and helped her kneel.

"Please leave," the girl managed to say just before her stomach turned inside-out. She heaved once, quickly, as if it were an encore, then staggered over to the sink, splashed cold water on her face and patted it dry with paper towels. "He swore it wouldn't make me sick," she muttered, "but he lied. I was almost late for work."

Ellie said, "Who swore what wouldn't make you sick?"

"Nico. He's a waiter here."

"Yes," Ellie said softly, "I know."

"He said vodka wouldn't make me sick."

"He took you out drinking?"

"He *invited* me. To share some vodka. With him. At his apartment. I was flattered. Most people can't see the passion that lurks beneath my outer surface."

Was I ever that young? Ellie wondered. *I was never that thin.*

"Nico can sense passion," the hostess continued. "He can see it."

"'With eyes that know the darkness of my soul,'" Ellie murmured.

"What did you say? I couldn't hear you."

"Nothing. Go on."

"He carried me to the car so I wouldn't get my shoes wet. Isn't that romantic?"

"Yes. Very."

"He carried me into his apartment and he gave me some vodka. I thought he wanted to…you know…but he kept giving me more and more to drink and asking how I felt. He seemed annoyed when I said I felt okay. I finally made the first move, took off my clothes. By then I felt numb, like a zombie. Nico put me to bed and I guess I passed out. He left the apartment. When I woke up, he was sleeping next to me and—"

"Wait a sec. If you passed out, how could you hear him leave?"

"I didn't hear him leave. But he must have because this morning his shoes were wet and muddy."

"That's understandable. Last night it rained."

"His waiter shoes were almost dry. His sneakers were wet and muddy. Then, after he woke up, he talked about how many times we did it. But we didn't do it. Wouldn't you know if you did it?"

Absolutely, Ellie thought with a blush. Out loud she said, "Were you here yesterday? During the lunch shift?"

"Yes, ma'am. Oh, God, I've got to get back on the floor or I'll lose my job. Thank you so much for listening." Her acne-scarred cheeks turned crimson. "I never, ever, blab to strangers."

"Don't fret. Strangers often blab to me. And if you tell me your name, we won't be strangers."

"Micki…M-i-c-k-i."

M-o-u-s-e, Ellie sang silently.

"I'll put you in Jon's section," Micki said. "Not counting Nico, he gets the most repeat customers. I mean, guests. Sara Lee…the waitress who was strangled? She got more request tables than anybody."

Everybody liked Sara Lee, Ellie thought. She pictured Sara as a feisty teenager and her heart ached for what might have been.

"Nico always has a black tongue," Micki continued, "because he licks his pen before he writes down an order. I think that's cute, don't you? He's so macho, and then he opens his mouth and his tongue is all inky. Nico makes lots of money. He and Sara Lee would have contests to see who ended up with the most money at the end of a shift. You know, the highest tips? Nico won every time. Last week Sara Lee pretended to punch him out when his tips were double her tips. She accidentally gave him a bloody nose, but he just laughed. And hugged her."

Before Micki turned away and scurried toward the restroom exit, her eyes flared with…anger? Resentment?

Every emotion except grief, thought Ellie.

TWELVE

BY THE TIME Ellie finished her Cobb salad, the early lunch rush had died.

Clutching two pots of coffee, one in each hand, Micki stood tableside, her gaze straying toward the croutons that seemed to march across Ellie's side plate like toasted soldiers.

"Everything was delicious," Ellie said with complete sincerity. "Do you think I could go into the kitchen and thank Vincent personally?" *And check the employee bulletin board?*

"Vincent isn't cooking today, ma'am. Al is."

"Then I'd like to thank Al, please."

"Vincent should be here in ten, maybe fifteen minutes. Theodora...the waitress who found Sara Lee? She picked up her tips, but she wants her paycheck, and Vincent signs the paychecks."

"Theodora's here now?"

"Yes, ma'am."

"Could I talk to her? She used to date my brother and I haven't seen her in years."

"I'll get her...and the theater brochure Jon said you wanted."

Theodora Mallard wore a white blouse under a blue-checkered pinafore. Above her platinum braids she sported a turban of bandages. She looked as if Dorothy had clicked her way back to Kansas, aged forty years, moved to Colorado Springs, bleached her hair and converted to Hinduism.

"I remember you," she said, sinking onto a chair. "Tab's sister, right?"

"Right."

"The hostess said you wanted to talk to me."

Ellie nodded. "If you don't mind, I'd like to question you about yesterday's murder."

"Why?"

"I'm a private investigator and Sara Lee's mother, Mrs. Leibowitz, hired me to—"

"That's bull! Mrs. L. doesn't have a pot to piss in. She can't afford a P.I."

"Okay, Theodora, I'll tell you the truth, but it's a secret. I'm a writer and I thought I'd write a true-crime novel. After the killer's been caught, of course."

"Cool. Will you mention me in your book?"

"Absolutely."

"Please use my nickname, Tad. Most people don't know me as Theodora." She patted her swami headdress. "I told the cops everything I can remember."

"Yes, but did they ask you what you saw *before* you found the body?"

"You're kidding, right? I saw the Dumpster. The puke-green, putrid, icky Dumpster! Then I saw Sara Lee. Her eyes were o—"

"I mean *before* you saw the Dumpster. You were in the alley. All the shops use the same alley. This is important, so please take a moment to think. Did you see anyone walking down the alley toward the parking lot or one of the shops?"

"No."

"Maybe someone who ducked into a shop through the back door?"

"No. Just Anne Marie and Raymond. They work at the beauty salon."

"Why were they outside?"

"Smoke break."

"Did they know Sara Lee?"

"Of course. They eat lunch here all the time."

"Did Anne Marie or Raymond have some sort of grudge against Sara Lee?"

"Heck, no. Everybody liked Sara Lee."

Unless I'm way off base, Ellie thought, *Micki didn't.*

"Theodora…did Sara Lee serve anyone who looked malicious?"

"Malicious?"

"Sinister. Different."

"No. Unless you count the man with the big mole on his face. He and Sara talked for a long time. She looked sad, then mad, and she bought him dessert. We all wondered about that because Sara Lee never gave anyone *anything* for free."

"Was the man with the big mole inside the restaurant when Sara Lee took her smoke break?"

"No."

"Who was? Inside, I mean."

"The cops asked me that, Ellie, and I told them I didn't remember. I think customers—guests should be entitled to their privacy, don't you? Waitresses are like psychiatrists and psychiatrists don't have to give out any information, not without a subpoena or something."

What's with everybody needing subpoenas today? "I totally understand, Theodora, but a crime writer has to get every single detail straight, otherwise a publisher won't buy the book."

"Yeah. That makes sense. Okay, let me think. There were eight tourists from Canada. I remember because Nico could add the tip. He was really happy about that. Most tourists don't tip worth sh—"

"And?"

"And a couple of bar regulars. They always drink shots. Sex on the Beach. Don't you think that's a funny name for a drink?"

"Yes. Very funny. Who else?"

"Two of Sara Lee's tables. A three-top…more tourists, I

think. And a lady, I never can remember her name, but she comes in twice a week, alone, and she reads books. We call her 'the book lady.' She sits at a four-top rather than a one-top, or even a two-top. It doesn't matter if the restaurant is crowded, either, which I think is very rude. What's worse, she doesn't read *real* books. She reads the stuff we used to have to read in school, you know, Shakespeare and Charles Dick—"

"Theodora!"

"Sorry. What was the question again?"

"Who was inside the restaurant when Sara Lee took her smoke break?"

"Oh, right. Gosh, there wasn't anybody else, except Mr. Lester and—"

"Matthew Lester? He was still here?" Staring at Theodora's face, Ellie hoped the woman didn't try to bluff at poker. "Do you know if Matthew Lester and Sara Lee were—" how to put it delicately; there was no way to put it delicately "—sleeping together?"

"Yeah."

"Yeah, you know? Or yeah, they were?"

"Were. Everybody knew. Everybody at Uncle Vinnie's, that is. But we all like—liked Sara Lee so much, we kept her little secret."

"Someone told me…I was under the impression…wasn't Sara Lee messing around with Nicholas?"

"Nico? They got it on a couple of times, but it wasn't serious. Nico messes around with everyone. Sara Lee had a thing for Mr. Lester. She was crazy-nuts about him. Uh-oh, there's my boss. Gotta go, Ellie. Please let me know when the book comes out."

"The book? What book? Oh, *that* book. You bet."

Ellie put a five-dollar tip on the tip tray. Should she visit the beauty salon, ask Anne Marie and Raymond if they'd seen someone lurking in the alley?

No. The police would have questioned everybody who worked nearby.

Maybe the best game plan was to drive home, walk Scout, and try to figure out a game plan.

As she collected her jacket and purse, she looked down at the *Hello Dolly* audition brochure. Try-outs started at 7:00 p.m.

Aha! J.D.C.T. Not Jewish something-or-other. John Denver Community Theater. According to his appointment book, Matthew Lester had a 7:00 p.m. engagement at the John Denver Community Theater. Was it a rendezvous with Sara Lee?

Deciphering J.D.C.T. must have honed her wits, thought Ellie, because she suddenly pictured the cartons inside Rachel Lester's upstairs storage room.

The boxes had been mailed to Rachel. The return address had emphatically stated "Houston, Texas."

Ellie couldn't recall the street address or zip code, her memory wasn't *that* good, but she remembered the name of the street. Mainly because it sounded, somewhat, like the name of one of her favorite actresses, Jacqueline Bissett.

And that brought to mind something Rachel had once said.

Rachel had said that her sister Margee worked part-time at Murder By The Book, a Houston bookstore on Bissonnet Street.

THIRTEEN

As ELLIE WALKED Scout, her mind raced.

What had she discovered so far?

Nothing much.

She wished now that she had questioned the two beauty salon operators, Anne Marie and Raymond.

At least her visit to Uncle Vinnie's hadn't been a *total* waste.

One: Sara Lee and Matthew Lester were having an affair and Sara was "crazy-nuts" about him.

Two: Sara had looked "sad" then "mad" while talking to a man with a mole on his face.

Three: everybody liked Sara Lee.

Four: Micki the hostess was tall and she didn't seem to like Sara Lee.

Was Nico the waiter tall? *Damn, I never thought to ask!* And what was all that nonsense about taking Micki home and getting her drunk enough to pass out? Was she supposed to be Nico's alibi? For what? Why were his sneakers muddy?

Heck, he could have left his apartment in the dead of night, during a windy rainstorm for any number of reasons. Maybe he was out of cigarettes. Maybe he wanted to buy drugs. Maybe he wanted to play in the mud. Maybe he planned to kidnap and kill Matthew Lester.

No. If there'd been an abduction, it had occurred before the storm. Unless Matthew had so much on his mind he'd simply *forgotten* to close the windows.

Did Nico have a viable motive?

Crossing the street, a large, chocolate-colored dog walked toward Scout. Ellie tightened her hold on the leash. The dogs sniffed each other.

If Sara Lee and Matthew Lester were having an affair, Ellie mused, Nico might have been consumed by a jealous rage. Maybe he had felt more than a casual interest toward Sara. Maybe he had been obsessed by her.

Except…a jealous lover was such a cliché.

So was a jealous husband. And, anyway, Tim Zachariah had an ironclad alibi. Two ironclad alibis.

Which brought Ellie back to Matthew Lester. He could have killed Sara before he was abducted from his house—assuming he *had* been abducted—but why? Because Sara had threatened to tell Rachel, that's why. Rachel had initiated a class action suit, litigated, ironically, by Peter's brother-in-law, the famous—some said infamous—Jonah Feldman. Matthew wouldn't want to sever his marriage until Rachel collected her payoff. Colorado was a community property state.

Then why had Matthew ended up as dead as a spawning salmon? What was the connection?

There was no connection!

"I know I promised you a long walk, Scout," Ellie said, turning toward home, "but I need to track down your mistress."

Maybe a connection could be found at tonight's J.D.C.T. audition. Dollars to doughnuts Peter would consider the auditions a waste of time, even if she told him about the entry in Matthew Lester's appointment book. Peter would say that, with Rachel out of town, her husband had simply scheduled a Sara Lee tryst.

Still, it couldn't hurt to attend the auditions.

And it wouldn't hurt to call Boulder and speak to her son Mick's fiancée, Sandra, who had once been an active member of the J.D.C.T.

First, Rachel.

Scout gleefully chewed the gingerbread-flavored biscuit. While Ellie phoned Houston information, Jackie Robinson sniffed at the new mouse, gave Ellie a you've-got-to-be-kidding-have-you-ever-tasted-rubber look, and began to stalk Scout's wagging tail.

Ellie took a deep breath and tapped out Murder By The Book's number. The man who answered identified himself as Dean James, and she stalled. No way would a bookstore give out an employee's personal telephone number. What excuse should she use this time? Maybe, this time, she'd tell the truth.

I should have asked Peter to call, she thought just before she said, "Mr. James, you have a part-time employee named Margee. I know she isn't there, at the store, but I need to get in touch with her sister Rachel. It's very import—"

"Margee's here today, doing inventory."

"She is? But I thought she was ill."

"Margee? She's so healthy she'd make a vampire think twice about immortality. Hold on and I'll get her for you."

Since Peter had told her not to say anything about Matthew, Ellie chickened out and hung up. Then she stared at the phone. If Margee wasn't sick and Rachel wasn't in Houston, where the heck was she?

Had she murdered Sara Lee?

And her philandering husband?

No. Rachel couldn't kill a fly.

Neither could *Psycho's* Norman Bates.

Maybe Rachel had hired an assassin, promised him or her a chunk of the class action suit payoff, then tootled off to…where?

Someplace where she could establish an alibi.

But if that were true, why hadn't she flown to Houston and used her sister as an alibi?

In any case, shy Rachel would never hire an assassin. Unless she could dial 1-800-GUN-FOR-HIRE, she wouldn't know where to start. It made more sense for methodical Rachel to first pretend to leave town, then do the dirty deed herself.

"Oh, Scout, please let me be wrong. Even if I don't solve Sara Lee's murder, please let me be wrong."

FOURTEEN

THE JOHN DENVER Community Theater rented a building that had once been a consignment shop. It stood—maybe a better word would be slouched—in between a bicycle shop and a Salvation Army thrift store.

Ellie knew that Weight Winners had tried to rent the building, but the J.D.C.T. had already signed a three-year lease. Inside the shabby structure, J.D.C.T. volunteers stored costumes and props. On an improvised stage, directors held their rehearsals.

And their auditions.

As she circled a couple of blocks, looking for a parking space, Ellie thought about her conversation with her son's fiancée, Sandra.

Sandra had said the theater group was "incestuous." They had four directors who cast the same people over and over again. Theater members who contributed the most money were given nonspeaking roles, for example the townspeople in *Our Town*. Yes, Sandra had heard about Sara Lee. Yes, Sandra remembered Sara Lee. The poor kid had desperately wanted a part, any part. To that end, she had worked the spotlights, painted sets, designed costumes, even joined the makeup crew, until the Peter Principle kicked in. Directors didn't want to cast her and forfeit her backstage expertise. Finally, Sara refused to do any more grunge work. Somewhat reluctantly, a director gave her a part in *Fiddler on the Roof,* one of Tevye's daughters, the Bette Midler Broadway role. The show itself was mediocre but Sara scored a huge success.

Audiences adored her. Directors didn't. She hadn't shown one teensy speck of gratitude. Or humility. She had thumbed her nose at them and they all had egos bigger than King Kong *and* Godzilla.

At that point, Sandra had moved to Boulder.

"What are you going to sing, Ellie?" she'd asked.

"Sing? Surely you jest. I don't plan to sing."

"You'd better. Otherwise they'll ask you to leave."

"Don't people just watch?"

"Nope. J.D.C.T. auditions, especially musical auditions, always draw crowds, and they're paranoid about fire laws. If you don't audition, you don't stay."

"Aren't you exaggerating just a little?"

"No, Ellie. You wouldn't believe how many people want to audition, even if they can't sing and end up looking dopey. Well, maybe you would if you've ever watched the tryouts for 'American Idol.' Mick says I should try out. For 'American Idol.'"

"Mick's right. Holy cow, Sandra, what on earth would I sing?"

"'Tomorrow' from *Annie*. Everyone always sings 'Tomorrow,' so the piano player will have it down pat and you won't have to bring sheet music. Unless you know songs from *Hello Dolly*. That's a plus."

"I know them, Sandra, but…well, to be perfectly honest, I don't want to be cast in the show."

"Then why attend the tryouts? Aha! You're sleuthing, right?"

"Yup. I have a feeling there's some sort of connection between the J.D.C.T. and Sara Lee's murder."

"One of your gut feelings?"

"Yes."

Ellie's gut feeling grew stronger as she entered the room.

Of course, the feeling in her gut could be hunger. She'd been too nervous to eat supper. Instead she had rehearsed

"Tomorrow." Scout had howled as if she were being tortured and Ellie had decided the only way she'd get through this audition insanity was to pretend she was singing to her diet club members.

To coin a cliché, the audition room was filled to the rafters. To coin another cliché, the noise was ear-splitting. If Matthew and Sara Lee had truly planned an assignation, where on earth would they have assignated? Even the staircase that led to a second-floor restroom swarmed with bodies and Ellie had a feeling fire laws were being broken right and left.

At the front of the noisy mob, facing the improvised stage, the director and his young female assistant sat behind a long, narrow table. The director stared down at a clipboard while his assistant handed Ellie a form. Aside from the usual contact information, the questionnaire asked for previous experience. Leaning the piece of paper against a patch of wall, Ellie wrote, "Snow White and the Seven Dwarfs. Third grade. I played Dopey."

Heigh-ho, she thought as she turned in the form.

She found a seat between a girl who looked no older than eighteen and a man who smelled of hairspray. She smiled and said, "Hi, I'm Ellie." *And I'm a chocoholic.*

"Tiffany," said the girl. "They call me Tiff."

"Ray Morass," the man mumbled.

The director, who looked like the villain in a melodrama, called for quiet. Immediately the room grew eerily mute. A nervous cough tickled Ellie's throat.

An hour later she was no longer nervous, just bored. This theatrical gamble had been a complete waste of time. No one appeared threatening, no one had the ambience of a murderer, there weren't any men with huge face moles, and her male seat companion's hairspray was making her nose run and her eyes tear.

Her other seat companion, Tiffany "Call me Tiff," was summoned. Tiffany announced that she would sing a song by rock star, Yogi Demon. The piano player gave it his all, but without a backup band and synthesizer, her voice sounded iffy.

Iffy Tiffy, thought Ellie, suppressing the desire to laugh. Damn, she was tired. And hungry. And frustrated. *But the sun'll come up tomorrow,* she thought, letting loose a brief, uncontrollable chortle.

The director obviously liked the girl's legs, or bosom, because he convened several male hopefuls and asked them to "Sing to Tiff." Then he told Tiff to stick around for the dance tryouts.

The hairspray man—Ray—cussed under his breath.

Finally the director said, "Ray Morass, get your butt on stage."

Tall, thin and muscular, Ray had a certain flamboyance. Ellie pictured the frou-frou interior of Reigning Cats & Dogs. Ray wore black jeans and a black turtleneck, but she felt he should have been appliquéd and embroidered like that adorable cat blazer. And although she desperately needed a restroom break, she wanted to hear him sing.

Nodding at the piano player, Ray said, "'So Long Dearie.'"

"That's Dolly's song," the director said.

"I'm trying out for Dolly," Ray replied. "A man's never played Dolly. Carol Channing played her on Broadway, then an all-black cast…" He took a deep breath. "I'm not suggesting you change Dolly into a man, but we have wigs and gowns in Wardrobe, and a man playing Dolly would be different, innovative."

"We don't want to be innovative. We want to sell tickets," the director said.

"But we *would* sell tickets. I think the audience would be intrigued—"

"Are you out of your mind?"

"In Shakespeare's time," Ray said, "men played women's parts."

"This isn't Shakespeare's time," the director snapped. "Either try out for a man's part or work the spotlights."

"I can't work the spots. Sara Lee—"

"Is dead," the director said. "Her vote's nullified. Which reminds me. Let's have two minutes of silent prayer, people. For Sara Lee."

With a scowl, Ray returned to his seat and bowed his head. Again, Ellie was almost overwhelmed by the smell of hairspray. Again, the room was eerily mute.

This time she didn't have to cough. Instead she heard an intrusive sound.

Several people glanced her way with unmistakable malice.

"You're supposed to turn off your cell phone during auditions," Tiffany hissed.

"Sorry," Ellie whispered back just before she bolted for the exit. She had undoubtedly blown any chance for a *Hello Dolly* role, even a small part, but only one person would call her cell phone after 7:00 p.m.

And tonight she carried her Weight Winners purse.

"Where are you?" Peter asked, his voice so low she had to strain to hear him.

"J.D.C.T. auditions. Long story. Where are you?"

"At your house. I was eating lasagna sauce when I heard the doorbell. Your friend Rachel's back in town. She stopped here, first, to collect Scout."

"Have you told her?"

"Yes."

"I'll be right there."

FIFTEEN

I<small>F THE</small> J.D.C.T. audition room had been eerily mute, Ellie's family room was as silent as the grave. The only hint of any resonance came from the kitchen, where Peter was preparing herbal tea. Ellie couldn't catch the sound of his shoeless footsteps, but she heard the clink of china and the mournful whistle of the teakettle.

The house smelled of lasagna sauce and dog.

Spread out across the patchwork quilt, all legs and legs, Scout gnawed a rawhide bone. Still pointedly ignoring his new rubber mouse, Jackie Robinson played tether ball with the license that swung from Scout's collar.

At long last, Rachel heaved a deep sigh and said, "I want to go home, Ellie."

"No, sweetie. You'll stay here tonight. I have a guest room and—"

"I want to go home."

"We'll talk about it, okay? I'll be right back. Don't move."

A stupid request, thought Ellie, since Rachel sat motionless on the couch. She didn't cry, just wrung her hands like a June Allyson-coiffured Lady Macbeth.

Inside the kitchen, Ellie said, "Rachel wants to go home, Peter. Is her house still a crime scene?"

"Not really. It's been combed and dusted, but we don't think Lester was killed inside the house."

"Where do you think he was killed?" Ellie asked.

"In the trunk of the car."

"How was he killed?"

"Plastic bag."

"Someone put a plastic bag over his head?" She shuddered at the image. "GLAD? Ziploc? Generic? What?"

"Unfortunately, Norrie, the killer didn't leave us a note. Or the plastic bag. We're hoping to learn more after the autopsy, but Lester's mouth was covered with duct tape and his hands were tied behind his back. He didn't tear at the bag, so we don't have fingernail scrapings or—"

"Have you traced the owner of the car?"

"Yes."

"And the owner is…?"

Peter started to run his hands through his hair, stopped. "Sara Lee."

"Sara Lee," Ellie parroted.

"The car's a demo from her husband's lot. Vincent said she kept her car keys in her apron pocket. There were no car keys when we searched the bod—"

"Are you telling me that somebody killed Sara Lee, stole her keys, stole her car, then stuffed Matthew Lester inside the trunk?"

"Yup. And before you ask, there were no fingerprints. Whoever stole the car wore gloves. There were no obscure clues, either, like you always see on those CSI shows, even though the car was full of junk. Water bottles, a hairbrush, a can of hairspray, maps to Nashville and Los Angeles, and…why are you looking at me like that?"

"How come Sara Lee's murderer didn't stuff *Sara Lee* inside the trunk?"

"We figure he was making a statement. He considered Sara Lee trash. That's why he dumped her in the Dumpster."

Ellie remembered Micki's hostile expression. But if the hostess thought Sara Lee was trash, what did she consider herself? A passionate nature trapped inside a dispassionate facade? Sara Lee was married, Micki single—at least, she didn't sport a wedding ring. Adultery was…trashy. Micki had worked the lunch *and* dinner shifts? Could she have had enough time to kill Sara, steal her car, abduct Matthew, kill him, then bus back to the restaurant in time for the dinner shift? Al had said the restaurant closed at three and opened again at five, so Micki's window of opportunity would have been less than two hours. She was tall enough to strangle Sara Lee from behind, but was she strong enough to overpower Matthew Lester?

Suddenly, Ellie realized Nico's window of opportunity would have been exactly the same!

Ellie didn't know what Nico looked like, but she figured him for a stud. Micki said he'd carried her from the restaurant to his car and from the car to his apartment. Ellie tried to dismiss the image of a hunky thug with a black, ink-stained tongue.

Suppose Nico had kidnapped Matthew Lester and left him in the trunk of Sara Lee's car? Suppose Nico had worked the dinner shift, driven Micki to his apartment and plied her with vodka until she'd passed out? Then, leaving Micki in bed as his alibi, he'd gone back to the parked car and killed Matthew.

"Norrie?"

"Sorry, Peter. I was trying to put the pieces together. Where was the stolen car found?"

"In a restaurant's parking lot."

"Uncle Vinnie's?" At Peter's incredulous stare, she said, "I didn't get much sleep last night, either. If Sara's car had been found in Uncle Vinnie's lot, it wouldn't have been stolen. Which restaurant?"

"Some kind of upscale rib joint on Academy, near the mall. It went out of business three months ago…the restaurant, not the mall. A woman didn't know it had gone out of business. She parked·her car, opened the door and her dog jumped out. The dog peed on Sara Lee's tires and the woman smelled something in the trunk and—"

"I get the picture."

The mall isn't all that far from Uncle Vinnie's, Ellie mused, *so Micki or Nico could have made it back to work on time. Let's say one of them caught Matthew by surprise and—*

"Ellie?" Rachel walked into the kitchen. "All I need is Scout's food and I'll be on my way." She turned to Peter. "Let me apologize again for my hysterics, Lieutenant Miller. You've been very kind."

"Mrs. Lester," Peter said.

"Rachel."

"Yes, well, I really think you should stay here tonight, Rachel. I have to leave again and Ellie could sure use your company. And Scout's."

Clever, Ellie thought. Except she could see by the expression on Rachel's face that Peter's subterfuge wasn't working. "Why don't I go home with Rachel?" she said. "Rachel has a second bedroom and…" She swallowed her next words. Supposedly she'd never been inside the Lester house.

But Rachel didn't catch the faux pas. "That isn't necessary, Ellie," she said. "Really it isn't."

"Please? It'll make *me* feel better."

As Rachel nodded, Ellie thought her sorrow was entirely genuine.

SIXTEEN

IF THE audition room had been eerily mute and Ellie's family room as silent as the grave, Rachel's house was as quiet as a tomb. The cops had turned off the upstairs TV.

Just like last night, a storm was brewing. Ellie heard the wind and the muted sound of distant thunder. "Would you like me to check the windows?" she asked Rachel. "Make sure they're all shut?"

"I'll do it."

"Sweetie, please sit down, lie down, drink some tea. When was the last time you ate?"

"Lunch. Zucchini à la Grecque Gordon. The recipe calls for three eggs. We laughed about that."

"We, who?"

"I'll bet I can donate more Weight Winners recipes than Charlene Johnson. Thing is, they're all called 'Gordon.' Quiche Gordon, Eggs Gordon, Zucchini Gord—"

"Rachel, sweetie, where have you been? You don't have to answer if you don't want to, but I know you weren't in Houston. Or if you were, you weren't taking care of your sick sister."

"You talked to Margee?"

"No. But I called Murder by the Book and Margee was there, healthy as the proverbial horse."

"I wonder why they always say that…healthy as a horse, I mean. I've seen documentaries about wild horses on TV, Ellie, and they looked starved and skinny and hungry, always hungry, for food, for affection, for *one* kind word!"

"Where were you, Rachel?"

Before she could answer, or sidestep the question again, the phone rang. It sounded very loud. Rachel snatched up the receiver. As she listened, a smile transformed her face. "I'm all right, Kurt."

Ellie hummed an off-key tune to distract herself from what was obviously an intimate conversation.

Finally hanging up the phone, Rachel said, "I borrowed a mountain cabin from Cee-Cee Sinclair. Do you know Cee-Cee?"

"Yes. I once helped her with a fund-raiser for Canine Companions. Why didn't you tell me about the cabin, Rachel?"

"I didn't tell *anybody,* Ellie, except Cee-Cee. I needed time alone to think, to make some sort of a game plan. I've wanted to leave my husband for a long, long time, but I was afraid."

"Why? Did he threaten you? Was he abusive?"

"No, not physically. I was afraid because of this." She extended her clawed hand. "Matthew made it very clear that no one else would want me, that I'd be alone for the rest of my life. I couldn't have children, but I've always owned dogs. First, Atticus. Then, Boo. Now, Scout. But dogs don't live very long, not unless you count every year as seven years…" Rachel shook her head as if to clear it.

"What did you decide to do?"

"I decided not to decide, the same decision I've made a hundred times before." Tears streamed down her face. "When the storm killed my phone, I decided to go home. Then I met a nice man…"

"Kurt?"

"Yes. You have to understand, Ellie. Matthew and I haven't shared the same bed for years. I asked him why, once. He said my hand repulsed him. He didn't even sugarcoat it, just came right out and…" She paused to wipe away tears with her sleeve. "He was always mean, like a sniper. He used words instead of bullets, and I learned not to fight back be-cause…well, that would only give him more ammunition. So you see, I can't really mourn him. My only feeling is guilt. If I had been home, it wouldn't have happened. Kurt sug-gested I leave the cabin, face up to Matthew, ask for a trial separation, but it was too late."

"Rachel, bad things happen. It's *not* your fault."

"Then why do I feel so guilty?"

"Because you're human. Let's go into the kitchen. I'll make us some tea and you can tell me about Kurt. Or would you rather try and sleep?"

"I'd rather keep busy."

"When I'm upset I clean house," Ellie said.

"I cleaned house before I left, but I was about to pay my bills and…why are you nodding?"

Ellie felt her cheeks bake. "I trespassed, Rachel, looking for Scout's missing food. I had a gut feeling…something felt wrong…so I checked out all the rooms. I discovered the scat-tered bills on top of your desk. I didn't look at them," she has-tened to add.

"The bills couldn't have been scattered, Ellie. I left them stacked in a neat pile. After I write a check and put a stamp on the envelope, I scribble 'paid' and the date across the in-voice. Then I file the invoice." Almost yelling, she said, "My CPA sends me a thank-you note every Dopey…every Doc…every *damn* year!"

"Calm down. Take it easy. Maybe Matthew…" Ellie swal-lowed the rest of her words as Rachel raced toward the study.

By the time Ellie joined her, Rachel was seated at her desk. She sifted invoices through her curled-up hand as if she sifted flour for a cake.

No, not invoices. Credit card receipts.

"I think you're right, Ellie," she said. "I think Matthew was searching for a specific charge. Maybe he bought his wait-ress a piece of jewelry and—"

"You knew about Sara Lee?" Ellie couldn't contain her surprise.

"Yes." Rachel scrutinized a credit card receipt. "Something's fishy. This is from Uncle Vinnie's Gourmet Italian Restaurant. That's not unusual, Matthew ate there all the time, but the tip is huge. Here's another receipt from Uncle Vinnie's. Again the tip's generous, nearly fifty percent." She paused to take a deep breath. "Matthew is—was a horrible tipper. When we ate out, I'd make some excuse, return to the table and leave more money on the tip tray."

"Maybe," Ellie said, "he was paying Sara Lee for special 'services.'"

"No. The name on the credit card slip…both slips…is N-I-C-Q. I wonder what *that* stands for."

"Nicholas. He's a waiter. They call him Nico and the hostess said he licks the nib of his pen before he writes. That's probably why the 'o' looks like a 'q.'"

"Here's another receipt. The name says Jon. The amount is $22.50 and the tip is $2.00. What the *hell's* going on?"

"I don't know. Yes, I do. My brother Tab worked one summer as a waiter. He said another waiter always earned big tips and nobody could understand why because he was a worse waiter than Tab…if that's possible. Turns out the waiter ran the customer's credit card through the machine twice. He handed one slip to the customer, who wrote in the tip and signed the slip. Then the waiter filled in a bogus tip on the second slip, forged the signature, and destroyed the first slip. He got caught, eventually, but the restaurant didn't prosecute because of bad publicity. If people knew about the doctored tips, they'd be standing in line, asking for their money back. And the restaurant, not the waiter, would have to pay. Is that Matthew's signature at the bottom of the receipts?"

"Yes." Rachel looked at the writing. "If this Nico person forged my husband's signature, he's in the wrong business. He should be forging van Gogh's name. Or Picasso's."

"Let me see a Nico receipt and the Jon receipt." Ellie stared down at the two slips. "Do you happen to have a magnifying glass?"

"Sure. Doesn't everyone?" Rachel opened a desk drawer.

"That's better," Ellie said. "I can see the difference now."

"What difference? That's Matthew's signature."

"Then why would he use one continuous slash to cross the three t's on the Jon receipt and two separate slashes on the Nico receipt—one for Matthew, one for Lester? Is there a Sara Lee receipt? Let me have it. Look, Rachel. One slash."

"He *always* used one slash." Rachel twisted her wedding band. "I never look at the receipts, Ellie. I never even look at individual charges, just pay what it says we owe."

"I do the same thing."

"So…Matthew discovered the discrepancy. Then what?"

"My guess is that he blackmailed Nico. How's the real-estate business doing these days? Was Matthew selling lots of houses?"

"No. He hit a slump. That's why he insisted I join Jonah Feldman's class-action suit."

"Yesterday Matthew ate lunch at Uncle Vinnie's," Ellie said thoughtfully. "Nico served him. Let's say Nico pulled his scam. Peter said there was a huge tip on the credit card receipt. Matthew confronted Nico and threatened to tell the owners, Vincent and Al, unless Nico coughed up some hush money. Let's say Sara Lee knew about the scam. Theodora Mallard, the waitress who found Sara Lee's body, said everybody at the restaurant knew about Matthew and Sara, so Nico probably thought Sara had told Matthew during one of their, uh…"

"Trysts. Go on."

"Nico grabbed some gloves, probably rubber dishwasher gloves, and exited into the alley. He strangled Sara Lee and tossed her into the Dumpster. It wouldn't have taken him very long. He stole her car, followed Matthew home, caught him by surprise, knocked him out, duct-taped his mouth and stuffed him in Sara Lee's trunk."

Rachel shuddered and Ellie said, "Sorry. Maybe I should shut up."

"No. Go on. Please."

"Nico drove around, looking for a safe place to kill Matthew and leave the car. But time was running out. He had to work the dinner shift and he had to take a bus to the restaurant, so he left the car in a vacant parking lot. He couldn't leave the car in Uncle Vinnie's lot because there were too many cops milling around, not to mention the nosy reporter who looks like a monkey. Let's say Nico spent the dinner shift trying to think of a way to kill Matthew and not get caught. He saw some plastic bags in the kitchen. He took the hostess home with him…to establish an alibi. He plied her with vodka, and when she passed out he took his car back to Sara Lee's car. He killed Matthew, but he couldn't move Sara's car to another, more secluded spot. How would he get back to *his* car? Buses don't run that late and walking was out of the question. The wind was almost gale-force and it was raining pitchforks."

Ellie felt her cheeks flush. "You probably don't understand half of what I'm saying, Rachel, but does it make any sense?"

"Absolutely."

"Then I'll call Peter. I think I have enough ammunition in my arsenal now."

Once she'd outlined her theory, she could practically *feel* Peter's skepticism.

"I'll bet if you pretend you know everything for a fact, he'll confess," she said. "Just read him his rights and lie like hell."

"That only works on 'Law & Order,'" Peter replied.

"The hostess said Nico licks the nib of the pen before he writes up tickets, Peter. Tell him you tested his spit and it matched the DNA found on Matthew."

"We didn't find any DNA ."

"Lie!"

"Before I can lie, we've got to have probable cause. I'll buy the credit card scam, but why would Lester shake down Nico? Waiters don't earn big bucks."

"Some do. Tab did, and he couldn't walk across the floor without spilling something on a customer... I mean, guest. Maybe Nico has a hidden stash and maybe Sara Lee just happened to mention it to Matthew."

"Then why didn't she mention Nico's scam?"

"Maybe she *promised* not to tell. From the photo they showed on TV, Sara Lee looked like she'd keep a promise through thick and thin, until her dying day."

SEVENTEEN

"NICO DIDN'T KILL Sara Lee," Ellie said.

She and Peter were snuggled together in front of the fireplace, their butts denting a soft-cushioned sofa, their bare feet atop a coffee table, their toes stretched toward the warmth of the fire.

"C'mon, Norrie," Peter said, glancing toward their celebratory bottle of Spumante Ballatore. "You were the one who figured the whole thing out, the one who caught the bad guy."

She shook her head. "Nico said Sara Lee knew about his credit card scam. But why didn't he confess? He admitted he killed Matthew, said it was self-defense. Why not admit he killed Sara Lee?"

"With Matthew, Nico can claim self-defense. I don't think anyone would buy self-defense when it comes to Sara Lee. Nico wanted to invest in some kind of computer chip. He'd saved up twenty grand. Sara Lee knew and blabbed to Matthew, who wanted half. Nico swears he didn't plan to kill Lester, just scare him. But if you believe that, I've got a bridge in Brooklyn—"

"Nico swore he didn't kill Sara Lee," Ellie mumbled, deep in thought.

"Right. And Clinton said he didn't inhale."

"Maybe Clinton didn't inhale."

Peter sighed and wiggled his toes. "Then who do *you* think did it?"

"I don't know."

"Wait. Let me write this down. Then you can date it and sign it. Ellie Bernstein doesn't know—"

"But I've been thinking about it a lot and…holy cow, Peter!"

"What?"

"Hairspray."

"What do you mean, hairspray?"

"Just a sec."

Barefoot, Ellie walked into the kitchen. Retrieving the telephone directory from the top of the refrigerator, she looked up a number and tapped it out on her phone.

"Oh, I'm so glad you're still open," she said. "A friend recommended a hairdresser named Raymond. Do you have a hairdresser named Raymond?"

"Norrie…"

She covered the mouthpiece. "Hush, Peter. I happen to know they have a hairdresser named Raymond." She uncovered the mouthpiece. "You do? What's his last name, please?"

"Norrie, what the hell are you doing?"

"What do you mean, I need a subpoena?" She implored the ceiling. "Look, my hair is very important to me and, believe it or not, more than one Raymond cuts hair in this town…Morass? Yes. Thank you. He's the one."

"Norrie!"

She held up her hand for silence. "Why should I book an appointment now? Is Raymond planning to leave town? Oh, he's going to cut down on his shifts because he scored a part in *Hello Dolly?* Good for him. I'll call you back. 'Bye."

Peter steered her to a chair. Applying pressure to her shoulders, he helped her sit. "What was *that* all about?"

"Theodora Mallard, the waitress who found Sara Lee, said—"

"When did you talk to Theodora Mallard?"

"Yesterday. If you ever spent more than five minutes with me, Peter, I would have told you."

"Low blow. I was investigating a homicide."

"So was I. Before she trashed the trash, Theodora saw two

beauty salon operators in the alley, Anne Marie and Raymond. I thought about questioning them, but decided the cops had already—"

"We questioned them…and everybody else in the strip center."

"If *I* had questioned them, I would have figured it out sooner."

"Figured what out?"

"Ray Morass, also known as Raymond, killed Sara Lee. I sat next to him at the auditions. He reeked of hairspray. Holy cow, Peter, didn't you say you found a can of hairspray in Sara Lee's stolen car?"

"Nico stole the car," Peter reminded her.

"Okay…so the hairspray was Sara Lee's. Ray reeked because he works at a beauty salon. And he probably went straight from the salon to the auditions."

"What's *his* motive?"

"I don't know. Yes, I do. At the auditions Ray was moody, petulant. He told the director he couldn't work the spotlights for the show and it had something to do with Sara Lee because the director said that Sara was dead so her vote didn't count. The exact word he used was 'nullified.' Her vote was nullified."

"Are you telling me Raymond the hairdresser killed Sara Lee so that he could work the *spotlights* for a community theater production?"

"No, Peter. I think Ray wanted a part *in* the production, and I think he thought Sara Lee would keep him from getting one."

"How could she do that?"

"Vincent's brother Al said she sounded 'more like Streisand than Streisand.' Mick's Sandra said audiences adored Sara Lee and—"

"When did you speak to Sandra?"

"In between my sleuthing at the restaurant and my

sleuthing at the auditions. If you ever spent more than five minutes—"

"Go on."

"If Sara Lee was cast as Dolly, she'd have enough clout to uncast Ray. Or maybe…"

"Maybe what?"

"He wanted to *play* Dolly. He said as much when the director called him up to the stage. The director wouldn't let him try out for Dolly, but Ray wouldn't have known that the day before."

"How could he strangle Sara Lee? He's a *hairdresser.*"

"Actually, he's a stylist. That's what the beauty salon receptionist told me. And please don't stereotype."

"I wasn't stereotyping."

"Yes, you were. Ray's tall and muscular and…hunky. Can we get a search warrant?"

"You know better than that. There's no probable cause. I suppose I could tell the judge you've already solved three homicides, but somehow I think—"

"Okay, let's pay him a visit."

"The judge?"

"No. Ray Morass."

"Seriously, Norrie, you've got to be kidding."

"Seriously, Peter, I'm not kidding."

"You can't just knock on somebody's door and—"

"I've a gut feeling Ray Morass killed Sara Lee. I need you to come with me. You're more astute than I am, more experienced. Your instincts are far superior to mine, not to mention your heroic strength." *And your badge!*

He snorted. "Flattery will get you nowhere, especially when it's insincere."

"Insincere? I'm hurt to the quick."

"I'll kiss your quick and make it better," he said, giving her a squeeze.

"If flattery will get me nowhere, how about bribery?" She

looked at the wall clock. "In a couple of hours *Jeopardy* will be on TV…" She paused to give him a sultry glance. "And tonight…it's the Tournament of Champions."

"YOU SHOULD HAVE CALLED for backup," Ellie said as Peter drove down Ray's street.

"Why do we need backup? I doubt he's armed."

"Are you stereotyping again?"

"I wasn't stereotyping the first time. But if it makes you feel better, I called Will McCoy and asked him to meet us here."

"Oh, good." Ellie adored Peter's partner, who possessed more street smarts and far less stubbornness than Peter.

"If you're wrong about your hairdresser, we pay McCoy's bar tab this Monday at the Dew Drop Inn. That means *you* pay."

"If I'm wrong, and I don't think I am, you'll have to lend me the money. I saw this adorable cat blazer at Reigning Cats & Dogs. I've decided to buy it, and the cost of one sleeve equals half my food budget."

"Marry me, Norrie, and I'll give you the cat blazer as a wedding present."

"How sweet, Peter. Is that Ray's house? The little house with the gingerbread trim?"

"Yes. I want you to wait in the car."

"No way!"

"Then don't say anything, not one word. I'll ask the questions."

As they walked up the path toward the front door, Ellie heard music. The soundtrack from *Hello Dolly*. Barbra Streisand was singing "Before the Parade Passes By." As she and Peter drew closer, she heard someone singing along with Barbra.

Peter rang the doorbell and the non-Streisand voice stopped singing.

Ray Morass opened the door and Ellie smelled hairspray.

Peter flashed his badge and said, "Mr. Morass, would you be good enough to answer a few questions?"

Ray looked around, as if searching for an escape hatch. Then he spied Ellie. "You! You sat next to me at the Dolly auditions. I remember because you were so much older than anyone else."

"Tell me, Ray," Ellie said. "Did you get the part you wanted?"

"What part?"

"Dolly."

"No."

"Then you killed Sara Lee for nothing."

"Who said I killed Sara Lee?"

"Theodora Mallard. She saw you."

"That's a damn lie! She didn't even step outside until after I'd already…"

"Killed Sara Lee," Peter finished. "Ms. Bernstein might have been the oldest person at the auditions, Mr. Morass, but *she* fingered you."

"Really!" Ray turned to Ellie. "Assuming, hypothetically, I killed Sara Lee, how did I give myself away?"

"When the director asked for two minutes of silent prayer," she said, "you scowled. People kept telling me everybody liked Sara Lee. Obviously you didn't."

Ray faced Peter again. "May I make a phone call?"

As Will McCoy pulled up to the curb, Peter nodded. "One call, Mr. Morass. My partner's here now, so I'll trust you not to try an escape."

Ray's smile was wistful. "Where would I go?"

Ellie thought he'd call a defense attorney, but the name she caught had nothing to do with lawyering. It was the name of the monkey-faced reporter.

If Ray Morass couldn't shine in the J.D.C.T. spotlight, he'd settle for the lights of a TV camera.

EIGHTEEN

THE NONDESCRIPT MAN smoked his last cigarette. He had started out with a full pack. His nondescript car was parked in front of a parking meter, but it was nighttime, well past six o'clock, so he didn't have to feed the meter.

Good thing, since he didn't have any quarters, didn't have any coins at all, just a thick wad of ones, fives and tens from pretty Sara Lee.

He wore nondescript clothes, purchased at the Salvation Army thrift store; jeans and an old, faded-from-washing gray sweatshirt that had, ironically, once boasted the words Colorado Springs Police Academy. On his feet he wore dirty sneakers. On his face, a mole like Robert DeNiro's, only much, much bigger. All eyes were drawn to the mole. If asked for a physical description, people always said, "He has a mole." For the life of them, they couldn't remember whether he was tall or short, fat or thin; even, sometimes, his ethnicity. Just the mole.

The mole was fake, a good makeup job. After tonight's job, he'd scrub it off.

He used a dozen aliases, but his favorites were Paul Redford and Robert Newman. For the past couple of months he'd been Robert Newman and he had asked pretty Sara Lee to call him Bob.

Through the clean glass of his windshield, Bob stared at the Dew Drop Inn. Its parking lot was full to bursting. So was the tavern. The marquee read:

MONDAY NIGHT FOOTBALL
BRONCOS VS RAIDERS
!!!!! FREE SHOTS !!!!!
WHEN THE BRONCOS SCORE

Ordinarily he'd be watching the game, but tonight he didn't care who won. Tonight he needed to score his own victory.

He flicked the ash from his cigarette. Due to the overcrowded Dew Drop Inn's parking lot, Tim Zachariah had parked across the street. Illegally. In front of a hydrant. He probably believed his football star status gave him unlimited parking privileges.

That was the attitude he had displayed on the showroom floor, when, inadvertently, Bob had given Zachariah an alibi. *I'm a football star,* Zachariah seemed to say, *so if you buy a car from me you can brag to all your friends.*

As Bob test drove what Zachariah had called a "new used car," Zachariah talked about his wife. How Sara Lee had trapped him into marriage by pretending to be knocked up. How she, and she alone, was the reason he'd been kicked off the Broncos squad. Why? Because every time he thought about the dirty trick she'd played on him, he'd lose his damn temper. Still, he said, the bitch doted on him and he treated her like a queen, even if she *was* a lousy cook.

Pretty Sara Lee told a different story and she'd had the bruises to prove it. She'd said she'd pay anything to have her husband out of the picture, out of her life. She'd said she couldn't leave him because he had threatened to kill her. Her tears had nearly drowned the Italian cheesecake she'd served Bob for dessert, free of charge.

Snuffing out his cigarette, Bob refocused on the Dew Drop's entrance. As he did, the front door opened and a couple of bouncers bounced Tim Zachariah, who was dead drunk, just as he'd been every night since his wife's death.

Until now, he'd always been accompanied by friends. Tonight he stood there—make that sprawled there—all by his lonesome. Obviously the game wasn't over yet. When it came to nursing a drunk buddy or watching the fourth quarter of a football game...

Sara Lee had paid all she could afford, five hundred hard-earned dollars, and she had promised to scrape together another five hundred after the hit.

Bob watched Tim Zachariah crawl to the curb.

There was no one to witness Zachariah vomiting into the gutter. In fact, there were no witnesses at all. Everyone was inside, watching the Broncos.

Zachariah stood on shaky legs and began to stagger across the street.

Bob turned the ignition key, maneuvered out of the parking space, revved the motor and pressed the accelerator pedal with his right foot.

All the way down to the floorboards.

Pretty Sara Lee had been killed before the hit, but a contract was a contract.

ELLIE WANTED to throttle Peter.

They had planned to watch Monday Night Football at the Dew Drop Inn, but Peter was stuck at the precinct. Too much paperwork, he said.

"You should ask Rachel Lester to organize your desk," she had told him, only half joking.

He had suggested she go and he'd join her later, but she said she'd watch at home and cook up some honey lasagna. He had called again, after the game, with a one-liner that sounded like a telegram. "Sweetheart, something's come up, don't know what time I'll be home, love you."

I love you, too, she now thought, *but sometimes I could throttle you.*

Restless, she strolled into the kitchen. Jackie Robinson

snoozed on his usual chair and yet the house felt lonely without Scout. Maybe she'd get a dog. A small dog. No, a medium-size dog so Jackie Robinson could curl up against its bell—

The phone interrupted her musings. Snatching up the receiver, she said hello.

"Ellie Bernstein?"

"Yes?"

"This is Susan, the J.D.C.T. assistant director. We've cast you in *Hello Dolly*. Rehearsals start next Sunday at one o'clock."

Ellie's first thought was, *Peter promised we'd go to the Dew Drop Inn next Sunday to watch the Broncos play the Kansas City Chiefs.*

Out loud she said, "How could you cast me? I never auditioned, never even sang."

"We cast you as Ermengarde, Dolly's friend. No singing. It's a comedic role." Pause. "You were the only one old enough to play the part."

Ouch! "If I remember correctly," Ellie said, "Ermengarde's the same age as Dolly, more or less."

"Dolly's ageless," said the assistant.

So is Sara Lee, Ellie thought. She pictured the teenage Sara in combat boots and T-shirt, staring at the camera with a brave "I'm gonna succeed no matter what" look on her face.

Before Weight Winners, Ellie wouldn't have set one foot on a stage, but maybe she owed it to Sara Lee to try to be the best she could possibly be.

As she said yes, she could have sworn she heard a ghostly laugh; a laugh that sounded like a cross between a puppy's playful growl and wind chimes.

DEATH TO DONUTS!

Cynthia P. Lawrence

ONE

It happened the summer that the Food Brigade started blowing up donut shops.

No one was too surprised that the attacks led to murder. I just didn't expect the target to be so close to home.

My boss, Nick Dellacasa, was worried. The Food Brigade had appeared from nowhere, promising to create havoc in Los Angeles. Its prey: donut shops, bagel purveyors, even Italian restaurants that were heavy on fats and carbs. Its mission, wrote the Brigade in notes sprayed with exploded powdered sugar and left at a half-dozen crime scenes, was to raise consciousness about the evils of foods that were making us a tubby nation. While deploring their methods, some of the media called the Brigade members messiahs; others said they were nuts or criminals. The police were baffled and offended. One patrol car team, the local press reported, suffered headaches after snacking on cheesecake energy bars during repairs to a favorite donut stop.

As I said, Nick was worried. The owner of Dellacasa's Restaurant in Westwood, near UCLA, he'd opened his first pizzeria in Brooklyn, serving up traditional Sicilian fare. Even though he'd added a California spin to his menu: you know, barbecued lamb pizza, Thai chicken and peanut sauce calzones, ravioli stuffed with blue and goat cheeses—his heart still belonged to spaghetti, heavy on the meat sauce.

I'm Cat Deean, his catering manager. Don't expect me to cook or carve ice swans. I bring in business: weddings, luncheons, corporate brunches. Planning menus is part of my job, working with Mario, our catering chef. I order supplies, scout party locations, bargain with clients who want vintage French wines at beer prices. I schlep a lot, work late and, since my divorce, take fencing lessons in my rare spare time to stay fit. My Aunt Sadie warns me that I'll wake up at age sixty-five with nothing but a scrapbook of other women's wedding menus. She may be right. I'll think about it tomorrow, or the day after.

"This goofy bunch scares me," said Nick. One powerful hand slapped the table and made our coffee cups shake. He'd joined Mario and me at our early Monday morning scheduling meeting. We were in Dellacasa's, drinking espresso strong enough to curl my eyebrows. I was surprised. Nothing appears sinister to Nick, except maybe pre-grated Parmesan in shaker cans.

"They say they're against pasta," observed Mario, "but they haven't hit any Italian restaurants yet."

"We could be the first," said Nick gloomily. "Our luncheon for Flavio might make them act. It's only two weeks away."

"They'd have trouble with access," I assured him. "I've already alerted the Bel Air security patrol. The party's at a private estate. We'll check invitations at the entrance. Guests, food critics and reporters will get in. That's all."

I was too complacent about security. To my mind, the Brigade was a bunch of misguided comic-opera buffoons. In view of what happened later, my thinking was dead wrong. A few private guards might have averted disaster.

If only Flavio Ricci had stayed in Rome, presiding over his five-star restaurant. But a chef's pride and a businessman's instincts had pointed him in a new direction. He'd rebranded himself as the Italian diet guru. He'd written his book, *Lose Weight, Enjoy Life with Pasta and Vino!* It had become an international bestseller, in a triumph of hope over experience. Now he was touring America to bring his message to a joy-starved nation.

Although this would be his first meeting with Nick, their family trees were intertwined through many generations in Palermo. Via e-mails and international phone calls, they'd discovered their shared philosophies about nourishment, Italian-style.

"Michelangelo's *David,*" said Flavio triumphantly. "Would anyone call him fat?"

"Botticelli's *Venus,*" replied Nick, riffing on the same theme. "Shapely, but not an extra ounce on her!"

Of course, there'd been Mediterranean diets before, based on plentiful seafood, fresh veggies and fruits. It had been Flavio's genius, however, to make his version an in-your-face attack on our national obsession with low-carb regimes. It was, I'd heard, his reaction to Americans who'd deserted his usually crowded Rome restaurant. Or, even worse, having to defend the glorious national cuisine to those brainwashed patrons who'd asked for soy-based spaghetti!

His book had already become a sensation at home, after sensitive Italian palates swiftly rejected the new pastas which, while virtuous, did taste like strands of cardboard.

His teachings had spread to gourmets in all of Western Europe, and now he was bringing his revelations to America. And soon to us, in Los Angeles.

In spite of our anxieties, Nick and his wife Rosie, Mario and me, and all of Dellacasa's staff were heady with anticipation. Flavio would bring his retinue, his *nuovo* recipes, and the sous-chef from his Rome restaurant to prepare them.

He'd have cookbooks to sign as gifts for the luncheon guests. I'd been reading the American edition in advance. Usually, I'm so involved with beautiful food as part of my job that I rarely have cravings. But lingering over Flavio's recipe for *Pizza Bianca/Bianca*—white pizza with herbed white veal sausage— and running my fingers over the glossy photos, I felt ready to cook voluptuously while dropping down to a size eight.

TWO

WE'D ARRANGED WITH FLAVIO'S New York publishers to find an appealing and safe location for the luncheon. One of Nick's customers, another transplant from Brooklyn, was thrilled to host.

Carlos, The Tango Teacher, born Ciccio Bosco, had made his fortune by introducing Angelenos to the tango; in recent years, he'd added salsa to the dance card.

His Bel Air estate, shared with his elderly mother and three maiden sisters, was a giant leap from the dark, crowded flat in Bensonhurst. But Serafina, the matriarch, still ruled.

She'd never given up her widow's black garments, the mourning jewelry, her faint moustache.

Nick, Carlos and I were drinking cappuccino on the upper terrace of the Mediterranean villa, basking in the genial morning sun that smiled down upon the green hills of Bel Air.

"Why you want to be such a big shot?" asked Serafina, who'd hobbled out on arthritic legs to join us. She pointed the daily newspaper in our direction, waving it like a talisman that could ward off evil.

"You could bring those crazies right to our front door! Look at this!"

I'd already seen the headline in my home-delivered paper: FOOD BRIGADE HITS TAKE-OUT PIZZA IN BURBANK. Warning Message On Window Scrawled In Tomato Sauce.

Carlos shrugged. "Please sit down, Mama. If they throw tomato sauce at us, we'll just add some garlic and have it for dinner."

Serafina scowled at him. "Don't laugh, read the story. They

broke in through the back of the store and shot holes in the pizza ovens! In ovens! With guns! They're not making jokes."

He patted her hand reassuringly. "Nick and Catherine promised that the Brigade won't get past our gates. Why should we act out of fear and miss a great honor?"

"Honor? To tell Americans how to lose weight? I hear Signor Ricci is from Palermo, but he served all those rich sauces, worse than the French, in Rome. Now he's at the age when he worries about his heart, so he's changed his mind again. But look at you, Ciccio. You never got fat on my honest Sicilian cooking."

I'd always thought that teaching tango had kept Ciccio/Carlos as supple as a gaucho's whip. Yet I'd seen him at Dellacasa's packing away heaping plates of pasta.

And Nick, broad-shouldered and muscular, chose lunch every day from his restaurant's kitchen. Perhaps there was something, after all, in keeping trim with pasta and wine. There were days, as I carried a tuna salad upstairs to my office and heard Dellacasa's happy diners, when I felt like a Roman who'd misplaced her ticket to the orgy.

My own shape is sturdy, inherited from Scottish forebears along with blue eyes and thick black hair that defies a comb. I work out when I can and try to be sensible about chocolate. I eat yogurt and whole grain breads, although I can't resist taking home a few leftover croissants after one of our catered brunches, a nutritional flaw I must have inherited from an uncle who, for unclear reasons, joined the French Foreign Legion.

The memory of my uncle gives me hope, when I feel restless, that my life can change from earnest, dutiful and, yes, long stretches of dull.

BACK AT DELLACASA'S, I returned a call from Sam Maguire, the New York publicist who was accompanying Flavio Ricci on his American book tour. Sam introduced himself and informed me he'd be arriving in L.A. a few days early. He wanted to check out the luncheon's guest list, confirm that the major food critics had sent RSVPs and that reporters from the newspapers and TV stations and West Coast magazine editors were coming.

The Italian consul in L.A. would attend, as well as a couple of Italian movie stars currently working in town. There'd be influential and very social ladies who lunch, and Flavio's local friends among an international elite of restaurateurs.

Mario and I could relax, said Sam. The menu was taken from the pages of *Pasta and Vino*; the author's sous-chef, Danté, would cook, bringing along his own pots and utensils. For our part, we'd supply the waiters and cleanup crew, do the table settings, order and place the floral arrangements. Oh, yes, plus security.

"Any problems you can see?" asked Sam. His voice was pleasant and cheerful, and I warmed to him at once.

"None at all," I replied with equal cheer, crossing my fingers and toes at the possibility that the Brigade could break in like a squadron of anorexic Attilas, throwing fat-free fluids on our parade.

"Come to Dellacasa's for lunch," I said, inviting him to meet Nick, Rosie, Mario and me. "I have a copy of the cookbook. We can prepare a meal from that."

"Thanks, no," said Sam, and chuckled. "I'm just promoting the book, I'm not living by it. Make me something rich and fattening. I won't tell Flavio."

I chuckled, too, hiding my surprise. Did I sense a rebellion simmering?

THREE

BY THE TIME HE ARRIVED, Flavio's book tour would already have taken him to Boston, Philadelphia, Chicago, Milwaukee, and Dallas. Los Angeles and San Francisco would be the last stops before Flavio headed back to New York and, finally, Rome.

"We could include ten more cities," said a jubilant if weary Sam, tearing into a thick slice of Nick's moist and fragrant garlic toast. "But Flavio closed his restaurant for all of August to do this tour, and he's got to get back in time to reopen."

"It's going well, then?" asked Nick.

"Incredibly well! We had lines around the block at just about every bookstore on the list. It helps that Flavio's such a good-looking guy. The ladies love it when he hands over their signed copy, looks up with those admiring Latin eyes and whispers, *'Bella!'* as if he really means it. And you know what? He does. Flavio appreciates women."

We were chatting over the remains of lunch at Dellacasa's. Nick had offered *Risotto alla Parmigiana,* a green salad, a plate of chocolate-dipped strawberries and mini Napoleons for dessert. I gave up my usual miserly tuna salad in honor of our guest. It was, actually, a sensible decision. Too much mercury in tuna these days, I've read. So I was guilt-free for the day, splurging on Nick's really rich risotto of chicken livers, sausage and cheese.

Certainly, Sam Maguire had no need of a diet. He was a trim six-footer, golden-haired and tan, with the clear blue eyes and calloused hands of someone who'd grown up around sailboats; I guessed Eastern Seaboard and Ivy League. In spite of being splendid, he was likable.

"I haven't been to Flavio's restaurant yet," said Sam, "but I'm hoping to get to Rome this fall. Personal invitation from Julia, you know, his daughter."

Sam colored slightly and I thought, *Aha! A dash of spice for the kettle!*

"So, you all got along well," said Rosie Dellacasa, who could give the CIA a course in subtly prying out secrets.

"Mostly. A little unhappiness about some of the hotels. Not my call," he added hastily. "Peak Publishing made those arrangements."

"Didn't like the hotel food?" asked Nick.

"Well, Milwaukee wasn't exactly a triumph. There was a convention going on at our hotel, and it was crowded in the elevators, the coffee shop, everywhere. Julia and Flavio's girl-friend, Loretta, were okay. Flavio and Danté seemed to think I was responsible."

He shook his golden head. "I shouldn't be telling tales, but it almost got ugly one afternoon there when we were late to a signing. Beg your pardon, Nick and Rosie, but you know those Italian tempers!"

Rosie and I exchanged glances. There might have been more, we told each other silently, than cold sausages in the hotel coffee shop.

"Well," Sam added briskly, "I've said too much. Honestly, everything went fine."

We all smiled and relaxed. The ample lunch was giving me an attack of inertia. I had work to do. The low-carb mania was making my head ache. It was complicating the box lunch menu we'd planned for an upcoming corporate meeting. How would the requested option of low-carb dressing affect the taste of our chicken, green grapes and walnut salad? Should we substitute lettuce wraps for our delicious panino sand-wiches? Is there really intelligent life after low-carb cookies?

Mario, who's made a specialty of liqueur-spiked cannoli, was on the verge of an anxiety attack. I needed answers and a few taste tests from our food suppliers.

I hastened up to my office and checked my voice mail. Most of it was the usual, except for one odd message. The voice was so cracked and husky, I wasn't sure at first if it belonged to a man or a woman. I pushed Replay and decided it was a woman trying to disguise her voice.

"I know who you are," she said. "Your cards are on the cashier's counter at Dellacasa's. You caterers are the *worst!* Everything you serve turns to fat on the hips of your innocent victims." The voice rose to a screech. "But your time is coming, Ms. Catherine! Find another line of work before we bury you in a big tub of butter! Goodbye from the Brigade!" There was a sharp click.

Well! Should I laugh? Should I shiver? I wasn't sure. What disturbed me most was that the Brigade had scouted out Dellacasa's, maybe had a meal here, and we hadn't a clue as to when, or what she (or they) looked like. I assumed she was thin, but maybe the Brigade had some chubbies who went berserk from their calorie-cutting. I've always felt that a zealot like Torquemada, for example, may have fasted so much he lacked essential fiber in his diet.

Nick needed to know right away about the phone call, and then we should inform the local police. I had mixed feelings about the Brigade. While I still chose to find something absurd in its donut shop raids, I wanted to be cautious about the cookbook luncheon. Nick was my mentor and friend, and it would be a blow to his honor if the event for a fellow Sicilian went bad.

FOUR

AS A LONGTIME BUSINESS OWNER, Nick keeps up cordial relationships with the West L.A. police. He put me on the phone to Detective Rubio, who snorted at my story.

"That bunch of loonies! So they're hitting the Westside now. Why? You putting double cream in your latte these days? I care. Got to watch my cholesterol."

Inwardly, I groaned. Fat intolerance was spreading, even to the cops.

"Drink espresso," I said. "Zero cholesterol."

"Gives me acid indigestion," he said mournfully. "Truth is, those cop shows on TV have it wrong these days. They always have us gulping black coffee out of soggy paper cups. Maybe in a place like Pittsburgh it's still true. But not in L.A. If they *really* looked around this station, they'd see a lot of us hugging bottles of fancy imported water. Crime isn't what it used to be."

We shared a moment of silence at the missteps in the march of progress.

"Um," I began in a gentle reminder, "the Food Brigade? Is there anything the police can do?"

I told him about the upcoming event. "That's what worries us. The first publicity was in the newspapers this morning. Just a mention that Dellacasa's would be hosting a private luncheon to launch Mr. Ricci's diet cookbook. We carefully omitted to say where it would take place."

"I don't see that there's much of anything we can do now. There's still very little we know about the Food Brigade. The

LAPD has a citywide threat management unit. Deals with stalkers, cases like that. I'll call them, talk it over.

"So far, yours is the only Italian restaurant they've threatened. And you, Cat, are the only person they've ever named as a target. Usually, they strike at night. So we'll have the patrol cars in your area keep a special watch on Dellacasa's. If the woman calls again, you might consider a security guard."

Swell. If a guard called too much attention to the need for security, Nick might have to reintroduce Dellacasa's special Tuesday, Wednesday and Thursday prix fixe dinners. Three courses with a glass of wine at the price of one regular entrée. A promotion sure to cut my end-of-year bonus. Delay my postholiday trip to Paris.

And yet, what if the Brigade shot up our catering kitchen? It was in the shop Nick had bought next to Dellacasa's when our catering business expanded. Separated only by a rear door and a corridor from the restaurant. Usually dark by nightfall after the canapés and I had left for the next cocktail party. Suppose, even in error, a bullet went through the walls and landed in some diner's tagliatelle.

I told Nick about Detective Rubio's suggestion. He called in Rosie and Mario and we agreed to hire a private security company. At least until the book tour was over and the celebrity chef had left town.

I used to worry that our portable pizza ovens would overload the circuits in the client's kitchen and cause a blackout. Or that a guest would be allergic to the peanuts in our Thai noodles and fall down in a fit. Or, although it had only happened once, while we were icing the champagne, that the groom would panic and leave the bride at the altar. Or... But that was in the good old days. Before I'd consider, in a fleeting moment of fear, packing a gun under my best powder blue linen pantsuit.

THE NOTE was slipped under the rear entrance to Dellacasa's sometime during the night.

Whereas….
The People of these United States are a gross
60% and more overweight—even obese—
in a conspiracy concocted by the
food makers and purveyors of such States
to make sales at the expense of
the health and happiness of said People,
it is our duty to start the revolution and overthrow
those who would offer fat, calories,
and really evil supersized portions,
using whatever means necessary including violence
to rescue this Nation from wretched excess.
As it has been truly said:
"A moment on the lips, a lifetime on the hips!"

                      —The Food Brigade

FIVE

THE *PASTA AND VINO* GROUP ARRIVED at LAX from Chicago with enough luggage to outfit a chic European duchy. Since Nick was busy with the lunch crowd at Dellacasa's, Sam Maguire and I were the delegated greeters.

The vivid photo on Flavio's book jacket—chef staring with hypnotic eye at an angry lobster—didn't quite capture the man's imposing presence. He was taller and leaner than most Sicilians I'd met, with curly, silver-streaked black hair. His profile was classic. You could imagine him in ancient days, heroic nose sniffing the erupting lava on Mt. Etna, leading panicked hordes to safety. Today, he was elegant in a lightweight tan silk suit, tasseled loafers and a cerulean-blue silk shirt open at the neck.

It would be easy to fall under his spell. I didn't envy his girlfriend, Loretta. She was model slim, with long straight black hair, thin nose, thin red lips expertly rounded with lip pencil. Stylish in a sleek black jersey pantsuit. And as wary as if her expensive black alligator handbag had hidden teeth.

She looked me over, from my flyaway hair to the sandals showing fading red polish on my pedicure. I had this sudden image of myself as a bare-footed, grape-stomping peasant scrambling out of the sticky vat. Overcoming my instant dislike of Loretta, I smiled.

"Buon giorno," I said in my fractured Italian. *"Come sta?"*

She smiled back, a cat-licking-cream smile. "Don't knock yourself out," said Loretta in a husky, lightly accented voice. "We all speak English quite well."

She turned to Flavio, dismissing me as no threat, slipping

her arm through his. "Let's go, darling. I'm famished enough to eat Los Angeles hotel food." They were staying in Beverly Hills, at a hotel whose restaurant rated high both with Zagat and Michelin.

Flavio was more gracious. He lifted my hand, kissed it lightly, caressed my fingers perhaps a trifle longer than manners dictated. Using restraint, I did not simper.

"Grazie!" said Flavio. "It is so kind of you to break up your day to greet us."

I said that Nick had asked me to help, during their visit, in any way I could. Flavio had already told Nick that he and Loretta were dining with a couple of restaurateur friends that evening. Which left it up to Sam and me to amuse Julia, his daughter, and Danté, the sous-chef. Julia was no problem.

Past the baggage carousel, she'd rushed to Sam, flinging her arms around his neck. *"Amoré,"* she trilled. "I have missed you so desperately!"

He disengaged her arms and said gently, "It's only been a few days, Julia. Let's not make a big deal out of it and upset your daddy."

"Of course," she said, lowering her head and fluttering big, brown, thickly lashed eyes. "I am so emotional. Too Italian. You must let me know if I'm embarrassing you."

She was a pretty young thing, about twenty, I guessed. Tall and dark-haired, like her father, but with softer features, straight little nose, a pouty mouth. Her summer dress looked couture: a lilac voile print with lettuce-edged miniskirt that showed off long, shapely legs. Not exactly the tee and denim skirt I usually wore for travel, but her doting daddy obviously indulged Julia's taste for expensive fashion. Flavio frowned as his daughter flung herself at Sam, and the publicist avoided his client's disapproving eyes.

Danté stood quietly in the background. He was a small, dark, wiry man, not much over thirty-five, I guessed, despite a receding hairline. Olive-green polo shirt, neatly pressed jeans, beige linen jacket carried over one arm. His brown eyes were partly covered with odd, droopy eyelids that gave him a sorrowful, hangdog expression. His thin face broke into a shy smile as I stepped up and shook his hand.

"Welcome to Los Angeles, Danté. I'm Catherine, Cat to my friends." I burbled on. "How was your flight? Is this your first trip to L.A.? Will you have time to do some sightseeing?"

"The trip was exciting. My first. We flew over the Grand Canyon. Please, call me Danny. In America, Danté makes me sound like someone still in the Middle Ages." And sensitive about losing his hair.

"I hope the four of us, and Mario, our catering chef, can have dinner tonight. There's a really good seafood place overlooking the ocean in Malibu."

"Yes, thank you. We've all been under pressure with this tour. It will be nice to relax for an evening."

Face impassive, Danny glanced over at Julia and Sam. Although they stood discreetly apart, one of Julia's hands moved thoughtfully up and down Sam's arm, as if she were deciding whether to roast, braise or devour him raw.

Relief on my part that Flavio would not be joining us tonight! Although a caterer is expert at soothing relatives with wounded feelings (the bride's parents are divorced, the groom's uncle broke the Spode gravy boat last Thanksgiving), keeping a hormonal young woman from being locked up by her father was beyond my skills.

And I thought the Food Brigade was my greatest worry.

WE DINED ON PLUMP CRAB CAKES and cioppino, goat cheese tart and pistachio-crusted salmon, mango sherbet and chocolate torte. We agreed on an amber-gold Napa Chardonnay. There was a full moon over Malibu, tranquil waves broke and curled against the stilts that kept our restaurant from falling into the Pacific, and I twirled my half-empty wineglass, as mute and stranded as a clam at low tide.

To one side of me at the oceanview table, Sam and Julia, with heads together, cooed like doves in mating season. On the other side, Danny and Mario chatted about herb gardens and horse racing.

Mario, despite his name, is not Italian. He's Afro-Ameri-can-Caribbean, one of a large family that settled in Los Angeles from Belize. His mother played Mario Lanza records during her pregnancy, hoping the lyrical accents of her native country would lead her son to a career in opera. Instead, Mario is a chef who wants to become a restaurateur.

He and Danny bonded like Sicilian blood brothers. By the end of the third bottle of Chardonnay, they'd decided to open the Danny & Mario Trattoria in Rome within the next two years. Why not? Dreams can come true if you're Italian at heart. And have talent and a backer.

Meanwhile, I faced the moonlit ocean and wistfully considered my own future. I didn't at all regret my divorce the year before. Gil is a decent man, steady, as predictable as oatmeal at seven every morning (he thoughtfully cooked it himself), valiantly battling the 405 to the office where he designs computer programs for engineers, home and asleep by ten. There were nights when I was working late that we didn't connect at all. Oh, he'd roll over when I slipped into bed, sleepily pat me on the shoulder, content that I was where I belonged, then drift off again. We'd been married for five years when I looked ahead with dismay to forty-five more years of an unexamined life before Medicare and a condo in Sun City.

He was hurt, but took the divorce well. Recently, though, he'd sent me two dozen roses on what would have been our anniversary. Was he hinting?

Single is a state to make you shudder when you consider the indignities of the dating scene in L.A. So many walking wounded, or adorable but untouchable gays, or the gym rats so buff they'd make Schwarzenegger look like the Pillsbury Doughboy.

(My phone rings.)

Him: "Hi, Cat, it's Gary. From The Fit Place. Haven't seen you around lately."

Me: "Well, I've been busy. How about you? Still working out?"

Him: "You bet. I've been hired part time to tend the juice bar. Stop by and I'll blend you my latest. Beet juice, crushed pineapple, organic non-fat yogurt, honey and filberts. My treat. In fact, come on Saturday morning and help me train for my next marathon."

Me: "Gosh, wish I could, Gary, but I'm catering a wedding that night."

Him: "So I suppose you won't want to run on the beach with me early Sunday morning? Afterward, I know a café with the most righteous granola. Your treat."

Me: "So tempting, but I have other plans."

Actually, I've been lucky. I'd always kept in touch with Nate Greene, a friend from UCLA undergraduate days. Back then, we'd both been too immature to go beyond a few casual movie dates. Now he's a reporter in San Francisco and, after a trip north, we'd started what I suppose is a long-distance romance. Planes fly every hour to the Bay area, and cell phone talk is cheap, so I'm really not alone. Except on a mellow summer night, caught up in the treacherous pull of the moon and the tides.

SIX

Sam had taken Julia and Danny to Disneyland on Saturday; the next day, they all slept in and lounged by the hotel pool. So I was able to devote my full attention to the Riley Johannson wedding on Saturday evening.

Chip Riley, the groom, was a Marine home on leave; Susanna, the bride, wanted a patriotic theme for the dinner. Everything red, white and blue, up to the miniature flags on stands at each table setting. The menu was a challenge for Mario.

He snarled and refused to put blue dye (the bride's suggestion) in the mashed potatoes. Creative chef that he is, he triumphed with a pretty dish of poached chicken breasts, ramekins of bourbon-cherry sauce, and buttery blue-skinned new potatoes. He arranged a salad of roasted beets and endive sprinkled with blue cheese. Dessert was a strawberry-blueberry fruit tart, followed by a whipped cream wedding cake topped with fresh red, white and blue flowers. No one worried about carbs or calories. It was a feast for the eyes and tummies, like the good old days.

So, I was in a terrific mood on Monday after our usual morning meeting. Hummed "God Bless America" as I checked my voice mail. Damn it, another message from the Food Brigade!

"You're not listening," croaked the voice. "I saw that Ricci goon being interviewed on TV this morning. All that crap about it's okay to eat linguini. That's like white worms squirming around in your stomach! Tell him to *stop* before it's too late!"

"I won't see America destroyed by white flour. Not as long as the Food Brigade lives!"

It was becoming our regular routine: I told Nick, who called the West L.A. police, who assured us that their patrol cars were alerted, and giving special attention to Dellacasa's day and night. All I had to do was multitask: ignore the threats, do my usual job and focus on Flavio's visit.

Los Angeles was in the August doldrums, snoozing before the start of the fall blockbuster season and the Oscar campaigns. Flavio was the most charismatic Italian to arrive since Fellini, and he'd become an instant celebrity. Three days of TV interviews and book signings before the luncheon on Thursday.

Many of the bookstores were in malls with a flow of foot traffic that presented security problems. We'd alerted Sam to the growing Food Brigade threats, and he'd arranged for a guard to travel with him to the signings. Flavio was outraged.

He'd insisted on being dropped off, alone, at Dellacasa's for a quick lunch with Nick, Rosie and me. Nothing heavy that could tire him during a long day of signing each book with a flourish and a smile. Grilled chicken salads, crusty rolls and sparkling water bottled near a therapeutic Italian mountain stream.

"Sam informs me that my publisher will not pay for a security guard," Flavio declared. "The cost will come out of my pocket. *My* royalties. I tell you, Nick, I am beginning to doubt the way Americans do business."

"We don't know who these crazies are," protested Nick. "It's better that you're protected, even if you have to pick up the cost."

"This Los Angeles of yours. I see it on CNN. The wild gangs. Young women in jeans pulled under their *ombelico*. Everybody in cars holding a cell phone in one hand and a dripping fast food burger in the other! Italian traffic is horrendous, but nothing like your freeways. Much more dangerous than your Food Brigade!"

His attractive nostrils flared in disdain. I thought I should change the topic.

"I've been wanting to ask," I said, "have any studies been done on your diet?"

He plucked a strip of grilled chicken from the greens and chewed it thoughtfully.

"Too new. A small Italian university wants to set up a study, and Danté is working with them. Don't get me wrong. I love America, but would your media look for the truth? I have my doubts. I observe Sam and today he's promoting *my* book. But next week, it could be the absolutely final word on yin/yang, or yang/yin, diets!"

"The public has a choice," said Nick mildly. "They make up their own minds."

The author shrugged. "Credibility. It's one reason why I'm doing the tour, and paying no attention to this ridiculous Food Brigade."

Flavio waved his fork, pointing it at any possible nonbelievers at our table, or in the world.

"I refuse to have my diet laughed at. It works! Pasta is the soul of it, mozzarella is the heart and a full red wine every day unclogs the arteries that lead to the brain! As my book says, moderation but not starvation. *'A firm body, a happy stomach, a spirit at peace.'"*

Nick, Rosie and I digested all of this, while Flavio beamed. I had skimmed through the book, but paid too little attention to the theory behind it.

"Mozzarella?" I asked timidly.

"It's well known that the minerals in cheese break down the fat faster. You could also grate a wedge of parmigiano over pasta and get a bowl full of fat-reducing benefits."

"But pasta?"

"I believe in carbohydrates!" said Flavio passionately. "Not the flabby macaroni and spaghetti with disgustingly sweet tomato sauce that Americans put in cans, or in little plastic tubs for the microwave. And then you feed it to your unfortunate children!

"You can import proud pasta from hardy Italian wheat. It has made Italians healthy and beautiful since the days of the Roman Empire, and it is time to restore it to its noble place in advancing world nutrition!"

I resolved to hit the supermarket tonight and stock up on proud pasta. Sauté a little garlic, throw in crushed fresh tomatoes, mix with the al dente pasta, top with a sprinkle of grated parmigiano-reggiano lifted from Dellacasa's kitchen. Pour a glass of red wine (did it matter if it was Italian or Californian? I'd have to research the book), put up my feet and have a happy stomach and a peaceful spirit. What a satisfying way to become a sylph! I want to believe, I do!

I wasn't the only new believer. There was a message from Aunt Sadie on my office answering machine. Sadie is my only living relative in L.A., a widow with a bouncy nature and a devoted band of male friends. During an empty weekend, she'd never feel, as I sometimes have since my divorce, as isolated as if I'd been handed my tiki torch and voted off the island. No regrets, Cat, move on.

I returned Sadie's call. She said, "I saw Signor Ricci on TV this morning. He's *so* dynamic. My book club ladies and I are going to one of his signings this afternoon. We want to do his pasta and vino diet. Have you tried it yet?"

"I'm thinking about it, Auntie. But what happened to your spa regime? Isn't it working for you?"

A sigh. "It takes such a long time to see results. And I'm getting awfully tired of miso soup and potassium cocktails. This sounds like much more fun. Besides, if it isn't all that Signor Ricci promises, our club is investigating another new diet. Fascinating! You're so literary, I think you'd love it."

"Shopping tips from Chaucer?" I snickered. "Ham dishes from Hamlet?"

"I won't say another word," declared Sadie. "We're going

to the book signing and then we're stopping for pastry and coffee in one last fling before we study our pasta and vino diet."

"Makes sense to me," I said. "Tell Flavio you're my aunt. Maybe he'll kiss your hand twice."

"You're getting silly," she giggled.

We hung up amid mutual expressions of fondness. Now I had to step next door and tell Mario that the Compassionate Matrons of Messina wanted low-carb chocolate soufflés for their fund-raising lunch.

SEVEN

THURSDAY DAWNED bright and hot. I'd ordered green canvas umbrellas, like giant lily pads, to shade the luncheon tables on Carlos's terrace. Pastel green tablecloths and orange napkins were a touch of Italian flag-waving. Flavio had parted with his menu in advance, so we'd know what dishes and cutlery were needed.

At my urgent request, he'd stopped at Dellacasa's on Tuesday evening after his last book signing.

"It's very simple, my lovely Catherine," he'd said. Supple fingers played romantic melodies on my shoulder, as a weary-looking Loretta, seated with a glass of Merlot and tapping a stiletto-heeled white sandal, glared at me.

"Everything for the lunch is from my cookbook. I want my guests to feel as if they are in Taormina, on a terrace facing the Mediterranean, dining on the bounty of the sea and the land and growing slender." He lifted his fingers long enough to touch his lips and blow a kiss into the air.

"Pasta! Cheeses! Wine! Olive oil, lemons, garlic, onion, tomatoes, and herbs so perfumed, they seduce your taste buds! Los Angeles will see, Catherine, that there is a better life ahead without burgers and tacos and, what do you call them? Those Dodger Dogs!"

"Oh, yes!" I breathed, overcome partly with yearning and partly with the necessity of planning. "Flavio, let me have your menu now! I'll be sure to have copies printed to put at each place setting."

"I appreciate that, bella Catherine. You take such good care of us."

Lose Weight, Enjoy Life with Pasta and Vino
Cookbook Menu of
Chef Flavio Ricci

~~~

Turkey Bacon, Lettuce & Tomato Personal Pizzas

~~~

Ragu of Prawns and Scallops

~~~

Spaghetti with Mozzarella and Parmigiano

~~~

Fresh Melon Slices
Figs Poached in Red Wine and Honey
Orange and Almond Cake

~~~

Selection of California Red Wines

~~~

Mineral Water. Coffee. Iced Tea

Mario had volunteered to assist Danny, who would cook in the kitchen of the Bel Air mansion. The day before, I took them for a dress rehearsal. Danny was happy with Serafina's spacious kitchen, even to the ochre-tiled counters and the dried herbs that hung in fragrant bunches above the kitchen sink.

"Like home," he said wistfully. "Like Sicily. Country cooking, from the land, not like the classic Italian I cook for Flavio in Rome."

"But you know him from Palermo."

"Not really." With pride, Danny said, "He hired me in Rome as an apprentice, and I worked my way up to sous-chef. But Flavio knows I can make a true *Pasta con le Sarde,* the magnificent dish of the Sicilian people!"

"*Sarde*?" I asked.

"Sardines. Spaghetti and sardines, so delicious mixed up with fennel and currants and pine nuts. It is the specialty of

Trapani, the fishing town where I was born. Your lovely dinner in Malibu, on the water, made me homesick."

He saw my concern. "Please, don't worry. I'm enjoying my visit to America. My second cousin—my mother expects me to call—lives in Santa Monica. Maybe he can explain what I don't understand on TV, like drinking yogurt through a straw on the bus, and calling it breakfast."

Mario smiled. "Our two top exports—democracy and fast food."

I led the two chefs up to the terrace, where we chose the placement of tables for serving beverages and desserts. It was a pleasant day; the three of us sat looking out at the hills and drinking the iced tea served by Serafina's oldest daughter, Maria. Since the last time I'd seen her, the young woman had bleached her moustache, so there were only glints of golden hair as she smiled at Danny. I liked Maria, and I hoped that Serafina hadn't pushed her into dreams that would likely never come true.

IT WAS ARRANGED for Carlos to greet the arrivals. After Sam checked invitations, Julia and Loretta would escort the guests to the upper terrace to meet Flavio and Nick.

I'd brought in my most reliable kitchen crew and waiters. They'd have had to be sudsed and sprayed in a car wash to be any cleaner. In spite of my nagging sense of unease, we'd left it to the private Bel Air patrol to provide security. Carlos had assured us that there'd never been a problem at his estate. And Flavio had already dismissed the bodyguards who tagged along with him to his book signings.

Besides, the Food Brigade had gone north. They'd struck two nights earlier at a popular Chinese restaurant in Berkeley. Who would've expected that pan-fried dumplings could upset them so? But they'd broken into the restaurant kitchen sometime after midnight and left the refrigerator door open after liberating three trays of ground pork morsels encased in dough, which they'd tossed into the alley. The police were clueless, although some stray cats were delighted.

The Brigade left a note taped to the back door.

> *"California needs to be awakened to the dangers of fatty pork in coffins of white flour. And then they're fried? In spite of bad press in L.A., the Food Brigade will persist! Let your newspapers know."*

I persisted when the florist arrived, insisting that our people unload his van and bring the table centerpieces into the kitchen. I poked through every bowl of fresh-cut flowers, feeling for explosives hidden among the gladiolas. All clear and safe.

But careful planning in the morning couldn't prevent the bloody afternoon.

What we missed—blame it on our own mild dispositions—was the murderous power of obsession.

EIGHT

To BEGIN WITH, the book-signing table was in the wrong place. It left only a narrow aisle for the waiters and that would be crowded once the guests lined up. As Loretta observed to Sam, with her usual disdain, the water pitchers would get more attention than the guest of honor. For once she was right, although Julia, hovering near Sam, sent poisonous glances at her father's extremely good friend.

Meanwhile, two cartons with Danny's special pans and utensils had been left behind in his hotel room. He'd called the hotel desk and arranged to have the cartons delivered, *Rush,* by messenger service.

Which meant the luncheon was behind schedule. A fuming Flavio and a calmly professional Sam decided to have the cookbooks signed and handed out during cocktails.

Danny had wilted like week-old romaine, but he and Mario kept busy chopping and slicing with knives borrowed from Serafina. It wasn't really a disaster; the two chefs had prepared the pizza dough, ragu and desserts yesterday, in Dellacasa's catering kitchen. However, it didn't help now that the maiden daughters, dressed in unfortunate shades of brown, stood in the kitchen doorway giggling like three Graces high on double lattes. Even Carlos couldn't move them away from the action. Serafina, black eyes sparkling, kept her promise to stay out of her kitchen, but huddled with the maidens and provided commentary in noisy whispers.

So we moved the book-signing table to the far end of the terrace and sat Flavio in front of the balustrade, facing his guests. Sam stood beside him, opening each *Pasta and Vino* to the title page and handing it on to the chef.

It was a lively crowd, the happiness level rising as lime-splashed wine coolers, artichoke crostini, and pomegranate-glazed wings were passed around. The women were lovely in summery dresses; I believe I sighted a Prada. A few edgy L.A. alternatives: black pantsuits or mirror image whites; tee-shirts discarded in favor of big cleavage. Jeans, tees and linen blazers for the men, although I spotted an all-black Armani and a pinstriped Lauren. There might even have been a Target or two among the freelance writers.

Flavio, although he wouldn't even brown butter today, sported his chef's whites. Sam was discreet (never upstage the client) in a beige linen suit and checked blue shirt, his tie the clear summer-blue of his sailor's eyes.

Nick, Rosie, Julia and Loretta disappeared into the crowd, while I did my usual last-minute check among the tables, straightening a fork, moving a wineglass. Until Felix, my waiter captain, distracted me. He was missing the small box of souvenir menus. A hasty search found them where they shouldn't have been—on the floor under the dessert table. We were pulling out the box when I heard, above the talk and the laughter, about six sharp cracks. My first reaction: a glass carafe of coffee had exploded and showered glass. Which explained the sudden shrieks. Then came the shattering cries!

"Those were shots!"

"They're wounded!"

"Oh, God! They're dead."

I scrambled upright to a scene of panic. Chaotic, like a terror attack on the nightly news, only I was no longer a spectator. This wasn't TV, the cool medium. Whatever had happened, it was hot and happening now.

A blur of movement, bright streaks of color like flowers in a hurricane, as guests in their finery crouched and scuttled toward the French doors leading to the stairs. A potential disaster as they blocked the doorway, pushing to get through. I saw Carlos, with the clout of an ex-Marine sergeant, hold them back.

"Calm down! Be calm! It's all over. You're safe! Safe!"

Shouts from the crowd.

"We're not safe!"

"There's a sniper out there!"

"Call 911!"

"Get the police! Stop the murders!"

So strange to see fifty guests and my staff stumbling as far away as possible from the balustrade. I stood as my head waiter, always efficient, drew his cell phone from a back pants pocket and dialed 911.

"For God's sake, Cat, get down!" Nick, voice trembling, was crouched at my side, pulling on my arm.

I looked around, bewildered. Nick was okay, but where were Flavio and Sam? Julia and Loretta?

The women, with Rosie Dellacasa, were down on their knees, gathered as if in prayer at the end of the terrace. Julia sobbing, making terrible keening sounds of mourning. Rosie comforting her. Loretta leaning forward, holding the hand of someone lying on the ground. I counted three bodies, two men and a woman, although I couldn't tell who they were.

At that moment, Mario and Danny, who'd left the kitchen, pushed past the mass of terrified people, saw the bodies and rushed toward them.

The Food Brigade, I thought. *They've done what they promised.* My fault! My fault! I didn't protect him enough!

I tried to tell Nick that I knew I was to blame, but he shook his head and raced to join the others. No doubt in my mind that Flavio was dead. So I stood there, blinking in the strong sunlight, unable to take a step, unwilling to face the bloody reality of the victims.

Victims! There were three bodies. Who else?

"Cat!" Felix was calm but insistent. "What do you want me to do?"

Yes, it was still my catered affair. Only now it was a crime scene.

"Help Carlos until the police come. Nobody should leave."

Swiftly he turned and headed for the doors where Carlos stood, arms stretched wide, preventing an exodus. Bless you, Felix—part-time waiter, part-time Hollywood stuntman, compact, muscled and cool.

The rush to safety had made the terrace a disaster area. I walked shakily past centerpieces overturned on the pale green cloths, smashed dishes littering the floor, wine and water glasses still rolling on the tables. Perhaps five minutes had passed since the shots, but for now time was suspended. There should have been a breeze, but it seemed that the air on the terrace had been sucked up into a giant vacuum. I found it difficult to breathe and couldn't decide if the earth had stopped turning for a brief time. Or whether it was a panic attack.

I forced myself to take three deep breaths before looking past the crying women.

There was Flavio, sprawled on the ground, blood seeping from his left arm and his shoulder, staining his chef's whites. But I saw his eyelids flutter and, as I watched, he groaned and moved deathly pale lips.

"Don't talk, *caro*," said Loretta softly, leaning over him. "The ambulance will be here soon."

So Flavio was alive. Then why was Julia, his daughter, tearing the sky apart with her cries? I stepped forward, into the little circle where she was cradling Sam Maguire's blond head in her arms, rocking back and forth. I saw that Sam was dead.

"I loved him! I loved him!" she sobbed to no one in particular.

The bullet, or bullets, must have hit the back of his head. The ground below Sam was wet with a dark pool of blood that had crept up the collar of his blue-checkered shirt and made blotches on the light-colored jacket.

I shuddered, glad that earth mother Rosie was there, smoothing Julia's hair, murmuring quieting words of comfort to the girl.

But there was a third victim, one arm flung wide, the other still clutching a copy of *Pasta and Vino* that she'd probably been holding as she fell.

She was a dark-haired, slim, fine-featured woman on the other side of middle age. Good legs under a brief, braid-edged pink tweed suit that could have been a real Chanel. It was untouched by her injury, a bullet hole on the right side of her forehead that left droplets of blood marring the side of her face.

"Who was she?" I whispered to Nick, holding tightly to his arm.

"I recognize her," he said. "Can't remember the name, but Flavio introduced me. She's the food critic for one of the big magazines."

I don't mean to be flippant, but it's not a bad way to die. Under a cloudless California sky, anticipating a fine lunch from a first-rate chef. She was most likely an accidental victim, waiting for her book to be signed, caught in the sniper's line of fire. I hoped she'd had few regrets in her life—that she'd given and received love, and that her critic's expense account had been generous—so she could have shared good bread, wine and occasional caviar with many congenial companions.

Why was I eulogizing this woman, whose name I didn't know? I suppose I felt that, at the moment, she was too lonely to ignore. The horror and pity were focused on the other two victims. And, truthfully, I wasn't able yet to face up to Sam Maguire's violent death.

It was apparent that Flavio's wounds weren't fatal. From what I could see, he'd taken bullets in his arm and shoulder. Sam, standing beside him to keep the line moving, had gotten in the way of the sniper's target. There'd been six shots. Either the killer was a wildly firing amateur or had coolly aimed at Sam and the Chanel woman, dropping them for a clear shot at Flavio.

First impressions. Too spacy to be trusted.

"I heard the shots, Detective. No, I didn't see anyone."

"Did Mr. Ricci have any enemies?"

"Well, the Food Brigade didn't like Italian food."

"Was that a good enough reason to kill?"

"It must have been. Sam and the Chanel woman, they're both dead. No, Chanel isn't her name, it's her designer. I'm not much help, am I?"

A patrol car was the first to respond. Two policemen called for backup and an ambulance. These screeched up, lights flashing and sirens piercing the air, drowning out the placid Bel Air sounds of birdsong and gardeners with power mowers.

Efficiently, the officers held back the crowd that had soon gathered around the victims. Paramedics quickly focused on saving Flavio, lifting his half-conscious body onto a stretcher, rushing him off to the nearest E.R.

Nick, face ashen but hands finally steady, volunteered to drive a distraught Loretta to the hospital. He spoke to Carlos, standing sentry-like at the French doors, who whisked them past the distracted police.

Julia still knelt beside Sam, holding his lifeless hand, until an officer gently told her she must move back. Danny had made his way through the crowd to help Rosie lift up the grieving young woman. They led Julia to a quiet corner of the terrace, where she could no longer see the body. She seemed oblivious to her father's near-death and injuries.

I tagged after to offer what help I could and became witness to the drama that followed.

"I loved Sam so much," she cried again to Rosie. "We were going to be married."

Danny had had enough. To my surprise, he grabbed Julia around the shoulders and snarled at her. "Stop it, you foolish girl! Stop it! You know that Flavio would never allow that marriage!"

Unfortunately, Danny had a voice that quavered under

pressure, when it should have commanded. It lacked the tim-
bre of Moses ordering the Red Sea to part or Henry V spur-
ring the English into battle. It didn't calm Julia. Her cries rose
to a hysterical pitch.

"He couldn't stop us. Only *death* could stop us! Maybe my
father planned this. Did he? Do you know?"

Danny stepped back, as suddenly as if he'd been slapped.
He raised his arms and reached out to her, begging, implor-
ing, his whole being asking her forgiveness.

"*Mi dispiace, Julia!* I'm so sorry. I spoke out of emotion.
Your father, he could have died. You didn't ask. I understand,
you were too upset."

Julia slumped into a chair next to a table scattered with
overturned dishes. Rosie joined her, reaching into a pocket
to find a tissue for Julia's tear-streaked face. Eyes patted dry,
Flavio's daughter settled into a frigid calm. She sat motionless, a statue carved from blue ice, incongruous in a floaty
minidress the color of vanilla. Its hem was stained with
Sam's blood.

"How *is* my father?"

"We don't know yet," answered Danny. "Wounded but not,
from what I could see, too serious. Some blood lost, but he
will recover."

"That's good," said Julia in the same dispassionate tone.

"As soon as the police allow us to leave," said Rosie, "we
can go to the hospital. I'll get Nick on his cell phone, find out
where they are."

Rosie stood and walked over to where I was standing.

"The girl's in shock," she whispered. "She needs a doctor."

I nodded in agreement, and Rosie returned to Julia's side.

There was a sudden buzz along the terrace. The detectives
had arrived. Two men in plainclothes talking to the uniformed
police. It was Danny's cue to rush to me.

"Cat, please listen to me!" His voice was low, the words
rapid. "Julia didn't mean what she said about Flavio. He loves

her, but he is an old-fashioned Italian father. He *never* took Sam Maguire seriously as a husband for his daughter.

"Beg your pardon, but Sam was too American. And besides, Julia falls in love too easily! Sam is only the latest of Julia's many crushes. A salesman for a French winery! The son of an Ecuadorian diplomat! A waiter from Brussels! And more!

"With some of them, Julia fell out of love as fast as she fell in. Others, Flavio paid off. I know, I was the middleman, the deal maker. Julia doesn't know or she'd hate me."

Danny paused for breath, turning his head in the direction of the police. "They mustn't hear what Julia said about her father. Please help. They would not understand."

I assured him that I wouldn't tell, and neither would Rosie. In my mind, I decided to have a discreet conversation with Nick the first chance I got. Flavio was his friend, his *compare* from the old country. And yet there were, after all, the murders of two innocents.

Of course, it was the Food Brigade that had committed the crimes. We all knew it. Even if they were obsessive fools, they were more dangerous than any of us had believed.

I didn't recognize the two detectives, although I was sure they were from the West L.A. division. They were occupied now with the crime scene, sidestepping the yellow tape that the first patrol had strung around the perimeter.

The medical examiner arrived and set to work. Next came the crime lab technicians with their equipment kits. Always competent, since O.J. they were meticulous. A police photographer circled in and out of the taped area. The two bodies lay like birds with bloody plumage, felled by a triumphant hunter.

I saw the detectives leaning over the balustrade, pointing toward the possible arc of the bullets. After a minute or so, they came over to question Carlos. He gestured toward our little group, and one of the detectives held up his hand to us to say "Stay!" and we did, as docile as well-trained dogs.

More cars were arriving, and voices rose from the driveway

below the bottom terrace. Unnoticed, I moved to where I could see over the balustrade. Blue uniforms and plainclothes detectives had begun a slow and careful search of the green hillside below Carlos's mansion. Where had the sniper stood? The lower terrace was hidden from my sight, but I heard muted conversation and a shout. "Here! Look over here!"

Then groans from the police as vans lettered with the names of two TV stations turned from the road into the driveway. The murders were fast becoming a media event. I saw some cops run down the driveway, waving arms.

"Stop right there! This is a crime scene. You can't come nearer!"

Shouts of protests from the occupants as their vans were pointed over to one side of the driveway.

I corrected myself. This was more than a media event; these were the Hollywood celebrity murders that L.A. had thirsted for after a long dry spell. Notorious homegrown terrorists attacking an enclave of the rich and famous, picking off a famous diet guru, a handsome New York executive and a noted authority on food. No sex angle in sight, but this was only Day One. I shuddered.

The glitzy film biz has its share of the desperate and deranged, but never in my catering career had I come across killers for a cause like the Food Brigade.

Finally, the detectives got around to us.

"Where's Nick?" growled the older man, obviously the senior member of the team. He was short and stocky, big dour face like a bulldog with an attitude problem. His partner, slim, blond and smiling, was the good guy. Both were bareheaded and sweating in dark suits on a day that was rapidly heating up.

"You know Nick?" Stupid answer on my part. Bulldog snorted.

"He's a longtime friend of our division. We've been keeping an eye on Dellacasa's for him ever since this food craziness started. I was told he left after the shootings. Shouldn't have done that. He's a key witness."

"He's at the hospital with Flavio Ricci, the third victim." I turned to Rosie, who released Julia's hand and stood. There was a streak of blood on the arm of her good green silk. I remembered she'd been leaning over Flavio, trying to stanch the blood.

"Here's Nick's wife."

"Hello, Rosie." The bulldog had backed down.

"Oh, Sal, this is so terrible. Flavio and Sam, these are our friends. And that poor woman, I don't know her name, who just got in the way. How senseless!"

"Irma Van Wolfington. That's her name. Did she know Ricci?"

"I—I don't think so. She was standing next to him, holding a book. I was carrying cold drinks to give Flavio and Sam when the shooting started."

"And you. Where were you?" Abruptly, Sal turned to me.

"Well, I was under a table, pulling out a box of menus. I didn't see anything."

"And who are these two?"

I introduced Julia and Danny to the detectives. Julia stared with blank eyes. Danny forthrightly put out a hand to shake. Sal frowned, as if the sous-chef's gesture would contaminate the evidence, and Danny pulled back, his olive skin reddening in embarrassment.

"We'll need statements from all of you," said the younger detective (we never did learn his name).

"But we're not going to be the primary on this," Sal told us. I thought he looked relieved. "We're assuming for now that the Food Brigade is involved, so this becomes a citywide investigation."

He paused for a moment. "Correction. Statewide. Last we know, they were in Northern California. Anyway, the case was turned over to downtown, to Robbery-Homicide. If the freeway is moving, their team should be here in a few minutes."

The bulldog showed yellow teeth in what passed for a smile.

"I heard that one of the detectives is an old friend of yours, Ms. Deean. You seem to get involved in more murders than any other law-abiding citizen in our fine city."

NINE

IMPOSSIBLE TO IGNORE the moustache. It was silky, black and droopy in the style of Charlie Chan, pudgy crime-fighting icon of 1930s movies. Only, Detective Paul Wang was tall for an ethnic Chinese, as slim and broad-shouldered as when he'd played quarterback for UCLA.

My heart lifted as he walked toward me. Not only do we share an affinity for crab wontons, but he's been my rock and my rescuer since we met during a murder investigation in wicked old Hollywood.

"Hi, Cat," he said. "Still stumbling over bodies?"

His tone was light, but his eyes showed sympathy.

"Oh, Paul! I'm so glad you're here. It's been horrible!"

He was calm and deliberate, pulling me from the blood-soaked plain where I'd been wandering.

"Judy and I were checking out a donut shop in mid-Wilshire when we got the call.

"We'd had a tip about a Food Brigade break-in, but it turned out to be two kids who just wanted to liberate some jelly donuts. We caught them, sticky fingers and all, running out the back door."

Judy. I'd hardly noticed his partner. Early thirties, I guessed. Short and trim in a crisp white shirt and knife-creased tan pants. Latina. Curly, light brown hair ending above her collar. Clear hazel eyes, a full mouth carefully toned down with pale coral lipstick. No wedding ring. If Paul was a slightly exotic species of cop, she was regulation LAPD.

"I should introduce my new partner. This is Judy Sanchez.

Judy, meet Cat Deean, my caterer friend. Be nice and she might even treat you to lunch."

We murmured our hellos. She appraised me with a cool though kindly glance that took in my pale lime pantsuit, now crumpled and grimy at the knees from kneeling near the bodies, and my unruly hair. No mascara is unconditionally waterproof; surely mine had run after a brief burst of tears. I suspected I looked like a drunk raccoon.

She said reassuringly, "Sure, lunch would be nice. Paul raves about the food at Dellacasa's."

I could guess they were already a smooth team. Judy pulled out a notebook as Paul asked, "Can we talk, Cat? I need your input while everything's fresh."

"Ask questions. I don't know where to start."

Paul cleared a space at a nearby table and we sat. He took me through the shooting while his partner made notes, then paused to find me a bottle of fizzy mineral water. My throat was as parched as if I'd been climbing over dunes in Death Valley.

Rosie, Danny and Julia were still waiting. I asked the detectives to see them soon; Julia really needed a doctor.

"Your turn," said Paul. With a nod, Judy Sanchez took her notebook over to our stunned little group.

"So tell me, Cat, is this a killing spree by the Food Brigade? Till now, they've only gone after property, not people."

With a tinge of guilt, I buried my memory of Julia's outburst against her father. No sense in taking it as truth. Time enough to tell Paul after I'd checked with Nick, who knew the Sicilian temperament much better than I did.

Sure, I'd read *The Godfather*, seen the movies. Gasped at the horse's head left between the sheets in a horrific act of revenge. Stayed home most Sunday nights with a veggie pizza and low-fat frozen yogurt to hang out with Tony Soprano. But that was fiction, right? Not the kind of thing that a charming friend of Nick would do merely to keep his child from marrying a slick (in his eyes), sexy American.

He hadn't had time to check the growing file, so I gave Paul a summary of my messages from the Brigade.

"We believe they're a small group," he told me. "Just a handful of loonies. Last I heard, our alerts to retail food places were working. They've become more cautious. That's probably why they moved their last attack up north."

"And came back to L.A. in time to shoot Flavio?"

Paul shrugged. "An hour by plane, just five hours if they drove. Think of the big publicity for their cause if they managed to kill him."

I had to agree. "It's possible they've been stalking me. I know from one of the phone calls that they've been to Dellacasa's. We were up here earlier this week. They could have followed us."

Sometimes my thoughts roam in strange ways. I could imagine members of the Brigade, faceless as yet, munching on celery stalks and raw carrots as they snaked through the low hills, somehow avoiding the security patrol.

As if reading my mind, Paul said, "We're checking out the local security. How did the Brigade get past the gated entrance? Did they drive? Find a way in on foot? We still have to interview your host, Carlos, see if he noticed any strangers around lately.

"Anything you can add? If not, you're free to leave now. Just give me your cell phone number so I can keep in touch. Your friends can go once Judy's taken statements."

He smoothed his black hair where the breeze had ruffled it.

"I'd been meaning to call you. My uncle Lucas is part owner of a new dim sum place in Monterey Park. Great smoked eggs and tiny meatballs in chili oil. And real Chinese breakfast porridge. It's always crowded for brunch on weekends, but I have influence. My cousin Grace is usually at the door, so I can get us past the red rope in seconds. If I'm not on duty and you're free on a Saturday or Sunday morning, let's go."

Paul knows my devotion to dim sum. If anything could distract me on this ghastly day, it was the vision of a turntable with small plates of Chinese delicacies floating by.

I managed a weak smile.

"Are you trying to comfort me? Hard-boiled cop turned sensitive man? I don't know about sensitive men. They'll swear that they understand your pain, but they don't."

"Honest, Cat, I don't want to deal with your wounded psyche. It's just that you can order more dishes when there's someone to share them. Last time I ate alone, I didn't have room for turnip cakes after I finished off the baby ribs."

"*That* kind of pain I feel! Oh, Paul, it's such a mess with Flavio and these killings. Nick and I will have to help him. I don't know how badly he's hurt and what he'll want to do about his book tour. We may be the only people he knows in Los Angeles. But after all this is over, lead me to the shrimp toast."

Paul rose from his chair, looked around, then kissed me gently on the forehead.

"Be well, Cat. And be very, very careful. Ricci may not be the only target. We're putting an officer outside of his hospital room, and what else we should do is under discussion downtown."

I promised and made my way toward Rosie. She'd called Nick at UCLA Medical Center, learned that Flavio was in surgery for a couple of flesh wounds. I decided to head to the hospital in my own car. The others could come later in the catering van.

It was still a crime scene, so the cleanup after the aborted luncheon would have to wait. I gathered my crew and put them on standby. Felix could salvage the food that had never been served. He'd work it out with Carlos and deliver everything to a soup kitchen of their choice.

Let the needy appreciate Flavio's talents. Although my only meal had been a power shake around dawn, I wasn't hungry. Correction. As the day wore on, my craving grew for justice for the victims.

I've always been wary of the super righteous. Even if the Food Brigade meant to salvage America's waistline, what it had done was slaughter two unlucky bystanders. Its crusade was too rigid, too rejecting of our human frailties. Life can be so tragic; we need our small indulgences. At least, that's what I believe. But then, my job, which I love, is planning parties, celebrations, a few hours of pleasure at a reasonable cost per person.

TEN

NICK WAS IN THE WAITING ROOM, navy jacket off, best red silk tie loosened, troubled eyes staring at a battered copy of *National Geographic*. Loretta sat still as marble, an ancient goddess in a plastic chair—silver eyelids half-closed, ivory dress draped like sculpture over shapely legs, silver fingertips holding tight to the chair arms. When I was thinking better, I might recall which deity she resembled.

They seemed to be in different worlds. Did Loretta blame Nick and the other Americans for the bloodshed? Certainly, she hadn't turned to him for comfort. But then she'd already made it clear that Flavio reflected Italian culinary genius, while the height of our drive-through culture was the Happy Meal.

I hurried to my boss for answers. We exchanged information. I gave him a quick briefing on progress at the murder scene; he assured me that Flavio would be okay.

"Two bullets, but neither one hit a bone or an artery. He's in recovery now, then they'll keep him in a private room overnight."

"Just one night?"

"He has the constitution of a bull. And, before he went into surgery, he told me he's determined to finish his book tour. San Francisco on Saturday and Sunday, then back to L.A., New York and home."

"But without Sam—" I caught my breath.

Nick sighed heavily. "I've had time, waiting here, to make a plan. Flavio asked me to talk to his publishers in New York. They'll notify Sam's family on Cape Cod and help them arrange to send his body home."

All the practical details that a death ordains.

Nick continued, "The publisher is sending another PR man to finish what's left of the tour. But he can't be here until Monday. Meantime, Cat, I'm putting you in charge. You go to San Francisco with Flavio and his people."

Though I'd have to rearrange my life, he made sense. There was no one else in California, excepting Nick who had a restaurant to run, who knew them as well as I did.

"But what about security?"

"Well, the LAPD is posting an officer outside his room here. Your friend, Detective Wang, has already called. Assuming that the patient can talk later today, Wang will be here to interview him. I think the police will agree to keep an eye on Flavio until we can put the whole bunch of you on a plane early Saturday morning.

"I haven't asked Flavio's permission, but I've contacted a security firm in San Francisco. They'll have a guard meet the plane, take everyone to the hotel—you need to make a reservation, Cat—and he'll stay until you come back on Monday.

"I've already changed Flavio's and Loretta's plane tickets to first-class, for safety and his comfort, and made a round trip reservation for you. Sorry, but you, Julia and Danny are sitting in coach."

In spite of my concerns, I was amused. I'd noticed that the great chef, though attractive in many ways, squeezed lira and dollars as fervently as flattening garlic in a press. Private security guards! First-class plane tickets! I hoped his cookbook would sell millions of copies to cover the costs of his American tour. He indulged his daughter's expensive tastes, but Loretta seemed to be left with the shorter strand of spaghetti. Well, she did wear diamond-drop earrings, but they were awfully *small* diamonds.

Detective Wang, Nick added, would be at Dellacasa's tomorrow morning for follow-up interviews. No reason, then, for me to wait here for Rosie, Mario and Flavio's entourage. There was enough to do before I took on my new role as Cat's Escort Service, Guide and Grief Counselor. On duty, not quite 24/7.

In my lascivious heart, I hoped I could meet up with Nate, my reporter friend in San Francisco, even stay overnight at his apartment on Russian Hill. (If you stood on tiptoe on his balcony, you could see the Bay.) I doubted that Flavio would be recovered enough to do more than rest at his hotel. He had friends in the city, he'd once said; they would surely want to visit him, hear his terrifying story and exult in his narrow escape.

Leaving me free to enjoy Nate's cool mind and warm bed. It had been a while since I'd seen him, and my nights in L.A. had become as bland as boiled rice.

We lead such busy lives. Nate is an investigative reporter. He'd just won a journalism award for his series on gaps in our Golden State's mental health system.

Though August is my slow time, I was already deep in Christmas party planning. It took a supposed terrorist attack to get me away from jingle bells and holly and on a plane to what might be a tense, possibly dangerous adventure with the Italians. I deserved time out for, what the heck, cable cars that go halfway to the stars and all the other enticements of San Francisco.

Right now, I needed to get to my office and book Olivia to replace me on Saturday night. Then call a favorite client to tell him, with true regret, that I'd be missing his intimate party for the talented, famous, and connected. For tonight, I'd used up my tolerance for Italian food. I'd stop at Foo Chow Gardens and take out BBQ Pork Buns and their sweet and tangy Chinese Chicken Salad. I'd have to find time tomorrow for a manicure, pedicure and hair trim. It is sometimes exhausting to be a love object, but better than a late night alone in my hotel room yawning over a rerun of *Friends*.

Where was the Food Brigade in all of this? In San Francisco to take another shot at Flavio? Back in L.A. to terrorize my friends and the patrons at Dellacasa's? Could they be stalking me and, if so, would I put Nate in danger? Or, now that they'd tried and failed to stop the chef who exalted car-bohydrates, perhaps they'd retreat and go back to blowing up donut holes.

ELEVEN

THE SHOOTINGS were already on TV breaking news. So it was no surprise that I had messages on my voice mail. The first call was from Aunt Sadie.

"Are you all right? I'm so worried. Call me immediately!"

I zipped to the second message. It had all the tasteful sympathy of a Hallmark card. The cracked, badly disguised voice I'd heard before said, "We're so sorry for your loss. But sometimes truth comes in through the back door." A click, then the dial tone.

I wanted to throw the phone at the wall. What nerve, such a mastery of clichés! Yet, thinking about it, the voice wasn't gleeful. It was almost sad. Well, it's a known fact that depression often follows an extreme high. What did the Brigade do to get out of the black hole? Sleep it off? Hit the treadmill? I doubt if they'd dug into half gallons of ice cream like your standard neurotics.

But catching the Brigade was a police matter. My job was shepherding my flock through a weekend of what was sure to be public curiosity mixed with private sorrow.

I returned Sadie's call, told her the bare details of the deadly luncheon, mentioned my upcoming trip to San Francisco and promised to call if I felt upset or threatened. She and her book group had already studied *Pasta and Vino* and planned to support Flavio's recovery by following his diet. Bless Sadie! I hoped her enthusiasm was a good omen. I wondered how San Francisco would welcome the stricken chef. Would fans line up to meet him, knowing he might still be a target for murder? I'd be exposed, too, standing at Flavio's side. Where was Sam Spade when I needed him? Well, it might be a crummy setup, but I'd do my part to make book-stores safer, sweetheart.

Play the last message, from a supplier. Our order of vir-gin olive oil, he apologized, was delayed by a dockworkers' strike in Naples. A decent everyday crisis.

I called Nate Greene on his cell phone, got him waiting to board a plane in Sacramento. He'd been covering committee meetings at the state capitol, and hadn't heard my news.

"Ohmygod! You could have been killed."

"Actually, no. I was under a table looking for stuff when the shooting started."

His sigh of relief, his tentative laugh.

"I'd rather picture you as brave and dodging bullets like Catwoman. I know you. You're not the victim type."

What a rush that he saw me as a gravity-defying superher-oine. I'd come a long way since our undergraduate days at UCLA when I was a frail Christina Rossetti and he was Hemingway swaggering through the Spanish Civil War. No wonder it took us years to reconnect.

But he was wrong. It was only this morning that I'd heard the screams, seen the bodies, and I still had the shakes. My fingers had been as slippery as flippers when I punched in numbers on the phone. I wanted to be held close for comfort.

Nate didn't disappoint. "They're calling my flight. Spend Saturday night with me. We'll have early dinner at a Thai place that has the best green curry, and rice whiskey like grandpa used to make. A few bottles and you'll forget how to even *spell* pasta! Call when you get to your hotel." Pause. "I've been missing you, Cat. Gotta run now."

Well, the weekend was looking better. I had one other call to make. An apology to Maurice Leblanc for not overseeing his party in person on Saturday night. It was to be a light sup-per for twenty theater lovers who might put up the money to

back Maurice's new musical. The playwright and the com-
poser would be there to run through the score.

He'd already okayed the menu. First, a classic cheese fon-
due with Gruyère and kirsch. Very retro. The host's well-
stocked bar. Lobster salads and warm cornbread, served with
champagne. Mango-strawberry granita, lemon bars and chocolate truffles.

Maurice was understanding about my absence.

"What a tragedy! Of course you'll have to stay with Mr.
Ricci for now. But I'm sorry you'll miss the run-through. It's
going to be a sensational show. Listen to this, it's 'The Wolf's
Lament.'"

He sang a few melodic bars, ending with a plaintive howl.

"You know Sondheim's *Into the Woods*? Well, this takes
Red Riding Hood a step further. We tell it from the *wolf's*
viewpoint."

"The wolf has an alibi?" I asked.

"Even better!" said Maurice triumphantly. "He didn't kill
grandma, and he proves it with modern forensic evidence. A
tale updated for the twenty-first century."

He laughed gleefully. "Would you believe—the woodman
is the perp!"

Maurice has a terrific record of Broadway hits. If anyone
could make an audience reconsider the nature of the beast, he
could. I expressed my real regrets and my client promised me
front row seats if my fabulous supper helped convince his
backers.

I hung up the phone thoughtfully. So the big bad wolf
didn't do it after all. He'd been condemned by his lousy reputation. The real killer was lurking deeper in the forest. Well,
every culture finds meaning in its twice-told tales. Was there
a lesson here? Probably not. What did this funny revisionist
fairy tale have to do with me?

TWELVE

DETECTIVE WANG delicately spooned up and sipped the foam on his cappuccino.

"Our search team found the rifle almost immediately. It was thrown into the grass just below the mansion. No attempt to hide it."

"So the sniper shot from the hillside," said Nick. Mid-morning on Friday, we were all seated around one of Della-casa's red banquettes.

"No. He—or she—stood on the lower terrace and aimed up. We found the casings scattered over the floor."

"A Winchester folding hunting rifle, easy to carry," said Detective Sanchez, putting down her coffee cup and holding up her nicely manicured index finger in a firing position. "But even with a telescopic sight, not as accurate as you might think. It takes pretty good shooting to hit three people at that distance."

"Even with a scope," echoed Paul. "That rifle has a kick. Plus, with a strong breeze and moving targets, the marksman has to make a few calculations to get it right."

"What I'm hearing," said Nick, who had done his service in Vietnam, "is that the shooter was no amateur."

The two detectives nodded.

"Someone with military—or police—training."

"Or an experienced hunter."

"Could you read the serial number?" asked Nick.

"Perps don't file down the numbers nowadays," said Paul. "A crime lab can use acid to bring up the ID again. No, the weapon we found had the numbers *drilled* out. We're dealing with a firearms expert. Or, he bought the altered gun on the black market. And, of course, there are no fingerprints on the rifle or the casings."

Rosie, Mario and I were the civilians at the table. I ventured a question.

"But does having the weapon help you narrow the list of suspects?"

Paul frowned and helped himself to an almond biscotti before he answered.

"We don't *have* a list. What we're doing, though, is checking into some local paramilitary groups. See if there's been any unusual action lately. Some of those cadres have pretty wild ideas, although I don't know any that care more about food than preparing for Armageddon."

We had little more to tell. None of us had looked over the balustrade, seen anyone on the terrace below. It was on the same level as the auxiliary parking lot for staff and deliveries, but the entrance forked off: one side accessed the terrace, the other led to the kitchen. No one busy preparing the meal had seen any strangers, the detectives told us.

"It's possible," said Judy Sanchez, "that the killer—or killers, there might have been two of them, probably not more— hiked up the hill, staying out of sight of the security patrols, and climbed onto the terrace."

She hesitated, looked around at the four of us who'd arranged the luncheon.

"Here's something we're not telling the press. About a redwood table. We found a note on it, pinned with a barbecue fork."

Paul spoke grimly, "It says, 'PASTA LOVERS! CHANGE YOUR WAYS OR DIE! THE FOOD BRIGADE.' If the Brigade wants publicity, they won't get it from us."

"Doesn't sound as if they'll give up easily," I noted with a sigh. "Flavio's signings could be as entertaining as a singalong on the *Titanic*."

THE LINE OUTSIDE THE MALL BOOKSTORE stretched past Teen Trinkets, Nell's Bras & Lingerie and Buckets O' Popcorn. I needn't have worried about wimpy fans in the city that was home to *Dirty Harry*. A crowd of intrepid buyers, having paid for their copies of the cookbook inside the store, joined the line behind the red rope, inching forward two by two until they reached Flavio's table against the back wall.

Willie, our private security guard, hovered to the right of the smiling chef, while I flanked him on the other side, moving each buyer along once Flavio had scrawled his bold signature. He was doing well, all things considered. The store had scheduled a two-hour signing and though he showed signs of fatigue after an hour, he was as happy as Columbus on the first Caribbean cruise.

With the bookstore crowded, Loretta, Julia and Danny had been banished to the mall's food court. Julia was still in the severe black dress, pumps and sheer black panty hose she'd worn on the plane earlier in the morning. She'd spent the day before shopping on Rodeo Drive, and I suppose that's where she'd found the antique mourning brooch she'd pinned to one shoulder. It was a gleaming hunk of onyx surrounded by gold and seed pearls, like a woeful flower that opened only at midnight. She'd pulled back her hair and tied it with a black scarf; her full lips were bare and a double coating of mascara couldn't disguise eyes rimmed with red.

Danny bustled around, bringing tall plastic glasses of lemonade to the women. Julia had no appetite and Loretta frowned at the food court offerings of corn dogs, pizza and Szechuan beef bowl. I'd visited during my brief break and found Danny absorbed in an enchilada combo plate. In spite of the hubbub in the mall, the three were living in a silent movie with no tinkling piano for relief. Julia stared at the pattern on the tiled floor; Loretta addressed postcards that showed a glittering night view of the Golden Gate Bridge.

It was a repeat of the morning flight and the taxi ride to the hotel. Flavio and Loretta sat in first class; she was as starchy as Nurse Nightingale in the Crimea, carrying a small duffel packed with bandages and tape to change the dressings on his wounds. I sat across the aisle from Danny and Julia, relieved that I could just drink bad coffee and not make conversation.

The sous-chef seemed to shrink into his clothes, his odd droopy eyelids blinking as white clouds bounced light back through the windows. He couldn't get Julia's attention although he tried—asking whether she wanted juice or coffee, a pillow, the shade lowered. She favored him with a small distracted smile, rejection of his offers, a relapse into apathy. I felt sorry for both of them.

Willie met our group at the gate. The security guard was a tall, burly, no-nonsense man in a charcoal business suit. He retrieved our small mountain of luggage, settled us in a black SUV big enough to hide a SWAT team and delivered us to our hotel. After check-in, he posted himself outside of the chef's suite until it was time to leave for the afternoon book signing.

Although I'd taken a room, Willie's presence gave me courage to think of absenting myself from the hotel on Saturday night. I called Nate; we'd arrived so early, he was still home and in bed. I resisted his invitation to join him immediately.

"What time can you break free of mission impossible?"

"The signing's over about five o'clock. But Loretta's asked Willie to drive us around for a short sightseeing tour of San Francisco."

"You want to see Fisherman's Wharf?" He was incredulous.

"No, not if you're available."

"Well, I'll be at a conference on renewable energy—this one could get a front page slot. I want to poke around during cocktails, but I'll leave when the delegates break for dinner, around seven. How about I pick you up at your hotel?"

I had my own plan. It's what I do when I'm stressed out.

"There's a multiplex at the mall. It doesn't matter too much what movie is playing. I just want to sit in the dark and gobble popcorn."

"Fine! Get a small popcorn. Save your appetite." A lowdown chuckle.

We arranged a time and a meeting place. I packed a small tote with overnight necessities, stretched out for a nap, changed into my day-into-evening-or-whatever deep raspberry jacket over a paler slinky wrap dress. I'd be flitting from Flavio to Nate. What I didn't expect, in the hours between duty and desire, was the Brigade at my back, breathing down my neck.

THIRTEEN

THERE WAS A CRAZY VOICE whispering in my ear. From behind, a bony hand grasped my shoulder: it was Death keeping our appointment in San Francisco. I shuddered and spilled almost half of my popcorn. The theater was dark and only partly filled. No one would notice a quick stab with a knife, or a gun with a silencer.

"It's all right if it isn't buttered, you know."

My heart stopped racing. If we could chat about nutritional values, perhaps I wouldn't be shot in the midst of a Dashiell Hammett film festival. Veronica Lake was pouting her way through *The Glass Key*, and I'd hate to miss the end.

"Plain popcorn is all right?" I asked with bravado.

"It's the fat in the butter that makes it evil!" she hissed. Definitely a female voice.

"I'll admit, I never thought about it that way."

The breath touching the back of my neck faded. There was a pause, then the voice said reproachfully, "You're patronizing me. You shouldn't. I know what you're doing, I'm not stupid."

I was genuinely contrite. Even though there was no cold steel prodding my back, I wasn't stupid, either. What if I turned around and talked it over face-to-face?

"Don't turn! I don't want you to see me. Suppose I was careless and got caught, and there was a lineup. You'd be able to identify me, and thousands of fat Americans would suffer."

Reasoning with her wouldn't work. I changed the subject.

"You must have been following me all day. Why am I so important to you?"

"I wanted to inform you that I—that is, the Brigade—didn't do it. We totally despise what Mr. Ricci stands for, but murder isn't part of our manifesto. We respect all human life."

Warned not to look back, I focused on the screen. Alan Ladd gave Veronica a look as cold as a loser on a morgue slab. She wiggled her hips, but it didn't shake him up.

I said, over my shoulder, "Then you should contact the police and clear yourself."

"Are you kidding? At the very least, they'd send us up for property damage. As if rescuing humanity from its baser instincts was a crime!"

Foolish of me to upset her, but I wanted to argue. "What's so terribly base about eating a donut? Or ravioli?"

"There have been three major diseases that destroyed entire peoples. The Black Plague, carried by rats. Malaria, from mosquito-infested swamps. And overeating, promoted by our major corporations through fast-food chains, supersize portions, and selling enough fatty, sugary foods to kill a pond full of freshwater fish. I know, I've done it."

"You killed off a bunch of fish by feeding them donuts?"

Defensively. "In the interests of research. I regretted my actions immediately. I thought the fish would just get a little sick, but they sank to the bottom of the pond in hours. I'd used jelly donuts and crème-filled long johns. They're the worst."

Useless to try to talk her out of her quest. If I were to accept that she wasn't the sniper, I needed more information.

"I want to believe you, but you'll have to help me. Where were you last Thursday around noon? You know, when the shootings started."

"Here, in San Francisco. The cops in L.A. were putting on too much heat. They actually had patrols near donut shops!" She snorted, a honking *hneh! hneh!* sound. "Of course, there are so many donut shops and bakeries in L.A. County, you'd have to call out the National Guard to cover them all. *Hneh! hneh!*"

"But you singled out Dellacasa's, right? You were actually in our restaurant. You left messages."

"You were giving that fraud, Mr. Ricci, too much publicity. He says his diet helps people lose weight. Well, red wine comes from sun-blessed vines. But all that spaghetti? I don't think so! We had to counterattack."

"So, natural foods are cool with the Brigade." Keep up the dialogue, Cat. Hopefully, learn something. "By the way, you know my name. What's yours?"

"*Hneh! Hneh!* That's good! I'll tell you that I have an advanced degree in philosophy. So don't try to mess with my head. I know a trick question when I hear it."

"I'd really like to call you *something*, instead of 'Hey, you!' Give me a break."

Another snort, a little cough. "Okay, call me Artemis. Like the Greek goddess of hunting. That's what I—uh, we—do. Hunt the sellers of disgusting ugly fattening foods."

"Artemis, thank you for giving me your name. Do you take care of your health? You sound as if you have a cold."

"Haven't bothered to see a doctor in years," she said proudly. "Doctors want you to eat too much. I drink carrot juice and herbal teas with lots of antioxidants. They're filling, so I don't need much food. My cold's almost gone. It was freezing in the back alley behind that Chinese restaurant in Berkeley. I waited for hours until it closed. You probably read about our success in the newspapers. It was death to dumplings that night!"

"So you know Berkeley pretty well," I ventured. "At least, where to eat. Lots of students from the university hang out there." It was an open-ended question.

Snort! "Hah, hah, you won't catch me with that one."

Alan and Veronica were smooching. The movie might be ending soon. She said, with feeling, "I'd better take off now. I just wanted to give you the truth about the Brigade. We did *not* shoot or murder anyone. Please tell the L.A. cops to call off the dogs. We're getting really pissed."

"Okay, Artemis, thanks for telling me. Keep in touch."

"Maybe, maybe not. By the way, I like you, Cat Deean, but you could stand to lose ten pounds. Skip the pasta, try peppermint tea."

I could feel the bony fingers as she patted me on the shoulder. Then she was gone up the aisle. So fast, I didn't see her when I turned around.

Lose ten pounds, indeed! Not much left of my popcorn, but I scooped up a handful with buttery fingers as *THE END* appeared on the screen and the lights came on.

I SAT IN THE LOBBY and dug into my tote for my cell phone. Detective Wang had been catching up on paperwork at Parker Center, and he'd just returned home. He whooped like roundup time on the prairie at my news about Artemis.

"Did you get a look at her? Could you identify her? Check out some mug shots? I've been pulling pictures of a few domestic terrorist suspects and militia groupies."

"Sorry, I was too scared to turn around. She's really one waffle short of a breakfast special. I never knew whether or not she had a weapon. I might be able to identify her voice."

"You did pick up some good information, though. San Francisco's already figured that she's familiar with Berkeley. The restaurant the Brigade hit wasn't in any tourist magazine. It's popular with locals and kids from the university. What she told you about her advanced degree in philosophy could tie her to UC. It's a lead."

"I keep thinking, Paul, about her bony fingers. It was like a skeleton's hand touching my shoulder. And her rejection of doctors. It figures, with the Brigade's proclamations, that she could be anorexic. There must be some campus clinics for the students, or what about doctors in Berkeley? You could check them out."

"I'm going to call the detectives up north right now. They could want to talk to you tonight or tomorrow. I know what hotel you're at, but give me Flavio's schedule for Sunday. How did the signing go today?"

I told Paul that it was such a triumph that we could expect a bigger response tomorrow in Sausalito. A TV crew had shown up to film the crowd, so we might even be on the local news tonight.

"I worry that Artemis has been stalking you," he said. "I'm going to suggest to San Francisco that they have some officers at the signing. Meantime, I hope you'll be careful at your hotel tonight. Order room service if you're not having dinner with Flavio and his people."

"Paul, I'm beginning to think that Artemis may not be our killer. I don't know, but she sounded plausible. Besides, I'm meeting an old school friend for dinner. Uh, I may not get back to the hotel tonight, but here's where I'll be staying." I offered Nate's home number, telling myself to answer his phone if anyone rang.

He hesitated. "Well, stay safe. Don't make any headlines." End of call.

FOURTEEN

OUR FORKS HAD JUST MET in a tangle of *Mee Krob* crispy, spicy noodles when Nate's cell phone sounded. He'd set up calls to be forwarded from his home phone—the *Post-Ledger* news desk never slept. Shrugging apologetically, he answered.

"This is Nate. Who did you want? She's right here. Can I tell her who's calling?" He lifted an inquiring eyebrow behind tortoiseshell-rimmed glasses. "It's the police."

"Not to worry. I gave them your number." He handed me the phone, picked up the amber bottle of Mekong whiskey and poured refills for both of us.

"Yes, this is Cat Deean."

"Inspector da Silva here. San Francisco detectives. Paul Wang gave me your name, Ms. Deean. Now that you know mine, please contact us directly."

He was too stern for my taste. I made a face, raised my glass and sipped the light, rum-like whiskey.

"Sure. What can I do for you, Inspector? We're at a restaurant, having dinner."

"Sorry to interrupt," he said briskly, "but I need to hear, firsthand, about your encounter with the Brigade. This is, you know, a murder investigation."

I'd been drifting into such a mellow mood—food, drink, Nate—I could easily have blocked out the memory of Artemis and her nonfat fantasies, the hand on my cringing shoulder. But the detective was right—this was about murder.

I gave the details to da Silva while Nate listened, transfixed. Later, I had to laugh, realizing that I'd been sitting straighter, talking tougher, weaving a story like a seductive broad out of a Hammett film. Veronica Lake. Mary Astor. Cat Deean. For a few minutes, I hadn't been *at* the film festival, I'd been *in* it. Dealing with the real fear that caught me in its grip when Artemis clutched my shoulder.

"We have an idea, Ms. Deean. Remember where you sat during the movie?"

"About halfway down on the left side. In an aisle seat."

"Aisle seat, good! That makes it easier. If she grabbed you with one hand, she may have held on to your seat back with the other. We want to dust for fingerprints. We'd like you to meet us at the theater and point out, as close as you can, where you were sitting."

"Now, right now?" I was aghast.

The inspector was reassuring. "No, the film festival is still going on. *The Thin Man* tonight. We don't have to empty the house. I don't expect too many people are going to be hanging on to the seat in front of them. Tomorrow morning will do."

Abruptly, he asked, "Artemis wasn't wearing gloves, was she?"

I thought about the hard grasp with the skeleton-thin fingers. "I doubt it. She's smart, Inspector da Silva, but I suspect she thinks she's invincible."

"Most of the kooky ones do. Most are harmless, this one isn't. How about eight in the morning? I'll have an officer meet you at the mall entrance."

"Eight o'clock," I repeated for Nate's benefit. He shuddered, then nodded okay.

"You can bring along your boyfriend, if he insists. He may have a story here, as long as he spells my name right. That's da Silva with a small *d* and a capital *s*, like the Portuguese pirate. Nate and I have met before. Say hello for me."

Now both the LAPD and the SFPD knew where I was spending the night. In spite of my new persona as a brazen temptress, I blushed.

I woke up around 3:00 a.m. in Nate's arms and softly began to cry. Good sex will do that, but this was more than satisfaction. It was a letting-go of all the horrors of—was it only three days since the shooting spree?

Nate stirred and wrapped his arms more closely around me.

"What? What's the matter? Why're you crying?" He sat up, wavy hair mussed, brown eyes heavy with sleep.

"S'nothing," I blubbered. "I feel so sorry for Flavio and Sam and that poor lady in the Chanel suit."

"Delayed shock," he said wisely. And added, "Too bad. When you raked your nails down my back a couple of hours ago, I thought maybe we had something going."

He fumbled for a Kleenex on the nightstand and tenderly wiped my eyes.

"I've been thinking about us."

I sniffled. "It was really a lovely evening. I enjoyed the green curry very much."

"Good God, Cat! I know you're still recovering from your divorce from that *sensible* guy, but maybe you're ready to move on. Sure, I know this is a lousy time to mention it, but—oh, hell, forget I said anything tonight. There'll be other times."

"I'm not changing the subject," I said, "but maybe the police should be looking a little further. I can't believe I'm saying it, but I *liked* Artemis."

Nate nibbled at my ear. "You need sleep. Uh, unless you have another idea."

"It's 3 a.m. We have a few hours until we have to get out of bed. Who knows when I'll get to San Francisco again?"

I held him fiercely.

FIFTEEN

EARLY ON SUNDAY MORNING, the mall was as desolate as a ballroom after the dancing stops. The loudest sounds were the whirl of floor polishers and the clatter of our feet as we walked to the first-level cinema.

Inspector da Silva waited impatiently. He was powerfully built and swarthy. Add a gold earring and a cutlass in his strong white teeth, and he'd be the very model of an ancestral Portuguese pirate. Today, he wore a Sunday-best dark suit, as if he'd detoured on the way to taking the family to church.

"This won't take long," he said, pointing to the small, tidy man in gray sweats who waited with him. "George here thinks he can bring up fingerprints if you can show him where you sat."

"I'll try."

The detective's sharp eyes took in the slightly creased raspberry jacket and clingy dress I'd had to wear again this morning. I'd taken along a change of underwear in my tote, but hadn't anticipated meeting San Francisco's finest before returning to the Fairmont for today's restrained blue pantsuit. Well, I never did earn my Girl Scout badge in disaster preparedness.

Nate and I had had a quick breakfast of croissants and coffee in his apartment, while I called the hotel for messages. Willie had left word that he'd be taking us by SUV and ferry to Sausalito. We were to meet in the lobby at noon.

Time enough for a kiss and a farewell to Nate, who'd be driving to Sacramento later today. *Arrivederci,* I'd say, and add silently, *Oh, love, I'll miss you!*

IT DIDN'T TAKE LONG to find the aisle seat where I'd had my encounter with Artemis. I'd noticed yesterday that the padded plastic armrest had been slightly ripped. To be absolutely sure, George took out his brushes and lightly dusted the backs of the seats in the rows before and after, as well.

I watched, fascinated, as latents appeared clearly on my seat's molded wood frame. With a triumphant smile for da Silva, George snapped photos of the prints, then pulled them up with tape for transfer to a card.

"Easy," said the tech. "No other recent prints on that seat back. I'll go to the lab now and start the search for a match."

"The Lord will look kindly at you, my son, for giving up your Sunday," said da Silva with a grin.

"All that and overtime, too," answered George. "It's okay. I hate to see this nut running around loose. Killing is bad enough. But she hit that donut shop on Geary. She blew up my favorite chocolate crullers. What a waste!"

It helped to have the crime lab tech remind me not to think too kindly of Artemis. People, as well as crullers, could be hurt when the Brigade went on its next rampage.

"Stay close to your cell phone," George told da Silva. "I'll call if I get lucky."

What struck me was their urgency. Three people had been shot; Artemis had to be identified and tracked down. If she was not the sniper—though the police considered her the number one suspect—then the real killer was out there, motive unknown. Flavio was still in danger this afternoon, and I could be another unlucky bystander.

As if reading my mind, da Silva said, "We're going to have a police presence in Sausalito. A couple of uniformed officers outside the bookstore and a plainclothes detective keeping an eye out for Artemis, or for any other action.

"Meantime, thank you for your help this morning. But I don't want you or your friends talking about it. Nate, I'm asking you to hold back for now. If we do get an ID, you'll get first crack at the story."

We agreed and left soon after. Nate drove me to the Fairmont. Yesterday, I'd told my group that I'd be staying overnight with my old school chum. Loretta's eyes had glittered, like a hawk discovering a titmouse, but I think they were all too absorbed with their own concerns to gossip much about an outsider.

That suited me just fine. Nate wove in through the traffic to stop at the hotel entrance, and we managed a hurried kiss before a limo driver honked at him to move on.

SIXTEEN

FLAVIO STOOD ON THE DECK of the ferry, so happy I thought he'd burst into song. It was a golden afternoon. The morning fog had lifted, and a stiff breeze had puffed the sails on a flotilla of small boats and sent them skimming over the blue waters of the bay.

The group was enthralled with my tale about Artemis, the meeting and the fingerprints—I thought I told it with a certain panache—and vowed to be on a lookout for a skinny woman with a hacking cough.

Earlier, the chef had thanked me and given the good news. Every copy of *Pasta and Vino* had sold at yesterday's signing. Saturday evening, he'd tracked down Harry, his editor at Peak Publishing, calling him away from a clambake in the Hamptons, to ask for extra cookbooks for today. Impossible on such short notice, but the editor, brushing the sand from his cell phone, had an epiphany.

The author who'd been shot for promoting spaghetti had overnight become a major celebrity.

The chef's story had moved from a Home & Entertainment feature to the front pages. Not to mention the mystery of the two murders, as yet unsolved. One of the victims, Sam Maguire, was mourned by his publishing colleagues and the industry. Harry raised his glass of white wine in a heartfelt toast to Sam and implored Flavio to extend his tour.

"We can get you on *Good Morning America* and *Oprah*. Maybe even *Larry King*. So please, decide now, Flavio. Sam's replacement will be in L.A. by late Monday afternoon, but New York can start publicity rolling immediately."

"What about a security guard?" asked Flavio cagily. "Will you pay?"

"Sure. No problem. We want you safe."

"Then I'll do it!" said Flavio triumphantly. "But just for another two weeks. Then I must return to Rome."

He'd told me all of this before we docked. The signing went even better than expected. It was in an airy, two-story enclave of shops, centered around a greenery-filled courtyard. Sausalito has always been an upscale artist's colony. A laid-back crowd was waiting patiently.

The celebrity chef made a gracious little speech sprinkled with *grazie*s and thank-yous, and then we settled in for the signings, Flavio at a table heaped with books, Willie and I again flanking him like sentries.

I'm not sure why, but I doubted that we were in danger this afternoon. The two uniforms were in evidence and I think I spotted the detective, but I'd lost the jittery feeling that had haunted me since the shootings. Had Artemis given up? I'd be relieved if she were caught, but something else had happened that I was still far from understanding.

Pasta and Vino sold out again, and the author accepted congratulations and a kiss from the bookstore owner, a serene woman in a caftan the colors of Monet's water lilies. We took the ferry back to San Francisco, and I pleaded weariness when Flavio invited me to join them and some hospitable friends for dinner. I settled for tea and a room service burger, a very good one with blue cheese and grilled onions. We'd return to L.A. early tomorrow, though I could think of a few excellent reasons to linger by the Bay.

SEVENTEEN

NICK WAS WAITING FOR US at LAX. He greeted the Italian contingent warmly and dropped the four of them at their hotel. Flavio, who'd ignored his healing wounds over the weekend, was feeling the strain and wanted to rest. The morning traffic had heated up, but Nick was in a curiously good mood as he took the slow-moving fast lane down Wilshire to Westwood and Dellacasa's. The restaurant would be quiet until it opened for the lunch crowd. I couldn't wait to tell him about my adventures, but he was bursting with his own surprise.

"Save your story," he said. "We have a guest for breakfast."

The airline served juice or coffee and teensy bags of peanuts on the short hop to L.A. I'd been dreaming of a double latte in my own mug, thick slices of toasted brioche with a chunk of creamy yellow artisan cheese from Sunday's farmers' market, perhaps a dollop of Rosie's homemade fig jam. Yes, it was good to be home.

I nearly forgot my food when I saw Paul Wang set down his cappuccino and hurry to meet me at the door. I believe he started to give me a hug, reconsidered, then pulled back and grasped my hand instead.

"Congratulations! You did it."

"I did? What?"

He held my hand and walked me back to the table, where Rosie and Mario stood smiling and joined Nick in applause.

"We have an identification," said Paul. "I got a call this morning from da Silva.

"They found a fingerprint match. We know who Artemis is!"

Practical Rosie said, "We're making your latte now. Sit down, you look hungry."

I would have fasted just to hear this news. Paul said, "She was in the San Francisco database. Her name is Amy St. Clair, and she was arrested at a Berkeley student rally fifteen years ago. Arrested, booked and fingerprinted!"

"What had she done? Was she violent?"

He shook his head. "No, the charges were trespassing and disturbing the peace. She was part of a small radical group picketing the globalization of fast-food restaurants. They had signs like, *Berlin: Say Nein To Big Macs! and Kentucky Fried Chicken: No Nuggets in Bangkok!*"

I was amused. "But all that sounds peaceful. Artemis exercising her right of free assembly. Why was she arrested?"

"It got touchy when they tried to move her off the university grounds. She hit a campus guard over the head with a picket sign. When a Berkeley cop came to his rescue, she bit him on the leg. A couple of her friends scattered, but the police got her. No arrests since. But she's a wild one, that Ms. Artemis."

Rosie had delivered my cup of steaming latte. I sipped appreciatively. "Did the police find a current address?"

"No, she's dropped from sight. They think she moves from one safe house to the next. Stays with other true believers for a few days and then moves on. But da Silva faxed me her picture. Fifteen years old, of course, but we'll get it on TV news tonight, and into the newspapers. That's what they're doing up north."

The brioche wasn't toasted and the cheese was Gruyère, but I dug in. I pride myself on soldiering on in the face of deprivation.

Paul showed me the old mug shot. I saw the vulnerable, still unformed face of a defiant adolescent. No makeup, no comb. Wild dark hair falling loose. Thin face, well-defined cheekbones. High-intensity eyes. Something mesmerizing about her.

"She may have slipped off the edge," I told Paul, "but she is definitely a leader."

"Until she talks her disciples into drinking poison."

"I don't think she has a death wish. And I have a hunch she's not our sniper."

The detective stared at me. "She drops in on you, sits in the dark and whispers some crap, and you believe her?"

"I think I do," I said stubbornly.

"Okay," said Paul, waving his arms in mock surrender, "but just bolt your doors and windows until we catch her. Trust me, she's not your chum. Now, tell me in full detail what you told da Silva."

I repeated my story for the benefit of the detective, Nick, Rosie and Mario. More subdued in the telling this time, in the stark light of Monday morning. When I finished, I felt as flat as a thirty-nine-cent burrito. Down from the high drama of the weekend.

Artemis was delusional, no doubt about it. Yet there was an honesty about her that made me question if she could take even one life, much less attempt to kill three.

I needed to know more about her, even as I tried to protect myself and my friends from a killer.

Paul was ready to leave which, for once, was a relief. I wanted to get to my office and call Nate. The *Post-Dispatch* would have clips of stories that dated back fifteen years. What had Amy St. Clair been doing before she emerged as the skinny crusader?

EIGHTEEN

NATE WAS IN SACRAMENTO, heading into another meeting on California's continuing energy crisis. I quickly gave him the news about Artemis.

"Great! I'll call da Silva during a break. Even if they release her mug shot to the media, I want to do a background story."

"Don't go too far with it yet. I'm not convinced she's the killer."

"You don't care that you're bucking the police up and down the state? That's my girl. But be cautious if she approaches you again. She may think bagels are aliens sending hidden messages to a mother ship."

"I'll tell her the signals really come through the cream cheese. Nate, you're in a hurry. When can you check the *Post-Ledger* files for background on Amy St. Clair?"

"Tomorrow morning, I'll be back in the newsroom. Meantime, remember we talked about Paris in January? Think about it."

"Oh, yes!" We exchanged a few mushy words and said our goodbyes.

I'd had an easy time with the Italian visitors, yet it was a relief to be free of responsibility. Later, I'd see the group for cocktails at their hotel and meet Sam Maguire's replacement. Meanwhile, it was a normal workday.

Mario and I had our usual Monday meeting. Coming up this week: Wednesday, a charity luncheon for the Patronesses of the Orphans of Ragusa, one of Nick's longtime

Sicilian connections. The Patronesses had ordered seafood salads, baskets of seasonal fruits, gelati and a pastry cart. They were sweet, chatty ladies and I enjoyed their annual fund-raiser.

On Thursday, we'd cater the fall kickoff brunch for Mind-hounds, Inc., our software client, at their headquarters. Brilliant nerdy types in short-sleeved shirts, Dockers or jeans, trading new visions of cyberspace as they plowed through conventional juices and fruits, ham and sausage, eggs, home fries, yogurt, muffins and croissants. No temperaments, and the company paid its bills within ten days.

Friday was the red carpet premiere of a summer blockbuster, cocktails and canapés before the show in the great lobby of an art deco movie house in Westwood. An event brimming over with glamour, already five revisions of the menu to accommodate the high-protein, low-carb, low-fat, live-for-today-to-hell-with-the-calories tidbits my staff would serve.

Old and new challenges, and nothing to fear but a guest who might collapse with allergies or a Hollywood chieftain too fond of scotch. My kind of week.

My clothes had wilted since I'd dressed for our flight at 5:00 a.m. in San Francisco. Mario drove me home to check the mail, ignore the sad offerings in my fridge, scrape off my old makeup and change to meet the *Pasta and Vino* people.

I'd pass the torch to the new publicist, Pete Drummond, wondering if he could succeed Sam in Julia's affections. Flavio didn't take kindly to American suitors, but perhaps the success of his book would mellow him.

SILVER-HAIRED PETE WORE a gold wedding band and the air of a man who'd made a career of conquering tigers. Julia, who'd been on a shopping trip, had given up total black for a bare-armed gray chiffon top and flowing pants, a transitional phase of mourning. She sulked in a brocaded armchair in Flavio's suite, accepting a glass of white wine from Danny, refusing a cube of pâté. Loretta lounged in her chair, watching them as if this were the hundredth rerun of a very boring movie.

Flavio was on the phone to Rome when I arrived, so I introduced myself to Pete Drummond. We sat at a small, gilt-edged white table at the far side of the room, away from the others. I told him what a shock Sam's death had been to all of us.

Pete glanced over at Julia and lowered his voice.

"She's still taking it pretty hard."

"I didn't realize," I whispered back, "it was that serious. She's so young."

"Well, Sam was crazy about her. He'd phoned me in New York to talk about the tour, but then he said something that floored me. He could see himself marrying Julia, he said, and moving to Rome to head public relations for Flavio's food empire.

"I was his mentor, and I told him to go slowly. He didn't know the girl or her family that well, and he had such a bright future at Peak Publishing."

"Did he listen?"

"He just laughed and said it was probably a fantasy. Sam's last words to me were," said Pete sadly, "'I'll be back in New York in a week. Let's drive up to the Cape and go sailing.'"

I wondered how much Julia had loved her handsome American. Enough to fight her father for him? I'd seen iron man Flavio up close this weekend and heard the story from Nick. The chef was so obstinate that the medics had had to pry the pen from his hand before they took him away on a stretcher.

NINETEEN

TRUE TO HIS WORD, Nate called me the next morning. I filled him in on Flavio's runaway sales, and on the tour that had been extended to La Jolla and San Diego.

"He's persistent," I said, and laughed. "He's finally coaxed the cost of a security guard from his publisher. "

Nate's news was even better than I'd expected. He'd accessed some old *Post-Ledger* stories and a more recent "Where Are They Now?" feature.

Amy St. Clair had graduated from UC Berkeley. Always a fanatic about fitness, she'd used a small trust fund to found a company selling Min-O-Phene ("M.O.P. Up Fat"), a weight-loss supplement. Unfortunately, M.O.P. proved lethal when taken with steroids. Two athletes had died.

St. Clair had felt so guilty that she'd suffered a breakdown and dropped out of sight. The reporter who traced her was granted an interview. After her company folded, St. Clair had spent much of her time, and the fortune she'd made, brooding about fat while cloistered in a succession of private sanitariums.

She told the writer that she intended to leave Meadowbrook Haven shortly, find an apartment and dedicate her life to public service.

"That's the last story we have on her," said Nate. "Two years ago."

"It's a new take on public service," I noted. " Preemptive strikes on donuts."

"We ran her picture in today's papers, with a police number to call. I'll check da Silva, see if they've had any response.

It's a brief story, doesn't mention the shootings. Just that she's wanted for questioning in several food shop bombings. Who knows? Maybe someone saw her performing an exorcism over an apple fritter."

"You're not taking this seriously," I protested. "I don't want her hurt."

"I don't want *you* hurt! You and your boss could be taking the heat while Flavio does a Kerouac along the California coast. With a private guard to protect him from the dolphins at Sea World."

"You don't think he's still in danger?"

"To be fair, I don't know what to think about him. I do know that Ms. St. Clair has approached you once and may try it again. The cops up here are making a real effort to find her. She might decide it's safer now in L.A."

"I'll talk to Nick," I promised. "After all, Dellacasa's was on the Brigade's hit list.

"Flavio will be back in L.A. at the end of the week. Even if Artemis isn't the sniper, the publicity over Flavio and his diet somehow led to the tragedy."

I sighed. "We'll all be safer when Flavio is back in Rome. But I'm puzzled. Yesterday you seemed fairly calm about Artemis."

"When I read the articles about St. Clair, or Artemis, whatever she calls herself, I realized she's been unstable for a long time. Probably harmless, but the donut bombings could be an escalation into real violence. Don't take chances, Cat."

There was another topic that would be easier to discuss with Nate, rather than alarm Nick or send the police into orange alert.

I told him about my talk with Pete Drummond. "He said that Sam Maguire was thinking about marrying Julia and moving to Rome. Danny bought off some of her other suitors—in other words, doing Flavio's dirty work. Could he be such a protective father that he'd try to hurt Sam?"

"You mean, hire a Mafia hit man who turned out to be a lousy shot and wounded daddy by mistake? I doubt it."

I mulled it over. "You're right. I'll keep the talk with Pete to myself—for now."

About as smart a move as entering a flourless chocolate cake in the Pillsbury Bake-Off.

I RETURNED AUNT SADIE'S WEEKEND CALL, told her just the good parts about my San Francisco visit—the fine weather and the success of the book signings.

"Everyone was so excited to meet Flavio. His cookbook is on its way to making the bestseller lists. Have you and your buddies tried the diet yet?"

"We did! Blanche, Myrtle and I got together in my kitchen on Saturday and cooked and ate bowls of pasta and shrimp, and eggplant in sauce and—I'm embarrassed to admit it—we finished off two bottles of red wine. I had to sleep late on Sunday."

"But did you lose weight?"

"Not yet. But we had a great time. And, just in case Mr. Ricci's regime doesn't work as quickly as he says it should—we've been on so many diets over the years, we've lost faith—ask me about our new project."

"Your literary diet?"

"Yes! You've probably been too busy to discover the Lewis Carroll theory."

"Lewis Carroll had a diet?"

"Oh, Cat! You *must* read it. Conrad Creem's *Beating Time With Alice In Wonderland* is filled with clues to staying young."

"But Carroll, that is, Rev. Dodgson, was a mathematician in his other life."

Sadie's voiced lowered to a conspiratorial hush. "You know, he liked young girls a little too much. He liked to take photos. Dodgson was just this side of being kinky."

"His hobby's well-known," I said. "What does it have to do with staying young?"

"Well, Creem's theory is that the mathematical riddles in Carroll's work lead to one conclusion. Carroll desperately wanted to keep his little girls youthful forever. And he found a formula that he hides in clues in *Hunting of the Snark, Through the Looking Glass* and some of the earlier poems. The final equation is in *Alice,* if we can solve it. Along the way, Creem quotes Carroll on food. The Mock Turtle's song about beautiful green soup, for one example."

"Oh, for heaven's sake, Auntie dear, I think you'd spend your time better with Flavio and another few bottles of red wine."

"Time. That's what it's all about," insisted my aunt. "I'm sure you haven't read the chapter on the Mad Tea Party since you were a child. Well, read it again. It will open your eyes. The Mad Hatter talks about time. *'Time won't stand beating,' says the Hatter. 'Now, if you only kept on good terms with him, he'd do almost anything you like.'* Creem has almost solved the time equation and will reveal it in his next book. Fascinating!"

I shook my head in wonder. Aunt Sadie is usually so practical, yet she worries about getting on in years. Her mind and spirit will always be youthful, but she doesn't see it that way. Nevertheless, I'm foolish to scoff. Even I want to believe that out there is a rabbit hole where I can plunk myself down into a new and fabulous self.

TWENTY

DELLACASA'S HAD CLOSED and I was alone, enjoying the after-hours calm. Once I'd opened the windows, my little office above the restaurant was cool for an August night. The only sound at first was the usual chatter from the street, UCLA on-campus students unwinding in the Village, those in extension classes stopping for a late snack before the commute home.

I was catching up on plans for the Liebling-Wongsawat wedding. He was Jewish, she was Thai. They'd met at UCLA, both sets of doubtful parents finally agreeing to celebrate ethnic diversity. A buffet dinner would satisfy the culinary tastes of both sets of guests.

Chopped liver and egg rolls. Brisket with sun-dried tomatoes, steamed salmon with herbs, green papaya salad and… Damn! This needed more work.

I rubbed my tired eyes and leaned back. In the stillness, I heard a faint sound. It was a creak from the staircase that led up to my office. That second stair always announced visitors. I sat up, ice cubes attacking my spine, instantly regretting that I'd never applied for that gun license. What could I use for a weapon? I grabbed at the brass paper knife with the fleur-de-lis handle and leaped up.

She was already standing in the doorway, the face more drawn than in her fifteen-year-old mug shot, hair still with the Medusa-like wildness, wearing a crumpled camouflage jumpsuit. A weary militant on the run.

"Put down that paper knife, please," she croaked. "You look silly."

I obeyed, relieved that the inevitable had happened, and said, "I'm not surprised that you're here, but how did you get in?"

"Your boss doesn't know much about security," she chided. "There's a good lock on the back entrance to the restaurant, and probably a security system, but he hasn't protected the back of your catering shop. It was as easy as slicing butter to force that lock, and then I came through the connecting door into Dellacasa's."

She was right. Nick had updated the cooking equipment when he bought the snack stand next door, but hadn't thought too much about preventing break-ins.

We'd never even been hit by vandals, much less domestic terrorists. I wondered if Artemis intended to blow up the cannoli in the unlocked fridge. I thought of ricotta and candied fruit flying all over our kitchen. What a mess it would be!

The silence stretched as I considered my options: try to talk her out of her next descent into anarchy, or rush her and hope that the sweaty work on my abs would pay off. Artemis spoke first. "Let's sit down. I just came here to talk to you. Obviously, I couldn't enter through the front door."

She sat in my client chair, and I could see the gaunt features, the wrists and hands bony enough to hire out on Halloween. The eyes still burned, but there were dark circles beneath them. The olive-and-brown camouflage suit swallowed up her tiny body.

She saw me appraising her and said proudly, "In spite of all those custards and milkshakes at Meadowbrook, I never gained too much weight. It was easier to stay trim once I'd checked out of there."

"Well, I'm glad," I said gently, because she seemed ill, "to finally meet you face-to-face. But you must have been following me. You knew I was working late."

"No problem. I got back to L.A. late yesterday. It was easy to follow you from Dellacasa's first thing this morning. You were feeding all those faces at that software company. So much food, so many carbs and fats! I had to restrain myself."

She saw me tense up. Leaning forward she said earnestly, "Don't worry. The Brigade never does any big, bad thing when there are people around. That's why I hung out in Westwood after you came back to your office. So I could talk to you again. I didn't go too far, and I planned to follow you home, but you worked late. So I broke in. I can't hide much longer. The cops are hounding me."

So she doesn't know where I live. A relief! My turn.

"Where are you staying?"

"It doesn't matter. One place or another, one night at a time. Ever since the shootings, even comrades who believe in our cause worry about hiding me."

She sighed in what I can only call pique. "So few believers burn with a pure flame these days. Their souls have become flabby."

The sounds from the street were dying down. Even the fast-food places were closing. Subdued as she seemed, I didn't want to be alone with her in the deserted town.

"How can I help you, Artemis?"

Her thin shoulders slumped forward. She ran a hand through the snarled hair.

"I'm so tired. I want to surrender. Just don't let the cops kill me. They'll listen to you. Tell them the Brigade never hurt *anyone!* Besides, they can't blame the shootings on me. I have an airtight alibi. Witnesses. The whole ball of low-fat tofu!"

I heard it then. The creak on the second stair. Artemis was so caught up in her appeal to me, she never noticed. What the hell? Had she left a door open and let in a burglar?

Whoever had entered was creeping up the stairs as quietly as a cat with a bird on its agenda. I had my paper knife. Should I alert Artemis? I still didn't know if she had a weapon. This could turn bloody.

I went weak in the knees when I heard the familiar voice.

"Don't move!" snarled Detective Paul Wang. He burst into the room, Detective Sanchez at his heels. They both had pistols out, pointed at Amy St. Clair. It was a scene I'd watched many times on *Law & Order,* and I could have applauded.

Artemis stood and, to their amazement, stuck out her skinny arms.

"Arrest me! Don't hurt me! Put on the cuffs. I'll go quietly."

"I'll do it," said Judy Sanchez. Before Artemis could change her mind, the detective pulled out handcuffs and snapped them on the outstretched wrists. Paul lowered his gun and stared at me, bewildered.

"Cat, are you all right? What's going on?"

I said protectively, "Ms. St. Clair came to see me. She was volunteering to surrender when you came in. How did you know she was here?"

He said, "We've been on surveillance, parked down the street all evening. The light was on in your windows. But it was getting so late, we checked to see if your car was still parked in back. And we found the broken lock."

"Why didn't you tell me you were watching Dellacasa's?" I couldn't resist raising an eyebrow and reciting the child's mantra. "The policeman is my friend."

Paul gave me an aw-shucks smile.

"Didn't want to alarm you. Downtown just decided it was good strategy, in case Ms. St. Clair came back to L.A."

I thought huffily that they may have feared I'd try to hide her, be out of my depth and end up dead. How irritating that they didn't trust my judgment.

Artemis spoke up. "I didn't do it! I can prove I never hurt anyone."

"She really has been very cooperative," I added.

"Well, she'll have a chance to convince us." He turned to her. "Are you ready to go, Ms. St. Clair?"

Detective Sanchez took the prisoner lightly by the elbow.

"I do have one thing to say right now," declared Artemis.

Looking kindly at Judy Sanchez as the detective led her away, she added, "You're an attractive woman, officer. But you could stand to lose five pounds."

TWENTY-ONE

"She didn't do it."

Detective Wang stifled a yawn and scowled into his cappuccino. It was midmorning Friday and Paul had stopped by to give us a report.

"Sorry, but I've only had four hours of sleep. Judy and I questioned St. Clair at the West L.A. precinct, and aside from giving my partner diet tips and lots of blah blah about the perils of fat, she was coherent as far as her alibi. We couldn't shake her."

"What's her story?" asked Nick.

"We checked it out first thing today. The week of the shootings, she was at a camp for urban warriors called Survival Tactics, in the San Jacinto Mountains near Idlewild. It's where the doomsday believers and messiahs like St. Clair spend their tax refunds to save America from the government, or from folks who don't think they way they do.

"The FBI keeps an eye on them, but most of what these guerillas do is wear camouflage, choose up teams, track each other through the woods and shoot blanks."

"And St. Clair was there the entire week?" I asked.

"Yep! The course was Methods of Urban Counterattack, and St. Clair was in the thick of it every day. The camp's owner confirmed her presence and said that thirty-two day warriors could vouch for her."

His coffee cup was empty. He shook it and said, "I haven't had breakfast. Any more of this? And maybe a roll?" I ordered another cappuccino from the bar and brought him some hard rolls, butter and a baby ball of fresh-milk mozzarella. It was still Brooklyn 1965 for breakfast at Dellacasa's.

"I'm glad she's cleared," I said.

"Well, not quite. She still faces charges on the bombings."

Nick growled, "If she's not the sniper, who is? Is Flavio still in danger? Are we?"

The detective broke a roll in half and carefully buttered the pieces.

"I came here first thing to put your minds at ease. If it's not the Brigade—and we do believe that St. Clair acted alone—then there's no threat to you folks and the restaurant."

Gloomily, he shook a few crumbs from his suit jacket. "We have to look more closely at this famous chef and who'd want him dead. Any ideas?"

Nick hesitated and then decided. "He has an ex-wife, Julia's mother. He told me she lives in Southern California. They were divorced while Julia was still underage, and it was very bitter. The wife got a lot of money, and Flavio got custody of their daughter. They don't keep in touch."

"When will Flavio be back in L.A.?"

"Sunday, they'll drive up from San Diego," said Nick. "He's very happy. This fellow Pete, Sam's replacement, arranged both TV and newspaper interviews. All in a few days. Big crowds in La Jolla and he still hasn't signed the cookbook in San Diego. He'll make a mint on his fifteen minutes of fame."

Nick smiled ruefully. "Flavio's spent years building up his restaurant and cashing in on his reputation as the chef of all chefs. Plus product endorsements, and now his diet book. Money gravitates to him. Just think of it. He gets wounded and even that makes him richer!"

THE BREAKTHROUGH CAME disguised as a jade pendant and two dozen long-stemmed red roses.

It was Monday morning. I was in my office, readying the bills for last Friday's movie premiere party. I'd been hungry all weekend, as if I hadn't had my fill yet of excitement and, yes, fear. Maybe my adrenaline glands are programmed to demand pizza. Mario is a gourmet pizza designer, and my favorite is the Brie with fresh blueberries. We'd cut a dozen of them into narrow slices for hors d'oeuvres, but I'd remembered there was a leftover half in the fridge. In my ravenous state, I wanted some of it cold and right now.

So I had sticky fingers and a blueberry stain on my white shirt when dapper Pete Drummond knocked on my door. I swallowed and stood.

"Come in, come in, what a nice surprise!"

He entered and found a clearing on my desk for a small package richly wrapped in gold paper. The bouquet of roses went directly into my arms.

"A thank-you," he said and bowed low, "from Peak Publishing. For helping our wounded and shook-up author survive San Francisco."

"It wasn't such a big thing," I protested, eyeing the gleaming package. "Really, Flavio and his people were very agreeable."

Pete sat himself in my client chair, crossed long legs in well-tailored gray pants, and said, "I hope you like the gift. My publishers asked me to pick out something special for you when I had free time in San Diego."

It was quite special—a circle of jade the size of a bonbon on a fine gold chain.

"Oh! It's beautiful!"

"Richly deserved. I just spent a weekend with the Flavio entourage, and I'm not sure how you managed to keep them all together."

"It was probably easier for me," I said. "Flavio was still hurting from his wounds, and Julia was so depressed after Sam's death she could barely move."

"Well, they're all recovering now. Saturday night, Flavio was picked up by an old buddy. I guess there are relocated Italian chefs all over California."

I confirmed: Italian is the top restaurant favorite in America, followed by Chinese.

One reason I have job security.

"Anyway, the two of them drove over the border to the jai alai games in Tijuana. Flavio thought the games might be too rowdy for Julia and Loretta. But Julia was getting bored, so Danny took her to see the animals at the San Diego Zoo. It's open at night during the summer."

Pete grinned, recrossed his legs and said, "That left me with Loretta."

"Beautiful, but *molto* bored," I said. "Not the type to feed the giraffes."

"Not the zoo type, indeed. Did you know she grew up poor in Rome? But she was ambitious and by the time she met Flavio, she'd become a top runway model. One of the fashion magazines had a party at his restaurant and, from what she told me, she made sure to introduce herself."

I'd clasped the gold chain around my neck, and the circle of jade glowed against my skin. I'd never yearned much for fine jewelry, as many otherwise sensible women do, but I could get used to being plied with semiprecious stones.

"You've learned more about Loretta in one weekend than I have since she and Flavio landed. I can tell you didn't bore her."

Pete pointed to his gold wedding band. "Neither one of us wanted a one-night stand. I'm seriously married, and she has too much invested in Flavio to stray very far."

"Do you think he'll ever marry her?"

"Not a chance. From what she confided over too many Cosmopolitans, he's never forgiven his ex-wife for the divorce settlement. He'd rather push a ravioli from here to Rome with his nose than let it happen again."

"He doesn't seem too generous with Loretta," I observed.

"She's resigned to what she can get. It's hardly a bad life. My job gets me into a lot of A-list parties in New York, and I can tell you, there aren't many gorgeous models over the age of thirty on the guest lists.

"Some of these beauties start modeling when they're around fourteen. Slap on enough mascara and lip gloss and they can pass for a young eighteen. Sorry, but no thirty-year-old woman has thighs as firm as an adolescent. It has to be even worse in Italy, where girls seem to mature earlier."

My God, but he was depressing me! I had passed my prime like a runaway train on a track to oblivion.

Pete peered at me with compassion. The crinkly lines around his clear gray eyes and the salt-and-pepper in his thick hair were reminders that many men became more attractive after they hit forty. Unfair!

"It's okay, Cat. You've obviously made a good life for yourself. You don't need a Flavio to take care of you. Besides, I don't think he strays. He's an old-fashioned Italian head of the family—working hard, doling out love and money as long as his woman and his kid stay on the right path."

Any more of Pete's painful, if accurate, views and I might forget about Paris with Nate and run back to my ex-husband, aging thighs, panic and all. Change the subject, Cat.

"So what did you and La Dolce Loretta do for the evening?"

"We had dinner at the Del Coronado, Teddy Roosevelt's favorite hotel. Loretta enjoyed it, but she was tired of traveling, she told me. Ready to get back to their apartment in Rome. And she did look stressed.

"She just picked at the expensive steak she'd ordered, and said proudly that the master chef loves her home-cooked meals."

"Loretta cooks?"

"Not often, but she says she knows how. Her specialty is this *Pasta con le Sarde*, spaghetti with sardines. An old Roman recipe, I suppose."

Where had I heard about this sardine dish? Danny had mentioned it, I remembered. But it was Sicilian, not Roman.

So what's the big deal, Cat? If Marco Polo could bring spaghetti from China, a sardine could take the ferry to Rome.

And yet, when I thought about it that night, I wondered if there was something fishy in the story of Loretta's past.

TWENTY-TWO

NICK HAS A SOUVENIR MAP of Sicily pinned to his office wall. Palermo is at the top of the map. Follow the highway west to Trapani, Danny's birthplace. South along the Mediterranean coast, then inland to Ragusa, my client's hometown.

Gina and Madelyn, luncheon chairs for the Patronesses of the Orphans of Ragusa, were coming in to thank us and bring a check. Today, I had another reason to be happy they'd be here in person. I had questions.

"Oh, yes," said Gina, a comfortable henna-haired matron in a jersey dress that clung to her spectacular bosom. "I know about the Perrino family in Trapani. They're the cousins of my brother-in-law's cousins."

"I'm asking," I said, "because I met a nice man who was born in Trapani. He's a chef. Have you heard of Danté Perrino?"

Madelyn, Gina's daughter, was trendy and chic in a lemon-yellow pantsuit. She made the connection. "He's with the chef who nearly was killed. Remember, Mama? It was in the newspapers."

"Of course," said Gina. "Flavio Ricci, from Palermo. I knew his aunt, she predicted he'd be famous." She shook her head in dismay. "So many of our talented young men have left Sicily. So much unemployment. They do better on the mainland.

"We read that Dellacasa's was helping at the luncheon when Flavio was shot. Just terrible. Is he all right now? What about you?"

I assured my clients that we'd all recovered. It had

brought us closer, I said. And I'd become so impressed with the sous-chef!

"Danté has been such a help to Mr. Ricci. But, confidentially, he's told me he may want to open his own restaurant soon."

"I wouldn't be surprised," answered Gina. "If I remember, he and his sister and a few cousins all left Trapani the year that a storm almost destroyed the tuna fishing boats. They were very poor. He was determined to be a success."

My ears pinged. "A sister? Danté never mentioned a sister."

"I heard," said Gina, "that she found a husband in Rome. Danté comes back to Sicily sometimes on the holidays. The cousin of my brother-in-law's cousin wrote that he still sends money to his mother. A good son."

"And the sister?"

"The gossip—although I never listen—says that Loretta thinks she's too good for the old ways. Why do you ask?"

"I'm just curious about people that I meet."

Gina looked me up and down with a keen matchmaker's eye.

"He'd be about the right age for you, Cat. You could live in Rome and start a catering business there."

I couldn't wait to usher the charming ladies out of my office. Marry Danny?

Loretta could be my maid of honor. My sister-in-law. But there were a few curious matters to attend to before that glorious day. It was not the right time yet for ordering the wedding cake.

"IT COULDN'T have been Danny," protested Mario. "He was in the kitchen with me the whole time. He'd been unpacking that box of pots and stuff that came by messenger. We ran up to the terrace together when we heard the shots and then the screaming."

"The messenger? Who was the messenger?" I asked.

"I was too busy to pay much attention. A young guy from one of the delivery services, and he was wearing the usual cap.

His van was in the parking lot outside the kitchen. I think it was a regular van, you know, with the name on the side."

"Think, Mario! What else do you remember about him?"

Mario's dark brow creased as he concentrated. He'd been working a round of pizza dough, but he now he pushed it aside and dusted flour from his hands.

"The second carton. I think he brought in two cartons. I can't remember seeing the smaller one again."

"It must have held the rifle. Could he have taken it out to the lower terrace?"

"Sure, and we probably wouldn't notice."

"Stop right there, Mario. I want to call Paul Wang."

TWENTY-THREE

IT WAS ALMOST DINNERTIME at Dellacasa's so Mario and the detectives crowded into my small office. Faint scents of garlic and oregano wafted up the stairs, but we were too hyper to enjoy them.

"We found the delivery service," said Paul. "One of their vans was stolen a couple of days before the shootings. They made a report."

He asked Mario about Loretta. "Did you see her? Did she come into the kitchen at any time?"

"Just for a few minutes. Flavio had started signing cookbooks for the guests, and she wanted to know how long before we started serving lunch. Danny said about half an hour, and she said something like, 'That worked out perfectly.'"

"Did she return to the upper terrace—take the stairs or the elevator?"

"I don't know. I was heating the ragu. She could have gone in any direction."

The detectives looked at each other.

"Could she have gone to the lower terrace?" asked Judy Sanchez.

"It's possible," said Mario. He was unhappy. "What I don't understand is why Danny would want to kill Flavio. He admired him."

"And what I don't understand yet," added Detective Sanchez, ticking off answers on her outstretched fingers, "if Loretta is really Danny's sister, what's her motive for killing her meal ticket? Doesn't make sense to me."

"We're not even sure yet that this is the right Loretta," said Paul. "They do have different last names. It's Danny Perrino, but Loretta Valente."

"The mysterious husband," I said. "The Patronesses told me she'd been married. She could have discarded Signor Valente before *or* after she met Flavio."

Paul scribbled a few words in his spiral notebook. "One more question to ask when—and if—we pick them up. We have nothing substantial so far. And it could be sensitive—accusing our Italian visitors of heinous crimes."

"But if the messenger didn't belong to the Brigade," asked Judy, "who is he?"

"Danny said," I recalled, "that he asked the hotel desk to have a delivery service pick up the cartons."

"Okay," said Paul, standing. "We start with the hotel clerk. Any other ideas?"

"Here's a possibility," I offered. "Danny mentioned that he was going to call a second cousin who lives in Santa Monica. His mother wanted to send greetings."

"My assignment," said Sanchez. "Look for a Perrino or a Valente in Santa Monica. Easier than approaching Danny or Loretta. They have passports. If we're right and they get alarmed, they could leave for Italy in a hurry."

The detectives left. Mario checked out the invoices I'd prepared, then hurried back to the catering kitchen. The party had gone well and Dellacasa's Catering had made a decent profit. This in spite of the starlet who'd arrived high, then tried to spray the movie's action hero with a full bottle of champagne. A production assistant pulled her away and called a taxi.

In the quiet office, my mind kept going back to motive. Everything could fall into place if *we* knew why Danny and/or Loretta might want to kill Flavio. There was a fragment of an idea floating around in my brain. It had something to do with Loretta. At one time, she'd reminded me of an ancient Greek goddess. I'd never figured out which one. If I could remember, it might help.

I AWOKE IN THE MIDDLE of the night, sat up and tried to remember my dream. Loretta, dressed in a Grecian tunic that showed her smooth thighs, was shooting arrows at a man whose face was hidden from me. It wasn't Flavio; the target was young and tall.

"Sam," I told the darkened room, "all along, it was Sam."

There was Danny, always clinging to Julia's side like a clownish pet monkey, doing Flavio's dirty work to drive away unapproved suitors. Of course, if Danny made himself indispensable, he could win Julia—and inherit Flavio's food empire.

And Loretta, dependent on Flavio for the good life. He'd never marry her, but her future would be secure if her brother married Julia.

I thought of calling Paul Wang on his cell phone, but it was only 4:00 a.m. I'd have to wait, though it might be impossible to sleep. How about a strawberry nonfat yogurt, Cat? It was the first time in weeks I'd wanted food that wouldn't land heavily on my hips. I practically skipped to the kitchen, polished off my treat and almost fell asleep holding on to my spoon.

TWENTY-FOUR

It was late afternoon before we gathered again at Dellacasa's. The two detectives, Nick and Rosie, Mario and me.

Early that morning, I'd called Paul on his cell phone, roused him out of sleep and gave him my theory.

"Pete Drummond gave me the clue. He'd told me that Sam intended to go to Rome in the fall. If all went well he'd marry Julia and work for Flavio."

Groggy with sleep as he was, the detective could see the inevitable next step.

"Danny and Loretta would be returning to Rome soon. They had to stop Sam before they left."

"I think Julia and Sam were genuinely in love," I said. "She'd have fought her father for him, and Flavio would eventually give in to make his child happy."

"So Sam had to die," said Paul. "And Flavio was slightly wounded to make him look like the intended victim."

"Poor Chanel lady," I added. "I doubt if the sniper intended to kill her. She just got in the way and, too bad, her death helped take attention away from Sam."

"It was still good shooting. Let's get off the phone. I want to wake up Judy and see if she's made any progress tracking the messenger."

By the time we met in the afternoon, Silvio Perrino had been arrested and booked.

"Almost too easy," said Detective Sanchez. "He was listed in the phone book, and he was still asleep when we knocked on his apartment door. He crumbled like one of these macaroons." She pointed to the plate of amaretti that Rosie had placed on our table. Guests never go hungry at Dellacasa's.

"Who's this Silvio?" asked Nick.

"A small-time hood," Judy explained. "One arrest and a plea bargain for squeezing protection out of a bunch of Westside dry cleaners, did minimum time. An ex-army sharpshooter. And, a distant cousin to Danny and Loretta.

"The hotel will testify that Danny never called the desk for a messenger. That wasn't in the script. We found the delivery company's cap in Silvio's apartment. He's up for killing two people and wounding a third, so he was ready to cooperate."

"He said," Paul continued, "that Danny called, told him it was a matter of family honor—although we think the ten thousand Danny paid him helped. And Loretta, well—she was in it up to her elegant eyebrows."

"Looking back," I said, "it falls into place. I remember her fussing about where to put the table for Flavio's signing. She picked a place where he and Sam would be exposed to anyone on the terrace below. I didn't think about it at the time, but she wasn't mixing with the guests for a while, until she popped up after the attack."

"That's right," said Judy. "She slipped away to check with Danny in the kitchen, make sure that Silvio was in place. He told us Loretta was the one who pointed Sam out, Silvio'd never seen him before. It was a cold-blooded contract killing."

"Flavio must be in shock," said Rosie. "And poor Julia. To think she innocently caused Sam's death!"

"We arrested Danny and Loretta at their hotel," said Paul. "They clammed up. Claimed they didn't speak much English."

"Well, here's to pasta and vino," said Nick, rising to pour his best red wine. "I'm relieved it's over. And Flavio will undoubtedly sell his story and make more millions!"

IT WAS SATURDAY MORNING in Monterey Park. I'd finished the breakfast porridge served personally by Paul Wang's uncle and snagged a plate of spicy meatballs.

"If I ever retire," said Paul, plying chopsticks on a turnip cake, "I'm going to buy into a dim sum place, maybe this one, and give up chasing murderers."

"You'd miss the adrenaline."

He carefully wiped a spot of turnip from the Charlie Chan moustache. "You think so? I'd miss the free cappuccino at Dellacasa's."

"You don't need a murder as a reason to visit. And, I wanted to show you this note. Loretta was the *second* Artemis, the huntress. That's what I'd been trying to remember. Her obsessive hunt for money and security. But the first Artemis just wrote to me from jail."

Hi, Ms. Cat Deean. I'm doing well, holding down my weight in spite of the baloney sandwiches that are a specialty of this institution. Come visit me. I'll show you the progress on my mss. It's like Emile Zola's J'Accuse, only I take on the fast-food establishment instead of the French army. I want to keep up my fight against fat, even if I'm restricted from blowing up donut shops. I never meant to do any harm. Artemis.

"What will happen to her?"

"Most likely a closed psychiatric facility until she's judged harmless."

"She has a point about fat, you know. Maybe we're the crazy ones."

"Have another dumpling. Life is short. Pleasure keeps us sane," said Paul sagely.

TORI MIRACLE AND
THE TURKEY OF DOOM

Valerie S. Malmont

THE GUESTS

Dr. Daniel Appleby	Cowardly Lion
Candace Appleby	Sexy Dorothy
Bob Burkhardt	Scarecrow
Mildred Burkhardt	Authentic Dorothy
Larry Diffenderfer	Wizard of Oz
Lorna Diffenderfer	Old Dorothy
Bernie Johanson	Tin Woodman
Ingrid Johanson	Nimmie Amee
Frank Kirchner	Flying Monkey
Kathy Kirchner	Tip/Ozma
Darren Worth	Cowardly Lion
Ramona Worth	Lullaby Munchkin

THURSDAY

IF I'D THOUGHT BRINGING the Land of Oz to Lickin Creek would be a much appreciated coup, I was dead wrong. Not only did the local citizens not know how popular Oz was, they apparently did not appreciate being labeled Munchkins in the newspaper article announcing the convention that I'd so carefully planned.

I had not actually referred to them as Munchkins, but my replacement at the Lickin Creek *Chronicle* seemed to hold a grudge against me, even though I was the one who was fired and she was the one who got my job. She must have thought it would be funny to get me into more trouble in the borough. I wonder how funny she'd find having to fend off dozens of angry citizens who thought I'd poked fun at their anatomy.

My name is Tori Miracle. I am a foreign service brat who was transplanted to New York City after college, found a great newspaper job, was fired, then moved for what I thought was love to Lickin Creek, Pennsylvania, which is located in Caven County, the most rural county in the commonwealth. I found work on the local paper, and once again I was fired. I've published two novels, both of which went directly from the publisher's warehouse to the remainder tables. I am on the downhill side of thirty. I live on pizza, Snickers bars and Diet Cokes. I have a relationship with my two cats, Fred and Noel, and that's the only satisfactory relationship I've ever been able to maintain. Perhaps that's because they don't demand anything in return for their unconditional love.

Last summer, my on-again, off-again boyfriend, Police Chief Garnet Gochenauer, was in Costa Rica, and I wasn't sure if he was ever going to come back. I was miserable living with Ethelind Gallant, an Anglophile college professor, who specialized in the use of contractions in medieval writings, wretched English cuisine, and pushing her nose into my business. To make things worse, I had lost my job at the paper where I had recently shifted from the position of acting editor to part-time reporter. It was then that Michael Thorne, who had inherited a castle in an area better known for its brick farmhouses and newer split-level homes, had approached me with an offer to be the events coordinator for the new Silverthorne Bed and Breakfast Inn.

The handsome actor had retired from showbiz to manage the B and B and had realized there must be a better way to drum up business than running his picture in a *Variety* ad for Silverthorne. All the ad had attracted were wannabe actors who hoped that some of Michael's glory as the star of several commercials and summer theater productions would rub off on them.

"Part-time is all I can offer," Michael had said right after explaining the job of events coordinator to me. "The pay isn't real great, and there are no benefits, but I can offer you free room and board in the inn. And of course you can bring your cats."

That was all it had taken to woo me, and I had accepted instantly. I had been absolutely thrilled not only to have a job, but also a means of escaping my landlady's clutches and her interminable stream of steak-and-kidney pies and toad-in-the-holes.

During the past year, my life had spiraled out of control when my stepmother, baby brother, and two of her servants had shown up as refugees from a revolution that had nearly killed my father. Ethelind had generously welcomed them into her fold, but there went my dreams of owning a small house of my own.

Then Garnet had returned from Costa Rica and had asked me to move into the historic Gochenauer mansion with him. He had even been willing to have me bring my family with me, but by then Ethelind had practically adopted the four of them and didn't want to let them go. They had agreed with her that it would be easier to wait for my father to join them there than to move once more.

I had tried to explain to Garnet that I had made a commitment to Michael Thorne to help him get his B and B off to a good start, but he had taken it wrong. No matter what I'd said, he couldn't seem to understand my point of view, that I'd made a promise and had to keep it. The situation had culminated one night over dinner at the American Legion when he'd lost his temper and snarled, "You've had a crush on that actor ever since the day you met him."

"I don't deny that," I'd said calmly as I sucked the cheese spread out of a stalk of celery. "He is the handsomest man I've ever seen, but that doesn't mean we have a relationship. Besides, Garnet, Michael is married."

"And just where exactly is his wife? I haven't seen her in the borough."

"Briana is living in New York. She's in the chorus of *Phantom of the Opera*." I hadn't mentioned that Michael had recently told me his wife had asked for a divorce, because I knew that would only cause Garnet more agitation.

Garnet had gulped his martini, nearly choked on the olive, slammed his glass on the table, and glared at me.

"So you're choosing him over me?"

"If that's the way you want to look at it, then I guess I am." I'd pushed back my chair, stood in a dignified manner and turned my back on him, ready to exit the club.

Although I'd lingered near the door for nearly a minute waiting for him to come after me, nothing had happened; I'd realized the end had finally come. Not in the steamy rain forests of Costa Rica, but in the overheated, fake-wood paneled dining room of Lickin Creek's most popular restaurant.

The next day, I'd waited until noon for him to call to apologize, then I'd moved into Silverthorne Castle to start my new career in the hotel business.

Which brings us to this Thursday evening in October, when the guests began to arrive for the fun-filled Ozzy weekend I had planned. I was excited and exhilarated. Until then my special events had been weekends featuring natural brown trout fishing in the Lickin Creek, overnight stays that included tickets for a play at the Whispering Pines Summer Theater ("See Stars Under the Stars"), and a disastrous mystery weekend where confusion reigned, the new cook turned out to be a raging alcoholic, and nobody was able to figure out who the murderer was supposed to be. To make up for it, I'd had to come up with something good, fast, and since I loved the Oz books and knew there was an enormous number of other Oz fans, I managed to talk Michael into letting me concentrate on throwing an Oz convention.

I made a few phone calls to people I'd known in my past life in Manhattan, sent out some press releases, and sat back and waited for the phone to ring. A few days later it did ring, and someone told me that the International Wizard of Oz Club held a Munchkin convention every summer in Harrisburg. My heart sank like the *Titanic* with all my hopes and dreams aboard, but within a few days of the publication of the first news articles, there was literally "no room at the inn." I couldn't believe my good fortune.

Tonight, the first guests arrived. The most crucial, in my opinion, was Antoine, the jeweler I'd known in New York, who had come through with his promise to bring a real emerald replica of the Emerald City. Pictures of the gemmed city had been featured prominently in all the news releases. It would have been a real disaster if he hadn't shown up, but he did, accompanied by his special friend, Roman. That was okay since I'd expected that and had booked him into a double room. While Michael manned the front desk, I led Antoine and Roman to the small room that I had designated for displaying the Emerald City.

Even though the city was insured for several million dollars, I'd taken extraordinary precautions to protect it. It was to be displayed in an interior room with no windows and only one door, which opened into the lobby. There was one key, and I planned on keeping it on a chain around my neck, night and day. Antoine agreed that the room would be perfect for his priceless work of art and set to work placing the glass case that contained it on the marble-top table I had put in the center of the room. The table was the only piece of furniture, and there was plenty of room for people to walk around and admire the exhibit. I had thought the Aubusson tapestry on the paneled wall would prove to be a distraction, but Michael had refused to take it down, saying it was too valuable to handle. Despite that one minor problem, I was ecstatic. Everything was going perfectly.

When Antoine was completely satisfied with the way the display looked, we stepped out of the room, which I locked behind us.

"What are the yellow bricks made of?" I asked Antoine.

"Canary diamonds. The most expensive of all stones."

I turned and checked the door to make doubly sure it was locked.

Behind the desk, Michael appeared to be in shock. "You won't believe how many people have already registered," he said, "four couples, and the convention doesn't officially start until tomorrow. You've done a wonderful job."

I felt my cheeks heat up. "It's going to be a super weekend," I was saying, when the castle's huge front doors burst open and two more people entered.

"I'll take over the desk," I told Michael. "You can be the charming host."

I smiled at the pair and asked for their names as they approached.

To my horror, Dr. Daniel Appleby and his wife Candace were not on the reservation list.

Although I kept running my pointer finger up and down the three-page list of names, Appleby did not magically appear.

"I'm sorry," I murmured, feeling the burn in my cheeks that indicated I was seriously embarrassed. "I can't find your reservation."

"We called late, but the person we talked to said it was okay," the young woman said. She appeared to be at least thirty years younger than her husband. "We came all the way from California. My husband is Dr. Daniel Appleby, dentist to the stars." This she said as if I should recognize him. I didn't, but then I seldom watch TV except for old movies, and I only read the gossip magazines while standing in line at the supermarket.

I wanted to say they had not talked to me, but didn't want to be rude to anybody who had the potential of actually paying for a weekend stay at Silverthorne Castle.

Michael, who had been listening while trying to appear as if he were busy with something else, stepped up to the desk. "Tori, we could put them in your room. That is, if you don't mind."

My jaw dropped as I tried to think of a snappy comeback. But before I came up with more than, "Uh…." a woman spoke from the doorway.

"But if you give them Tori's room, where will I sleep?" The familiar woman's voice came from the front doorway. I turned and gawked at the female who was over six feet tall and had long, streaky blond hair.

"Alice-Ann!" I choked. "What are you doing here? And what do you mean 'where would I sleep?'" Alice-Ann had been my best friend since we'd met in college, and she was also the reason I'd first come to Lickin Creek. She was not a big fan of Oz, and she was the last person I'd expected to see here.

"I called a couple of days ago to see if there was anything I could do to help out with the convention. Michael told me you could use some support, and that I could bunk with you."

"That's very thoughtful of you," I said to Alice-Ann, then spun to face Michael and hissed at him, "Now you've given my room away twice. What is the matter with you?"

He firmly pulled me from behind the desk and backed me into a corner, far away from Alice-Ann and the Applebys. My back was against a seventeenth-century Gobelin tapestry, and his two very muscular arms were on either side of me, preventing me from slipping away.

He leaned very close to me and said, "Listen to me, Tori. We need the income from every single person who shows up this weekend. There's a room behind the kitchen where you and Alice-Ann could sleep for a couple of nights. It's a nice room. Used to be the scullery maid's room. Think *Upstairs, Downstairs*' only you'll be down instead of up. Only for a few nights." His sapphire-blue eyes glowed in his deeply tanned face. His prematurely white hair reflected the multicolors of the Tiffany lamp that hung from above. His personally blended cologne smelled wonderful. All I could think of was he was the handsomest man I'd ever seen in my life, so even though I hated myself as I did it, I giggled like a teenager hoping for a prom invitation and said, "Okay."

"Hey, did you catch that?" Dr. Appleby asked of no one in particular. He was watching the Weather Channel on the small TV in the cozy lounge area of the great hall, now used as a lobby. "Looks like we're due to have some serious weather. How many people were you planning on coming?" he asked.

I watched the television for a minute. "Quite a few," I said. "They're calling for heavy rain in the Pennsylvania Grand Canyon area. That's hundreds of miles north of here. It shouldn't affect us."

Candall Appleby said, "But it's moving south through the Appalachians, and flooding is a possibility. Aren't we in the Appalachian Mountains?"

"The Appalachians cover a huge area," I said. "We don't need to worry about it."

The front door opened again, and Michael and I, hoping for another guest or two, leaped to attention, but this time it was the snippy reporter from the Lickin Creek *Chronicle*. The one who had replaced me for less money and because she had her own photographic equipment. Her personal camera was slung around her neck, and she clutched a stenographer's notebook against her chest. "I'd like to get a picture of the Emerald City made of genuine emeralds," she said to Michael, ignoring me.

Michael nodded, and I reluctantly unlocked the door to the exhibit room. The Applebys traipsed in behind us and emitted orgasmic sighs to express their awe upon seeing the Emerald City for the first time. The reporter snapped a dozen pictures from different angles and said she'd like to interview some of the attendees.

Fortunately there were three couples in the lounge area, the Burkhardts, Worths and the Diffenderfers, who didn't mind being interviewed, because the Applebys declined with Candace saying, "We want to have a relaxing weekend without any of the fanfare that usually accompanies a man of my husband's fame."

Michael caught my eye, and I covered my laugh with a polite cough.

Candace Appleby was still talking about not wanting to be interviewed and volunteered the information that her friends call her Candy Apple. "Isn't that cute?"

To give the *Chronicle*'s Lois Lane credit, she neither gagged nor burst out in laughter, but went about her business of asking the couples in the lounge why they were there, how long they had been Oz fans, and what they wanted to get out of the weekend.

While they talked, I examined the guest book. We now had ten paying guests, with another twenty due to arrive in the morning. Most importantly, there were nearly one hundred central Pennsylvanians who had signed up for Saturday-only participation. This was going to be a great and profitable weekend! Michael flashed a brilliant white smile in my direction and my knees wobbled from pleasure.

Our guests had all gathered in the great hall for the promised light supper, which had not yet appeared. Bernie Johanson asked where the bar was. When I told him we didn't have a liquor license, he blanched. His wife, Ingrid, patted his hand and told him she'd take care of it. She disappeared up the grand staircase and returned in a few minutes with an oil can and a glass from a bathroom.

"The oil can is part of his costume," Ingrid explained to anyone who might be listening. "He's going to be the Tin Woodman, and I'm going to be his lost Munchkin sweetheart, Nimmie Amee." Mr. Johanson seemed content with his glass of oil mixed with a little water.

"Where's supper?" someone asked.

"Should be ready in a few minutes. I'll check on it," I said and left the assembled group to make the long trek through the dining room and the pantry in search of the cook. All the way I was saying a little prayer that our new cook did not suffer from the same "disease" as our recently departed chef.

Verna Fogal was standing at the stainless-steel counter in the center of the kitchen, neatly arranging cold cuts on a platter when I walked in. Little remodeling had been done to the room when Michael opened the castle as an inn, because the castle kitchen had been used for many years to prepare food for hundreds of people at one time. Verna smiled at me and used one forearm to push her bifocals higher on the bridge of her nose. Not a hair of her neat gray bun was out of place, and she looked as cool as if she'd spent the day in air-conditioning instead of the castle's steamy kitchen.

"Let me help," I said, surprising myself with the offer. I put three kinds of rolls into several large baskets, found a huge still warm bowl of German potato salad on the counter and several bowls of ice-cold grapes in the refrigerator, and put it all on the large stainless-steel serving cart. Verna scooped mustard and homemade mayonnaise into antique pressed-glass dishes, produced a platter of deviled eggs from somewhere, and we were ready to roll.

"Nothing to worry about, Miss Tori," she said. "I've got everything under control."

"I was sure you would," I said, hoping she wouldn't know I was fibbing.

She pushed the cart while I followed carrying an aluminum tray on which she'd placed a pitcher of green lemonade in honor of the Emerald City and eighteen brilliant green antique oatmeal glasses.

Verna arranged the food on the mahogany buffet. The table had already been set with the castle's second-best china and crystal. I hadn't noticed this in my haste to get to the kitchen earlier. The guests began to enter, and Verna left abruptly— the perfect servant—always invisible. "Use the intercom if you need anything," she whispered to me as she slipped out of the room. "I'll leave brownies and coffee on the counter in the pantry."

Michael sat at the head of the table, looking relaxed and elegant and every inch the way the owner of a castle should look. I sat opposite where I had the perfect position for admiring him.

After the promised light supper, which seemed to please everyone there, I stood and tapped my water goblet with the edge of my knife to get everyone's attention. When they were quiet, I announced, "Tomorrow morning you may all start wearing your costumes. Prizes will be given at dinner on Saturday night. The top prize will be awarded to the person who remains truest to his or her Oz character.

"In the morning, while we wait for the rest of our guests to arrive, I will lead you on a 'walk on the Yellow Brick road,' really a nature walk to explore the castle grounds. Please think of me as your very own Glinda the Good. I will be your guide through the land of Oz for the next three days."

Scattered applause greeted my announcement. Candace, or Candy Apple if you wish, stretched and yawned in an exaggerated manner and said, "I'm so tired I could go to bed right now. That is if I had a room."

"Give me ten—no fifteen minutes—and I'll be out of the room," I told her. "Come on, Alice-Ann. I'll need your help. Let's get the serving cart from the kitchen. We can put everything I own on it and have a shelf left over."

Verna was reluctant to let me take the serving cart. "I'll need it back," she said with a grunt. "For clearing the dining room."

"You'll have it," I said, thinking she was being a little pushier than necessary.

Alice-Ann followed me into the dark hallway behind the kitchen. Michael had once told me that the castle was built in the days before electricity was commonly used, and after the castle was wired for conversion to electricity, nobody bothered to put light fixtures in the hallways, making a trip to the nearest bathroom an adventure worthy of H. Rider Haggard.

We groped our way down the murky hall to where a former storage closet had been converted into a small elevator by the castle's previous owners, Michael's mother and aunt. The two of us barely managed to squeeze in with the cart, but after we sucked everything in that could be sucked I pulled the brass grille shut. The elevator rose with a moan and finally jerked to a stop. "Second floor. Ladies lingerie," I said, tugging the grille open.

Alice-Ann giggled, threatening the stability of the small elevator.

"You have to stay perfectly still in here," I warned, "or else it could break down. Let's go."

I pushed the cart noisily down the dim flagstone hallway to my room. "This thing's loud enough to wake the dead," Alice-Ann said, cheerfully.

"Thankfully, we have no dead here to wake." I flung open the door.

Alice-Ann sniffed, then said, "Cats. You've got your cats here."

"Of course I do. Where else would they be?" The sweet animals in question jumped off the dresser and coiled around our ankles. Unfortunately, Alice-Ann was wearing black slacks that showed every hair they left behind.

"What's wrong with him?" she asked, pointing at Fred. "Does he have a skin disease?" She ineffectively tried to wipe the hair away while I emptied the dresser drawers onto the serving cart. I removed my few decent outfits from the closet, hangers and all, and laid them on top of the drawer contents.

"There's nothing wrong with him. I simply dyed him pink with food coloring so he could be Eureka, the Pink Kitten from *Dorothy and the Wizard in Oz*." There was an extra set of sheets on the closet shelf, and I remade the bed while I talked.

"He looks hideous," Alice-Ann said. "You'd better keep him hidden this weekend if you don't want to gross out your guests. Pink Kitten, my foot. He looks like the most foolish feline I've ever seen. He's all blotchy, as if he has a rash. You should be reported to the Humane Society for doing that to him."

I ignored her silly tirade. Fred, I knew, liked extra attention and had enjoyed being dyed. "My toothbrush! Wait a minute while I go get it." The reason I'd picked this room was that it had a connected bathroom. A few seconds later, my makeup kit and personal toiletries had joined the collection on the food cart.

"Just grab the litter box and the food and water bowls," I directed. "I'll tuck a cat under each arm and…"

"You grab the litter box," Alice-Ann said grumpily. "I'll do the cat tucking."

We bumped our way back down the hallway and into the elevator, where the cats howled in concert with the moans and groans made by the ancient mechanism.

The scullery maid's room was at the end of the same dark kitchen hallway that held the elevator.

"Charming," Alice-Ann snarled. "This is going to be a delightful weekend." She made sure the door was closed and put the cats on the floor. They immediately began to investigate their new quarters. "I'll go get my suitcase."

"Would you return the serving cart to the kitchen on your way, please?" It had taken only a few moments to unload my personal belongings onto one of the two single beds.

"My pleasure," Alice-Ann said in a way that sounded almost sarcastic.

I still had one thing to do. That was to get the Applebys settled in my—I mean—their room. I quickly put my clothes away then headed down the shadowy hall. Alice-Ann and I crossed paths there. She was pulling her wheeled suitcase behind her, making a terrible racket. The look on her face warned me not to make any comment about the noise.

As I passed through the kitchen, I saw that Verna had nearly everything cleaned up and put away. "I guess you didn't need the serving cart to clear the dishes," I remarked.

"Mmmm. There wasn't all that much to carry."

"You are prepared for tomorrow's breakfast, aren't you, Verna?"

She laughed. "It's the worst meal I've ever served, but if that's what you want, that's what you'll get."

"They'll love it," I told her.

"Mmmm. We'll see."

"Did you take enough turkeys out of the freezer for Saturday night's dinner? As you know we'll have the regular guests plus about one hundred who signed up for Saturday only."

"They're thawing in the refrigerator. Quit worrying, Miss Tori. I done told you I have everything under control."

I then escorted the Applebys up the grand stairway to their room. They didn't seem terribly impressed by the private bathroom, but that was probably because dentists to the stars are accustomed to staying in castles.

When I came back downstairs, I saw Michael at the registration desk and took the opportunity to have a little quality time alone with him.

He was looking at the registration book. "Candy Apple," he muttered with a frown on his face. "Sounds more like a stripper than a dentist's nurse."

"Wife," I reminded him.

"She used to be his nurse. You missed her telling that story while you were upstairs the first time." He suddenly changed the subject. "Have you heard the weather report?"

I shook my head. "I've been rather busy," I said, hoping for a little appreciation for the time and effort I'd put into everything.

"It's pouring in the Pennsylvania Grand Canyon area," Michael went on as if he hadn't heard me. "The storm is supposed to be moving toward us rapidly."

"The Grand Canyon is a long distance away," I said.

"I hope rain doesn't ruin our weekend."

"I'm sure it won't," I assured him. "Besides, except for tomorrow morning's walk down the Yellow Brick Road, everything is going to take place inside." Despite my optimism, his frown stayed in place.

When Michael began to blur, I realized I was exhausted. I excused myself, saying, "I really need to get some sleep so I can be ready to go in the morning."

Michael nodded his agreement. "Me, too," he said. "By the

way, have you seen what the cook has on her menu for breakfast tomorrow morning?"

"Of course I have. I selected it."

"Sounds horrible to me."

"The guests will love it," I told him and left the lobby area before he tried to talk me into changing the breakfast menu.

Alice-Ann was snoring, ever so gently, indicating she was already sound asleep when I finally reached my room. I slipped between the sheets, and the cats immediately curled up on top of me.

I think I had just dozed off when I heard the sound of a woman talking quietly outside my bedroom door. It must be Verna, I thought, half recognizing the deepness of her voice. But whom was she speaking to? Her voice was so soft, I couldn't make out what she was saying, but I did distinguish one girlish laugh that was cut short as if someone had slapped a hand over her mouth.

"Alice-Ann," I whispered. "Wake up."

Alice-Ann sat straight up in bed and shrieked. "What? What's the matter? What do you want?"

That was the end of the conversation on the other side of the door. I slipped out of bed and hurried to the door, which I opened cautiously. There was nobody in the hallway.

My voice was weary as I said to Alice-Ann, "Go back to sleep. I thought I heard something, but I must have been wrong."

"Good grief," Alice-Ann mumbled from beneath the covers. "I'm never going to get any sleep if you keep this spooky nonsense up."

I thought her snores indicated she'd been sleeping pretty soundly, but I didn't argue with her. For the first time in several months I really missed Garnet.

FRIDAY

MY ALARM WENT OFF at six, before any light had struggled into the room through the one narrow window. The cats tried to convince me to stay and snuggle with them, but I told them I had to get up. Today was the first day of my Oz convention, and I was eager to get started.

Alice-Ann rolled over and glared at the clock, then at me. "This mattress feels like it's stuffed with corncobs," she grumbled. "I didn't get a wink of sleep all night. Seems to me even scullery maids deserve better than these mattresses."

I ignored her complaints and padded barefoot down the cold flagstone hallway to the bathroom where I took care of my morning ritual. When I returned to the room carrying a stainless-steel bowl of fresh water for the cats, I was startled to find Alice-Ann dressed in a silver robe, over which she wore an embroidered organdy apron. She was both beautiful and elegant.

"Who are you?" I asked in awe.

"I'm Mrs. Yoop, the Giant Yookoohoo."

"From *The Tin Woodman of Oz*," I said, almost in shock. "How did you know about her?"

"To prepare for the convention, I decided to read some of the forty-two Oz books you've given my son over the years. Becoming an 'Artist in Transformations' appealed to me. I'm glad you knew who Mrs. Yoop was. Who are you going to be? Someone really clever and obscure?"

I pulled my pink tulle store-bought Halloween costume from the wardrobe and spread it out on the bed.

"You're doing Billie Burke as Glinda? That's not very original."

"I promised I would be their Glinda this weekend, guiding them toward the Emerald City, and I figured it would be nice if they recognized me."

Mrs. Yoop smiled graciously, knowing full well her costume choice was much better than mine.

The guests were already gathered in the dining room when we arrived.

I was glad to see that most of them had also purchased Halloween costumes. Bernie Johanson, the Tin Woodman, appeared well lubricated and in no danger of rusting. His ever-present oil can sat on the table next to his coffee cup. His arms and legs were wrapped in aluminum foil, a tin funnel, secured by an elastic band, was perched on his head, and he carried a plastic ax from a toy department. His wife was the Tin Woodman's Munchkin sweetheart, Nimmie Amee, in a bright blue dress and a white apron.

One of the two Cowardly Lions, wearing his mask on the top of his head like a cap, said to me, "This is the worst meal I've ever eaten in a public place." I recognized him as Dan Appleby. Beside him sat Candy Apple in a too-small store-bought Dorothy dress.

"I have to agree," Michael said. "Oatmeal, scrambled eggs, and plain white bread. It's totally unimaginative."

"Boring ain't the word," added the dentist. "Me and her," he nodded at his wife, "have got sensitive stomachs. We're used to better."

As he grumbled, he helped himself to more scrambled eggs.

Antoine and his friend Roman were dressed as identical scarecrows. I remembered that Roman was a professional costume designer for the New York theater, which explained why the costumes they wore could have come from a Broadway production of *The Wiz*.

There were three other costumed couples at the table. Mildred Burkhardt and Lorna Diffenderfer were also dressed as Dorothys. Ramona Worth was a Lullaby Munchkin from the movie. Her husband, Darren, was another Cowardly Lion. Larry Diffenderfer was the Wizard himself, and Bob Burkhardt was a Scarecrow, whose Giant Big-Mart costume was shamefully ordinary next to those worn by the jeweler and the costume designer.

They all protested the dentist's and Michael's opinion of the carefully chosen breakfast. A Dorothy, not Candy Apple, said, "I think it's wonderful. It's Dorothy's supper after the near fatal adventure in the 'Deadly Poppy Field.'"

The others all nodded in agreement. "Brilliant choice."

"How clever of you."

"Absolutely charming."

I beamed with pride and took my place at the foot of the table where I had an unobstructed and pleasurable view of Michael. He was not in costume, having told me much earlier that he had to draw the line somewhere. Perhaps all those years dressed as a bunch of dancing grapes in an underwear commercial had turned him against the wearing of costumes. Instead, he was wearing tight jeans and a plaid shirt, the unofficial uniform of the Lickin Creek male. On him, it looked good.

"Love your costume," one of the Dorothys, on the plus side of fifty, said to me. "You look very pretty in pink. It flatters your dark hair and eyes."

Alice-Ann's rude snicker was disregarded by the assembled group.

The same Dorothy who had just spoken turned to Alice-Ann and said, "My name is Lorna Diffenderfer, and this—" she nodded her head in the direction of the Wizard "—is my husband Larry. I've been an Oz collector for years, but I am afraid I don't recognize your costume."

"I'm Mrs. Yoop," Alice-Ann said.

"Of course—should have realized. It's very nice, dear."

Lorna Diffenderfer turned back to me and inquired, "Is the castle haunted?"

It seemed like an innocent question, but I cautiously asked, "Why do you want to know?"

"I woke up in the middle of the night to use the 'facility.' As I walked down the hall I thought I saw a woman in white disappearing into a room."

"That's odd," Mildred Burkhardt, another Dorothy, chimed in. "I had the feeling there was someone in my room, but I was too scared to open my eyes."

"There are no ghosts at Silverthorne," Michael assured them. "I've lived here all my life and should know if it's haunted."

Mildred continued as if I hadn't spoken. "This morning I noticed a piece of jewelry that had been on my dresser was missing."

"Oh my, this is serious," I said.

"Don't worry. I probably didn't put it where I thought I had. I often misplace things. Besides it was just a cheap souvenir pin that spelled out Oz in rhinestones. I bought it at the Library of Congress exhibit back in 2000." Candy Apple stood and walked to the sideboard to refill her coffee mug. Her blue-and-white checked dress was not only too small, it was too short, and we all had an eyeful of her lace-trimmed bloomers. All I could think of was thank goodness she isn't wearing a thong.

The grandfather clock in the great front hall struck eight. "Time for our walk down the Yellow Brick Road," I said, as I picked up my magic wand and brushed the white bread crumbs from my pink tulle. "Don't forget to stay in character to be eligible for a prize on Saturday night."

The couples paired up as we stepped outside. First came Dorothy, aka Candy Apple, and her dentist/husband, the Cowardly Lion. Roman and Antoine in their dazzling Broadway costumes stood apart from the other couples. Lorna Diffenderfer as Dorothy walked beside her husband Larry, the Wizard. Bernie Johanson, the very loose Tin Woodman, and his wife Ingrid, the Munchkin maiden Nimmie Amee, came next. The third Dorothy, Mildred Burkhardt, clung to the arm of her Bob, the store-bought scarecrow, while the Lullaby Munchkin, Ramona Worth, in a pink tutu almost as garish as my pink gown, held hands with husband Darren, the second Cowardly Lion. I was pleased that I'd managed to remember all their names.

"Looks like it might rain," said Mildred, looking up at the sky, which was filled with scudding clouds. "I'd hate to ruin my costume." Like the other Dorothys, she wore a commercially made blue-and-white checked dress, but I mentally gave her bonus points for wearing a pink sunbonnet and silver shoes as described in the book instead of the ruby slippers worn by Judy Garland in the movie version.

Michael and Alice-Ann chose to stay behind at the castle. "Somebody's got to get some work done," Michael said.

"What I'm doing is work," I reminded him. "Given my choice, I'd still be in bed with my cats."

He smiled. "Sorry to sound unappreciative, Tori. You're doing a great job. I just hope it doesn't rain."

"I'm sure it won't rain before we get back, and then it doesn't matter since everything else is going to take place indoors."

"Tori, have you ever heard of a low-water bridge?"

I shook my head. "I have no idea what you're talking about."

"It's what we have here, and it's the only way to cross the Lickin Creek to get to the castle."

"So?"

"It's made by laying pipes in the creek to carry the water, then pouring concrete over them to make a cheap bridge. If it rains, and the creek overflows, the bridge will be underwater. It's very dangerous to try to drive across a bridge you can't see, and if a car slips off most likely it would be carried off down river."

I was beginning to understand why he was worried. "You're telling me if it rains, nobody will be able to get in?"

"That's exactly right. And we're expecting twenty people to arrive today, and one hundred more to come tomorrow for the day."

"Do you know any rain dances in reverse?" I asked.

He looked up at the threatening sky. "I think it's too late for magic. Let's just hope the bad weather passes quickly and keeps moving south."

With my happy face on, I skipped over to the Oz characters. "Let's get started," I said.

The Tin Woodman groaned as if he needed more lubricant. "My knees are killing me; I can always tell when there's going to be a change in the weather."

"Now, now, this is going to be great fun," I assured them. "Follow the Yellow Brick Road." I tried to skip as Judy had done in the movie, and tripped over a flagstone. "Please be careful," I warned the others in a movie-Glinda tone of voice. "We don't want anybody asking the Wizard for new body parts, do we?"

We followed the flagstones straight ahead for about thirty feet. There the walkway stopped at the edge of a circle of white pebbles, which enclosed a small fountain surrounded by chrysanthemums. Two narrow paths branched out from the circle in opposite directions. From within the circle, I pointed out the spectacular view of the hazy blue mountains behind the castle, and then I pointed out Silverthorne Lake backed by a forest of vermilion and carnelian trees. "When in doubt, go left," I said after everyone had admired the scenery.

"I thought it was 'when in doubt, go right,'" said a Dorothy.

"Not in the Land of Oz," I said cheerfully. Actually, I'd noticed the lake was fuller than usual and my reason for taking them around to the back of the castle was to steer them away from the banks of the Lickin Creek, just in case its waters had already begun to rise. I knew that the borough of Lickin Creek, with its countless streams, often flooded before it began to rain, due to runoff from deluges higher in the Appalachians. Someone might notice the rising waters and decide to leave while there was still a chance of getting out, and I had a gut feeling that could start a stampede of Oz fans desperately trying to escape the Emerald City.

As we turned the corner and approached the side of the castle, we passed a large gazebo, enclosed on five of its six sides with lattice panels trimmed with Victorian gingerbread.

"What's that?" Ramona asked, pointing to it. "It's really charming."

"Used to be an outdoor seating area," I said, "but I understand the gardener now stores his supplies in there."

"Why is it open on one side?" she continued.

"So he can drive his lawn mower out," I told her.

"And that adorable fenced-in area over there?" Lorna asked, pointing to an enclosure about fifty feet from us. "It looks like a little secret garden."

"That's the Thorne family cemetery," I said.

"A cemetery in the yard? That's disgusting," Larry Diffenderfer said.

"It's a common custom in Pennsylvania," I told him with the authority of someone who'd lived in Pennsylvania for over a year.

A cool wind had arisen, the sky was turning blackish-blue, and teeth were beginning to chatter.

"I don't want to get soaked," the dentist said. "Let's go back in."

"In a minute. Let's move along," I said, waving my magic wand, and attempting my best Billie Burke imitation. "There's so much to see."

Lorna Diffenderfer proved there was more to see than I had imagined by sprawling face down in the grass.

"What happened?" I screamed, as I rushed to her side.

She sat up rubbing her right ankle. "My foot got caught in a hole," she said through her tears.

"Gophers," her husband said, after he had examined the hole in question.

"They're a terrible problem here. I'll get the gardener on it first thing Monday morning," I promised. "He's got stuff to get rid of them." I asked Lorna if she was all right.

With her husband's assistance, she stood and gingerly put some weight on her right leg. She smiled and sighed with relief. "Guess nothing's broken. I do think I should go back to the castle though and put some ice on it."

I agreed, and told the group we'd be heading back for coffee. Most looked grateful.

I walked in front, to keep an eye out for more gopher

holes. Suddenly a noise behind me caused me to stop and turn around. One of the Cowardly Lions lay face down on the grass. *Not again!* I thought. *Those gophers really do have to go.*

Candace Appleby was on her knees next to the fallen lion. "He's got a heart condition," she wailed. "We have to get him to the hospital right away. Someone call an ambulance."

"It will take forty-five minutes to an hour for one to get here from the nearest hospital," I told her.

"Then I'll take him myself," she said, looking up with a tearstained face. "Stay here with him. I'll get my car."

She ran down the path toward the gravel parking area with her short Dorothy skirt flipping up behind her to reveal shapely legs and ruffled bloomers. We hovered over the unconscious dentist. *Can it get any worse?* I wondered. First someone practically breaks a leg falling into a gopher hole, then another guest has a heart attack.

It did get worse, almost immediately. A drizzle at first, then a torrent, accompanied by spectacular bolts of lightning and rolling grumbles of thunder.

"You people go back to the castle," I ordered. I pointed toward the glass addition that jutted out at a right angle from the near side of the castle. "You can get in through the conservatory. The inside door will bring you in under the grand staircase in the front hall. I'll stay here with Dr. Appleby."

They were quick to follow my command, and in a few seconds I was alone with the sick man. I felt for his pulse. Still there. I hoped that was a good sign, but I really knew nothing about heart attacks. Since the rain was pooling beneath his head, I turned his face to one side. It was bad enough to have a heart attack; the man didn't need to drown because of it.

A green sedan roared across the lawn. Candace jumped out, leaving the engine running. "Where'd everybody go? I need help getting him into the car," she said.

"They went inside," I said, gesturing toward the great glass-domed conservatory. "But I can help you."

Candace lifted him under the arms while I picked up his

feet, and together we slid him into the back seat. He uttered a slight moan, but didn't regain consciousness. I leaned in the front window and gave Candace some quick directions on how to find her way to the hospital in Hagerstown.

She nodded her thanks. "I'll call from the hospital and let you know how he is," she said. The car backed up, made a U-turn on two wheels, and disappeared around the front of the castle.

I sloshed back to the castle. The downpour had washed all the starch and pink dye out of my tulle Glinda-the-Good dress. It was totally ruined. My tall pink crown had collapsed and felt like a stack of soggy pancakes on my head. Thankfully, I had planned ahead and there was a backup costume hanging in my closet.

After answering a dozen questions from the concerned guests about Dr. Appleby and making sure they were comfortably settled with coffee and cookies in front of the stone fireplace in the great hall, I went to my room to change.

Passing through the kitchen, I saw Verna hard at work preparing the next meal, and I stopped to ask a question I should have asked days ago.

"Do you have enough tables to seat all the expected guests? And where do you plan to set them up?"

The cook sighed, but patiently answered. "I got enough folding tables from Shopes Rentals to seat everyone in Lickin Creek, should they be foolish enough to show up. And them what won't fit in the dining room can eat in the library and the great hall. When the time comes, I'll need your help setting up the tables."

"No problem," I told her and continued on my way to my room.

I changed costumes, throwing the bedraggled gown, limp wand and soggy sequined crown in the trash. However, when I went to the closet shelf to get my replacement crown, I couldn't find it. Although I searched for several minutes, it was not there. Still wondering where I had left it, I finally decided it wouldn't hurt to be a crownless Glinda the Good and headed back to the public rooms of the castle.

About an hour later, as Verna was collecting the cups and saucers and the last of the Girl Scout cookies she'd found in the freezer, the front door blew open and Candace Appleby appeared. At first I thought, *Her costume didn't hold up any better in the rain than mine.* Then, remembering what she was going through, I felt ashamed of myself.

A buzz of questions greeted her. She held up her hands, pleading for silence. "He's in critical condition," she explained. "I'm going to pack up my things and go back down to Hagerstown. There's a motel fairly close to the hospital where I'm going to stay till he gets better."

With that, she left us to go upstairs.

"Alice-Ann," I said. "Could you take a tea tray up to her? Maybe she'd like some cookies, too."

"No problem," Alice-Ann said, and bustled into the kitchen as if she were glad to have something to do.

Once again, the front door opened, revealing a miserable-looking, waterlogged couple.

"We're the Kirchners," the taller one who wore a raincoat said. He pointed to a shorter figure under an umbrella. "She's Kathy. I'm Frank.

"Welcome to Silverthorne." Michael came out from behind the desk with his hand extended. "So glad you're with us."

Frank ignored the outstretched hand, removed his sodden raincoat and handed it to Michael. "You won't be so glad to hear what I'm going to tell you. The road's washed out. We got through, but I could see it sliding away behind us. Nobody else is gonna make it in. And that bridge—it's a disgrace. I thought for sure we was gonna drown."

I had stepped forward to take the new guests' wet coat and umbrella.

When I heard what he said, I grabbed Michael by the arm and drew him aside. "Did you hear what he said? The road is out."

"I heard," Michael said, his face grim. "There goes the weekend."

"Who's going to tell Candace?"

"I don't see what—oh, I do see what you're getting at. She won't be able to drive back to the Hagerstown hospital."

"Better take the Kirchners to their room," he said. "I'm going to start figuring out how much money we're going to lose this weekend."

"Please follow me," I told the new guests. "I've got a lovely room for you overlooking the lake, and lunch will be ready in the dining room after you've unpacked and hung up your things to dry."

The couple trudged slowly up the staircase behind me. The others, near the fireplace, had evidently not yet recognized the seriousness of the situation because they continued their conversations in muted voices.

I settled the Kirchners in a bedroom. It could have been any bedroom, since we now had about ten rooms that would remain vacant, but I had promised them a view of the lake and they got it. The lake, however, had brimmed over and lost its form, and water was now lapping at the base of the castle like the Nonestic Ocean on the border of the Kingdom of Rinkitink.

"Lovely," Kathy Kirchner said. Her frown told me she really didn't find it lovely at all.

"I'll see you downstairs in a bit. You can put on your costumes if you like. We're going to give an award tomorrow night for the person who stays in character all weekend."

"Lovely," Kathy Kirchner said again. I had the feeling we would not be seeing her in costume any time soon.

I was heading for the kitchen to see if Verna needed any help with lunch, when the telephone behind the desk rang, startling us all.

"Can you get it, Tori?" Michael called from the office.

I answered with my most professional desk-clerk voice. "Hello. Silverthorne Castle, where the Lickin Creek meets the Land of Oz."

The connection was very poor. The telephone lines crackled so loudly, I could barely understand the speaker.

"Doctor who?" I yelled.

"…Richland…Hagerstown…calling from…hospital."

"Yes, go ahead. I can hear you."

"…Mrs. Appleby…information…husband…"

"I'm sorry there's no telephone in her room," I said. "If you can hold a minute I'll go get her."

"…tell her…husband…passed…ten minutes ago…massive…cardiac…"

"My God! You mean he's dead?"

The guests turned to stare at me, mouths agape.

"…call me…questions…301-555…"

"I can't hear you," I shouted. "What was the number?"

Too late, the phone was dead.

"I couldn't hear the number, but that's okay," I said to Michael who had come into the room when he heard my shriek. "I can look it up in the directory."

"Even better," he said, taking the receiver from my hand. "I'll get it from information." A few seconds later, he slammed the phone down. "It's dead," he said. "The lines must be down."

"Oh, no!"

The guests were beginning to look unsettled.

Questions spun around us. "Did you say the lines are down?"

"I heard those new people say the road had washed out."

"Is Dr. Appleby really dead?"

"What's going to happen now?"

"Don't worry about a thing," I assured them. "We will continue with our activities just as if nothing was happening outside."

"But first," Michael whispered in my ear, raising goose bumps all over my body, "you and I need to go tell Candace her husband is dead."

"Michael and I have something we must do. We'll be back in a few minutes," I told the dubious guests. "If cook announces lunch is ready, please go ahead and get started."

"Can't you tell her alone?" I muttered to Michael on our way down the hallway to my old room.

"I think it would be better for a woman to be there for her to lean on after I tell her what has happened."

He tapped on the closed door, and after a moment or two Candace Appleby opened it and stared at us as if she'd never seen us before. "May we come in?" Michael asked politely.

Her answer was to open the door wider and step back. I saw an open suitcase on one of the beds, half-full of Candy's clothes. Her husband's clothing was stacked in a neat pile on the other bed. My attention was caught by something brown and furry.

Candace saw me looking at it. "It's my husband's extra Lion costume," she said with a smile. "He's very fastidious. Doesn't like to wear things twice. I thought I might as well take everything with me," she explained. "I don't know how long he'll be in the hospital, so I…" Her voice faded away. "What is it?" she asked. "Why are you here?"

"Please sit down," Michael said calmly.

Candace fell rather than sat on the wicker rocker in the corner. "It's bad news, isn't it?"

"I'm afraid so," Michael began. "Tori, tell her about your phone call."

The look I shot him would have killed anyone else. So much for him doing the telling and me being there for her to lean on.

I gave her the bad news as quickly and as kindly as I could. Tears flowed down her cheeks. "I can't believe it. Did the doctor say what happened? When I left the hospital they seemed so sure he was going to recover."

"These things are in the hands of God," Michael said, revealing a spiritual side I'd never before observed.

"Thank you for telling me," she said as she blew her nose into a tissue. "If you don't mind, I'd like to be alone for a little while. When I'm able, I'll head into Hagerstown to make the necessary arrangements."

"I'm afraid I have some more bad news for you," Michael said. "The road is out. You won't be able to leave for a few days."

Poor Candy threw herself from the rocker to the bed, knocking her husband's clothes onto the floor. She cried hysterically, while Michael patted her hand in vain and I ran into the bathroom to get a glass of water for her.

"Go away," she mumbled into her pillow. "I want to be alone."

After placing the water glass on the marble-topped end table, Michael and I backed clumsily out of the room and slowly descended the staircase.

I fancied that Michael and I looked like the lord and lady of the manor as we led the twelve hungry guests into the dining room. Verna had done wonders with my luncheon menu. In the center of the sideboard, she'd created a map of Oz from fresh fruit. Sliced green kiwis represented the Emerald City. Above it, or rather to the north, she'd placed purple grapes for the Gillikin Country. South of the Emerald City, standing for the Quadling Country, were ripe, red strawberries, ordered at great expense from California. Bananas on the left were for the yellow Winkie Country, and on the right a bowl of fresh blueberries depicted the Munchkin Country.

The guests applauded upon seeing the display.

When everyone had taken their seats, the same ones they'd taken at breakfast, Verna wheeled in lunch on the stainless-steel serving cart. What everybody saw were square paper lunch boxes with metal handles, so often associated with Chinese carryout.

Michael's comment was "Huh?"

But Mildred Burkhardt could hardly contain her excitement. "It's what Dorothy ate in *Ozma of Oz,* right after she was shipwrecked with her pet chicken Billina. Am I right?"

I nodded, pleased she'd recognized the meal for what it represented.

Mildred's husband Bob said, "Then it's going to be ham sandwiches, isn't it?"

Again, I nodded. "With sliced cheese, a pickle, and an apple, and we'll finish up with sponge cake for dessert, just as Dorothy did. And of course the fruit from the map of Oz. We also added a hard-boiled egg to each lunch box in case we need to fight off the Nome King."

"Nomes are allergic to eggs," Kathy, the new guest, told her husband. It was obvious that she, not he, was the Oz fan in their family.

Michael looked as if he couldn't believe what was happening as he watched the Oz fans dig into their paper lunch boxes with gusto.

During lunch, I thought I heard the front door open, but I didn't want to be rude and end the conversation I was having with Mrs. Johanson, the Munchkin Nimmie Amee, about whether or not the Gillikins were really northerners or southerners. When I did manage to get away for a minute to see if a new guest had miraculously managed to get through to us, I found the great hall was empty. There were still some wet spots on the floor where the Kirchners had dripped, and I wiped them up with a scarf I found hanging in the hall closet before returning to the dining room. The last straw would be if someone slipped on the flagstone floor and broke a leg.

While the sponge cake was being sliced, Larry Diffenderfer excused himself to make a phone call.

"But the lines are down," I commented to his wife. "How can he make a call?"

"He has his cell phone with him." With a sigh, she added, "He can't leave business at home for even a day."

Larry returned only a minute later with a thoroughly disgusted look on his face. "I couldn't get through," he said, glaring at his cell phone as if it had betrayed him.

Michael said, "Cell phones never work very well here at Silverthorne. It has something to do with the thick stone walls and the mountains on three sides. Bad weather always makes the problem worse."

"Swell," Larry said. "Now I'm stuck here in *Fawlty Towers* with no phone and no way to get out. We're stranded here like the cast of a cheesy version of *Survivor.* I'll probably lose millions on the stock market today." The disgruntled man slumped in his seat and glowered at me.

I tried to liven up the party by announcing that an Oz quiz would be next. The guests chose instead to go to their rooms for naps. I couldn't argue with them. There was something about having one of your guests die to put a damper on the party. Also, I was exhausted. "It's okay," I said to their backs. "We can do the quiz before dinner."

After the group had left, I asked Michael if he needed me for anything. "No thanks," he said. "Get a little rest while you can. I'm going up on the roof and see if I can't temporarily patch some leaks. The third floor is getting drenched. Verna and I put buckets up there, but there's not enough buckets in the world to catch that much water. I'm particularly worried about the wall tapestries. Some are priceless."

I understood his distress. The Aubussons and Gobelins I had already recognized, but there were many others I wasn't familiar with that were equally as valuable. I'd been told earlier by Michael that some dated from medieval times.

Alice-Ann and I went to the scullery maid's room, stripped off our costumes and stretched out on our lumpy beds. I set my alarm clock to ring in two hours. Fred and Noel, who had been ignored for many hours, purred loudly to tell me how happy they were to see me.

"Tonight, we'll move upstairs," I promised Alice-Ann and the cats. "Since the other guests couldn't make it through the rain, there's plenty of room for us."

She answered with a gentle snore. My last conscious images were of poor Candy Apple upstairs, sobbing over her unexpected widowhood. Despite the noise of the driving rain and my thoughts about Mrs. Appleby, I drifted off to sleep in a minute or two and probably added my own snores to Alice-Ann's.

I hit my snooze alarm several times before finally hauling myself from my warm bed. The only light in the room came from the silver-gray beam struggling to squeeze through the narrow window set high in the wall. Through it, I could hear the driving rain. If anything, it was worse than before.

After donning my pink gown, I awoke Alice-Ann.

"No," she moaned, trying to cover her head with the pillow.

"Verna could use your help in the kitchen, Alice-Ann. Or did you forget the reason you're here is to help out?"

She groaned and swung her feet over the side of her bed onto the cold stone floor.

There were only two couples, the Diffenderfers and the Burkhardts, in the lounge area, so I decided to postpone my Oz quiz until after dinner and instead popped one of the silent Oz films made by L. Frank Baum's film company into the VCR. I hoped *The Patchwork Girl of Oz* would entertain anybody who wandered in after their nap.

"It's nice to see you're staying in character," I commented to the two Dorothys, the Wizard and the Scarecrow.

"Not much else to do," Larry Diffenderfer grumbled. "Millions. I've probably lost millions...."

His wife, Lorna, winked at me. "He'll be all right," she said, cheerfully. "We can afford to lose millions."

"I need to check on dinner," I said, leaving them staring at the TV. While I walked toward the kitchen, I pondered what it would be like to have millions to lose. It was something I'd never have to worry about.

Verna and Alice-Ann had everything under control. "No need to dig out the rental tables," Verna said. "I can easy put fourteen people around the dining room table. I made a few changes to the menu, since eighteen people didn't show up." My cheeks must have reddened, because she added quickly, "Don't worry. I'll make it good."

Whatever she was cooking did smell wonderful, so I left them to their work and rejoined the guests in the lounge. Kathy Kirchner, the newest guest, surprised me by cleverly dressing as the boy Tip, who was actually the royal girl ruler of Oz. I gave Kathy some bonus points for originality. At least this proved she'd read more than one Oz book. Her husband was a Flying Monkey, which was also rather unique.

When Kathy saw me, she jumped to her feet, stood arms akimbo, and said, "Someone stole something out of my room." She was glaring at me as if she were sure I was the guilty party.

"What was it?" I asked.

"My tiara. I was planning to wear it tomorrow when I dress as Ozma. You know, after her transformation from boy to girl."

"Was it very valuable?" I asked. It wasn't a stretch to go from the Diffenderfers being worth millions to the Kirchners bringing a real diamond tiara to an Oz convention.

"Not really. It's made of rhinestones, but it has a great deal of sentimental value for me. I wore it to my senior prom in 1989."

Mildred looked away from the TV for a minute. "Maybe it was stolen by the same ghost who took my rhinestone Oz pin."

"That's funny," Lorna Diffenderfer said. "After my nap, I couldn't find the red sequined sneakers I'd made to go with my Dorothy dress. Maybe there really is a ghost here. One who steals sparkly things."

Antoine appeared at that moment, his eyes wide with fear. "Sparkly things…oh my God…my Emerald City!"

"There's no need to worry," I assured him. "The key is still hanging around my neck."

"Open the door, please," he begged. "I have to see for myself."

Ridiculous. Nobody could have gotten in. I unlocked the door to the display room and threw it open. There was nothing on the marble-topped table in the center of the room. *Impossible.*

Antoine slumped to the floor in a faint.

Michael knelt beside him and felt for his pulse. "He's not dead," he said.

"That's a relief," I said, fingering the key on my bosom. There was no way, absolutely no way, anybody could have gotten into that room without my knowing it.

Roman, in his Scarecrow outfit, dropped to the floor and cradled Antoine's head in his lap. "Somebody call a doctor. Call the police. Do something."

"We can't," Michael reminded him. "The phone lines are down, and the road is out."

"Then at least help me carry him to our room."

"Use the service elevator," I told Michael. "It should be easier and more dignified than trying to haul him up the stairs."

Antoine was a slender man, not very tall, and Michael was able to lift him by himself and carry him out of the display room. From habit, I locked the door behind me.

"That's really locking the barn door after the horse escaped," Darren Worth said.

I hadn't even heard him come in. Ramona, as usual, was right next to him, clutching his hand.

Coming down the staircase were Mr. and Mrs. Johanson. Mrs. Johanson's cheeks were still bright red from her nap. A few minutes later, Candy Appleby, face streaked and swollen but still in costume, joined us.

"I got hungry," was her ingenuous explanation for being there.

"I believe dinner should be on the table," I said to the assemblage. "Let's go in."

Alice-Ann and Verna were just finishing putting out the last dishes when we crowded around the table.

Michael and Roman came in right after the rest of us had sat down.

"Antoine's awake," Michael quietly confided in me. "He wants to rest."

"This has been a terrible shock," Roman added. "He may never be the same."

What ran through my mind was *Here comes the first lawsuit of the weekend.*

Verna had indeed prepared a delightful dinner. Nothing Ozzy about it, but neither was it any of the Pennsylvania Dutch food I had half expected. There were four full tureens of beef bourguignone, garnished with sautéed mushrooms and tiny cooked onions. With the bourguignonne, Verna served hot French bread, buttered peas, crisp tossed salad with a balsamic vinaigrette dressing, and fluffy white rice. There wasn't much conversation after the guests began to eat.

They nearly emptied the tureens, but not quite. I hoped there was enough left for Alice-Ann and Verna.

"Dessert time," Alice-Ann chirped cheerfully, as she came

in pushing the serving cart on which sat several pies. *"Tarte aux pommes,"* she announced.

"À la mode, of course, only with green ice cream in honor of the Emerald City," Verna added. She, of course, had no idea that the real Emerald City had disappeared, or I'm sure she would not have mentioned it.

The ice cream, despite being bright green, was French vanilla and the perfect accompaniment for the warm tart.

Most of the guests were on their second helpings, when Mr. Johanson pushed his chair back noisily. "I don't feel good," he announced. "I'm going to my room to rest for a few minutes." His wife did not accompany him.

"Should we be worried?" I asked her.

Ingrid leaned over to me and whispered in my right ear. "It's more or less a code phrase. What he really means is he needs a drink." She saw my questioning look. "He has to keep his blood-alcohol level up to a certain level to appear normal."

"Oh my," I gasped. "Is there anything we should be doing for him?"

She shook her head. "I've been a member of Al-Anon long enough to realize it's his problem, not mine. He'll be back in a few minutes, good as new."

When fifteen minutes went by and he still hadn't returned, Mrs. Johanson began to look anxious. After a few more minutes passed, she rose from her chair, "I think I'd better go see how he's doing."

As she left, the guests finished their desserts. "Now what?" Larry Diffenderfer asked.

Although earlier I had said we'd have the Oz quiz, it didn't seem right to start it with three people out of the room. "More videos," I said brightly.

"And the fun continues," Larry sniped.

The guests dutifully followed me into the lounge, where I placed the video of *The Magic Cloak of Oz* in the VCR. As I adjusted the volume, we were startled by a ringing sound coming from the great hall.

"What was that?" someone asked.

I stared at the television. *A malfunction?*

The sound repeated, and I recognized it this time. "The phone. The lines must have been repaired."

"Great," Mr. Diffenderfer said. "Now it's too late to call my broker."

I ran to the desk and grabbed the telephone. "Hello," I cried, feeling joyful to be reconnected to the outside world.

"Tori, it's Garnet."

"Thank God," I sighed.

"I've been trying to get through to you since last night. I've missed you, and I want to get back together with you after this weekend."

I couldn't believe my ears. This was as close as Garnet ever came to an apology. Suddenly, I knew I still wanted to be with him, as attractive as Michael might be.

"Are you there, Tori? Is everything all right?"

"No. Everything is not all right. We're stranded here, Garnet. The road's gone, the bridge is gone, nobody can get in or out, and one of our guests died this morning."

"Died? What happened?"

"Dr. Dan Appleby from Beverly Hills. He's known as 'the dentist to the stars.' He had a heart attack while we were on a walk this morning. His wife managed to get him to the Hagerstown hospital, but he died there."

"...a shame..." Garnet's voice spluttered.

"And the Emerald City made of real emeralds was stolen this afternoon," I wailed. The line crackled.

"I can't hear you," I yelled, but it was too late. Our connection was gone. I immediately tried to dial the police department, thinking I'd at least get the girl who answered for both Hoopengartner's Garage and the police, but the phone was absolutely dead.

"Psst."

I glanced around but saw no one.

"Psst. Tori."

This time I saw Mrs. Johanson standing on the staircase. She gestured for me to come forward, which I did.

"It's my husband," she said quietly. "Can you and Michael come take a look, please?"

I motioned to Michael to come along, and we followed her to her room. Mr. Johanson was sprawled upon the four-poster bed, still clutching his oil can. The antique quilt was stained with vomit, and the man's face was contorted as if he were in terrible pain.

"He was having a convulsion when I came in," she said. "Then he became very still. I'm afraid...I don't know what's..."

For the second time this evening, Michael knelt next to a recumbent person and felt for a pulse. He shook his head as he stood up. "I'm sorry," he said.

Ingrid Johanson staggered but did not fall. "I didn't think...I mean, he always disappears for a drink after dinner...he can't be..." She changed from being confused to angry as she looked me in the eye and asked, "Just what did you put in tonight's food?"

Michael took her hand and once again said, "I'm very sorry, Mrs. Johanson, that your husband has passed away. However, I'm positive it wasn't anything he ate. After all, everybody else is all right. Tori," he said to me, "there's a bathroom two doors down. Please get a glass of water for Mrs. Johanson."

Please let everybody else be all right. I ran down the hall to the bathroom and stopped, stunned by what I saw there. On the counter, next to the sink, stood a container of gopher poison. So as not to disturb fingerprints, if there were any, I wrapped my right hand in a towel, picked up the can by the rim, and found it was empty. The main ingredient listed on the label was strychnine.

Forgetting the glass of water, I ran back to the bedroom carrying the empty can with me.

Mrs. Johanson and Michael both gasped when they saw it.

"Where did that come from?" Michael asked me.

"I found it in the bathroom on the counter, but I assume it

came from the garden shed. The gardener's been trying to get rid of the gophers for months."

Michael took the oil can from the dead man's hand and sniffed at the contents. "Ugh," he grunted. "There's something in here, besides whiskey, I mean."

"You're saying someone intentionally poisoned my husband?" Fear glimmered in Mrs. Johanson's eyes.

"It looks like that's what happened," Michael said awkwardly.

I distanced myself from them. *Don't be an idiot, Michael. She was the only person who was up here with him for any length of time. Police always look to the spouse as the prime suspect.* But there was someone else up here, for an even longer period of time, I recalled. Antoine, my jeweler friend from New York City.

Ingrid whimpered and dabbed at her cheeks. "I always thought his drinking would eventually kill him…but…not like this."

Michael said to me, "Tori, go try the phone in my bedroom. See if you can get through to the police."

I did as he ordered but had to come back and tell them the lines were still down.

"I hate to mention this," I told them. "But with no way to get Mr. Johanson out of here, we need to make some sort of arrangements for…uh…keeping him in a safe place." *Where he won't begin to smell.*

"But where…?" Mrs. Johanson asked.

"There's the walk-in meat freezer downstairs," I told them. "I think it would be best not to let the guests know about this. There's no point in scaring them. Nobody will see us if we take him down the elevator. We can keep him in the freezer until the road is open."

Mrs. Johanson was so ashen I feared she might faint, but after a moment or two she agreed we had to do something.

"Give me a minute to strip the bed," Michael said, looking at the stained quilt.

"Don't you dare," I told him. "This is a crime scene, and we can't disturb it." I turned to Mrs. Johanson. "We'll move you to another room right after we…" I nodded in the direction of the dead man and tried to phrase it gently "…after we relocate him."

Michael and I carried the body down in the elevator. Alice-Ann was just coming out of the kitchen as we exited the lift.

"What on earth…?"

"Shhh," I warned. "We don't want the other guests to know."

"Is he dead?"

"I'm afraid so," Michael said. "Apparently it was strychnine poisoning."

Alice-Ann's hand flew to her mouth. "My God!"

"Have you been in the dining room in the last few minutes? Are the other guests all right?" I asked.

"I just left there. Everybody's fine."

"That's a relief," I sighed. We stopped in front of the stainless-steel door of the meat freezer. "Can you please open the door?"

Alice-Ann swung the heavy door open, and Michael and I carried Mr. Johanson in. "Hold the door open," I told Alice-Ann. "We don't want to accidentally get locked in."

"There's no lock," Michael said.

"Hold it open, anyway. I get nervous in enclosed places."

"Should we sit him up in a corner or stretch him out on the floor?" Michael asked.

"I think he'd be better off stretched out," I said. "He'll freeze in whatever position we put him in, and he'll look less odd lying flat than sitting up when the ambulance people carry him out on a stretcher."

We laid Mr. Johanson on the steel floor, directly under several frozen sides of beef, and backed out.

"Come on, Alice-Ann," I said. "We're moving upstairs. I want to keep an eye on things up there. And you can help me move Mrs. Johanson to another room."

"I'll get the cart," she said and scurried down the hallway toward the kitchen. A few minutes later, we had the shaken new widow situated in a different room and our belongings stashed in an upstairs bedroom.

When the last guest had said good-night, Alice-Ann and I wearily trudged upstairs to the bedroom we had chosen mainly for its proximity to a bathroom. Remembering that Mr. Johanson had been murdered by someone in the castle, I carefully locked the door before getting into bed.

Despite my worries, I fell asleep rather quickly. And I slept soundly until an unfamiliar creaking sound awoke me. Too afraid to move, I opened one eye and waited for it to adjust to the darkness. It must have been a clap of thunder I heard, I decided, when I saw something that chilled me to the bone. The door to our room, the one I'd meticulously locked before going to bed, was closing slowly on its rusty hinges.

I saw a flash of white just before the door made a gentle clicking sound as it stopped moving.

I waited for a few seconds to make sure it didn't open again, and then got out of bed. Ever so slowly, but not very quietly, I swung open the door and peered out. In the dimmest far reaches of the hallway, I saw a figure in a long white gown moving away from me. I got the impression that it was female with flowing blond hair. *The castle ghost!* Before I had time to call out for help, it had disappeared. Wishing I had some of the Cowardly Lion's courage, I ran down the hall to where she had been before vanishing. There was nothing to be seen, and the bedroom doors on either side were locked.

Once again, I entered my bedroom, locked the door, and went to bed, but this time I did not fall asleep.

SATURDAY

AFTER A RESTLESS NIGHT, I got out of bed and woke Alice-Ann. She climbed out of the four-poster bed immediately, without complaining, which was very unlike her.

"I think I saw the castle ghost last night," I told her. "It was in our room."

"You should have locked the door," she said.

"I did. Somehow it still got in."

"It must have been your imagination," Alice-Ann said. "You've been working too hard."

I dragged my Glinda costume from the walnut Eastlake wardrobe and reached for my magic wand, which I'd left on the dresser. It was gone. "This proves it wasn't my imagination," I said. "My wand is gone. The ghost stole it because it was covered with sparkly silver dust."

"It's certainly not very discriminating in its tastes," Alice-Ann remarked. "There's a big difference between a miniature castle assembled from real jewels and your tacky magic wand made from a cheap dowel rod with a cardboard star glued to the top."

"It wasn't tacky," I muttered, knowing full well it really was. "Come on, Alice-Ann," I said. "It's time to get to work."

I went down the hall to the nearest bathroom, and when I returned, found her dressed in a loose straight gown of white silk from which hung many multicolored scarves.

"Polychrome," I guessed.

"Right. The Daughter of the Rainbow. Do you like it?"

"I love it. I can't believe you've been so clever with your costumes." *A lot cleverer than me with my store-bought pink tulle.* "With all this rain, I only hope we see your father, the Rainbow, soon."

"Mark helped me," she admitted. Mark was her son, the eight-year-old boy I'd been giving Oz books to since he was born. By now, he probably knew more about Oz than I did.

I paused in front of Mrs. Johanson's door at the end of the hall and tapped softly. The door opened quickly, so I knew she must not have been in bed. A soggy tissue hung from one hand and her face was swollen from crying. "Is there anything I can get you?" I asked.

"Maybe some coffee," she replied with a sniffle.

"I'll bring it right up," I assured her.

Alice-Ann had gone into the bathroom and now came out carrying the empty gopher-poison can.

"What's this doing in there?" she asked.

I shut Mrs. Johanson's door quickly, not wanting her to be reminded about what had happened last night.

"You've ruined it," I pointed out. "It probably held the poison that killed Mr. Johanson and now your fingerprints are all over the can."

"Then you shouldn't have left it in there," Alice-Ann said.

"It's a crime scene," I explained. "We have to leave everything just as we found it. I suggest you find Michael and ask him to lock the door, and also the door to the Johansons' former bedroom. We don't need anybody else mucking around with evidence."

"I wasn't 'mucking,'" Alice-Ann complained but headed obediently toward Michael's room.

Instead of using the grand front staircase, I conserved my energy by riding the creaky elevator down to the first floor.

As I pulled the grating open, I heard an unfamiliar sound coming from the kitchen. My first guess was someone had tripped and fallen and needed help. The hall was dark as pitch as I ran down it, my footsteps echoing against the arched stone ceiling and flagstone floors.

When I entered the kitchen, I encountered a ghastly scene. The body of the Cowardly Lion lay on the stone floor, face down in a pool of blood. Standing over the body was Verna Fogal, eyes blank and unseeing, a large turkey clasped in her arms.

It had to be Darren Worth, dressed as the Cowardly Lion. What was he doing in the kitchen? "Help me turn him over," I ordered.

Verna still seemed to be a thousand miles away, so I relieved her of the turkey, which I found was partially frozen, and sticky with blood and matted hair. I suddenly realized I was holding the murder weapon and knew I'd probably never eat turkey again. I let it fall to the floor with a disgusting thud.

Not only was the turkey covered with gore, but the kitchen cabinets and the stainless-steel countertop were also spattered with droplets of blood.

When Verna made no effort to help me, I gingerly reached out and rolled the lion over onto his back. Despite my revulsion, I placed my fingers on his neck to try and find a pulse. Although his skin felt warm beneath my fingers, there was no life to be found. I pulled the lion mask off and for the first time caught a glimpse of the victim's face. "I can't believe this!" I choked.

The man in the lion costume, lying dead on Silverthorne's kitchen floor, was not Darren Worth as I'd thought, but instead was the other Cowardly Lion, the same man who had been lying near death on the lawn yesterday morning—Dr. Dan Appleby. The same Dan Appleby who had been declared dead at the Hagerstown hospital.

"This is impossible," I muttered as I struggled to my feet to stand next to Verna. "He's been dead since yesterday. How did he get here?" The frozen turkey lay on the stone floor where I had dropped it.

Verna's eyes were blank. She looked at the clock on the kitchen wall, then turned to me. "I gotta get breakfast ready." With that, she calmly stepped over the body and the pool of congealed blood, opened the refrigerator and pulled out a large glass pitcher, which she handed to me.

"Orange juice. Can you take this to the dining room?"

She was obviously in shock, but I couldn't stop her from going about her morning chores.

"I'm going to fix scrambled eggs and bacon. The coffee should be ready. I started it about half an hour ago. I already put sticky buns and doughnuts on the sideboard. That should be enough."

She glanced down at the turkey as calmly as if it were not lying next to a dead man. "I suppose I'd better look in the freezer to find something else to cook for dinner tonight," she said. Lucky we won't have as many people as you originally expected."

"Please do," I said weakly. Verna bustled out of the kitchen as if someone had not recently been murdered in her kitchen.

I stood near the sink wondering if preparing meals in a kitchen where somebody had recently been murdered would meet the board of health's sanitary requirements, when I had a terrible thought. Verna didn't know Mr. Johanson's body had been stashed in the freezer. "Oh, no," I breathed.

"Oh, no, what?" Alice-Ann asked, coming into the kitchen with Michael. "Oh, no," she screeched when she saw the dead man on the floor.

"It can't be," Michael said, when he recognized the man. "He's already dead."

Verna's shrill scream from the back hall interrupted us. Alice-Ann seized Michael's arm to steady herself.

"What was that?" she asked in an abnormal, high-pitched voice.

"I'm afraid Verna's found the Tin Woodman," I told them.

"Did Verna kill him?" Alice-Ann asked, pointing to Dr. Appleby.

"Did you come through the dining room?" I countered.

Michael and Alice-Ann nodded.

"Was anybody missing?"

"No," Michael said. "I mean yes. Mrs. Johanson didn't come down. But the good news is Antoine did and seems to be all right. They were all drinking coffee and talking about what they are going to do today."

"Then either Mrs. Johanson sneaked downstairs, encountered Dan Appleby who was already supposed to be dead, quickly murdered him for no apparent reason in front of the cook, and left in a hurry before I came in, or Verna did it," I said. "I'm betting on Verna, since the alternative is preposterous. And he was still warm when I felt for his pulse, so it must have happened just seconds before I came in. And that was only a few minutes ago.

"We'd better go help Verna," I said. "Even if she did kill Dr. Appleby, she's got to be shocked by finding a body in her meat freezer."

"Maybe she murdered him, too," Alice-Ann said.

I admitted the thought had already crossed my mind.

We ran down the hall to where the stainless-steel door to the freezer stood open. An ashen Verna Fogal was leaning against the sill, gaping at the corpse, and clutching at her chest.

"Are you all right?" I asked.

"Heart…nitroglycerin…help me."

Alice-Ann pushed me aside. "I know about nitroglycerin because of Richard's father," she said, referring to her deceased husband's father. "A person with angina usually carries little tablets in a metal container that hangs around the neck." She groped Verna's chest. "Here it is." She quickly unscrewed the container, removed a tablet and placed it beneath Verna's tongue. Within seconds Verna's color returned.

"Thanks," she breathed to Alice-Ann.

"We'd better get her to bed," Alice-Ann said. "Where's her room?"

Michael said, "Up the staircase in the pantry. She has a small suite of rooms on the next level, which is over the kitchen."

"Staircase? I never saw a staircase leading out of the pantry," Tori said.

"It's got a secret door," Michael said. "Hard to see unless you know it's there. As a kid I thought having a hidden staircase was cool. Very Hardy Boys and Nancy Drew-ish."

I was incredulous. "This means Mrs. Johanson could have

found the secret staircase and actually might have been able to get in and out of the kitchen without anyone seeing her."

Michael shook his head. "The staircase only goes up to the cook's suite. There's no other way in or out. Come on, Verna," he said, gently taking her arm. "You need some rest."

"But the food…" she protested.

"I'll take care of it," I said, wondering what it was I could do. My usual means of serving a large crowd was to have pizza delivered, but even that option was out because of the road outage.

"There's some nice pork roasts in the freezer," Verna said with a shudder. "Maybe if you started them roasting now, they'd be ready for dinner."

"Yuck," said Alice-Ann. "I don't want to eat anything out of the freezer."

"Look, Alice-Ann, we have to serve something. Please don't mention this to the guests."

"What are you planning to do with the other body?" Alice-Ann asked. "I don't mind helping with the cooking, but I refuse to do it with a dead man in there."

Michael looked over his shoulder. "We'll have to put him in the freezer, too. We can move him as soon as I get back."

"I'd better take the juice to the dining room," I said, eager to leave before Michael came back and asked for my help with that unpleasant task.

Alice-Ann huffed mightily but really had no option except to wait for Michael to return.

Carrying the pitcher of orange juice, I stopped in the pantry and examined the secret doorway that led to Verna's rooms. If I hadn't watched it close behind her and Michael I never would have noticed the seams that blended flawlessly with the stone-block walls.

In the dining room almost all of the guests, with the exception of Mrs. Johanson, were cheerfully discussing what was planned for the day. The stack of sticky buns was nearly gone and the platter of doughnuts had been ravaged. I knew Verna had planned to serve bacon and eggs, but I pretended that breakfast, as served, was complete and nobody objected.

Striving for a conversational tone of voice, I asked, "Did anyone come through here in the last five or ten minutes?"

"Sure," Ramona said. "Michael and Alice-Ann."

"Anybody else?"

Heads shook all around the table.

I looked intensely at Candace Appleby. "How are you coping?" I asked.

"Pretty good," she sniffed. "But I really want to get out of here to make arrangements for my husband's funeral. You have no idea of how much I want to see him one more time."

"Your opportunity may come sooner than you think," I said.

Candy looked questioningly at me, but I turned my attention to pouring juice into the green oatmeal glasses on the sideboard.

My movements agitated Antoine, because he unexpectedly began to whimper into a handkerchief. Roman put a reassuring arm around his shoulder, then looked at me. "The emerald color of the glasses makes him think of the stolen Emerald City. It's very upsetting for him."

"We'll get your Emerald City back," I reassured Antoine. "There's no way anyone could get it out of the castle. We'll find it for you."

Antoine answered with a loud sniff, but he did put his hanky back in his pocket and managed to smile weakly at me before he gulped down half a cup of coffee.

"I'll be right back," I said and ran back to the kitchen. If we were to have pork roast for dinner, it probably should come out of the freezer and be put into the oven now. Alice-Ann and Michael were closing the freezer door when I sailed around the corner.

"Leave it open," I cried. "I need to take something out for dinner. I couldn't eat turkey if you paid me."

I averted my gaze from the side-by-side bodies and found several pork roasts.

"Help me," I said to Alice-Ann, as I raced with my arms full of meat back into the kitchen. "I have no idea of how to cook this."

She took the pork from me. "Pork loins. They're the best. I'll take care of dinner," she said. "But I still don't like the idea of eating meat from a freezer where dead bodies have been stored."

"Just think of all meat as dead," I said.

"That doesn't sound particularly appetizing. I may become a vegan." But she began to move about the kitchen as if she knew exactly what she was doing.

"May I watch?"

"If you want. There's a first time for everything. I'm going to put the roasts in the microwave for a few minutes to thaw them out a little."

While the microwave hummed, she opened and closed kitchen cabinets, occasionally removing something out of one, then another. By the time the microwave stopped, she had several flavorings and a flour canister on the counter.

Alice-Ann stirred about one teaspoon of salt and a half tea-spoon of paprika into a cup of flour and mixed it all together. She then sliced a large garlic clove in half and rubbed garlic juice over the pork, which she then sprinkled with dried rose-mary. After dredging the meat in the seasoned flour, she placed the roasts fat side up in a shallow greased pan.

"I'm going to cook it at about four hundred degrees. Roasts this size would normally only take one and a half hours, but since they're still partially frozen they'll need to cook longer." She opened the huge oven and put the roasts inside. "I'll check them later with the meat thermometer to make sure they are thoroughly cooked."

"Where did you learn to do that?" I asked admiringly.

"When you're married and have kids, you have to learn how to cook. You'll find out one of these days."

I doubt it.

"What should we serve with it?" I asked.

"Leave it to me. I saw sweet potatoes in the pantry. There's plenty of food to choose from. We need to come up with something for lunch. Any ideas?"

"Cold cuts? Anything at all. I don't care."

Alice-Ann sighed. "I'll take care of the lunch menu. You go back to the guests, and I'll work on thinking up something."

The last of the sticky buns had disappeared when I returned to the dining room.

"I'm afraid to ask what's next," Larry Diffenderfer muttered.

I'd grown accustomed to his grumblings, so I ignored him and said cheerily, "Now, we'll play the Oz Quiz Game. No need to move. I'll pour some more coffee for each of you, and then we can begin."

"Where are the Johansons?" Mildred Burkhardt asked.

"Probably sleeping late," I fibbed. I took advantage of her question to ask one of my own. Perhaps someone else had seen the castle's mysterious ghost. "Was anybody's sleep disturbed last night?"

They all shook their heads and stared at me as if I were from another planet.

"Did something happen?" Antoine asked.

"Heavens, no. Just want to make sure everyone slept well." I poured coffee so gracefully, I might have been in service all my life. Michael trailed behind me offering cream and sugar. When everyone was ready, I announced, "All questions are based on the books, and not the movie."

I waited for the groans to subside. Our guests, with a few exceptions, were definitely fans of the movie and not the books.

"Are you ready? First question: What color were the magic shoes Dorothy took from the Wicked Witch?"

"Red," two people volunteered.

"Silver," Mildred said.

"Silver is right," I said, as Mildred beamed proudly.

"How did the Sorceress Mombi hide Ozma from the world?"

"That's easy," Kathy Kirchner said. "She turned her into a boy named Tip."

"What did Tip call Jack Pumpkinhead?"

"Dear father," Kathy answered. I wasn't surprised she got the two questions right seeing as how she was dressed as Ozma today and was Tip yesterday.

"Who was the surprise guest at Ozma's birthday party?" I answered for them when no one knew. "Santa Claus.

"What was the name of Ozma's maid?"

"Jellia Jamb," Roman said.

"Who was accused of eating Ozma's white piglet?"

To my surprise, Ingrid Johanson quietly entered the room. "You forgot my coffee," she said to me.

"Oops, I'm sorry. Things got hectic."

Roman answered the last question. "Eureka, Dorothy's pink cat."

"What Oz character was inspired by L. Frank Baum's mother-in-law, the famous suffragette, Matilda Gage?" No one knew, so I told them, "General Jinjur."

Ingrid Johanson filled a cup with coffee, added a little cream and slipped out of the room. Thankfully nobody asked where her husband was.

"What country did Dorothy's uncle Henry move to?"

"Australia," Lorna Diffenderfer piped in.

"Right. And what barrier keeps the Land of Oz safe from the outside world?"

"The Deadly Desert," Roman volunteered. "Really, Tori. These are much too easy."

"How many officers are in the Royal Army of Oz?" Blank stares all around. *Guess I showed him. Much too easy indeed.* "Twenty-eight officers," I told them.

"How many privates are in the Royal Army?"

Roman again knew the answer. "None. They were all promoted to officers."

"What was the name of Ozma's cousin, the Rose Princess? Ozga," I said when nobody knew.

"In what book did the Shaggy Man first appear?"

"The Road to Oz," Alice-Ann said. She had finished in the kitchen and joined the party.

"Who took over the series immediately after Baum's death?"

"Ruth Plumly Thompson." Again, it was Alice-Ann who knew.

"Name the two best-known illustrators of the Oz books."

"W. W. Denslow and John R. Neill," Roman answered quickly before Alice-Ann had a chance to respond.

"Was there ever a book called *Dorothy of Oz?*"

Roman shook his head. "No."

"What did the Wizard make the Scarecrow's brains out of?"

Mildred knew. "Bran, pins, and needles. 'Bran-new brains,' was the pun. And the needles sticking out of his head showed how sharp he was."

"Last question. What kind of courage did the Wizard give the Cowardly Lion?"

"Liquid courage," Alice-Ann said.

"You all did great, but the Oz Quiz winner is Roman."

The costume designer clasped his hands together and raised them above his head in a gesture of triumph. Antoine grinned as if he were the proud father of the winner of the state spelling bee.

"I'll give you your prize at the banquet tonight," I told Roman. "Let's go into the lobby and have our costume parade."

"Costume parade! Good grief! Is the girl mad?" Larry Diffenderfer griped. "We've all been in the same clothes for two days. What's the point of…"

Lorna punched his shoulder. "Shhh," she said. "You'll hurt her feelings."

My feelings were already hurt, but I held my head up high as I led the guests into the lobby. "Michael and Alice-Ann will be the judges, giving our opinions of each person's costume and how well you have stayed in character."

Alice-Ann leaned toward me and whispered, "I've got to start getting lunch ready."

"My apologies," I said to the group. "Michael and *I* will do the judging."

Larry Diffenderfer, cell phone in hand, walked right out the front door, letting it slam loudly behind him.

"He's going to see if he can get his phone to work outside," Lorna explained. "He's terribly worried about the market."

"Can't do much about it on Saturday," Antoine said. "Even if he does get through."

The guests made some minor adjustments to their costumes and one at a time walked in front of Michael and me. Darren was first and growled dramatically at us just like a real lion would. Ramona, as the Lullaby Munchkin, as usual was close behind him. I thought Frank Kirchner's blue Flying Monkey suit made him look like a satanic imp, but the others applauded when he pulled some hidden strings and made his wings flap.

Kathy Kirchner, as Ozma the girl queen of Oz, looked beautiful even without her tiara. She had chosen to portray Ozma as originally drawn by John R. Neill in *The Land of Oz*, before Ozma's long tresses of ruddy gold had turned to ebony, and she still wore robes of silken gauze, which floated around her like a cloud.

"Points for originality," I wrote on my notepad, which I slid over to Michael.

"I guess," he wrote back. "Who's she supposed to be?"

"Trust me. It's a good costume."

The three Dorothys chose to come by together. I had already mentally cataloged them. Candace was the sexy Dorothy, Lorna was the old Dorothy, and Mildred was the authentic Dorothy since she wore silver shoes and a pink bonnet. Candace sauntered by us, appearing unusually cheerful for someone whose husband had died two days ago, but I was glad to see her join in. I wasn't looking forward to telling her that her husband had died—again.

After the Dorothys came the three Scarecrows, Antoine and Roman identically dressed in their Broadway finery, and Bob Burkhardt in his store-bought costume.

Larry Diffenderfer unintentionally entered the contest as he stepped inside. I thought his soggy Wizard of Oz costume matched his personality—Oz, the great humbug—and I decided to give him a prize for that, but in my opinion it was Kathy Kirchner who deserved the prize for the most originality in dressing both as Tip and as Ozma, thus depicting both the male and female aspects of the rightful ruler of Oz. Mildred would receive the second prize for originality.

"I got through to Mac," Larry said to his wife.

"You got a connection?" I interrupted.

"Yeah. But I had to stand in the rain to do it."

I turned to look at Michael. "How can that be possible?"

"Sometimes a signal can get through if you're using a cell phone outside," he explained.

"Let me borrow that." I snatched Larry's phone from him before he could protest and ran across the lobby.

I entered Garnet's number at the police station before I opened the door, and as soon as I was outside I pushed Send. I heard no ring at the other end, and remembered Larry had said he'd had to stand in the rain to make his call. Thankfully, the torrential deluge had turned into a gentle drizzle, and puddles had replaced the overflowing lake. There were even a few spots where muddy hillocks poked through the water. I waded through dangerous and dark, swirling eddies to a high grassy spot and tried the police number once more.

This time the phone rang, but nobody answered. "Drat." I punched End and tried Garnet's home. He picked up on the second ring.

"Tori," he said when he heard my voice. "Thank God. I've been so worried about you. I've been trying to call every hour on the hour. Listen, this is important. The dentist you thought died at Hagerstown hospital, didn't die there. In fact I checked yesterday after you called, and he wasn't even admitted. That sounded suspicious, so I ran a computer check on him. There's no dentist named Dan Appleby listed with the American Dental Association. For certain, he's not a Hollywood 'dentist to the stars.'"

"I know," I said.

"You do? How?"

Pennsylvania grammar, I was tempted to say. "Just a hunch. Garnet, I don't know how long this connection will last, so listen carefully. I knew Dan Appleby didn't die because he came back here, but someone hit him over the head with a frozen turkey and he's really dead this time. He's in the freezer right now."

"What?!"

"That's not all, Garnet. Another guest died of strychnine poisoning. I've got him in the freezer, too."

"Tori…something horrendously wrong…out there."

"You don't need to tell *me* that. Garnet, you're fading out."

"…can't hear you…you're…terrible danger. Keep an eye on… Appleby… Don't let her leave."

"I don't think there's any chance she can."

"…sleep with…bedroom door locked. I love…"

"Garnet…are you there?" The phone had gone dead, again. I immediately tried redialing his number, but it was hopeless. I felt helpless and alone. And what had he been saying when his voice waned away? "I love…"? Was he finally making a commitment? Was I ready for that?

I turned off the phone and splashed my way back to the castle. My gown was once again bedraggled. *It doesn't matter,* I thought. By now, everybody knew I was Glinda. There should be no problem with dressing like myself.

Inside, the costumed Oz characters sat in the lounge area, waiting uncertainly for me to return. The TV was turned to the Weather Channel, which promised partially clearing skies on Sunday. As if to prove it was wrong, a clap of thunder shook the castle.

"The connection broke up," I told Michael, as I returned Larry Diffenderfer's phone to him.

"Sorry. That's pretty typical of cell-phone reception here at Silverthorne. It comes and it goes," Michael said. "I'm going to help Alice-Ann get lunch on the table."

"Are you going to announce the prizewinner now?" Kathy asked me. She probably knew full well that she was the winner.

"No. I'll do that tonight at the banquet."

"Speaking of food," Larry interrupted. "Are we going to get some lunch soon? Those sticky buns did not stick to *my* ribs."

"I'll check with the cook," I told him.

I didn't have to, for at that moment, Alice-Ann threw open the dining-room door and announced, "Luncheon is served."

As everyone took their regular seats, Alice-Ann carried in

the largest bowl I'd ever seen. It was full of spaghetti, lightly coated with red marinara sauce.

Lorna Diffenderfer clapped her hands and squealed with enthusiasm, "It's a Quadling lunch."

Larry looked up from unwrapping the paper napkin that held his silverware to ask curiously. "What's that mean?"

"Food that is red, representing the Quadling Country in the south of Oz," Alice-Ann answered, as she placed several bowls of extra sauce and baskets of hot, crusty rolls on the table.

"Dig in," she ordered, and they did so with enthusiasm.

With coffee, Alice-Ann served a large sheet cake with white butter frosting, which was cleverly decorated with a map of the four Oz countries surrounding the Emerald City. It won everyone's approval.

I was astonished by Alice-Ann's ability to make an unplanned, delicious lunch in such a short time and then convince the guests it had an Oz theme. After lunch I told her so.

"It's nice to feel needed," she said with a smile. "The cake was from a mix," she confessed, "but I made the butter frosting myself. I shouldn't tell you this, but it was really an easy meal to prepare. There are certain basic foods any well-stocked kitchen will have in its larder. All I had to do was look, and there they were. I developed a repertoire of a few quick and easy things to fix for large crowds when I was still married to Richard. He often tried to make an impression on people he thought were important by inviting them home for a meal on the spur of the moment."

Michael stayed in the kitchen with Alice-Ann to help her load the dishwasher, while I joined the guests in the lobby. According to schedule, the hours after lunch were to be devoted to a show-and-tell of various Oz collectibles, and the visitors had taken advantage of the time I'd been gone to fetch their Ozzy treasures from their rooms.

Unfortunately, with the small number of participants that were here, it was obviously not going to take as much time as I had allowed. In the next quarter of an hour, we were treated to a first edition of *The Royal Book of Oz* with only one color plate missing, a map of Oz drawn by Dick Martin, a poster for *The Wizard of Oz,* which was a reproduction not an original, and a set of hand puppets made by Proctor & Gamble as an advertising giveaway. After we looked at a latch-hook rug that depicted the four main movie characters, and a set of the same characters that had been hand-crocheted by someone's maiden aunt, I showed them my collection of Oz bobble-head dolls, and Alice-Ann displayed her Oz Christmas ornaments, most of which I had given her. Mildred brought a Dorothy figurine from Avon.

During the presentations, Candace excused herself and went upstairs. I thought she was going to get her treasured collectible to show, but when she came back, her hands were empty and she appeared agitated.

Show-and-tell was over. It had taken less than fifteen minutes. "Now we'll watch *The Wizard of Oz* and synchronize it with Pink Floyd's *Dark Side of the Moon.* You won't believe what you hear," I said.

"I vote we all take naps, now," Larry Diffenderfer said.

"I'm not tired, but I think I'd rather read a book," Darren Worth said.

"Me too," said his ever-present wife.

No one seemed interested in the VCR/CD presentation. Most of the group picked up their toys and headed upstairs. The Burkhardts drifted into the library with Antoine and Roman to play bridge.

I slumped on the sofa and contemplated the ruins of my convention. *One more meal to go and this day will come to an end.* It was the longest weekend I'd ever experienced, and it wasn't even over.

Alice-Ann's banquet that night was amazing. The roast pork was done to perfection with a delicate, spicy crust on the outside. To accompany it, she served applesauce, mashed sweet potatoes and oven-roasted green beans, seasoned with onions and garlic cloves.

I ate enthusiastically, even while dreading the approaching day when I'd have to face the scale.

For dessert, Alice-Ann had prepared homemade cheese-cake that melted in the mouth. I sighed with pleasure and gladly accepted a second piece.

While the guests were finishing their dessert, I rose and tapped my water glass with my knife to get their attention. "It's time for the awards to be—uh—awarded," I said. "Candace Appleby gets fourth place for her glamorous Dorothy costume." She stood and bowed, displaying her bloomers again. I handed her a small loving cup from the Dollar Store. "Mildred Burkhardt gets the third-place prize for the authenticity of her Dorothy costume." I handed Mildred her loving cup and congratulated her, saying, "Most people don't even know the magic shoes in the book were silver."

"Frank Kirchner, as a Flying Monkey, wins the second-place trophy, and his wife Kathy, as Tip/Ozma, is our first-place winner. Candace Appleby gets the prize for staying in character all weekend, despite suffering personal tragedy. Special participation awards are given to Ramona and Darren Worth, Bob Burkhardt, and Lorna and Larry Diffenderfer."

"That's everybody, isn't it?" Alice-Ann said, disappointment clearly showing in her face. I thought her Polychrome costume was unique, but had decided earlier that "staff" could not win prizes.

"Special rose awards have been set aside for the hard workers who made this weekend so special by wearing costumes all weekend," I improvised. "Alice-Ann, Antoine and Roman, please step forward." I removed three red roses from the vase on the sideboard. "Here you are," I said, handing each of them a flower.

I presented another small trophy to Roman for having won first prize in the Oz quiz competition, and gave everyone who had brought a collectible to show-and-tell a trophy for participating. I still had a box full of loving cups, so I gave everyone an extra one for "being special" and staying in character all weekend.

"That concludes the banquet, but we do have some Japanese Oz cartoons to watch," I said.

"Shhh," Bob Burkhardt said. "Do you hear that?"

"What?" I asked.

"Nothing," he responded. "There's no noise outside. The rain has stopped."

"Maybe we'll actually be able to get out of this miserable place tomorrow," Larry said eagerly.

"The road might still be out," I told him.

"I can always hope."

After inserting the animated Japanese film into the VCR and turning up the volume level, I joined Michael and Alice-Ann in the kitchen for cleanup duty.

"Did you drink regular coffee tonight?" I asked Alice-Ann when we were done.

"No. I never do."

"Then I suggest you have some now. You and I are going to stay up tonight and watch for the ghost."

She groaned, but did pour mugs of hot coffee for both of us.

Michael shook his head in disgust. "You two are nuts. There are no ghosts here or anywhere. But if you want to stay up all night, be my guests."

When the movie dragged itself to a conclusion, and the company went upstairs to their rooms, Alice-Ann and I changed into jeans and dark sweatshirts, moved a pedestal that held a bust of Shakespeare out of an alcove in the hall, and sat down on the cold, hard floor. From our hiding place, we had a good view of the hall while remaining out of sight of anyone who wasn't specifically looking for us. For once I was glad Michael's forebears hadn't installed light fixtures in the castle's halls.

SUNDAY

ALICE-ANN JABBED ME in the ribs with her elbow as she whispered, "Tori, wake up."

My eyes popped open. "I'm not sleep...." I stopped in mid-sentence, both thrilled and chilled by what I saw unfolding in front of me. The door to my bedroom was slowly opening, and after a moment a woman in white slipped through, allowing the door to close quietly behind her. She leisurely walked, almost floated, down the hallway in the same direction as I'd seen her go the previous night. The only reason we could see her at all in the darkness was because of the long, light-colored gown she wore. Once again, she reached the end of the hall and simply vanished.

"Let's go," I whispered to Alice-Ann and tried to get up. "Darn! My foot's asleep." I sat back down and rubbed my right foot to restore the circulation while Alice-Ann impatiently rocked from one foot to the other.

When the pins-and-needles sensation subsided, I struggled to stand, took Alice-Ann's hand and crept down the hallway to the place where our ghost had disappeared. Once again, we were at the end of the long hallway, with locked doors on either side.

"There has to be a way out of here," I said. "She couldn't have just dematerialized."

"She could have if she really was a ghost," Alice-Ann said. The hairs on the back of my neck stood, but I refused to allow myself to believe in ghosts.

"The tapestry," I said. "I'm so used to seeing them hanging in the castle, that I didn't really notice it. Lift it a little, so I can slip behind it."

The smell of mildew assaulted my sinuses as Alice-Ann pulled the tapestry away from the wall. I slipped in behind it. "Don't drop it," I warned, and of course she did. With the heavy material pressing against my back, I groped around the stone wall until I found what I expected to find—a narrow slot, just deep enough and long enough for me to slip my fingers into. It was an exact duplicate of the door in the pantry. I tugged gently, and a door opened. "Alice-Ann, look."

She stuck her head around the tapestry. "Wow! Do you think it's another secret passageway?"

"Of course. The one leading to the cook's room couldn't be the only one in the castle. I'll just bet there are more...." My mind jumped to the tapestry hanging in the Emerald City display room. It probably screened another secret door from view. No wonder someone had been able to enter the locked room and steal the precious jeweled city.

I couldn't blame Michael for not knowing. He hadn't lived here very long as an adult, and those musty tapestries obviously hadn't been taken down for a cleaning since his grandfather's day. The secret doors and passageways had probably been long forgotten by everyone. The only reason anybody knew there was one leading to the cook's suite of rooms was that there was nothing hanging in front of it.

"Come on," I said. "We've got to see where this goes."

Alice-Ann protested but gamely followed me as I slipped inside. The door swung shut and we were in absolute darkness.

"I'm getting out of here," Alice-Ann squealed.

"I have a flashlight," I said, producing one from the kangaroo pouch in the front of my sweatshirt. "It's basic equipment for a ghost hunter."

I moved the flashlight in an arc and saw a tunnel that ran straight ahead about ten feet, then branched out in a T shape in two directions. Of our ghost, there was no sign.

"When in doubt, go right," I whispered.

"I thought you always said you should go left when you're in doubt," Alice-Ann whispered back.

"Go left, then. But I'm going right."

"No way. We're staying together."

We turned right as I suggested, took about twenty steps, and found the passageway again turning right. This time there was no choice to be made. I had already determined our tunnel was running along the outer wall of the castle.

We moved forward, following the spot of light on the stone floor. Once we came to a place where the ceiling of the passageway dropped quite low and we had to duck our heads.

"Why do you think the builder did that?" Alice-Ann asked.

"I think that's where a bedroom window is. Remember how high they are set in the walls? We just walked under one. There must be a secret door somewhere around here. Help me find it."

We both ran our hands over the wall and sure enough I eventually encountered a wooden door.

"Over here," I told Alice-Ann. I caught her hand and guided it to the wall next to where I was standing.

"Oh my," she said. She ran her hand back and forth across the area where the wood met the stone wall. "I feel hinges!"

"That's what I thought. Help me push."

The door swung open so effortlessly that one of us could have easily moved it alone. It was also so noiseless that I was sure someone must have recently oiled the hinges. When the door was slightly ajar it came to a stop as if something were in front of it, preventing it from opening any farther.

It was, however, open just wide enough for me to slip through, and I found myself behind another moldy tapestry. I stepped clear of it into a large bedroom, where someone lay sleeping. I tried to back up, but it was too late. The person in the bed sat straight up, saw me and screamed for help.

I'd expected the room to be empty, having forgotten that we'd moved Mrs. Johanson to it after her husband's death. "Don't scream," I warned, as I scurried to her side. "It's me, Tori. And Alice-Ann. We've found a secret tunnel that passes through the walls. I believe there are hidden entrances to every bedroom from it."

"You nearly scared me to death." Ingrid fell back against her pillow with her bosom heaving dramatically.

"Have you seen the ghost come through there before?" I asked, pointing to the tapestry that hid the door in the paneled wall.

She shook her head, then burst into tears. "I have something to tell you," she sobbed. "I should have told you right away, but I was too scared."

I sat on the edge of the bed and took her hand in mine. "What is it?"

"Friday, during nap time, my husband went to the bathroom. He was gone about ten minutes, and when he came back he was shaking pretty badly. I thought he needed another drink, so I poured one from his oil can. He did need the drink, but that wasn't why he was so terrified. He told me as he came out of the bathroom the first time, he saw the ghost of a young woman materialize right before his eyes."

"She probably just slipped out of the hidden door at the end of the hallway," I told her. "What do you mean 'the first time' he came out of the bathroom?"

"He was terrified when he saw her and ducked back into the bathroom, hoping she hadn't seen him. He peeked out after a minute or two and saw a person he thought was Darren Worth, sort of wrestling with the female ghost."

"Darren Worth?"

"That's what he thought, because of the Cowardly Lion costume. He saw the lion take something away from the girl that was a brilliant green. When the lion turned around, my husband saw his face. It wasn't Darren at all. It was another ghost."

"What do you mean?" I asked.

"It was the ghost of that dentist who died that morning. And he was holding what looked like the jeweled Emerald City in his hands.

"My husband tried to duck back into the bathroom out of sight, but he believed the ghost saw him. After a few minutes, he looked out again and both ghosts were gone. That's when he came back to the room and told me what had happened."

I was incredulous. "Why didn't you tell me, or Michael?"

"Because my husband had been drinking and we knew you'd think he was having hallucinations. We even considered that ourselves—you know—like some people see pink elephants. We decided to go downstairs as if nothing had happened. If the Emerald City was still on display, we'd know he had imagined the whole thing."

"But it was gone, and you still didn't say anything."

"My husband was frightened. He feared the ghost, or whatever it was he'd seen, would be after him. He begged me to keep quiet about what he'd told me and said after dinner we should quietly adjourn to our room and lock ourselves in until the rain subsided and we could leave safely. He suggested that he would go up first, and that I should wait a few minutes then come up to join him. He thought that would be less obvious than both of us getting up and leaving at the same time. But when I came up to join him, I found him having his last convulsion. One or maybe both of the ghosts must have slipped in here, probably through that hidden door, and put poison in his oil can while we were at dinner."

"Why didn't you say anything when Michael and I came in?" I asked.

"Because at first I was too shaken, and then after you came back with the can of poison, I felt it had been left in such an obvious place as a warning to me to keep my mouth shut if I knew anything—or I'd be next."

"You poor dear," Alice-Ann said. "What a terrible ordeal this must have been for you."

I felt less sympathetic. If she had spoken up at dinner, her husband would most likely still be alive.

"I never believed in ghosts," she moaned. "But this is proof. After all, we all know Dr. Appleby died at the Hagerstown hospital."

"He *is* dead," I assured her. "But he didn't die in Hagerstown. He was murdered in the kitchen yesterday morning. So your husband really could have seen him."

"I don't under—"

"There's still the girl ghost. How do you explain her?" Alice-Ann asked me.

"I don't know, but I'm going to find out. First, I want to see if there's a door hidden behind the tapestry in the Emerald City display room. Real ghosts don't need secret doors. From everything I've read about them, they can just walk through walls. If there is a door, then what we've seen is no ghost, and we can move on from there to find out who it is.

"Let's go," I said to Alice-Ann.

"Wait for me," Mrs. Johanson said. "I don't want to be alone. Anybody at all can come charging through that door over there, just like you did."

We waited until she had slipped into her robe, then cautiously opened the door to her room and peeked out. I don't know what I had expected, but I was glad there was nothing to be seen in the hall.

I motioned for the two women to follow me, and let the flashlight circle usher us on our way.

"Look," Alice-Ann said breathlessly. "On the floor over there." She had reached over my shoulder and was pointing to something on the floor. I directed the circle of light in that direction and saw something small and shiny. She darted over and picked the article up. "It's a red sequin," she said. "I bet it came off of Lorna Diffenderfer's stolen red sneakers." She tucked it into a pocket of her jeans.

We continued down the stairs and into the lobby, where I unlocked the door to the display room. I flicked the light switch and turned off my flashlight. The table that had held the priceless Emerald City was still bare. Sure enough, a Gobelin tapestry hung from the wall opposite the door. And as I expected, there was a door behind it set so cleverly into the wood paneling that you wouldn't see it if you weren't specifically looking for it.

"You see, it wasn't a ghost after all."

"Who was it then?" Alice-Ann asked. "Nobody wore a ghostlike costume this weekend."

"I think our ghost is Verna Fogal," I told the two women.

"But the ghost we saw had long blond hair," Alice-Ann protested. "Verna's is gray."

"Even though she wears it in a bun, it is long. And maybe at night the gray color would look blond. Think about it, on Friday Mr. Johanson witnessed Dr. Appleby take the Emerald City from a woman dressed as a ghost—and he died later that day. Saturday morning, Appleby was murdered by Verna, possibly as she was trying to get the treasure back from him."

"You do make it sound as if she's our murderer," Alice-Ann agreed. "But how did Dr. Appleby manage to die two times?"

"There are parts of this puzzle I haven't had time to think about," I told her. "We'd better make sure Verna's still in the castle and hasn't gotten away with it."

"There's no way for her to leave here," Mrs. Johanson reminded me.

"Then we need to hurry and find her before the roads are fixed."

I rushed through the lobby and dining room. The gray dawn was pushing its way through the castle windows, allowing me to turn off the flashlight. It was reassuring to see that the rain had indeed stopped, but that made it imperative to get to Verna quickly. In the pantry, I easily swung open the almost invisible door in the wall and led the way up a curved flight of steps. From the curve, I determined we must be inside one of the castle's many towers.

The door at the top of the stairs was unlocked, and we burst through to face Verna who was standing in front of us with a fireplace poker gripped in one hand.

"Put it down, Verna," I ordered, hoping I sounded more authoritative than I felt.

"It's you," she breathed and dropped the poker to the floor with a loud clang. She actually appeared to be relieved by the vision of three crazed women bursting into her parlor.

"Get the poker, Alice-Ann," I ordered.

Alice-Ann gingerly reached for the weapon and held it behind her back.

"We know what you did, Verna," I said. "We want the Emerald City back, now. Then you'll have to face murder charges for killing Dr. Appleby."

She bowed her head. "I don't have the Emerald City," she said softly. "But I did kill Dan Appleby. He weren't no dentist, and Appleby wasn't his real name."

"You'd better explain," I said. "What do you know about Appleby? And why did you kill him?"

"Me," said a voice from behind the open door to the bedroom. From the bedroom stepped the infamous castle ghost— a young, blond woman in a white cotton nightgown. "Me kill Daddy. Daddy hurt me."

Verna's lower jaw dropped. "Did you hear that? That's the first thing she's said in twelve years." She flung her arms around the ghost and hugged her as if she didn't ever want to let go. Before the embrace, I had time to notice that the girl wore a rhinestone tiara and an Oz pin. Something told me she would also be wearing red-sequined sneakers.

I recalled the kitchen as it had looked immediately after Dr. Appleby had been killed. Blood had been splattered everywhere. Except, that is, on Verna. Her apron and cotton dress had been spotless. Why hadn't I noticed that before? She had not had time to kill the dentist and change out of blood-stained clothing before I came in and found the still-warm body.

"Daddy?" I asked, looking directly at Verna. "You'd better explain."

Verna reluctantly let go of the girl. "May we sit down?" she asked.

"I think we all should," I said. Verna and the girl sat stiffly on the edge of the sofa, and I motioned to Alice-Ann and Mrs. Johanson to pull up chairs.

"His name was Daniel Aldrich. He was my husband," Verna said, staring blankly at a spot above our heads. "This is my daughter, Lynnie. Our daughter."

The girl, Lynnie, grasped her mother's hand.

"He did things to her when she was just a baby," Verna said. "Awful things. I can't say them. When she stopped talking at six I took her to a doctor, and that's how I found out. She never said another word in all these years. Not till this morning.

"I took Lynnie and left him. We hid, but he found us. Twice more we ran away. When I heard there was a cook's job open here, I thought it was the answer to my prayers, that we'd be safely hidden at Silverthorne, but I almost died when I saw him walk into the dining room Thursday night."

"That's why you left in such a hurry?" I asked.

"I prayed all night that he hadn't seen me. When he didn't come after us, I thought maybe we was safe. Especially if Lynnie and I kept out of sight. I shouldn't have been surprised at him showing up at your convention. That Emerald City would have been too tempting for a crook like him to pass up. He's done time twice for jewel theft.

"I didn't tell Mr. Thorne or you about Lynnie because I was afraid you wouldn't let me have her here. I kept her in my room during the day. She slipped out sometimes at night, though, and found the secret doors. She's not stupid, only mute."

"What about the—uh—the things she took?"

Verna smiled and fingered the Oz pin at the girl's throat. "She likes things that sparkle. I was going to return them."

"When did she start collecting sparkly things?" I asked.

"Right after the first time Dan found us. She would go outside and pick up sparkly rocks and take pieces of my jewelry to play with in her room."

"Did she take the Emerald City from the display room?"

Verna looked at the girl, who nodded.

"What happened to it?"

"Daddy took it. Daddy hurt me."

"I understand now what happened," Alice-Ann said. "Dr. Appleby must have recognized Verna, but he pretended he hadn't seen her. He knew Lynnie would be with her, and that the girl would be attracted by the Emerald City. He faked a heart attack so nobody would suspect him of everything and came back to the castle and hid. All he had to do then was wait until Lynnie took it, then snatch it from her."

"I think you've got it," I said. "Right after he took it from her, he caught sight of Mr. Johanson trying to hide in the bathroom. He poisoned him to keep his secret safe." I patted Mrs. Johanson's hand. "I'm so sorry."

"He was in the wrong place at the wrong time," Ingrid whimpered as she pulled a wad of tissues from her bathrobe pocket. "I would have been next if Verna hadn't killed her husband."

Lynnie shook her head vigorously. "Me kill Daddy. Daddy bad."

"She doesn't know what she's saying," Verna protested. "Of course I killed him."

It was obvious to me that Lynnie, not Verna, had murdered the man. But without witnesses, the police would only have Verna's confession, and surely they'd charge her with murder because of it. How could Lynnie survive without her mother? Especially now that she'd broken through the wall of silence that had surrounded her for so long. Briefly, I wondered what Garnet would do, then put that out of my mind. Garnet was sworn to uphold the law and would do so even if it went against his personal conviction.

I knew then that I had to make a quick decision. Unlike Garnet, I wasn't sworn to uphold the law, and even if what I was going to do was wrong, I believed the end result would prove me right.

"Verna, listen to me. I think you and your daughter are trying to protect each other. In my opinion, the best thing to do would be for you both to disappear. Do you agree?" I asked Alice-Ann and Mrs. Johanson.

"Absolutely."

"Of course."

"Is there someplace you know of in the castle where you can hide for a few days?"

"We can leave," Verna said.

"But the bridge, the road…"

"There's an old logging road that's been forgotten for years. It crosses the mountain behind the castle. My truck has four-wheel drive. We can get out that way."

"But it could be blocked after all this time," I protested.

"It isn't," Verna said with such confidence that I believed her.

"How long will it take you to gather up your belongings?"

"No more than ten minutes," Verna said. "I'll leave the things Lynnie took on the dresser."

"Do it. Quick," I said and added, "Promise me you'll get her counseling. I think she'll recover, with help."

"I most certainly will."

Verna and Lynnie began throwing their things into two small, cheap suitcases. Without being told, Lynnie found all the items she'd taken and arranged them neatly on the marble-topped dresser. Even my Glinda crown and magic wand were there.

"Don't worry about breakfast," Verna said. "I wanted to use some of the thawed turkey. Don't look so nervous, I didn't use *that* one. I made brunch casseroles last night. They're in the refrigerator, all fixed. All you need to do is take the dishes out for thirty minutes to reach room temperature, cover them with foil, and bake them for an hour. Take them out, spread with sour cream, and sprinkle Parmesan cheese on top. Bake it uncovered for about ten more minutes. There's juice. And coffee in the…"

"We'll figure it out," Alice-Ann said. "Now get going."

"We've got to get going, too," I said. "Aldrich's wife, Candace, must have the Emerald City. She'll probably try to get out with it today, now that it's stopped raining."

Verna snapped her suitcase shut and said, "That woman weren't his wife. Me and him was never divorced."

"It doesn't matter," I said. "Go!" I gave Verna a gentle push toward the door. "I don't want to ever see either of you again."

"I'll walk down to the truck with them," Mrs. Johanson volunteered. "To make sure they really leave."

I thanked her with a smile. After they had run down the stairs, I said to Alice-Ann, "Let's go get Candace."

We hurried down to the pantry, which was already empty. Verna and her daughter had wasted no time in escaping the castle.

We rushed into the great hall, intent on getting upstairs to Candace's room as quickly as possible, but what we saw by the open front door stopped us dead in our tracks.

Candace, with a small suitcase clasped under one arm, and—my worst nightmare come true—Fred tucked snugly under her other arm, stood framed in the arched doorway.

"Stop," I shrieked. "Please stop."

She paused and turned to face us, a wicked smile on her face. "So you did figure it out," she said. "I thought you would eventually."

"Most of it," I said, keeping an eye on Fred, whose eyes were angry slits. "I'm guessing your husband faked the heart attack, and you only pretended to take him to the hospital."

She smiled and nodded in agreement.

"And it wasn't a doctor from the hospital, but Dan who called on his cell phone and pretended to be the doctor telling us he had died. The bad reception probably made it sound even more authentic than you had hoped. When you drove back into the castle grounds, he must have been concealed in the back of your car. Where did he hide out? In the castle?"

"Not at first," Candace said. "He stayed outside in the garden shed. That's why his cell phone worked. He waited there until everyone was at lunch in the dining room, then I let him in through the conservatory door. Thanks for pointing it out to me. I might never have realized there was another way into the castle. Our original plan was to steal the Emerald City, then I'd pretend to go to Hagerstown to be with him, only we'd really take off and you'd never know what became of us. When we learned you had the key around your neck, I thought we'd have to kill you to get it."

"Kill me?" That possibility had never occurred to me.

"But then the rain started, and we had to change our plans because we couldn't get out. Luckily, that first night, Dan saw his ex-wife in the dining room, and we decided to use the time we were trapped here to devise another plan. He knew his ex would never leave her daughter, so she had to be here. And Dan knew her tendency to collect sparkly objects. We decided to keep an eye on her. There was a good chance she'd do our work for us. And she did."

"Where did the strychnine that killed Bernie Johanson come from?" I asked.

"After Dan told me he'd been seen taking the Emerald City away from that brat of his, I remembered while we were on our walk you said the gardener had been trying to kill gophers for a rather long time. I recalled my father used to use strychnine to kill gophers, so I asked Dan if he'd seen gopher poison in the garden shed. He said that he had. He sneaked outside to get it while the other guests were still napping. Then when you all went down for dinner, I sneaked into the Johansons' room, filled his oil can with the poison, and joined you downstairs in the dining room."

"You killed him! I thought it was your husband who did it."

"That gutless wonder! He wouldn't have had the nerve to poison a gopher, much less a person. Somehow he ducked out on me, but I have the jewels. I'll be a lot better off without him, especially when I take the gems out of this overpriced toy and sell them."

"He didn't duck out on you," I said. "He was murdered."

She threw back her head and laughed. "Tell me another funny story," she said.

"Give me my cat," I said, taking a step forward.

"You come any closer, and I'll wring his neck," Candace said.

Fred mewled plaintively, and I backed up, stopping only when I bumped into Alice-Ann. Despite the thick sweatshirts we wore, I could feel the trembling of her body.

"I'm getting out of here," Candy said. "And I'm taking this creature with me. If you try to follow me, his carcass will be the first thing you see. His death will always be on your conscience."

"You can't escape," I pointed out. "The flood…"

"The Weather Channel just announced the rain has stopped in this area. It also said the road's been repaired. All I have to do is drive across the bridge, and you'll never see me again. Bye-bye."

The great front door slammed behind her.

"Let's get her," Alice-Ann said.

I put out a hand and restrained her. "She's got Fred."

"Tori, he's only a cat, for goodness sake."

"He's my best friend. I can't take a chance on her hurting him." As I spoke, I moved to one of the front windows and looked out. Candace's green car was speeding down the muddy driveway in the direction of the Lickin Creek.

"Now," I said. "She's gone so far, she won't be able to see us." We ran outside and splashed through nasty mud puddles as we followed the ruts her car had made. We could tell by the grooves in a grassy knoll that Candace had swerved off the drive once to avoid an area that was still badly flooded.

"How can we stop her?" Alice-Ann puffed behind me.

"I don't know that we'll have to," I said, stopping suddenly. Before us roiled the Lickin Creek, its water dark and turbid. It swirled over the low bridge that spanned it and surged violently to where the outline of the lake was barely visible.

Candace's car was spinning crazily in the agitated water as it moved toward the deeper water. Candace was in the front seat. Her screams shattered the quiet morning air.

"Isn't there anything we can do?" Alice-Ann asked me as we watched helplessly from the riverbank.

Before I could tell her there was nothing anybody could do, the car hurtled forward and was gone, swallowed by the churning waters of Silverthorne Lake.

Before we'd had a moment to recover from the shock of seeing a woman drown before our eyes, a truck pulled up on the far shore, and Garnet Gochenauer jumped out.

"Are you all right?" he yelled across the river.

"My cat…" I burst into tears. "He's dead."

"I'm coming across," Garnet called.

"No. It's too dangerous," I warned.

"I've got a gadget here that will shoot a rope across the river. Stand back."

We moved away and Garnet aimed something that looked like a giant harpoon in our direction.

"Grab it and tie it around that tree," he yelled.

After we had done so and made sure it was secure, Garnet used it to walk, swim and pull himself across the river.

I fell into his strong arms and began to cry.

"There's a car in the lake. With a woman in it. Fred, too," I sobbed.

"We'll get it out as soon as the water level goes down."

"She's got the Emerald City in there with her."

"I'm not even going to ask what that is," Garnet said.

Garnet held me close and stroked my hair while I sobbed.

"Hey, there. What's going on?"

I recognized Michael's voice and turned to see him approaching with Fred snuggled in his arms. "I found your cat outside," he said to me. "He's all wet and covered with a sticky pink goo. Smells a lot like bubble gum."

I took Fred from him and hugged him close even though the pink dye on his fur stained my skin. Although he was wet and obviously miserable, he recognized that he was in the safety of my embrace and began to purr loudly.

Michael kept right on moving—toward Alice-Ann. "Darling," he said. "I was so worried when I couldn't find you this morning."

Darling? What was going on? I recalled all the hours Alice-Ann and Michael had spent alone together, while I had been entertaining our guests. That time had obviously been spent doing far more than preparing meals, serving food and cleaning up the kitchen. I shouldn't have been surprised at the end result.

Suddenly his porcelain smile, liposuctioned abs and gym-hardened body didn't look quite as attractive to me as they had before. Garnet, on the other hand, was one hundred percent real. Still clutching Fred to my chest, I nestled back into Garnet's arms. We were safe. I was home.

RECIPES

ALICE-ANN'S CHEESECAKE

¼ lb. butter
1¼ cups graham cracker crumbs
1 tbsp sugar
1 (3oz) package of lemon gelatin
1 cup boiling water
1 (8 oz) package of cream cheese, softened
1 cup sugar
1 tsp vanilla
1 cup whipping cream

Melt butter in a skillet or microwave. Add graham cracker crumbs and 1 tablespoon sugar and stir gently to mix. Line bottom of two pie plates with half the crumbs or one pan 8 by 12 by 2 inches. Save the rest of the crumbs for the top of the cheesecake.

Dissolve gelatin in boiling water. Place in refrigerator until gelatin begins to harden.

Beat cheese, sugar and vanilla with a mixer until smooth. Beat in gelatin.

Whip cream until it is stiff. Fold it into the cream cheese mixture.

Pour mixture over graham cracker crumbs. Sprinkle the reserved crumbs on top. Chill for at least 4 hours or overnight.

(Makes about 12 servings)

QUADLING COUNTRY SPAGHETTI

1 large onion
1 green pepper
2 tbsp olive oil
1 lb lean ground beef
1 bay leaf, finely broken
¼ tsp hot red pepper flakes
oregano, to taste
1 clove garlic, minced
3 or 4 cloves
2 cans (28 oz size) peeled tomatoes, chopped
1 can (6 oz size) tomato paste
1 can (4 oz) sliced mushrooms in butter
18 oz water
3 or 4 tbsp dry white wine
salt, to taste
1 package (about 8 oz) spaghetti
Freshly grated Parmesan or Romano cheese

Finely chop onion and green pepper and simmer in olive oil in a skillet until soft. Add ground beef and cook until meat is thoroughly browned. Add bay leaf, red pepper flakes, oregano, garlic and cloves. Remove from heat.

In a deep pot combine canned tomatoes tomato paste and mushrooms. Stir in 3 tomato-paste cans of water and the white wine. Add the ground beef mixture. Add salt to taste, and simmer, the longer the better.

Have ready a deep kettle of boiling salted water. Place spaghetti in water. Cook about 7 minutes, until tender. Drain and place spaghetti in a large bowl. Stir in some of the sauce and toss gently. Serve with bowls of extra sauce and lots of freshly grated Parmesan or Romano cheese.

Serves 4.

VERNA FOGAL'S EASY SUNDAY BRUNCH

2 lbs turkey sausage, commercially prepared or made from recipe below

TURKEY SAUSAGE:
2 lbs ground turkey breast
½ tsp garlic powder
½ tsp onion powder
1 tbsp paprika
2 tbsp chili powder
½ tsp cayenne
½ tsp salt
¼ tsp crushed red pepper
¼ tsp oregano
¼ tsp thyme
¼ tsp sage

Combine turkey sausage ingredients and set aside.

CASSEROLE:

1½ loaves day-old French bread, crusts removed
4 tbsp butter, melted
4 oz Monterey Jack cheese, grated
4 oz cheddar cheese, grated
12 oz Swiss cheese, grated
4 large scallions, finely chopped
16 eggs
2 cups milk
½ cup white wine

1 tbsp dry mustard
pinch cayenne pepper
¼ tsp black pepper
1½ cups sour cream
6 oz Parmesan cheese, grated

Coat two 8-by-13-inch baking pans with nonstick spray, or rub with butter. Lay bread flat in the pans, drizzle butter over bread. Stir together first three cheeses and sprinkle over the bread. Cook turkey sausage in a skillet, add scallions and place on top of cheese layer.

Beat eggs, milk, wine, mustard, cayenne and black pepper until foamy. Pour over ingredients. Refrigerate overnight.

Remove pans from refrigerator 30 minutes before baking. Preheat oven to 325°F. Bake covered for 1 hour. Remove from oven, spread sour cream over top, then sprinkle Parmesan cheese. Bake uncovered, until golden brown, about 10 more minutes.

Serves 20.

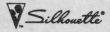

Silhouette®

SILHOUETTE **Romance**®

From first love to forever, these love stories
are fairy tale romances for today's woman.

Silhouette®
Desire®

Modern, passionate reads that are powerful and provocative.

Silhouette®
SPECIAL EDITION™

Emotional, compelling stories that capture the intensity
of living, loving and creating a family in today's world.

Silhouette®
INTIMATE MOMENTS™

A roller-coaster read that delivers romantic thrills
in a world of suspense, adventure and more.

eHARLEQUIN.com

The Ultimate Destination for Women's Fiction

Becoming an eHarlequin.com member is easy, fun and **FREE!** Join today to enjoy great benefits:

- **Super savings** on all our books, including members-only discounts and offers!

- Enjoy **exclusive online reads**—FREE!

- Info, tips and **expert advice** on writing your own romance novel.

- FREE romance **newsletters,** customized by you!

- Find out the latest on your **favorite authors.**

- Enter to win exciting **contests and promotions!**

- Chat with other members in our **community message boards!**

To become a member, visit www.eHarlequin.com today!

INTMEMB04R

HARLEQUIN®
INTRIGUE®

WE'LL LEAVE YOU BREATHLESS!

If you've been looking for thrilling tales of
contemporary passion and sensuous love stories
with taut, edge-of-the-seat suspense—then
you'll love Harlequin Intrigue!

Every month, you'll meet six new heroes
who are guaranteed to make your spine tingle
and your pulse pound. With them you'll enter
into the exciting world of Harlequin Intrigue—
where your life is on the line
and so is your heart!

THAT'S INTRIGUE—
ROMANTIC SUSPENSE
AT ITS BEST!

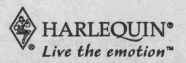

HARLEQUIN®
Live the emotion™